JANITORS

JANITORS

TYLER WHITESIDES

ILLUSTRATED BY
BRANDON DORMAN

SHADOW
MOUNTAIN

Text © 2011 Tyler Whitesides
Illustrations © 2011 Brandon Dorman

All rights reserved. No part of this book may be reproduced in any form or by any means without permission in writing from the publisher, Shadow Mountain®. The views expressed herein are the responsibility of the author and do not necessarily represent the position of Shadow Mountain.

Visit us at ShadowMountain.com

All characters in this book are fictitious, and any resemblance to actual persons, living or dead, is purely coincidental.

First printing in hardbound 2011.
First printing in paperbound 2012.

Library of Congress Cataloging-in-Publication Data
Whitesides, Tyler, author.
    Janitors / Tyler Whitesides.
        pages cm
    Summary: A sixth grader stumbles upon a secret that threatens to turn school-children everywhere into mindless automatons.
    ISBN 978-1-60908-056-3 (hardbound)
    ISBN 978-1-60907-065-6 (paperbound)
    [1. Students—Fiction. 2. Monsters—Fiction. 3. School custodians—Fiction. 4. Schools—Fiction.] I. Title.
    PZ7.W58793 Jan 2011
    [Fic]—dc22   2011007692

Printed in the United States of America
RR Donnelley, Harrisonburg, VA

20   19   18   17   16   15   14   13

*For mothers and custodians everywhere,
who seem to sweep and vacuum endlessly.*

And for Connie, who swept me away.

CONTENTS

Contents

CHAPTER 1

"YOU'RE GOING TO GET AN F."

S pencer shifted the papers on his school desk and looked for a hundredth time at the graffiti in the corner. Last year's occupant of the desk must have spent hours etching the message into the wooden surface.

Mrs. N Smells like cabbige

Dummy, Spencer thought. *Couldn't even spell cabbage.*

Truth be told, Mrs. Natcher did smell a little like cabbage sometimes, but she was still tolerable. Today, however, a strong Bath and Body Works fragrance filled the sixth-grade classroom and Mrs. Natcher was nowhere to be seen.

In her place was a thin, younger woman who had short, stylish hair streaked with pink highlights. She

1

wore high-heeled red shoes and a skirt so short that Mrs. Natcher would have croaked. Turned out that Mrs. Natcher *had* croaked—well, almost—which was why Miss Leslie Sharmelle had been called to Welcher Elementary that morning.

Spencer glanced at the clock on the wall. Only a half hour until lunch! The morning had flown by. After a lesson on geography, Miss Sharmelle had started the students creating maps of imaginary lands. Spencer traced a crooked line from his pencil-sketch mountains to the coast.

"Keep working on your maps, boys and girls," Miss Sharmelle instructed. "I've got to buzz over to the copy machine for a sec." With half a dozen papers in her hand and her heels click-clacking on the floor, she disappeared into the hallway.

Instinctively, Spencer swiveled his head to glance at Dez Rylie. Sure enough, there was already a soggy wad of paper coming out of the boy's big mouth. Only a desk away, Spencer's map was an easy target. But with the substitute out of the room, Dez wouldn't settle for a small target like Spencer. Dez was going to spread the fun (and the spit) to everybody.

With a whoop, he tossed the mass of chewed paper into the air. It made a lazy arc across the room, showering everyone below with drops of Dez-juice. The spit bomb made a fast descent and landed with a *splat* on Jen McNeal's new back-to-school shoes.

Jen screamed, jumping up and shaking her foot wildly. She danced in the aisle as though an army of ants had decided to bunk in her sock. The vigorous foot shaking sent out a spray of spit, and the wad dislodged, flinging sideways and skidding across Juan Rivera's map. Desperate to save his island, Juan snatched up his map and flipped the spit wad forward.

The wad (no longer soggy, but still unpleasantly moist) rolled off Juan's desk and quickly came to a halt between the backrest of the chair in front of him and the girl sitting in it. Instantly, she began to cry.

As the back half of the classroom erupted into chaos, Dez Rylie threw his head back and laughed at the ceiling. Spencer, who was still shielding his map, noticed that almost everyone else who wasn't dancing, screaming, or crying was doing the same. Those who had escaped the first onslaught were watching Dez like rabbits in headlights.

Everyone except Gullible Gates.

Daisy Gates was seated in the front left corner of the classroom, far out of spit's way. She might have been humming softly, as she often did, but there was too much noise in the room to be sure. One thick, sandy-colored braid reached halfway down her back. She sat hunched over the desk, her nose an inch away from the forest she was drawing. She scribbled more pine needles onto a tree, somehow oblivious to the upset in the room.

Dez scowled when he saw her. Spencer opened his mouth to shout a warning, but cringed, unwilling to make himself the target. Dez pushed himself out of his desk and tromped down the aisle, intentionally treading on somebody's notebook that had fallen to the floor. The back of the room had quieted. Juan was holding his wrinkled map in front of the fan. Jen was alternately blotting off her shoe and drying the tears of her sobbing friend.

It wasn't until Dez Rylie's shadow fell on Daisy's desk that she looked up. Seeing the bulky kid standing before her, she quickly looked down again, vigorously scrawling pine needles. Dez bent down to examine her work and the entire class held its breath. If Daisy had been humming before, she was definitely not doing it anymore. The clock ticked loudly. Twenty minutes to lunch.

"Nice map," Dez said.

Daisy stopped drawing and looked up. A reluctant smile spread across her face. "Uh, thanks, Dez."

"It looks pretty good . . . except for one thing."

"What?" Daisy asked, looking at her map as though it had betrayed her.

"You weren't listening when Miss Sharmelle told us about forests." Dez's fat finger pressed down on Daisy's pine trees. "Forests can't grow next to mountains. You're going to get an F."

Daisy sat stricken for a moment, then fumbled for her large pink eraser. With hasty movements that tore little marks in her paper, she scrubbed at her forest until it was nothing but a gray smudge next to the mountains.

Across the room, Spencer's body tensed. That was wrong. Daisy's forests could grow wherever they darn well pleased. Taking a deep breath, Spencer began to say "Daisy." But all he could manage was "Dai" before Dez silenced him with a threatening glare. Spencer felt the "sy" catch in his throat and he swallowed it down.

"Where *can* I put my forest?" Daisy asked.

"Forests only grow on tiny little islands a hundred and two miles from the coast. In geography, we call them Gullible Islands." Laughing, Dez snatched Daisy's pencil and drew a big *F* at the top of her map.

"You're so dead, Dez." Jordan Height broke the silence. Jordan wasn't as tall as Dez; no one in the class was. But Jordan was usually the first to stand up to the bully.

"Shut up, pretty boy," Dez replied, folding his beefy arms.

"I mean it," Jordan said. "Miss Sharmelle's going to drag you to the principal's office so fast."

"I don't care," Dez shrugged. "In fact, I kinda hope so. Maybe Miss Sharmelle will hold my hand. She's a hottie."

The students gasped collectively and Spencer averted his eyes, ashamed to even be sharing air with Dez Rylie.

"You *will* be going to the office, Dezmond." Miss Sharmelle's voice cut through the gasps. She was in the doorway, a large stack of papers in her hand. Her face looked a little flushed, but not as red as Dez's.

The bully turned to face her, regaining his composure. "Let's go," he said.

Miss Sharmelle crossed the room, set the papers on her desk, and returned to the open doorway where Dez was waiting for her with a stupid grin on his broad face.

"And *no*," she punctuated, "I will *not* be holding your hand."

CHAPTER 2

"THAT SOUNDS NEAT."

T he yellow school bus rumbled to a stop and released a hiss of air before the door opened. Four children with matching brown hair and a smattering of freckles moved to the front of the bus. James took two steps per stair because he was in first grade. Holly held the handrail and descended by hopping on one foot because she was in third grade. Erica jumped down all the steps because she was in fourth grade. The last one thanked the driver and moved down the stairs like a civilized human. Because, after all, Spencer was in sixth grade.

Once outside, the bus driver checked her mirrors and motioned the kids across the street. Spencer herded his siblings, wondering why the driver had even bothered to check the mirrors. There was never a car on this road anyway.

When the children were safely across, the flashing red stop sign tucked away and the bus ambled down the road.

Without a sidewalk to follow, the four kids moved along the weed-infested edge of the road. September was brown in southern Idaho, but the farmers still fought it with huge sprinklers that launched water in glittering, sunlit arcs across the fields.

They passed a rundown farmhouse and Spencer turned his siblings up a steep side road. Suddenly, the neighborhood changed. This newly developed area on the hill seemed too fancy for the rest of town. Like pearl earrings on a pig.

Two blocks into the wealthy subdivision, the kids arrived at their gaudy, three-story home. A few months ago, the lot had blended nicely with the neighborhood. Green lawn and tidy landscaping. But, for better or worse, Spencer's family had a way of making things their own.

In the weeks since they'd arrived, the lawn had withered to a dry and crispy brown. A clunker station wagon was parked mostly in the driveway, with one wheel on the dying grass. The car meant Mom was home. The bad parking job meant she was in a hurry.

The house, too, had once been a monument to wealth. Now it looked recently blown in from Kansas. On the porch, cobwebs hung scalloped from pillar to pillar like someone had hired Spider-Man to do the decorating. The "welcome" mat didn't look too welcoming, all caked in dry mud so that only the *w* and *e* were legible.

Spencer opened the door and stepped inside, his little

7

brother and sisters following. There was a clank of pans from the kitchen and Spencer heard his mother's voice. Probably on the phone.

A three-year-old rounded the corner with a bottle of soapy bubble solution in his hand. The other hand waved a bubble wand, flicking soap onto the hardwood floor.

"What the . . . ?" Spencer grabbed the wand from the child's hand. "Who are you?" A second later, two more three-year-olds came careening into view, one with a butter knife, the other with a pair of scissors.

"Whoa!" Spencer said, seizing his littlest brother by the arm and prying the scissors from his grasp. "If you're going to play inside with friends," Spencer lectured, "then you have to be respectful of Aunt Avril's house."

Max merely hissed at his older brother, exposing a chipped front tooth. He made an attempt to grab the scissors back and then ran off.

Spencer was alone in the entryway. His other siblings had dumped their backpacks on the floor and quietly crept downstairs. Afternoon cartoons on the big flat-screen TV attracted them like moths to a porch light. Not the porch light at Spencer's house, though. It had been left on 24–7 and burned out weeks ago.

Spencer sighed. For a house with so many windows, it surely seemed dark. He crossed the room and twisted the wooden blinds to let some light in. Something darted out from behind the leather sofa, nearly stopping Spencer's heart. It was a cat. Since when did they have a cat?

Spencer picked up a toy dump truck and kicked some

stuffed animals out of his way. The mess in this house was maddening. He would clean things up after dinner, but right now, Spencer needed some time in his sanctuary.

"Spencer!" his mother called as he headed toward the stairs.

"Here, Mom!" he answered as if she were calling roll.

"Spencer, come in here and tell me about your day."

Resignedly, Spencer left his backpack on the first step and walked into the kitchen. His mother was a whirlwind. Alice Zumbro was stooped down, digging for the colander while balancing a steaming pot of noodles in one hand and trapping a spatula between her knees as she pinned the phone to her shoulder with her cheek. Her apron nearly tripped her when she stood up, colander in hand, and crossed to the sink.

Spencer stood obediently near, wishing he could help, but knowing that his mother preferred to do everything on her own. Especially since Dad had left.

Finally she turned to him, her face moist from the steam of the noodles and her hair sticking in strands to her forehead.

"How was school today?" she whispered around the phone.

"Fine."

"What did you do?" she asked.

"Mom," Spencer protested. "You're on the phone. I'll tell you later."

Alice shook her head. "Tell me now. It's just your Aunt Avril." She carried the dripping noodles across the room and set them on the table, steaming water still oozing out of the colander. "Well?" she mouthed as she passed him on her way to the stove.

"Well?" echoed Spencer. "The bus ride was boring this morning," he began. "Boring and long."

"Uh-huh," his mom responded, though Spencer wasn't sure if it was intended for him or Aunt Avril.

"I sat by myself because James and Holly and Erica have all made friends."

"Uh-huh."

"Mrs. Natcher was gone and we had a substitute named Miss Leslie Sharmelle. She was nice, but some of the kids were mad because we didn't get morning recess."

"Oh, Avril, don't worry about that," Alice scolded into the phone. Then she looked right at Spencer and gave him a very clear "uh-huh," answering his question about who the grunts were intended for.

"Then this big kid, Dez, went berserk and chucked spit wads all over, so Miss Sharmelle took him to the office."

"Uh-huh."

"In P.E., I was picked last for kickball. I ate lunch by myself and accidentally spilled ketchup on my shirt, see?" Spencer stretched his shirt to show his mom the red spot. She tried to glance, but got distracted by the can opener.

"Then, at lunch recess I met some aliens. They were pretty cool and showed me their ray guns and stuff. So I zapped everybody except Daisy Gates, 'cause everybody picks on her. Then the aliens gave me a lift back to our *real* home in Washington."

"That sounds neat, Spence," Alice answered. She gave him a dismissive smile, said, "Oh, I know," to Aunt Avril on the phone, then said "Shoot!" because she realized that she hadn't put the noodles in a bowl and the colander was leaking hot water everywhere.

Spencer ducked out of the cluttered kitchen—*Aunt Avril's* kitchen—and made his way back to the stairs. His backpack was still there, but someone had flicked soapy bubble solution on one of the shoulder straps. Spencer picked it up carefully and jogged up the stairs, dodging piles of dirty clothes and an open can of soda as he went. He moved quickly, hopeful that there would be no more distractions.

With a sigh of relief, Spencer opened the door and stepped into his bedroom. Everything was clean. Everything had its place. And everything was *always* in its proper place . . . except for a heap of pillows in the middle of the floor!

"Max," Spencer muttered disapprovingly as he put the pillows back—two on the bed and two in the padded window seat. Spencer hung his backpack on a hook and sat down on a chair to remove his shoes.

It was Monday. Two lonely weeks at Welcher Elementary were over and another had just begun. Fifty more weeks until Aunt Avril and Uncle Wyatt would return from business in Thailand and claim their house back—or whatever was left of it.

Spencer wanted a snack. He had some treats in his top drawer, but he hadn't washed his hands from school yet. He couldn't bring himself to snack without washing and he couldn't wash without leaving his tidy sanctuary. For a moment he sat perfectly still. He closed his eyes, letting the school day settle behind him.

Something wet flicked across his face. For a terrible moment Spencer thought that Dez Rylie had somehow thrown a spit wad so far that it had penetrated his sanctuary. Spencer's eyes opened and he saw one of Max's friends emerge from hiding, bubble wand in hand. The kid was making a break for the door, giggling wildly.

Spencer would have zapped him if he'd had a ray gun.

CHAPTER 3

"DISGUSTING."

Miss Leslie Sharmelle gave them morning recess the next day. It was only a ten-minute break, but at least it was ten minutes that Spencer could get away from Dez's grubby hands. The big bully had been poking Spencer all morning. His trip to the principal's office obviously hadn't been enough to inspire good behavior.

Spencer cursed the seating chart after recess as Dez plopped down beside him again. Miss Sharmelle had thrown out Mrs. Natcher's lesson plans and decided to teach algebra. Daisy Gates, who had only briefly heard about algebra, thought it was some kind of deep-sea creature. Dez encouraged the myth, giving life-sucking tentacles to the dangerous algebras. Daisy, who had wholeheartedly forgiven Dez of his cruelty the day before, was ready to believe him.

But then the lecture started and Miss Sharmelle (wearing a shirt that said X + Y = XOXOXO) shot down the myth.

Miss Sharmelle, who had previously been so exciting, suddenly delivered the most dreadfully boring lecture possible. Spencer's head began to bob like a basketball dribbling in slow motion. The first time it drooped, he jerked up, embarrassed. He'd had this problem in his old school—falling asleep even when he really wanted to learn what the teacher was explaining. Glancing around, Spencer noticed that several others were fading too.

Not Dez. He slouched forward with a melty handful of M&Ms. Carefully, he placed a candy up his nose. Plugging the other nostril, he exhaled hard, blowing out the M&M and catching it on his waiting tongue.

"Disgusting," Spencer muttered. Repulsed beyond description, he turned away from the brute. He tried to focus on Miss Sharmelle's voice. His head bobbed again . . . and again. Spencer almost wished that Dez would start poking him again—if the bully washed his hands first.

Finally unable to resist, Spencer put his head onto his desk, X + Y equaling Zzzzzzz.

CHAPTER 4

"WEIRD."

Spencer felt someone shaking him. His eyes were sticky and he had to squint against the light. Suddenly remembering where he was, he shot upright in his seat. The glue seal on his eyes snapped and he glanced around the classroom.

He was alone.

Well, not alone, because Miss Sharmelle had a hand on his shoulder, bringing him around. But all the other students were gone!

"I'm sorry, Miss Sharmelle," Spencer said. "I don't know . . . sometimes I . . . I'm sorry."

Miss Sharmelle smiled attractively. "It happens, Spencer. Algebra affects everyone differently."

"What time is it?"

"The bell just rang. I bet your classmates aren't even in the lunch line yet."

Spencer shook his head in shame and began scooping his belongings into his backpack. "I won't fall asleep again, Miss Sharmelle. I really am sorry."

"Don't worry about it. I won't tell Mrs. Natcher or anything." But then, as Spencer stood and faced her, Miss Sharmelle gasped. Her green eyes, under a pair of fashionable fake glasses, studied his cheek and forehead.

"What?" Spencer asked, his stomach sinking. "What's wrong with my face?"

Without answering, she motioned him over to her desk. From her pink leather purse, Miss Sharmelle withdrew a round makeup compact, flipped open the lid, and held the mirror out for him. Although the mirror was marked with several smudges and dusted with powder, Spencer caught the reflection of his left cheek. $x + y = z$ was sloppily tattooed in black marker across his face. On his forehead was another algebraic equation, and by his chin, a third one had been started but left without an answer, probably because the bell had rung.

"Dez," mumbled Spencer angrily. He told Miss Sharmelle that he would wash it off in the bathroom and gave her the mirror back.

"Terrible thing, permanent marker," she said, examining her own reflection before replacing the makeup mirror in her purse.

"It'll come off," Spencer said.

"Good luck."

The nearest bathroom was just across the hallway. Spencer kept his face down and walked—fast. He pushed open the door with his elbow and stepped inside just as someone flushed the toilet and turned to face him.

Dez.

"Hey, Doofus," the bully said. Spencer paused, trying to decide whether he should flee immediately or attempt to get past Dez and wash his face.

"Nice equators," Dez smirked.

"What?" Spencer asked, his fist clenched like a grenade.

"Maybe you should look in the mirror, smarty-pants," Dez answered. "You've got math equators written all over your face."

"*Equations*," Spencer said. "Math *equations*."

"Yeah, whatever. You still look like a dork." Dez snorted and Spencer was afraid for a moment that the bully would launch a gob at him. Nothing came out, so Dez shifted gears. "You thought about standing up for Gullible Gates yesterday, didn't you?"

"That's why you drew on my face?" Spencer asked.

"No," said Dez. "Actually, I drew on your face because Nancy Pepperton thought it would be funny." Dez dug in his jeans pocket (a difficult task when the jeans are a size too small) and withdrew a crumpled strip of paper. "She passed me this during algebra."

Half expecting the paper to grow teeth and bite him, Spencer took it from Dez's hand.

Spencer is so out. Draw something on his face.
—Nancy

Spencer crumpled the paper and stuffed it into his own pocket. He barely even knew Nancy! What did she have against him?

"Anyway," Dez said. "Stay out of my fun with Gullible Gates and life will be easier for you. I like to play with her mind. It's soft like Play-Doh but doesn't dry out as fast. Next time you think about being a hero, I'll spell a different equator for you. It's called Fist + Nose = Blood. Deal?" Dez extended his beefy hand to seal the bargain, but Spencer just stared, trapped.

"Deal?" Dez repeated, unaccustomed to having his victims think before they agreed.

"Deal," answered Spencer finally. "It's a deal."

"Why won't you shake on it?" Dez demanded, his hand still extended.

"Well," Spencer hesitated, wondering if honesty would win him a face-plant in the toilet. "You just went to the bathroom and you haven't washed your hands yet."

Dez exhaled a breathy puff of disbelief that turned into a mocking laugh. Spencer stood rigid, ready for anything. After a good chuckle, Dez reached out and gently patted Spencer's cheek. "Washing's for sissies." He pushed Spencer aside, flung open the bathroom door, and announced his arrival in the hallway with a loud belch.

As soon as the door clanged shut, Spencer took three quick steps to the sink and turned on the water. Dez's bathroom hands were a second incentive to a thorough face washing. In the mirror, Spencer saw the ink equations more clearly. He must have been sound asleep not to feel Dez's marker.

Grateful that no one else had seen the math-work, Spencer splashed his face with water. Reaching over, he gave two solid pumps to the soap dispenser on the wall.

Nothing.

Spencer began pumping violently on the dispenser, but it was hopeless. There was no soap. Spencer scanned the room desperately. The next bathroom was all the way down the hall and around the corner. He would never make it without someone spotting Dez's artwork.

Spencer's eyes suddenly fell on a small bottle resting on the edge of the next sink. His face still dripping, Spencer reached over and snatched it up, hopeful that it might contain something that could remove his facial graffiti. Turning it over in his hand, Spencer saw that it was actually a hotel shampoo bottle from a Best Western. Quickly deciding that shampoo might do the trick, he unscrewed the cap.

There was the tiniest bit of gelatin-like substance in the bottom of the bottle. Spencer squirted the glob onto his palm, surprised to see that it was bright pink and looked more like soap than shampoo after all. The soap smelled fresh, if a little chemical.

Spencer worked the pink gel to a foamy lather between his hands. He rubbed his cheek, watching X and Y melt away with surprising ease. Then he closed his eyes and lathered his whole face.

Burning hot!

Icy cold!

"Yaaaaaggghh!"

Spencer frantically began rinsing his face. The soap was in his eyes now, stinging like crazy. He plunged his entire face directly under the faucet, letting the lukewarm water flush out his eyes. Spencer reached out blindly and pumped a roll of paper towels. Blotting his face with the paper helped make the tingling sensation fade.

Spencer opened his eyes and stared back at his reflection. The front of his shirt was soaked from his rapid and reckless rinsing. His brown hair was damp and clinging to his forehead. And his face . . . it was as red as a tomato and still burning. But at least there was no sign of Dez's algebra.

Spencer picked up the bottle, blinking rapidly in hopes that his eyes would stop stinging. He smelled the soap again. It was strong—definitely not Best Western shampoo. It might have been paint remover, for all he knew. Whatever it was, Spencer decided he was allergic. He was lucky to have found it first. What if some little baby first grader had washed his hands with the napalm soap?

Feeling like he was doing the world a favor, Spencer tossed the bottle into the garbage can, where it sank out of sight beneath crumpled paper towels.

Suddenly, a flash of movement caught his eye in the mirror. Spencer blinked, still trying to focus. The stall door was open, but he thought he'd seen something duck out of sight.

Spencer took a cautious step toward the bathroom stall

and peered in. Seeing nothing, he gently pushed the door. It swung on its hinges to reveal an empty stall, nothing but scraps of toilet tissue littering the hard floor.

"Weird," Spencer muttered, still blinking against the eye-tingling sensation. Dispensing another small piece of paper towel, he used it to open the bathroom door. Then he headed for the lunchroom.

CHAPTER 5

"BETTER HURRY UP."

Miss Sharmelle's afternoon lessons were back up to par. The students sat on the floor for the last twenty minutes of class listening to her read aloud from some novel about the Civil War. Spencer had read the book on his own the year before, but he didn't mind hearing it again. Anything was better than algebra.

As Miss Sharmelle turned another page, her voice escalating with the narrative, Spencer glimpsed movement by the bookshelf. There was something crawling across the top of the books!

Before Spencer could say anything, something sprang forward, unfolding leathery, batlike wings. It had the bald head and hooked beak of a vulture. The rest of its black body, no bigger than a softball, was covered in short, bristly hair.

From the bookshelf, it flew in a jagged arc over the students, turning only inches away from Miss Sharmelle's pink-streaked hairdo.

"Ahhh!" Spencer cried, flattening himself to the ground. "Look out!"

As soon as the words left his mouth, the winged creature arched back and dove as fast as a falcon behind the teacher's desk.

"Spencer?" Miss Sharmelle said, looking up from the novel. "Is something wrong?" The other kids were staring at him, some trying to suppress giggles.

What? Impossible! Of course something was wrong! Some hideous bat thing had just come out of the bookshelf. Spencer glanced toward the teacher's desk. The creature was hiding now. Probably waiting for the perfect moment to swoop down and scoop out everyone's eyeballs.

"I thought I saw something," Spencer said. "Did anyone else . . . I mean . . . did anyone see anything?" His classmates slowly shook their heads with looks on their faces that might have condemned him to a lifetime in the loony bin.

Finally, someone broke the silence. "Yeah. I saw something." Spencer turned. It was Dez. "I saw some doofus put his face on the floor and shout, 'Look out!'" This won laughter from several kids, but Miss Sharmelle killed it.

"Spencer, what exactly do you think you saw?"

"Well," Spencer said, unsure how to explain it. "It was kind of hairy, with black wings and a sharp beak."

"Like a bat?" one of his classmates asked.

"Yes!" Spencer said. "Kind of like a bat."

"Uh, bats don't have beaks, Doofus." This was from Dez, who clearly thought everyone was taking Spencer too seriously.

"It came out of the bookshelf over there," Spencer explained, rising to his feet. "It flew right down here, close to Miss Sharmelle. But when I saw it, the thing just shot down behind the teacher's desk."

Instant stampede. About half the kids in the class rushed over to Mrs. Natcher's desk, surrounding it from every angle.

"There's nothing here!" shouted Daisy. "It's gone."

"Of course there's nothing," answered Dez. "Spencer just imagined it. See, Daisy. He's got that flu I was telling you about. The only way to stop it is by doing this." Dez stuck his thumbs up his nose and put his pinkies in his ears. Then the bell rang and he jumped up, grabbed his backpack, and ran out of the classroom screaming.

As the students poured out of the room, Miss Sharmelle called Spencer over. "I'm a little worried about you," she said. "I don't know what Mrs. Natcher usually tolerates, but you've been kind of disruptive today. Now, I won't tell her about this, or about how you slept through math. But I surely hope you weren't *trying* to make a scene."

"No, ma'am," Spencer promised. "I'm pretty sure I saw something."

"Well, maybe you did. I'll keep my eyes peeled." Miss Sharmelle gave him a heartwarming smile. "See you tomorrow."

Unable to resist, Spencer took a few steps forward and peeked behind the desk.

Nothing.

It took Spencer a few moments to gather his things; by the time he entered the hallway, most of the kids were outside loading into the busses. It would be a long walk if he missed the bus. And Spencer really didn't want to bother his mother for a ride—assuming that the station wagon started in the first place.

Spencer rounded a corner, heading for the main doors, and stopped in his tracks. There it was, nestled in the trash can, its bat wings sticking up over the top edge. Frozen, Spencer watched it rummage through the garbage, poking its bald head in a Kit Kat wrapper.

"Get down!" someone shouted, and Spencer instinctively dropped to the carpet. Dez appeared behind him, waving his hands at invisible objects above his head. "Save us, Batman! They're everywhere!"

Dez's sixth-grade buddies showed up laughing. "Good one, dude." Dez stopped swinging his arms and joined in the laughter.

One of the bullies pointed as Spencer scampered to his feet. "That's the weirdo from your class? What a loser."

Spencer looked instinctively at the garbage can. The vulture-headed creature was still there. Lifting a chocolaty beak from the Kit Kat wrapper, it ruffled its wings and flew off down the hallway.

"Come on." The bullies burst through the school doors. Spencer's face still might have been a little pink from the soap that morning, but now it was bright red. Dez was telling everyone! It was bad enough that he didn't have any friends at Welcher Elementary. But it would be far worse if everyone in the school thought he was crazy.

Then, as if to seal his insanity, something else moved down the hallway, scuttling low to the floor. It was the size of a prairie dog but as round and bushy as a bath loofah. It had long, gray fur that was so dingy it looked like a giant mothball rolling down the hallway. The dust gopher stopped in a dirty corner where the carpet met the wall and began chowing down on . . . dust?

Suddenly, a broom sailed out of nowhere and slammed into the corner by the dust-ball critter. Spencer jumped as the gopher ran for it. It dashed to a doorway across the hall, but the way was instantly blocked by a huge, oafish man with a vacuum.

Hearing the vacuum rev to life, the dust-ball scurried back just as the vacuum hose came down. The suction came so close that Spencer saw the creature's fur change direction, bits of dirt tumbling out and rattling up the vacuum hose. In an instant, the dust-ball escaped, racing back toward the lunchroom.

Casually, as though nothing strange had happened, the bearlike janitor dragged his vacuum hose along the edge of the carpet, picking up tiny bits of paper that had fallen near the garbage can. With his other hand, he grabbed his leather belt, laden with a large ring of heavy keys and a walkie-talkie radio. His dirty white shirt came untucked as he hiked up his sagging pants.

"Better hurry up," the man said without looking. "Don't want to miss the bus."

Spencer backed away slowly, unsure if he should feel better because he wasn't hallucinating or worse because there really were demon creatures roaming the halls of Welcher Elementary School.

One thing was sure: No one could see them but him and the janitor. And Spencer had a feeling that he wasn't supposed to be on that list.

CHAPTER 6

"YOU BELIEVE ME?"

The morning was crisp and cool when Spencer coasted into the parking lot of Welcher Elementary School. He'd found a bicycle in Aunt Avril's garage. The tires were low, but he'd found a pump, too. It was still very early—school wouldn't start for another twenty minutes. But Spencer needed that time to investigate.

At home, in his tidy bedroom, Spencer had replayed the previous day over and over again, sorting out all the information and trying to determine what made him different . . . or special . . . or psycho.

It wasn't hard to figure out, just hard to accept. Everything had been normal until he had washed his face. Right after he'd dried his eyes, with his face still tingling unnaturally, he'd seen movement in the bathroom stall. Then

29

he saw the bat thing during reading, then more little monsters after school.

The janitor guy saw them too, which made perfect sense because the janitors were in charge of all cleaning supplies in the school. They must have accidentally left that burn-your-face-off soap in the bathroom.

Spencer chained his bike to the empty rack. He needed to tell someone what he'd seen. His mother was too busy to help. On Monday, Spencer had told her that he'd been abducted by aliens on the playground and she had said, "That sounds neat, Spence." No, he needed to tell someone who would take time to listen. Spencer hoped it would be Miss Sharmelle.

Spencer wiped a bead of sweat from his forehead. The morning was cool, but it had been a long ride from his house to the school. He tugged on the door.

Locked.

"They'll open it in five minutes," said a voice from behind a tree. Daisy Gates appeared, book in hand. "I always like to be the first one in the school, so I get here early and read until they open the doors. I don't live far away. Just like three blocks."

"Yeah," Spencer said. "I wanted to get here early too." He studied Daisy. Her long, thick hair was in its usual braid down her back. She was taller than some of the boys, and when she smiled big, her mouth was full of teeth. Despite her extra height, she still seemed small. She looked truly impressionable, which made sense since Spencer knew that she believed anything anyone said.

Gullible Gates. Suddenly, Spencer realized that she was exactly who he needed.

"Hey," he said, walking over to the grass. "There's something I've been meaning to talk to you about."

"About Dez?" she said, tucking a bookmark into her novel. She looked down and began backing away. "I know. People tell me all the time that I shouldn't believe him. But sometimes he says some really interesting things."

"Actually," Spencer said, "it's about yesterday. Remember when I said I saw something during the read-aloud?"

"Yeah."

"Well, I'm *sure* I saw something."

"The little bat?"

"It was more than a bat. It was . . ." Spencer took a deep breath, putting all of his hope in Daisy's gullibility, "a little flying monster."

All right. Now that he'd said it aloud, it sounded absolutely stupid. Daisy stared at him for a long time. Her eyes got wide.

"What did it do?" she asked intently.

"You believe me?" Spencer cried in disbelief.

"Wait a minute, are you tricking me?"

"No! No. I'm serious."

"How come no one else saw it?"

"The janitor did. He tried to vacuum one up after school, but it got away."

"Marv," she said.

"What?"

"The janitor. Was it the big guy with a shaggy black

31

beard and a bald spot on his head?" Spencer nodded. "His name is Marv Bills," she said. "He's really nice. Marv does most of the work, but John Campbell is really the head janitor."

"You're friends with the janitors?"

"No," Daisy said. "I just study the yearbook and memorize people's names."

Spencer wanted to tell her that was kind of weird. But then, he'd just told her that he saw flying monsters, so he had no room to talk.

"Yeah." Daisy nodded. "The yearbook's great. You probably don't have one yet 'cause you're new around here. Anyway, did you have monsters at your old school?"

Spencer couldn't believe that she was taking him seriously. But that was Daisy's greatest weakness. "It all started when I found some magic soap . . ."

That was it. Spencer had pushed it too far. He saw Daisy's eyebrows furrow in skepticism. If he'd only said "special soap" or "unusual soap"—but no. He'd said the "m" word.

"You're tricking me."

"I swear I'm not," Spencer pleaded. Daisy turned and put her book into her backpack. "Come on," he begged, "I'm not like Dez. I don't stick M&Ms up my nose."

"Why don't you prove it? I'd love to see little critters crawling on the walls."

"It's not really fun, Daisy. It's actually kind of freaky."

"How do you expect me to believe you if I can't see them?" she asked.

"Well, I don't know," said Spencer. "You seem to believe Dez just fine."

Daisy stalked away, pushing open the now unlocked door to the school.

Great! Spencer thought. *Even Gullible Gates doesn't buy my story.* But what if he *could* show her? He could show Miss Sharmelle, too. And the principal. They could call an exterminator!

Spencer caught up to Daisy halfway down the hall. Other kids were entering and Daisy had failed at her daily goal to be the first one inside.

"I've decided to show you, Daisy."

She raised her eyebrows as they walked side by side. Spencer could tell she was having some kind of internal battle: the Daisy who got tricked a lot versus the Daisy who wanted to learn something important. Silently, Spencer rooted for the latter.

"Come with me," he said. "Let me get the soap out of the garbage and you can try it for yourself."

They walked in silence. When they reached the bathroom, Spencer pushed open the door and ran inside with the urgency of someone who'd been "holding it" for hours. He reached the garbage can . . . and his hopes shattered.

A fresh sack lined the can. All of yesterday's garbage was gone—disposed of by the janitors. Spencer's plan was falling apart.

"It's not there," Spencer said, emerging slowly from the bathroom.

"That's okay," Daisy said. "I'm sure the janitors have more."

Spencer paused thoughtfully for a moment. "That's a good idea, Daisy," he said. "Come on. We've still got ten minutes."

In a moment, the two kids stood at the top of a few stairs. The short flight descended into the janitorial area. It was a large space for storing extra garbage cans, trash bags, chemical cleaners, wax for the tile floors, and, Spencer hoped, magic soap.

"Wait!" Spencer caught Daisy's arm at the top of the stairs. "Why do we need the soap?"

Daisy looked at him as though he were an idiot. "So I can see the little critters and you can prove that you're not lying to me."

"Well, yes," Spencer said, rolling his eyes. "But we're not going to tell the janitors *that*."

"What're we going to tell them, then?"

"Well, *I* needed it because I had marker on my face. The soap took it off, no problem." Spencer quickly unzipped his backpack and pulled out a ballpoint pen.

"What are you doing?" Daisy yelped as he reached for her face.

"I'm giving us a reason to ask for soap."

Daisy whimpered at first, but gradually became more co-operative. It was over in a flash. Daisy had blue ink flames leaping up her cheek.

"I'll do the talking," Spencer said. "Come on."

The two kids quietly descended the stairs until they

stood at the doorway to the large storage closet. From this angle, Spencer could see a small desk with a computer nestled among the janitorial boxes, bottles, and canisters. It seemed that the closet doubled for an office.

"Hello?" Spencer called into the dimly lit room.

Almost immediately, a head of shaggy black hair popped over a stack of boxes. Marv Bills stepped out, studying the two kids skeptically. He dusted off his hands, clapping them together like two thick slabs of meat.

Marv wore the same dirty white shirt as the day before. If anything, his faded jeans were sagging further down his behind. He looked a few years older than thirty, but it was hard to tell with his bushy beard. Really the only difference between Marv and a grizzly bear was that Marv could speak.

The burly janitor took a few steps forward, the massive ring of keys at his side tinkling like the bells on Santa's sleigh. Marv grunted when he saw Daisy's face. "Tattoos? In elementary school?" He shook his head and muttered, "What's this world coming to?"

"It's not a tattoo. We need soap," Spencer blurted. Instantly, he wished he'd made some small talk or said something to make it sound less desperate. "Hi, how are you?" he tried again, but it was like telling the joke after the punch line.

"Soap?" Marv asked. "There should be plenty in the girls' bathroom. I filled the dispensers yesterday."

"But she's got ink on her face," Spencer said. "We need soap that'll take it off fast. You know, the strong stuff."

Marv folded his arms. "You kids shouldn't be down here."

"Sorry," Daisy said. "We'll go."

Spencer grabbed her arm. "Not till we get some soap." Spencer stared at the janitor. With a swift motion, Marv reached over and grabbed something off a shelf.

"Think fast," he said, tossing a small rectangular box across the room. Daisy caught it, then fumbled, but caught it again before it hit the ground. Spencer reached for it anxiously, but she evaded his grasp and turned to read the label on the box.

Irish Spring.

"What?" Spencer muttered, finally pulling the box from Daisy's hands. He tore open the little flaps on the end and dumped a green bar of soap into his left hand.

"Not this." Spencer shook his head at Marv. "I want the *special* stuff. The pink gel soap that takes off marker and makes your face tingle."

"Why don't you just be glad for what you got and scram?" Marv flicked his wrist at them. "One kind of soap works just like another. There's no special stuff down here."

With those words, Daisy suddenly went rigid. Warily, Spencer glanced over at her. The blue ink flames outlined on her cheek were turning red. She slowly twisted her glare to meet his eyes.

"Bully," she whispered. Her eyes looked like they might be sprouting tears sometime in the next ten seconds.

"No, Daisy, I promise, I—"

"Dez tells me that forests only grow on islands and tricks

me into putting my thumbs up my nose. But you—you pretend to be my friend so you can draw doodles on my face and scare me into thinking that little monsters roam the school." The first tear departed, running down her cheek and sizzling on the flames. "Gullible Gates! Yeah, right! I'm not believing anyone anymore." Daisy turned and ran up the stairs, covering her graffitied cheek with one hand. Spencer started to follow, but a firm hand gripped his backpack.

"What do you know about monsters?" Marv hissed in his ear.

"Let me go!" Spencer slipped out of his arm straps and began a tug of war with his pack. Daisy had blown his secret!

"Where'd you get this special soap?"

"*You* know!" Spencer said. "You left it lying around!"

Marv suddenly released his backpack and Spencer staggered sideways a few steps. "You've got yourself into real trouble, boy," Marv whispered. "Stuff like that's not meant for you."

The bell rang to announce the beginning of class. Spencer moved toward the stairs.

"I haven't seen the last of you," Marv said. "But tomorrow, we've got an even bigger problem, so you'll have to wait. What's your name?"

"I'm not telling!" Spencer raced up the stairs.

"Then I'll find out!"

CHAPTER 7

"LOOK OUT BEHIND YOU!"

When Spencer reached the classroom, the Bath and Body Works fragrance of Miss Leslie Sharmelle had been replaced by a slight odor of cabbage.

Mrs. Natcher was back.

"Good morning, class," Mrs. Natcher said.

"Good morning, Mrs. Natcher," the class recited in unison.

Along with smelling like a steamed veggie, Mrs. Natcher was very conservative and formal. In her late fifties, she didn't bother to dye her graying hair or paint her nails. After Miss Sharmelle's flash and flare, Mrs. Natcher seemed drab and boring.

Daisy ignored Spencer all morning. The liquid soap in the girls' bathroom had taken the blue flames off her face—mostly. Her cheek was scrubbed raw and her determination was clearly set. Even Dez knew something was wrong with Daisy when she refused to believe that his tennis shoes had once belonged to the president of the United States. Gullible Gates had finally decided that *no one* could be trusted.

With the events in the storage closet as a prelude to his day, Spencer stayed far away from the janitor's stairwell. Before lunch, he entered the boys' bathroom to wash up, ducking past Marv in the hallway.

In the bathroom, he encountered a third type of creature. This one was slimy, pale yellow, and looked like a salamander. It was perched on the rim of the sink, its long black tongue working at some grimy film that had built up next to the tap. Spencer froze to watch, but the creature quickly sensed him and slid into the bowl of the sink. Its body flattened as though bones were optional and quickly slithered down the drain.

A few minutes later, Spencer was looking at a tray of mediocre cafeteria food, trying not to think that gross little creatures might live in the kitchen.

"'Sup, Batman?" Dez turned away from his food, shouting at Spencer over his shoulder. Dez was surrounded by his usual knucklehead buddies. "See any bats with beaks today?"

Spencer froze, his lunch tray gripped firmly. *Don't even look over there*, he told himself. *Just keep walking*. But it was a good thing he looked, because there *was* a bat monster perched right on Dez's milk carton. Its bald head bobbed as it wedged a sharp beak into the carton for a slurp of milk.

"Look out behind you!" Spencer shouted at Dez,

winning the attention of everyone in the cafeteria. Whether it was the sincerity in Spencer's voice or the suddenness with which he shouted, Dez whirled around in genuine surprise. His clumsy turn tipped the milk carton, sending the invisible creature into the air and cold milk into Dez's crotch.

The noisy room erupted with laughter at Dez's blunder. Across the cafeteria, Spencer glimpsed Daisy looking up from her sack lunch. Spencer watched the creature's jagged flight pattern until it ducked out the doorway. When he looked back down, Dez was coming right for him.

Sudden loss of appetite, coupled with the urge to run, made Spencer dump his lunch directly into the nearest garbage and head for the door. Bursting outside, he raced across the playground, not daring to check over his shoulder until he reached the far side of the soccer field. There was no sign of pursuit, so he slumped against the goalpost.

Tears were trying to surface. Spencer shut his eyes. His sixth-grade year was turning out to be worse than he could have imagined and he wanted to shut it out, to pretend he was at his old school. But shutting his eyes wasn't such a bright idea, since he was surrounded when he opened them.

Spencer scrambled to his feet, ringed in by Dez's friends. The bully stood right before him, an embarrassing wet mark down the front of his shorts. In his hand was a new milk carton that he tossed from left to right like a hot potato.

"So," Dez said. "You tried to get me with the oldest, stupidest trick in the book?" He held up his hands in mock fear. "'Oh! Look out behind you!'" he shouted in a high-pitched voice. "That's what *you'd* better be doing, Doofus. Because I'm going to be right behind you from now on."

"But it wasn't a trick," Spencer said. "I really did see something on your lunch tray. It flew off when you turned around."

"Whatever," Dez said. "You made me look bad in the lunchroom and you're going to pay for that." Dez took a step forward. "Do you know what this is?" He held the carton close to Spencer's face.

"Milk?" Spencer hoped.

"Yeah, it's milk. But take a look at the inspiration date."

"Very inspiring," Spencer said. "But it's actually the *expiration* date."

"Whatever," Dez said. "The point is—it's old. Steve's been keeping this in his desk since the first day of school. Should be nice and rotten by now. We've been saving it for a special occasion. This might be special enough. Unless . . ."

"Unless what?" Spencer asked. He stared at the deadly milk carton. Swimming inside were countless bacteria and germs galore. "What do you want from me?"

"Just a simple apology," Dez answered. "And explain to my homies that you lied about the invisible bats."

"But I didn't lie . . ."

"Hold him, guys."

The nearest bullies grabbed Spencer's arms. He tried to jerk free, but their grip was tight. Dez peeled back the cardboard flaps on the milk carton and gagged at the rotted smell. Then he slowly tipped the carton forward.

"Wait! Wait!" cried Spencer. "I'm sorry, okay? You're

right! I didn't see anything on your lunch tray. I never saw anything in the classroom. I lied about all of that. I was just making it up to get attention!"

Dez grinned and stepped back. "That's what I thought." Spencer tried to relax as the bullies released his arms. "See, Batman," Dez continued. "Isn't it easier when you do what I say? We both get what we want. I get to hear you confess about your dumb lies. And you? Well, this should get you plenty of attention."

With that, Dez hurled the milk carton. It struck Spencer in the chest with an explosion of putrid milk. The bullies ran off, laughing and whooping.

Spencer stepped away from the spot where the carton fell, glugging out yellowish milk. His shirt was ruined. It absolutely reeked. He wiped his face and noticed someone standing near.

It was Daisy. She looked sad and upset. Spencer was grateful that at least one person cared. But then she opened her mouth.

"You really did lie to me," she said, and Spencer knew she wasn't sad about him. "I heard you say it. You just made it all up for attention. *And* so you could draw on my face."

"Look, Daisy," Spencer said, rising to his feet, "I never lied to you. I really did see a creature on his lunch tray. I just had to tell those guys that I made it up so they'd leave me alone."

"Why?" she said. "If it's true, why did you tell them it wasn't? No one will ever believe you if you don't stand up for what you know is true."

"But you saw. They were going to dump bad milk on me."

"So you denied it."

"Yeah. I denied it to them."

"And they dumped bad milk on you anyway." Daisy shrugged. "Either way, you got bad milk. Seems like it would have been better to stand up for the truth." Daisy waved awkwardly, as if she were bidding him farewell forever.

Spencer stood alone on the soccer field. "Man," he said. "This stinks."

And it did.

CHAPTER 8

"WHAT KIND OF MAINTENANCE?"

Spencer started the next day at school with the secretary's voice crackling through the old intercom. "Good morning, boys and girls. We have a few announcements to make. Tomorrow there is a morning assembly. D.A.R.E. Officer Jacobs will be teaching us how to stay drug free.

"After-school clubs will not convene today. The Bureau of Educational Maintenance will be meeting with the janitors immediately after the bell. We ask that everyone leave the building as quickly as possible so the folks from the Bureau can do their routine checks. Have a great day."

Click.

Spencer, who had been twirling his pencil around his thumb, stopped suddenly, and the pencil rolled off the edge of his desk. Bureau of Educational Maintenance? Like, *building* maintenance? A bureau of janitors, perhaps? If that was true, maybe he could get some info about them at lunch.

Spencer felt tired through all of Mrs. Natcher's morning lessons. Not algebra-tired, like before, but still tired enough to ruin his focus. He hadn't slept much the night before. Every time he closed his eyes, the scene with Dez and the milk carton replayed.

When he watched the instant replay in his mind, Spencer bravely stood up for what he knew was right and took the rotten milk like a man. Then Daisy believed him and together they tried to convince responsible adults to acknowledge that Welcher Elementary had a major pest problem. Together they investigated the janitors and found out more about the creatures.

But that version of the story wasn't real. Spencer had denied the truth, shattered any hope of Daisy believing him, and still been hit with the sour-milk bomb. He was too ashamed to even tell his mom. The stinky shirt had gone straight into the garbage.

Spencer felt like a real loner. Dez hated him. Daisy wouldn't believe him. If he wanted to learn more about the janitors, he would be doing it alone.

When the lunch bell rang, Spencer made his routine stop at the restroom to wash up. Then he kept an eye out for big Marv as he quietly made his way to the front office.

Spencer had entered the office only once before, with his siblings, a few days before school began. They'd been living in Aunt Avril's house all summer, but of course his mom had waited until the last possible moment to register them and fill out the paperwork so the four Zumbro kids could be admitted to their new school.

"Can I help you?" asked the same voice that gave the announcements. Without the crackle and pop of the intercom, the secretary sounded much younger. Spencer had always imagined that the voice belonged to someone with an extraterrestrial in her family tree, but Mrs. Hamp was actually far too normal looking.

"Hi," Spencer said. "I had a question about the announcements this morning." He stayed a few apprehensive feet from her desk.

"After-school clubs will *not* be convening today. To 'convene' means to meet. Put it together. No after-school clubs today, sorry," she answered mechanically, as though a dozen other kids had already been in to bother her about it.

"I know. I'm not in a club. I just had a question about the bureau that's coming."

"The Bureau of Educational Maintenance?"

"Yeah," Spencer said. "What do they do?"

Seeing that his question was a cut above those of the pesky kids complaining about the cancellation of their clubs, Mrs. Hamp pasted on a friendly face. "The BEM is a very old agency. It oversees the maintenance of schools across the U.S."

"What kind of maintenance?"

"Structural integrity, environmental conditions, HR," she began with an I-know-big-words-and-you-don't look on her face. She chuckled at her overabundant wisdom and glanced at Spencer with a look of feigned apology. "In other words, they make sure the building is safe and sound and everything is running correctly. The BEM is in charge of hiring and firing janitors across the nation."

Then she tilted her head sideways and absently picked up a stapler. "But mostly they just do mundane things like deep cleaning and checking to make sure all equipment is functioning adequately."

"And someone from the Bureau will be here after school today?" Spencer pressed. "To meet with Marv?"

"Marv?" Mrs. Hamp asked. "I think not. I would imagine they'll meet with John Campbell."

"Because he's Marv's boss?"

Mrs. Hamp set down the stapler. "My, you have a lot of questions," she said, regaining her initial level of annoyance.

"I'm just interested in that kind of stuff," Spencer lied. "Maybe someday I'd like to work for the BEM."

"Ho, no," Mrs. Hamp said, shaking her head. "You want to scrape up chewed gum and shampoo carpets for the rest of your life?" She tipped back in her chair. "Close the door when you leave. I have to eat lunch too, you know."

Spencer could see that he'd exhausted Mrs. Hamp's knowledge of the BEM, but it was enough. He shut the office door and headed to the lunchroom. He replayed his confrontation with Marv the day before. *"Tomorrow, we've got an even bigger problem, so you'll have to wait."*

One thing seemed clear: Marv was nervous about the BEM's visit. And since he had said *"we've* got a problem,"

Spencer guessed that John Campbell was also involved. But what could the janitors at Welcher Elementary possibly have to hide?

To Spencer, the answer was right before his eyes, scuttling across the carpet, leaving a wake of gray dust.

CHAPTER 9

"THERE!"

Spencer's focus was even worse after lunch. Knowing that he might get answers from the BEM gave him anxious stomach butterflies. He also knew he would be breaking a rule to talk to the BEM, since the school was supposed to be empty for the routine checks. But Spencer was already planning a way around that.

Mrs. Natcher was droning on about what makes America great when Spencer felt drowsiness pull at his eyelids.

Not again! He sat up tall in an attempt to ward off the sleepiness. Then he caught a dreaded flash of movement that made his gut turn over. There, under the chalkboard, where white dust fell thickly to the carpet, Spencer saw a creature. It was one of the dust gophers, really enjoying a meal of carpet dirt and chalk dust.

Spencer stared for a moment, then glanced hopefully at his classmates. The creature must have truly been invisible, because to Spencer it sat in plain sight, only a yard from Mrs. Natcher's boring shoes.

Ignore it, Spencer thought. *Just ignore it and it will go away.* But even as he thought this, Spencer pointed a silent finger toward the creature.

"There," he whispered. The word was inaudible, but once he felt it form on his lips, it was easier the second time.

"There." The word got some attention this time and a few kids, including Dez, started looking where Spencer pointed.

"There!" This one was almost a shout and stopped Mrs. Natcher midsentence.

"If you have something to say," she instructed, "please raise your hand and I'll consider calling on you."

"THERE IT GOES!" Spencer jumped to his feet as the dust gopher took off across the room. He traced its run with his finger.

"What is it?" one student shouted.

"A spider?"

"A mouse?"

In seconds, the classroom was out of control. Kids were screaming and climbing onto their chairs. To add to the chaos, Dez knocked over Jen's desk, spilling pencils and notebooks.

Spencer watched the creature disappear into the hallway. He looked to see Daisy's reaction, but all he saw was

Mrs. Natcher coming right for him. She took him by the arm and dragged him to the front of the room.

"Class! Class! You will be silent in three, two, one." Mrs. Natcher clapped her hands and, like magic, the room fell quiet. "I'm sure Spencer would like a chance to explain himself."

Not really, Spencer thought. But it was too late now. Mrs. Natcher wasn't giving him an option. "Well, I thought I saw something."

"Not again," Juan moaned.

"*Again?*" Mrs. Natcher inquired. "Has this happened before?"

Cutting Spencer off, Dez took over. "While you were gone, Spencer thought he saw a bat. But just like this time, he was making it up." Dez turned to the class. "Come on, did anyone actually see anything?"

"Nope."

"Nothing."

"That's right," Dez said. "Nothing to see. Spencer made it up for attention. Told me so himself."

Mrs. Natcher clucked her tongue at Spencer. "That behavior is inappropriate and unacceptable in my classroom. Apologize to your classmates."

Spencer shifted uncomfortably. Couldn't they tell he was speaking the truth? Why would anyone make this up? Sure, he was getting attention, but it wasn't the good kind.

"Sorry," Spencer said. "I didn't mean to be disruptive. I thought I saw something, but maybe . . ." Then Spencer made the mistake of looking at Daisy Gates. Her eyes were trained on him, bolts of energy piercing him. *No one will ever believe you if you don't stand up for what you know is true.*

"I . . . I mean . . . I . . ." Each stammer was like the crank of an engine, slowly building up the power to take off. He looked at Dez. The bully was massaging his fist, like he was itching to pound somebody.

"I see creatures in the school. Some are slimy, some are furry, some have wings. I don't know why the rest of you can't see them. I'm trying to figure that out. I don't want to freak you guys out, but I had to tell you what I've seen."

Dead silence.

Then, like an avalanche: laughter. *Laughter!* Even Mrs. Natcher was chuckling in her own stuffy way. Spencer looked from face to face, sheer embarrassment and disappointment in his eyes. Then he saw Daisy, the one who wasn't laughing. Instead, her brown eyes gave a silent applause.

CHAPTER 10

"WALK WITH ME."

Spencer leaned his head against the pop machine and felt its steady vibration. Was that the machine's way of laughing at him too? Spencer could barely see the clock from where he was hiding. A half hour after school ended and Spencer could still hear his whole class laughing at him. Mrs. Natcher's tone lingered in his mind: "Sit down and remain silent."

All that had hurt deeply. But hurt wasn't the only feeling in his heart. A thread of courage had formed when he told the truth. Courage to stand up for what he knew was right. Courage to move forward with his plan to meet the BEM after school.

He was wedged between two vending machines in the teachers' lounge. Spencer had never even been in a teachers' lounge, let alone hidden out in one. But he'd also never seen demon dust gophers and slimy lizard things lurking around the school. Desperate times called for desperate hideouts. The bus was long gone, carrying his younger brother and sisters back to Aunt Avril's house.

With no idea how long the BEM's routine checks would last, Spencer could afford to wait no longer.

Spencer slithered out of his hiding spot. His backpack had gone home with his sister Erica so he would be able to maneuver swiftly if he needed to. He walked past a table and two couches before gripping the doorknob.

Spencer's plan was simple. He would secretly locate one of the BEM representatives and share his concerns about Marv and the creatures. It might be tricky to isolate one of the reps, but Spencer was willing to wait for the opportunity to arise.

Silently, Spencer pushed open the door, hopeful that the coast was clear. Instead, he found himself face-to-face with shaggy Marv. Beside the janitor was a man with a sinewy neck, thick as a tree trunk. His blond hair was buzzed in a military crew cut.

Spencer's first thought was to scurry like a dust gopher back into the teachers' lounge. But that was a dead end. He could try to dart past them and sprint for the front doors. Hopeless. So Spencer decided to change his tactic altogether.

"You from the BEM?" Spencer asked the man with the thick neck. The stranger wasn't very tall, but he seemed as tough and bulletproof as Kevlar. Next to Marv, the man looked sharp and clean, no trace of whiskers on his square chin.

"Garth Hadley, regional representative for the Bureau of Educational Maintenance," the man affirmed with a curt nod.

"No kids allowed in the school right now," Marv ordered. Spencer could tell that Garth Hadley made the grubby janitor nervous and twitchy. Marv began chewing on his fingernails, which were, Spencer thought, probably not very clean. Neither man seemed to mind that a sixth grader had just walked out of the teachers' lounge.

"I'm working on a project," Spencer lied, racking his brain. "It's about . . . mops."

"Mops?" Garth Hadley repeated.

"Yeah." Spencer smiled. "Mops through the ages. It's for a history unit. I heard you were going to be here and I wondered if I could interview you, Mr. Hadley, sir."

Marv, shaking his dark head, took an intimidating step toward Spencer, his hairy belly peeking through a hole in his white T-shirt. "Get moving!" Marv said in a tone he might have used to scare a stray dog.

Spencer felt a chill run through him. There was no telling what the big janitor might do to keep Spencer away from the BEM rep. Spencer backed away from Marv's intimidating bulk. The boy was silently pleading that Mr. Hadley would intervene before the janitor used Spencer's face as a prototype for a new mop.

"Mr. Bills," Garth Hadley said to Marv. A slow smile spread across the man's square face, and one muscular hand gestured for Marv to back off. "I'll see that the boy gets outside," he said, directing Spencer by the shoulder. "And we'll talk mops on the way."

Instead of taking Spencer to the nearby front doors, Hadley led him down a long hallway to the exit that opened on the parking lot.

"How old are you? Eleven?" the man said.

"Twelve, actually. I just had a birthday at the end of August. I'm old for my grade."

The small talk was nice, but Spencer had more important things to discuss. Glancing over his shoulder, Spencer made sure that Marv's hulking form was out of earshot.

"It's not mops, really," Spencer said quietly. In his peripheral vision, Spencer caught sight of a winged vulture-bat cutting a jagged path toward the lunchroom. "It's the janitors, Mr. Hadley."

"What about them?" asked the thick man.

Now that Spencer had Mr. Hadley alone, he didn't know exactly how to say it. He couldn't risk becoming the brunt of another joke. The last thing he wanted was for this new stranger to have a laugh at his story. Spencer decided to start small and go from there.

"The janitors are . . . weird."

Mr. Hadley snorted. "Every profession has its drawbacks."

"No." Spencer decided to approach from a new angle. "It just seems like they can see things that other people can't."

"Like an extra layer of grime around the sink in the restroom?"

"Yeah," Spencer said, preparing to dive in. "Like an extra layer of grime that can tuck back its tail and slither down the drain."

Garth Hadley froze, one hand on the metal bar of the door. He was apparently in some kind of deep meditation. Spencer studied his clean, strong face but was unable to read the emotions there.

"Get outside," Hadley said firmly. At first, Spencer thought the man was angry. But to the boy's surprise, Mr. Hadley also stepped out, closing the school door behind him.

The September afternoon was hot and dry. Spencer could feel the sun's rays soaking into the asphalt parking lot, making the few remaining vehicles shimmer.

"What else have you seen?" Garth Hadley whispered, intensity in his eyes.

Spencer felt a rush of exhilaration. Mr. Hadley was believing him! Of course, Daisy had believed at first, but Spencer had gone too far and she was thrown off. Spencer chewed on his lip, carefully deciding how to pace his story.

"Sometimes I see bats in the garbage can . . . and rodents scurrying down the halls."

Mr. Hadley shook his head. "But they're not quite bats, are they? And they're not really rodents." He stooped to look directly into Spencer's eyes. "It's important that you tell me *everything*."

With this encouragement, Spencer spilled all. He

started at the beginning, with the soap he'd found in the bathroom. Then he explained each creature in detail and told how Marv could see them too. He told about his conversation with Daisy Gates and his confrontation with Dez and the sour milk. He ended with his confession to the class and the resulting bitter laughter.

Telling the whole story made it sound even more unbelievable, but the grave look on Garth Hadley's face assured Spencer that he was right about everything.

"Your story confirms our suspicions," Mr. Hadley said. "Walk with me."

They crossed the sweltering parking lot to a white van. On the driver's door was a circular seal with the United States eagle, *e pluribus unum* written on a banner in its beak. In one talon it held a broom; the other clutched a dustpan. "Bureau of Educational Maintenance" was scribed in fancy letters above the eagle's head. Other than the seal, the van was blocky and plain, with no other windows and no additional doors except at the rear.

Garth Hadley pulled Spencer around to the back of the van, the vehicle's shadow cooling their legs. Hadley dug in the back pocket of his black pants and withdrew a wallet. Spencer saw his driver's license and legal BEM certification card. After rifling through the contents for a moment, Hadley produced a photograph.

"Have you seen this man in or around Welcher Elementary School?" Hadley asked, passing Spencer the photo.

The person in the picture was old—at least mid-sixties.

The man's hair was wavy and white. His face was lean and wrinkled, with a full mustache and goatee. It looked like a professional photo with a blue cloth background. The paper it was printed on was dull, the borders showing jagged scissor marks. Clipped out of a school yearbook, perhaps.

"Never seen him," Spencer said, handing the photo back. "Who is he?"

"His name is Walter Jamison, but we have reason to believe that he's going under the alias of John Campbell."

"John Campbell?" Spencer asked. "The secretary says he's the head janitor here. But I've never seen him, just Marv. What does he have to do with the creatures in the school?"

"The little monsters you've been seeing are very dangerous, especially to children. They inhale brain waves of young people and exhale certain toxins that affect children's ability to learn. Walter Jamison has been gathering them with the intent to extract, shall we say, *magical* properties from the creatures."

Spencer stared, dumbfounded. An adult had just dropped the "m" word in all seriousness. This was awesome. Spencer was finally getting some answers.

"So Marv is helping him?" Spencer clarified.

Hadley nodded. "You told me that Marv was trying to capture that dust gopher in the hallway after school. They are wild little beasts. Very difficult to contain. The few you've seen around the school must have slipped through Walter's fingers."

"So why don't you just fire Marv and Walter?" Spencer

asked. "Isn't the BEM in charge of hiring and firing janitors all over the U.S.?"

"I'm sure he'll be fired soon. But it would be unwise to fire Walter now that he is finally within our grasp." Mr. Hadley tapped his square chin in thought. "Walter Jamison has grown very powerful. Should we fire him now, he would vanish for a time, then pop up again somewhere else. Like a bad weed. But we have a chance to cripple him here and now—to put an end to his experiments before it's too late."

"What are you going to do?"

"I'm going to finish my routine inspection of the school and leave. While representatives of the BEM are around, the janitors will be overly cautious. It will be impossible to do what it takes to break Jamison."

"If you guys aren't going to do it, then who is?" Spencer asked.

"I was hoping *you* might help us." Garth Hadley opened the back doors of the van. Spencer was too stunned for words. Maybe he would end up with a career in the BEM after all. And sooner than he thought. Spencer's thread of courage was growing, bolstered by these newfound answers.

"What do you say?" Hadley asked, crawling into the back of the van. Instead of seats, the van was full of custodial equipment. There were two different kinds of vacuums, several brooms, some dustpans, and a couple of boxes full of miscellaneous items.

"Sure," Spencer managed at last. "What can I do?"

CHAPTER 11

"SWEET."

It's pretty complex," Garth Hadley explained. "Walter Jamison can only perform his warlock experiments within the walls of this school. He has fortified Welcher Elementary, using an ancient hammer to drive a bronze nail somewhere into the structure. The hammer gives him power, and the nail sets up a link with the building."

"What do I have to do?" Spencer asked.

"I need you to pull out the nail," Hadley explained, "with the same hammer that put it in."

"Whoa," muttered Spencer. "I don't know. I'm not really great with tools."

"You can do it," Hadley said. "It will be difficult. We have every reason to believe that Jamison keeps the bronze hammer on him at all times."

"That's why you want me to get it? Because he won't suspect me until it's too late?"

"Right," said Hadley. The man was on his knees, digging into a box in the back of the van. Spencer stood awkwardly by the bumper.

"Once I get the hammer, where will I find the nail?"

"We don't know. That is part of the reason we've scheduled these inspections." Hadley seemed to have found what he was looking for and began a backward crawl out of the van. "Once we get more details, I'll contact you and instruct you how to proceed."

Garth Hadley stood up and held out the two objects he had gathered from the box. His curiosity piqued, Spencer accepted the offerings. One was a small plastic flashlight with a red switch, the other, a used latex glove.

"Thought you might need these," Hadley said, shutting the back door of the van.

"Thanks," Spencer said, raising an eyebrow.

"There's more here than meets the eye," Hadley explained. "The flashlight bulb is charged with the same power that fuels Walter Jamison's projects. When you turn it on in the dark, you might not think it's doing much. However, other magical items will draw out a strong beam of light. That should help you find the nail and hammer.

"The glove is a dangerous item that we recovered from a raid of Walter Jamison's last experiment station. Jamison, it seems, somehow knew we were coming and was gone by the time we got there. Much like today, in fact."

"Where is he?"

"Marv said he was out of state at his brother's funeral. An unlikely story. But the glove," Hadley explained, "will be vital to your success."

"What does it do?" Spencer asked, dangling the limp, yellowish glove between two fingers.

"Put it on," Hadley encouraged.

Spencer looked at the used glove with apprehension. Who knew where this had been? What kind of germy hands had slipped into this glove before him?

"Nothing to fear," Hadley said, sensing his hesitation. "The glove won't harm you."

Spencer peered into the opening where his hand was supposed to go. Maybe it didn't look so bad inside. He pulled a face. Anyway, Garth Hadley was waiting for him. Taking a deep breath, Spencer plunged his hand into the glove, finding plenty of extra space at the end of each finger.

Hadley suddenly reached out with a sharp motion and grabbed Spencer's arm above the elbow.

"Ow!" Spencer winced at the iron grip and jerked away. To Spencer's surprise, his arm stretched and slipped easily through Hadley's grasp—as though the man were gripping a blob of Jell-O.

"Sweet," whispered Spencer.

Garth Hadley smiled. "As long as you're wearing that glove, no one will be able to hold you down." Spencer pulled it off, feeling the latex stretch and watching the glove turn inside out, a bit of sweat moistening the rubber.

"One exception," Hadley said, "although it's very

unlikely it will occur. If your opponent wears a similar glove, both become able to catch the other. Understand?"

Spencer nodded, still trying to believe that this was actually happening.

"Even with this gear, you'll need to be extremely clever and fast," Mr. Hadley continued. "You'll need some pretty potent distractions to occupy the janitors while you go snooping around. Be thinking—I'll be thinking too."

"What about Daisy?"

"Who?"

"Remember," Spencer said, "the girl whose face I drew on? I'd really like to show her the creatures. I think she could help me too."

"I thought she didn't believe you," Hadley said.

"She didn't," said Spencer. "But with your help, and some soap, she will."

"You want me to give her soap?"

Spencer nodded.

Hadley exhaled slowly. "Intentionally expose a child?" he whispered to himself, obviously caught in some moral dilemma.

"Out of everyone I've told, she's the most likely to believe," Spencer coaxed. "She wants to believe, but she gets tricked a lot." In his mind, Spencer saw the future playing out more hopefully. He would prove to Daisy that he wasn't a prankster, and at the same time he'd gain a friend to help him with Mr. Hadley's assignment.

Garth Hadley began to nod almost imperceptibly, his lips pursed. He led Spencer around to the driver's door and reached between the seats. He handed a clear plastic bottle to Spencer, half full of the strong pink soap. "Swear one thing," he said.

"What?" said Spencer, noting the intensity in Hadley's eyes.

"That soap is shared with Daisy alone. Once her eyes are opened, you'll give the bottle back to me with the bronze hammer and nail."

"Yes, sir."

"One more thing. As you've probably gathered by now, all this stuff is top secret. That means you'd probably better let things drop with your classmates. For your own good as well as theirs."

Spencer nodded. "They're going to tease me about what I've already said."

"Ignore it. This is dangerous business. We don't want to get anyone else involved. If they tease you, be silent and strong. Focus all your energy on your secret mission and bring Jamison down."

Hadley snatched a paper from the dashboard. He clicked a pen from his pocket. "You have a cell phone, Spencer?"

"Nope."

"How about e-mail?"

"SpenceZ@wahoo.com," replied Spencer. Hadley scribbled it down.

"If you run into trouble, just contact me," Hadley explained. He replaced his pen in his pocket and withdrew a business card with his name, phone number, and e-mail address printed on it. "The BEM doesn't want anyone getting hurt. If you think this is too much, don't hesitate to call. We can find some other way. But personally, I think you'll hit Walter Jamison so hard that he won't know what happened." Mr. Hadley patted Spencer's shoulder. "Good luck."

"Wait," cried Spencer as the man walked back toward the school.

"Go home, kid," Hadley shouted back.

Spencer leaned against the white van, wondering if the president of the United States knew that one of the government agencies had just enlisted a twelve-year-old.

CHAPTER 12

"THEM'S THE WORST KIND OF FOLKS."

The Gates home was small and rundown, the polar opposite of Aunt Avril's mansion on the hill. The single-story structure had been painted blue several times over the five decades that it spanned. The cement walkway sported cracks so large that the path looked tiered. A maple tree had been planted too close to the driveway. Now taller than the house, the tree roots reached far and limbs overhung the front porch.

Spencer found the house easily. After leaving Hadley's white van in the school parking lot, he had biked four blocks to a Chevron gas station. There, shuffling through the pages of an outdated directory at a dilapidated pay phone, he'd found the Gates's address. A two-block ride through the afternoon sun had brought him to the edge of Daisy's property.

The grass was mostly dry and crispy brown—at least Aunt Avril's house shared that feature after three months of Zumbro housekeeping. There was a large garage apart from the house. The garage door was open and a Buick was jacked up inside. There were two other cars parked on the broken driveway and a truck on the street.

Spencer stepped off his bike and put down the kickstand on the sidewalk. He reached into his pocket and felt the little bottle of soap. Would Daisy believe him now that he had told the truth in class? She wouldn't want to get tricked again, but Spencer had a plan to help her believe. The first step was knocking on the front door.

Spencer stepped onto the first tier of the walkway. As though he had tripped some unseen sensor, a black dog came tearing around the corner, barking, teeth bared. Spencer jumped backward off the walkway, but the dog seemed to have dinner on its mind. The boy stumbled into the street, tipping over his bicycle.

There was a sharp jangle of chains and the barking snapped short. Spencer glanced over his shoulder to see the dog, chain pulled tight around its neck, halfway across the yard.

Movement in the garage caught Spencer's eye. A pair of legs was sliding out from under the Buick! The legs gave way to torso, arms, and finally a head as a man stood up, staring into the street and wiping his grease-smeared hands on his blue coveralls.

Spencer stared. The man stared back. In his left pocket,

Spencer was fingering the latex glove and wondering if he could slip through dog teeth if the chain snapped.

"What's up?" the man called, walking down the driveway. His face was round and he was balding. Spencer guessed he was in his late thirties.

"Looking for Daisy Gates," Spencer said. "Does she live here?"

"Most certainly does," answered the man. His voice had a casual drawl. "But she ain't home right now. She's on a business trip to California."

"Dad!" Daisy exclaimed, appearing beside the Buick in the garage. Mr. Gates began to laugh as his daughter strolled down the driveway toward them.

"Aw, shoot," the man said, slapping his leg. "You heard me?"

"Hi, Daisy." Spencer waved awkwardly. It had been two days since he'd drawn blue flames on her cheek. He knew she'd been intrigued, frustrated, embarrassed, and disappointed in the past few days—all because of him. Suddenly, standing in front of her house seemed really uncomfortable.

Daisy gave him an unreadable stare before saying, "Hello, Spencer."

"This a friend of yours, Daisy?" Mr. Gates asked, gesturing at Spencer with a shiny, oiled finger.

"He's in my class," Daisy answered. Spencer painfully noted how he hadn't gained *friend* status yet. "What are you doing here?" she asked Spencer.

"I missed the bus," Spencer admitted.

"So you came to my house?"

"I looked you up in the phone book at the gas station."

Mr. Gates whistled through his teeth. "Darn resourceful, this kid."

"I was really hoping that you might give me a lift home. I live kind of far." Spencer gave Daisy a pleading look.

"You've got your bike." She pointed to the sidewalk where the back wheel of the toppled bicycle spun slowly.

"It's uphill." There was a moment of silence. "Please?"

"Don't look at me," Daisy finally answered. "*I* can't drive." Spencer shifted his plea to Mr. Gates.

"You bet," he said. "It might do me some good to get away from that Buick for a bit." He slapped the empty pockets of his coveralls, then said, "Daisy, run grab the truck keys, will you?"

Spencer quickly spoke up. "I was wondering if I could come inside for a minute. To use the bathroom," he explained, somewhat self-consciously.

"Take him in, Daisy," the mechanic said. "Just look out for the dog. She only bites a few times before she decides if she likes you or not."

Spencer followed Daisy through the garage, across a patch of hard, dry dirt, up some side steps and through a screen door, narrowly missing the dog. They entered through the kitchen. Gratefully, Spencer saw plenty of clutter on the countertop and dining table. Daisy didn't notice as he swiped a small paper and pen from the mess and tucked it into his pocket.

"The bathroom is yours," she said after leading him

down a narrow hallway with old, creaking floorboards. "I'll meet you outside."

"Thanks," he said, stepping into the small bathroom and shutting the door. Immediately, Spencer removed the paper and spread it on the counter next to the sink. There was a grocery list hastily scribbled on one side, so Spencer flipped it over and started to write.

Daisy,

This is the soap—the real stuff. Wash your face with this tonight. If I'm lying, you have nothing to lose. I'll never know that you used the soap and you never have to talk to me again. If I'm telling the truth, then tomorrow you'll see what I see.

I need your help. Please try it.

Spencer

He read over the note once more, adding a comma that he'd missed the first time. Spencer pulled out the top drawer, revealing a tube of toothpaste, some fingernail clippers, and a single toothbrush. Removing the little bottle from his pocket, Spencer placed the note and the soap in the drawer next to the toothbrush.

A moment later, he was outrunning the dog and climbing into the Ford truck idling by the curb. Mr. Gates had already loaded Spencer's bike in the back. The boy pulled the truck door shut and strapped on his seat belt. Daisy occupied the middle seat, but the cab was still spacious.

Daisy's father put the truck in gear and rolled away from

the Gates home, leaving his garage door up and the house unlocked. The driver's side window was down and the wind blew what hair was left on his head.

"Where we going?" Mr. Gates asked.

"Hillside Estates," Spencer said.

Mr. Gates whistled through his teeth again. "We've got a big shot here, Daisy," he said.

Spencer felt his face turn as red as the truck's paint. He wanted to explain that the house wasn't really his—that they were just living in it because Uncle Wyatt was away on business and Aunt Avril felt bad that Spencer's dad had left them in the lurch. Instead, Spencer just fumed silently for a moment, wishing that *he* had a dad who drove a Ford truck and trusted the world enough to leave the house unlocked.

The silence became awkward and Mr. Gates turned on the radio. When the stations only came in fuzzy, he snapped it off and turned to his silent passengers. "You go to school together, right? Don't you two have anything to talk about?"

"I haven't decided about Spencer yet," Daisy said to her dad as though they were alone in the truck.

"Decided? What do you mean?" her dad asked. With each comment, Spencer grew more uncomfortable. He watched out the window in desperate anticipation for Hillside Estates.

"Well, he's very confusing. He told me the truth and lied to another boy. But that made me wonder if maybe he lied to me and told the truth to the other boy. Now I'll never know for sure. He says some really interesting things, but I'm afraid he might be a chameleon."

"A chameleon?" Mr. Gates slapped a hand to his fore-head. "Them's the worst kind of folks."

Spencer cleared his throat to remind them that he was actually still in the vehicle.

"And he drew on my face," Daisy said. "But it washed off."

Another bout of silence hit the truck like a black hole.

"Could someone please explain why I'm a chameleon?" Spencer finally muttered.

"A chameleon," Mr. Gates said as he turned into Hillside Estates, "is a type of lizard that changes color. Might be green one moment and black the next. It changes to fit the environment around it, sometimes to blend in, sometimes to stand out."

"But what does that have to do with me?" Spencer pointed out Aunt Avril's house and the big Ford rolled into the driveway.

"You don't get it?" Daisy asked, a faint smirk on her face. "In our family, a chameleon is someone whose story changes. They might tell it one way, then totally twist it around and tell a different version. People do it when they're insecure. Sometimes to blend in, sometimes to stand out."

Spencer wasn't pleased about being called a color-changing lizard. He had a comeback worked up, but he let it die on his lips. Just wait. The soap was in Daisy's drawer. Soon she'd see that he wasn't a chameleon.

"Thanks for the ride, Mr. Gates," Spencer said, slip-ping off the edge of the seat. He checked his pocket for the flashlight and the latex glove. With both items secure, he walked to the back of the truck, but Mr. Gates had beaten him there. With a smile, Daisy's dad lifted out the boy's bike. Spencer jumped on and pedaled up the driveway. Ditching the bike on the steps, he opened the front door.

The house was its usual mess. Spencer hadn't seen the station wagon out front, which meant that his mother wasn't home. She would most likely bring back dinner. His mom flaked out on a lot of things, but the kids could always depend on her for some kind of dinner. The house was quiet. Max was probably with Mom. The other kids could be anywhere.

Spencer waded through a three-month-old box of clothes yet to be unpacked and found his way down the hall to the computer room. Photographs of Aunt Avril and Uncle Wyatt flashed across the screen until Spencer wiggled the mouse. Compared to the school computers, the internet seemed faster at Hillside Estates, and he had his e-mail open in no time.

Spencer felt his heart race as he saw that there was one unread message from ghadley@bem.gov. *"Instructions"* was the subject heading.

With a nervous hand, Spencer opened the e-mail.

CHAPTER 13

"I GOT MORE INFO."

Spencer and Daisy crouched behind the corkscrew slide on the playground. Daisy was breathing hard, as if she had just run a half marathon. In reality, she had barely run from the back door of the school to the playground before Spencer had intercepted her on his bike. Now the bike was ditched in the bark next to the tire swing and the two kids were using the slide for cover.

"How can you go in there with those . . . those *things* crawling around the hallways?" Daisy asked again, shaking her head in disbelief. The second bell rang, making them both officially tardy for Mrs. Natcher's class.

Spencer was relieved and delighted that Daisy had tried the soap. Now that she had seen the creatures for herself, Daisy was the best listener. Spencer had told her all he'd learned from Garth Hadley about the BEM and how he'd been enlisted to stop the janitors at Welcher Elementary.

"So they want you to do dirty work for the Bureau of Educational Maintenance?" Daisy asked. "I don't know." She sighed. "I met John Campbell when he came to Welcher at the end of last year. He doesn't really seem like the magical-experiment type of guy."

"You don't believe me again?" Spencer cried. "You think I'm still being a chameleon?"

"I know *you* are telling the truth," she said. "But what if the BEM is wrong about the janitors?"

"Don't be crazy," Spencer said. "The Bureau's a government agency." He opened his backpack. "I got more info," he said, handing Daisy a printed e-mail.

She read intently, mumbling every fifth word or so. But Spencer didn't need her to read it out loud. He'd read the message so many times he almost had it memorized.

To: SpenceZ@wahoo.com
From: ghadley@bem.gov
Subject: Instructions

Spencer:

I believe we were able to determine the location of Walter Jamison's bronze nail. At the end of the hallway by the gym is a boy's bathroom. The restroom has been labeled "out of order."

The door is normally locked, but I managed to jam the lock during our routine inspection. Somewhere in the bathroom is the nail. Before you go for the hammer, you must know exactly where the nail is. Here's the plan:

At precisely 11:06 tomorrow morning, the power will go out at Welcher Elementary School. The power will remain off for eight minutes. You should be able to get inside the bathroom without anyone seeing. Also, with the lights off, your flashlight will come in handy. Use the flashlight to locate the nail, then get back to your classroom and wait for more instructions via e-mail. Be careful, and watch out for the janitors!

Garth Hadley
BEM regional representative

"I always wondered about that bathroom by the gym," Daisy said. "It was out of order for months last year. Wonder why the janitors haven't fixed it yet."

"Because it's not broken," Spencer said. "They just *say* it's out of order so they can hide the nail in there and nobody will go in." Spencer checked his watch. "Hmm— 11:06. That's only two hours from now. Are you coming with me?"

"You only have one glove," Daisy said.

"We shouldn't need it," Spencer answered. "Remember, this time we're just scouting for the nail."

"Yeah." Daisy swallowed hard. "I'll come."

CHAPTER 14

"TAKE THE HALL PASS."

By the time the clock showed 11:00, Spencer's hands were sweating. He kept glancing at Daisy. Her eyes shifted nervously from the clock to her worksheet and back to the clock. What was she doing? Daisy was supposed to be out of the classroom with the hall pass by now.

Spencer checked his wristwatch. The digital screen showed 00:00. Since Mr. Hadley's 11:06 might not be the same as Mrs. Natcher's 11:06, Spencer was ready to hit "start" on his watch the minute the power went out. From there, he would have eight minutes to rendezvous with Daisy in the hallway, check the "out of order" bathroom, and get back to the classroom. If Daisy would ever leave!

Finally, at 11:01 and a half, Daisy's hand shot up, the gesture screaming urgency.

"Yes, Daisy?" Mrs. Natcher said, peering over her glasses in the usual manner.

"May I please go to the restroom, Mrs. Natcher?"

Mrs. Natcher breathed deeply through her nose as she looked at the clock. With three pairs of eyes on the clock, Spencer wondered if the minute hand would freeze under pressure. Evidently deeming it a good time to grant Daisy's wish, Mrs. Natcher simply said, "Take the hall pass," and looked back at the computer screen on her desk.

Mrs. Natcher, for some odd reason, used a bald baby doll wearing nothing but a diaper for a hall pass. Whatever the teacher's reasons, the doll (nicknamed Baybee) usually embarrassed students enough to prevent unnecessary trips out of the classroom. But at 11:02, Daisy leapt up, snatched Baybee without reserve, and disappeared out the door.

The next four minutes passed like hours for Spencer. His worksheet was untouched on his desk. He quietly clicked his tongue with each movement of the red second hand. Dissatisfied by the sluggish tempo of the clock, he began clicking twice for each second.

"Shut up," Dez grunted at his side, but Spencer didn't hear him.

Five . . . four . . . three . . . two . . . one . . .

11:06.

Nothing.

Spencer glanced up at the fluorescent tube lights on the ceiling. Not so much as a flicker. Spencer's stomach began to twist nervously.

Then, without a sound, the lights turned off. The fan

in the back of the room gradually slowed and Mrs. Natcher looked up from the black screen of her computer with an annoyed look, as though the power outage was planned. Well—it *was*, but Mrs. Natcher had no way of knowing that.

Spencer hit the button on his watch and the seconds started rolling.

Dez immediately jumped to his feet and did some awkward dance move while chanting, "Power's out! Power's out! Wahoo!"

The classroom had one large window in the wall, but Mrs. Natcher kept it covered with outdated paisley curtains. Under the curtains was a shade that she'd pulled down the first time the overhead projector was used and she'd never put it up again.

"Everyone sit down," Mrs. Natcher said. "The power will return at any moment." She crossed the room to pull up the window shade and let in the now-needed sunlight.

Spencer waited until Mrs. Natcher's back was turned. The class was still in mild chaos, and he attracted no extra attention as he slipped out the door.

It took Spencer longer than he wanted to find Daisy in the dim hallway. At the sight of Marv, Daisy had retreated to hide in a remote corner, clutching Baybee as if it were her own child. Spencer wandered several halls before they found each other.

Three precious minutes had passed by the time they stood before the boys' bathroom with a wrinkled "out of order" sign thumbtacked to the wooden door. Spencer was holding the little gray flashlight in his hand, but he was afraid to turn it on. Baybee dangled in Daisy's grip by one plastic arm, the doll's diaper crooked from Daisy's run down the hall.

Here, by the gym, it was rather dark. Spencer knew that without a window in the restroom, it would be pitch-black inside. Not willing to waste any more time, Spencer clicked the flashlight's switch with his thumb. A dull, yellow glow appeared at the end of the small bulb. As Mr. Hadley had explained, it wasn't even bright enough to illuminate the door two feet away.

Spencer was reaching out for the door when suddenly a bright white beam of light shot from the flashlight, angling sideways across the hallway. Spencer and Daisy jerked around to see the beam land on a winged vulture-bat. It was hanging upside down from the ceiling, but when the light touched it, the creature took flight. Spencer's light tracked the jagged flight pattern masterfully, even though the flashlight was motionless in his hand.

The flying beast dove and touched the ground. Wriggling forward, it disappeared through the gap under the gym door. The flashlight returned to its dull glow in Spencer's hand.

"What happened?" hissed Daisy in his ear.

"Mr. Hadley said that other magical objects would draw out the light. I guess that means creatures too." Spencer finally pushed open the bathroom door. A small card fell to the hard floor. Hadley must have used it to stop the door from latching.

81

Spencer picked up the card. "Come on," he urged, using the Indiglo feature on his watch to see that five minutes had passed. Daisy didn't move. "What's wrong?"

She hesitated. "I've never been in a boys' bathroom before."

"Oh, please," Spencer muttered. "They're just like girls' bathrooms, except *we* have couches and entertainment systems with surround sound."

"Really?" Daisy asked, her gullibility setting in again.

Daisy stepped into the bathroom and Spencer inserted the card over the latch and carefully shut the door over it, plunging the restroom into nearly complete darkness. In the dim light from the flashlight's weak bulb, Spencer saw two urinals on the wall next to a single stall. There was one sink with an old soap dispenser and a roll of paper towels.

Suddenly, the flashlight flared to life. The white beam split the darkness, pinpointing its target near the sink. Then the beam flashed a different direction, toward the wall of the bathroom stall. Erratically, the light jumped between two objects.

The target near the sink crawled forward. When the next flash of light highlighted it, Spencer and Daisy saw that it was one of the salamander creatures. The flashlight shifted targets and Daisy backed up, fearful that the little monster would crawl up her leg in the darkness. The next time they saw the creature, it was stretching its pale body through the grate on the floor drain. Then it was gone.

With only one magical target now, the flashlight shone a steady white beam at the silver wall of the bathroom stall.

All of the light honed in on one small area no larger than the head of a nail.

"There!" Daisy whispered. They had just taken a step toward the stall when the wooden door of the bathroom banged shut behind them. Spencer whirled around, but the flashlight changed to a weak glow as he faced away from the nail. Spencer felt Daisy draw closer to him. The boy's bathroom was almost completely dark again.

But *three* people were breathing in the darkness!

"Ha ha!" laughed the intruder. "Gotcha!"

That voice was much too familiar—and the last one that Spencer or Daisy expected to hear.

"Open the door, Dez," Spencer spoke into the darkness. They'd seen the nail and, according to Spencer's timer, had two minutes before the lights came back. Spencer had hoped to take a closer look at the bronze nail, but there wasn't time now.

"That's a wimpy flashlight," Dez said. His voice had drawn a step nearer.

Spencer reached into his pocket and felt the latex glove. Then he quickly withdrew his hand, realizing that Daisy would be stuck in the boys' room alone with Dez if he used the glove to escape. Facing away from the nail, the little flashlight wasn't doing much. Spencer didn't want to arouse Dez's curiosity further, so he switched off the light.

At seeing the dim bulb turn off, Dez laughed. "You can run, but you can't hide!"

Spencer grabbed Daisy's hand and jerked her against the wall as they heard Dez lunge through the blackness.

"Oh, ho." Dez chuckled. "Not bad, lovebirds." The big kid was swiping his arms through the darkness, dirty fingers eager to find them. Spencer held close to the wall, dragging Daisy around the urinals toward the door.

Thirty seconds left on Spencer's watch.

They were almost to the exit, Dez still blundering behind them, when Spencer and Daisy froze. On the other side of the door, they heard a heavy sigh followed by the sound of jingling keys. Someone else was trying to get in! Someone with a big ring of keys. In Spencer's mind, that narrowed it down to two people: Marv, or maybe Walter Jamison himself!

"Back, back!" Spencer hissed in Daisy's ear.

"I *hear* you," Dez whispered back, trying to make his voice low and menacing.

"Listen, Dez!" Spencer warned. "Someone's trying to get in and we've got to hide fast." Spencer was across the room, braving the germs on the bathroom wall and pushing Daisy into the stall.

"What?" Dez asked. Obviously this was the last thing he expected Spencer to say. On the other side of the door, they heard a mumbled curse. It was definitely Marv. And he seemed to be having trouble finding the right key in the darkness.

"Just get in here and shut up," Spencer ordered.

"In where?" asked Dez, taking a step toward Spencer's voice.

"The stall," answered Spencer impatiently. Then, suddenly, the lights went on. Spencer blinked against the brightness and Daisy shielded her eyes. Dez stumbled across the bathroom toward them. Outside, Marv managed to get the key into the lock.

The door opened and Marv stepped in.

CHAPTER 15

"WHAT'S SO FUNNY?"

The bear of a janitor glanced around the bathroom and then snorted. Marv didn't see the three kids and the baby doll balancing silently on the cold rim of the toilet, holding on to each other and bracing themselves against the wall. The stall door was shut and latched, but Marv didn't seem to notice details.

Spencer could barely glimpse the burly figure through the space between the hinges. Marv approached slowly until he stood only inches from the bathroom stall. On the other side of the thin wall, Spencer, Daisy, and Dez held their breath. Marv checked for the bronze nail, grunted unintelligibly, and then turned away.

The kids heard the bathroom door open, then bang closed. They heard the muffled sound of keys in the lock.

Marv snorted once more, apparently trying to dislodge something from his sinuses. Then there was silence.

Of course, Dez was the first one to move. He jumped down from the toilet seat, chuckling to himself. "Good thing I told you guys to hide. We'd have been busted. That dude looked like he wanted to eat someone."

"Quiet," Daisy whispered. "He might still be out there."

"Relax," Dez said. "He didn't see us."

Daisy and Spencer stepped off the toilet seat as Dez unlatched the stall door. "We've got to get back to class," Spencer said. "Mrs. Natcher's going to freak when she sees that three of us are gone."

"You're not going anywhere," Dez said, stepping in front of them. "I've still got to clean out some toilets with your heads."

"Get out of the way," Spencer said, brushing his hand at Dez like he was a pesky fly. A few days ago, Dez had been the most intimidating foe. But ever since the milk incident, ever since Spencer had discovered the courage to stand up for the truth, Dez seemed smaller. Indeed, compared to the wicked janitors and demented creatures that Daisy and Spencer were up against now, Dez looked about as frightening as Baybee.

"Hold it," Dez said, unaccustomed to people ignoring his threats. Spencer and Daisy stepped past him and Spencer pulled on the bathroom door.

Locked.

Marv had locked the deadbolt, making sure to keep everyone out while unintentionally trapping Spencer, Daisy, and Dez in. Unwilling to believe, Spencer pulled again . . . and again. But the door was secure. They weren't going anywhere.

Dez began to laugh.

"What's so funny?" Daisy said.

"It's perfect," answered Dez. "It's the perfect excuse not to go back to class . . . and to give you lovebirds endless swirlies."

Ignoring Dez, Spencer and Daisy began brainstorming. Hitting the door and shouting for help was out of the question. Picking the lock was impossible. Daisy got on her hands and knees, putting her cheek dangerously close to the bathroom floor, and tried to peek under the door.

"Hey." She carefully reached forward. A tiny bit of paper was visible under the door. Daisy trapped it with her fingernail and dragged it into the bathroom. It was the card that Garth Hadley had used to stop the lock. Daisy flipped it over. It was Hadley's business card, the same kind that the BEM rep had given Spencer.

"Yes!" Spencer said, taking the card from her hand. "That's got Hadley's phone number on it. He told me to call if we get in trouble."

Daisy smiled, showing her teeth in all their glory. "Hurry up," she said, "call him. I want to get out of here."

Spencer's shoulders slumped. "You don't have a cell phone?"

The girl shook her head, long braid swinging.

"Me neither."

Behind them, Dez emitted an obnoxious, look-at-me

sigh. Daisy and Spencer turned to find the boy operating a cell phone with both hands.

"All right, Dez!" Spencer said. For the first time, he was actually pleased with the bully. "If you let me borrow that for a minute, I can get us out of here."

"Hang on," Dez said. "I'm busy texting the sewer police. Got to tell them to expect two newcomers from toilet number one." He grinned maliciously and snapped the phone shut. "You think I want to go back to Mrs. Natcher's class?" Dez faked a yawn. "Yeah, right."

Spencer and Daisy exchanged a glance. They had to get the phone from Dez before the janitors found out that they were missing from Mrs. Natcher's class. If Marv's threats carried any weight, he would already have figured out Spencer's name and classroom.

"Why are you here, anyway?" Daisy asked, hands on her hips.

Dez tucked the cell phone into the pocket of his shorts and began to chant, "Spencer and Daisy, sitting in a tree, K-I-S-I-N-N . . . K-I-S-I-N-G . . ." he trailed away. "You guys came into class together this morning—late. Then, when the power went out, I figured Spencer went to find you. I usually don't like to watch kissing, but I wanted to know where you were going."

"So you followed us in here," Spencer said.

Dez nodded. "Not a very romantic place for your first date, Doofus. But I thought it might be fun to crash the party. Besides, I've been looking for a way to get back at you."

"For what?" Spencer asked.

"Yesterday's little speech to the class. You can lie to *them* about seeing monsters, but I know you're a fake."

Spencer swallowed and ignored the taunt. Just like Garth Hadley had advised, he focused on their secret mission. "Give me the phone, Dez."

"No way!" Dez pulled out the phone to tempt them again. "Minutes aren't free, you know."

"I'll pay you back," Daisy promised.

"You'll pay me now," Dez stated, pointing at the toilet aggressively. "Two swirlies for every minute on the phone. Deal?"

"You're disgusting," Spencer said, wondering if Dez actually had the guts to stick someone's head in the toilet and flush it. He wondered for only a moment.

Dez leaped clumsily at Daisy. She spun aside, and the bully turned quickly. He tripped on an untied shoelace and went down, grabbing Daisy's leg as he fell. Both kids tumbled to the hard floor, Dez struggling to get a controlling grip on Daisy.

Without thinking, Spencer plunged in. He'd never punched anyone before and it ended up hurting his hand a lot worse than he thought. Spencer's fist pounded into Dez's shoulder. The bully released his grip on Daisy and the girl crawled toward the stall. Dez's cell phone spun across the yellow-brown tile and stopped under the sink. Spencer went for it, but Dez's big foot kicked out, catching Spencer in the knee and sending him to the floor.

Dez grabbed the phone and jumped to his feet. His face

was twisted in anger like Spencer had never seen before. One punch from those meaty hands would probably put Spencer out cold on the floor—the dingy, *germy* bathroom floor.

Losing his courage, Spencer retreated to the stall, where Daisy quickly shut the door and latched it tightly. The walls of the stall didn't reach all the way to the ground, so there was still room for Dez to crawl under. But Spencer was prepared to stomp on any part of Dez that appeared.

"You're dead, Doofus. Sooner or later you'll have to come out—and I'll be waiting."

"Sooner or later, you'll give us that phone so we can all get out of here," Spencer said.

"Whatever! I'll wait a week if I have to."

"Without food? Yeah, right."

Dez fell silent. Apparently he hadn't thought about long-term food storage for his siege on the bathroom stall. Spencer and Daisy watched him pace for a while, then slump down against the wall. He pulled out his phone and, judging by the sound effects, started playing Pac-Man.

Spencer pulled Daisy aside and whispered in her ear. "I'm going to get the phone. Stay here."

"What?" Daisy shrieked.

"I hear you," Dez said, ending his game. But before he could slip the phone into his pocket, before Daisy could protest any further, Spencer threw open the door and lunged at Dez.

Spencer's right hand closed around the cell phone, jerking it free of Dez's grip. Instantly the bully had a heavy hand on Spencer's arm, twisting it painfully. Then Spencer stretched and slipped free, passing through Dez's grasp like his arm was made of Jell-O.

Spencer's left hand was sweaty inside the oversized latex glove. He had the phone and was only a few steps from the safety of the stall.

Dez sprang, grabbing both of Spencer's legs. But it was useless. Spencer's feet kept moving, his legs tearing free of Dez's hands without effort. Dez was left facedown on the dirty tile as Spencer flung himself into the stall, Daisy pushing the door shut.

"Here!" she shouted, thrusting the BEM business card at Spencer. He tore off the glove, flipped open the phone, and rapidly started punching in the numbers. Just as he hit the green *send* button, Dez's head appeared under the stall door. Daisy screamed and swung Baybee like a sledgehammer. The plastic doll smashed into Dez's face.

"Mr. Hadley?" Spencer asked. "We need help—quick!" he paused. "Yes, we found it. But we're locked in the bathroom with the nail!"

Daisy was going wild with Baybee. Dez's hands protected his face and he struggled to retreat. With one swing, Dez managed to grab onto the doll, and the two kids played tug-of-war with the hall pass. Dez came out with Baybee's torn diaper and Daisy fell onto the toilet with the unclothed doll.

"Thanks," Spencer said into the phone. "Okay, we will. 'Bye!" As soon as the conversation was over, Spencer closed the cell phone, bent down, and slid it along the floor. Dez turned like a dog going for a ball.

"You all right?" Spencer asked, helping Daisy to her feet. The girl nodded, hefting the nude hall pass like a club. "Good job," Spencer praised her combat skills.

"What'd Hadley say?"

"He's sending someone to get us out."

"When?"

Dez suddenly punched the stall door, causing both kids inside to jump. "Not before I'm done with you!"

CHAPTER 16

"THE ISSUE HAS BEEN RESOLVED."

To: ghadley@bem.gov
From: SpenceZ@wahoo.com
Subject: Thanks

Dear Mr. Hadley,

Just wanted to thank you for bailing me and Daisy out of the bathroom yesterday. We found the bronze nail and we're ready to go for the hammer. Do you have any ideas on how we can get to Walter Jamison? I think we should act fast. The janitors are already suspicious of me. Let me know what you want us to do.

Thanks,
Spencer

Spencer moved the cursor and clicked *send*. In a moment, the sent mail was confirmed and Spencer went to log off. He sat staring at the monitor for several moments, thinking. It was Saturday, and his siblings were all outside enjoying the warm weather and open spaces that their Aunt Avril's home in Welcher provided. His mother had gone to the store an hour ago. Spencer had spent the morning cleaning up the disheveled house, wiping down the mirror and sink in his bathroom, and vacuuming up a colony of ants that was working away at a long-abandoned cookie.

Yesterday was still vivid in his mind. After his phone call to Garth Hadley, Spencer and Daisy had spent a good half hour keeping Dez out of the bathroom stall. At last, help had arrived in the form of a nineteen-year-old, pimply guy with a shaved head and skinny legs. The guy was wearing the orange vest of a Welcher Elementary recess aide, but Spencer and Daisy had never seen him on the playground before.

The recess aide had opened the bathroom door and ordered Dez out. Once the bully was gone, Spencer and Daisy left the stronghold of the bathroom stall. The guy said he was undercover for the BEM. He'd swiped an aide vest and gone to the janitors, claiming to need their keys to unlock a door and get basketballs for the kids outside. With the keys, he had opened the "out of order" bathroom and rescued the kids.

The imposter recess aide had even given Spencer a slip of paper that he presented to Mrs. Natcher after lunch.

"What's this?" Mrs. Natcher took the note, plucking it out of Spencer's hand with two fingers. She unfolded it and read aloud: "Please excuse Spencer Zumbro, Daisy Gates, and Dez Rylie for their unexpected disappearance from class this morning. I had quite a discussion with them in my office. The issue has been resolved—Principal Poach."

Mrs. Natcher raised her eyebrows. "I hope you three learned your lesson. The principal is known to be harsh when occasion arises."

Spencer studied the carpet. The note had nearly convinced Daisy that she'd actually been to the principal's office. Dez had remained silent, brooding, probably waiting for the perfect opportunity to strike Spencer.

Which was another reason why Spencer was grateful for Saturday.

The weekend came just in time. It would provide two full days with no angry Dez. Two days without janitors and creepy crawlers. Two days without Welcher Elementary.

Spencer dug into a drawer and rifled through some computer games. He didn't feel like fighting evil Jedis, and the strategy games would make him think too hard. Spencer abandoned the idea and went to the internet again. Only a moment had passed, but why not obsess over his inbox?

There it was. Sent only two minutes ago.

To: SpenceZ@wahoo.com
From: ghadley@bem.gov
Subject: RE Thanks

Spencer,

Glad to be of help. Thanks for being willing to get the hammer. I think we have a working plan.

On Monday evening, there is an ice cream social at

the school from six to eight. The social will be held in the cafeteria, with games on the lawn outside. Other than the cafeteria and entry hallway, the school is supposed to be closed off. Marv Bills and Walter Jamison are both scheduled to work the event.

Spencer, you need to make a mess in the cafeteria—a large mess. It needs to be something that cannot be ignored. Something that will require both janitors to clean it up.

Meanwhile, Daisy needs to clear a path to the bathroom. That means opening doors, so she'll need to pick up a master key. Every teacher should have one.

Once Daisy gets the doors open, shine the flashlight on Walter Jamison. The beam should show you where he is carrying the bronze hammer. Wearing the glove, you need to grab the hammer and run to the bathroom. Once you've pulled the nail, I'll meet you at the southwest corner of the school in a blue Toyota to help you get away.

Good luck!

Garth Hadley
BEM regional representative

CHAPTER 17

"YOU *ALWAYS* MAKE A MESS."

Monday came. Spencer didn't think it would, but it certainly did. After letting his anger stew for a whole weekend, Dez was sure to make Spencer eat wood chips on the playground. Spencer had been lucky to evade the janitors on Friday, but there was no telling what secret councils had been held to get Spencer on Monday morning. That was why Spencer had decided to be sick.

He'd already made plans with Daisy on Sunday afternoon. Spencer had biked to her house, eaten pie with Mr. and Mrs. Gates, and secretly given Daisy the printed e-mail. They had solidified their plans for the ice cream social and then Mr. Gates had given Spencer a ride home, tossing his bicycle in the back of the red Ford truck again.

Spencer felt comfortable in the Gates home. Aside from its being ten times quieter than his house, Spencer felt relaxed and accepted there. Daisy, being an only child, received more attention from her parents in one day than Spencer did in a month.

Mr. and Mrs. Gates talked to Spencer like he was an honored guest, a fact that Spencer later found out was true. Daisy, in all her six years of schooling, had never had a friend come to visit. He was a valued commodity in the Gates home.

Every moment, Spencer was more grateful for Daisy's help. She'd given him courage in the beginning and now she was proving rather courageous herself. It would just be impossible without her.

Spencer's siblings had been home from school for over an hour on Monday before their mother returned. She entered the house, her face beaming. She'd been to a job interview with Quick 'n' Speedy truck stop and Mr. Aldez had hired her. It was her fifth interview in a month, and her success warranted a celebration. Alice had passed the school on her way home and seen folks putting together a giant, blow-up bouncy castle for the ice cream social. Her unexpected announcement made Spencer's stomach do a pirouette.

"We're *all* going to the ice cream party tonight!"

Max toddled up and began cheering for ice cream. Holly's head appeared around the corner, eyebrows raised.

"Yes! We're *all* going," Alice announced as though she'd just won a million dollars. "Now, let's eat some supper and head out."

With her victory at Quick 'n' Speedy and her offer to take the kids to a school activity, Alice had overlooked dinner. She hastily prepared some pasta from a box and microwaved some frozen peas. Hard rolls rounded out the dinner as five hungry kids sat shoulder to shoulder at the table with their elated mother.

Spencer had little appetite. His task of making a giant mess at the social had been daunting before. Now that his whole family would be there, Spencer wondered how he could do it without shaming his mom.

Before he had the answers he needed, the six Zumbros were piling out of the old station wagon in the school parking lot. There were already a lot of kids at the party. On the lawn outside was the bouncy castle with a pile of shoes beside it. A line of kids snaked toward the entrance, each anxious for a turn to bounce.

"Let's try to stay together," Alice said, ushering her children up the back cafeteria steps like ducklings. Spencer absorbed every detail along the way, wondering what would be to his advantage in mess making. Before he entered, Spencer got his bearings and scoped out the southwest corner. There was no blue Toyota yet.

As they entered through the cafeteria's back door, an oldies song assaulted them through tall speakers against one wall. The tables and chairs in the cafeteria had been arranged in a U shape. There were big white buckets on the center tables—gallons of ice cream in a variety of flavors. On the adjacent tables were bowls of optional toppings. Through gaps in the people, Spencer saw cookie crumbs, gummy bears, M&Ms, nuts, and an assortment of sticky syrups. At the end of one table were two ice chests brimming with cans of root beer for those who wanted to make a float.

Spencer studied the crowded cafeteria. There were no janitors on guard, and, gratefully, no sign of Dez Rylie. Spencer checked his watch. It was almost six-thirty. Daisy would be waiting for him by the front door. Now he just needed to get away from his family.

"I'm going to grab a drink real quick," he said.

"Good," his mom replied. "Take little Max with you; he's thirsty."

Without a word, Spencer grabbed Max's hand and led him out of the cafeteria toward the drinking fountain. In the hallway, the chatter of the crowd and the beat of the song faded. Spencer peered left down the entry hall. The janitorial storage closet that was also the janitors' office was at the end of the hall just before a set of double doors that closed off the rest of the school. At the other end of the hallway was the school's front entrance.

Spencer led Max to the drinking fountain. He boosted his three-year-old brother and the little kid began slurping up water. Soon he reverted to splashing water onto the floor and Spencer had to set him down.

"I want some ice cream!" Max shrieked, his cute little face smiling mischievously, showing off his chipped front tooth.

"You'll probably get it everywhere," Spencer said. For every ounce of effort that Spencer put into cleaning, Max threw down a pound of destruction. "You *always* make a mess." Spencer suddenly paused, staring at his little brother with newfound appreciation.

Suddenly, the sound of footsteps approached from behind. Spencer whirled around.

"You're late," Daisy said. "Are you ready?"

Spencer exhaled, relieved to see that it was only Daisy. He patted his pockets to show her that he had the flashlight and glove.

"Good. Here's the soap we're supposed to give back to Mr. Hadley today." Daisy handed Spencer the little bottle. "You should keep it."

Spencer shoved the soap bottle into his pocket as Daisy pointed at Max. "Who's he?"

"Oh, this is my little brother, Max."

"You brought your little brother?" she asked.

"I didn't mean to," Spencer said. "But he's great at making messes."

Daisy nodded, understanding the importance of Max's talent. "Well." She took a deep breath. "Let's get started."

CHAPTER 18

"IT'LL BE TOO LATE TO STUDY."

The first person Spencer and Daisy saw when they reentered the cafeteria was Mrs. Natcher. She wore a denim dress, and her gray hair was wound up in a bun. There was a purse dangling on her arm and a small bowl of plain vanilla ice cream in her hand. Yeah, that seemed right. Mrs. Natcher was a plain-vanilla kind of person. To Spencer's mild surprise, the dowdy teacher scooped a conservative helping of crumbled peanuts and let them cascade down her ice cream.

Spencer and Daisy exchanged one final you-be-careful glance before parting ways. Spencer headed toward his family, who stood huddled in the corner.

"Hey, Mom," Spencer said, "I'll help Max get some ice cream, okay?"

"Actually, Spencer," she said, "we're going to have a

bounce on the castle before ice cream. I don't want you kids getting sick on a belly full of sweets."

Spencer swallowed. His mom was supposed to say, "That sounds great, Spence. Thank you very much." But Spencer wasn't ready to give up so easily. He bent down to eye level with his small brother. "Do you want to bounce, Max, or do you want ice cream?"

"I want ice cream!" he shouted. Well, at least the three-year-old was going along with Spencer's plan.

"Spencer, did you really just . . ." Alice put her hands on her hips and took a deep breath. "If you have ice cream now," she told Max, "you can't bounce later."

"I want ice cream!" the stubborn little guy demanded. That seemed to settle the matter. Alice led the other kids out the back door of the cafeteria toward the blow-up castle while Spencer led Max to the ice cream table.

•   •   •

As Spencer and Max accepted bowls of caramel cashew and chocolate chunk, Daisy began some negotiating of her own.

"Hello, Daisy," Mrs. Natcher said, examining the girl below the rims of her glasses. The teacher always seemed to look over or under her glasses, never through them.

"Oh, Mrs. Natcher. It's a good thing you're here. I left my spelling review sheet in my desk after school. I need to study it tonight. I was wondering if I could go get it."

Daisy had often spread false information, believing it

was true. But to tell an outright lie would almost be impossible for honest Gullible Gates. Which was why she had *purposely* left her review sheet in her desk after school.

"The school is all locked up. Just get your review sheet tomorrow."

"But the test is tomorrow, Mrs. Natcher. It'll be too late to study."

Mrs. Natcher ate a nibble of ice cream, thinking. Then she sighed. "Pneumonia," the teacher said expectantly.

"P-N-E-U-M-O-N-I-A," Daisy answered.

"Correct," said Mrs. Natcher. "Aqueduct."

Daisy crossed her fingers, hoping that Mrs. Natcher wasn't going to drill her on all twenty words. Daisy began the word correctly before suddenly realizing the need to misspell. "A-Q-U-A-D-U-C-K."

"Incorrect," Mrs. Natcher said with a frown. Then the teacher gave the correct spelling and said, "Colonel."

"K-E-R-N-E-L."

"Incorrect." Mrs. Natcher began to correct her, then frowned deeper. Digging in her purse, she produced a ring of keys. "Goodness, you *need* the review sheet," she said, handing Daisy the keys. Daisy accepted with sweaty hands. "Bring those keys right back or you'll be in an undesirable P-R-E-D-I-C-A-M-E-N-T. You understand?"

Daisy nodded, backing away from Mrs. Natcher while trying not to let the look on her face betray her success. Before she exited the cafeteria, Daisy glimpsed Spencer and Max, who had moved on to the toppings. Then she broke into a speed-walk down the hallway.

• • •

"Okay, Max," Spencer said. "Do you want chocolate syrup on yours?" Max hadn't refused a single topping and his ice cream was unseen beneath a layer of goodies. As expected, Max nodded vigorously.

"Here's what we'll do," Spencer whispered to his brother. "These four syrups are just for us, but I need you to take them to that table over there, okay?" Spencer pointed to the table farthest away across the cafeteria. "Can you do it?"

"I think so." Max nodded with excitement. There were strawberry, caramel, butterscotch, and chocolate—four bottles of syrup just for him!

In a flash, Spencer untwisted the squirt caps on all four syrups. Then he set the caps loosely on top of the plastic bottles, only the sticky residue holding them in place. Spencer quickly loaded the bottles into his little brother's arms. Max toddled away, struggling to keep a good grip on all four bottles while still carrying his Styrofoam bowl of loaded ice cream.

As soon as the disaster was on its way, Spencer changed directions and headed for the ice chests full of root beer cans. He casually grabbed two cans, shook them, and slipped them into his pockets. A second later, he snatched two more cans.

"Whoa!" someone shouted, and Spencer heard Max's syrup bottles hit the floor. A shout went up and all of the adults in the room reached for Max. Their arms shot out like frog tongues going for a fly. Max was whisked away from the multicolored, sticky mess, dropping his ice cream in the process.

Parents converged on the syrup spill, each armed with a roll of paper towels. In the confusion, Spencer snatched as many soda cans as he could and retreated to the opposite side of the cafeteria.

Across the room, Max was attempting to recover his inverted ice cream. The mess was good, but the janitors hadn't been summoned yet. Of course, the parents thought they could handle it.

Spencer had his cans lined up—eight on the floor, with two more in his pockets. The cans were pressurized and ready to burst. Spencer had shaken each one for ten seconds. In the middle of the cafeteria, a stranger had Max by the arm, asking him where his parents were.

Just as the adults thought they had the syrup mastered, two cans of pressurized root beer slid across the cafeteria floor. The top was punctured just slightly to allow a tall geyser of brown soda to spurt out. Two more soda grenades followed, spraying root beer onto kids, parents, and all over the floor.

Spencer cracked two more soda cans and lobbed them into an adjacent corner. Kids were crying, parents shouting. The cafeteria had been plunged into Dez-worthy chaos.

Spencer had the seventh can opened when the first parent saw him crouched behind a table and stack of chairs. It was time to go. Spencer tipped over the tower of chairs to block his retreat, then sprinted out of the cafeteria into the entry hall.

Marv had emerged from the janitors' storage/office and was racing toward the cafeteria like a firefighter on call. There were several other people in the hallway. If Spencer could turn his back to Marv, he might blend into the crowd. He walked casually toward the drinking fountain, but his insides were trembling. Spencer lowered his lips to the stream of water, but he was too anxious to actually drink. With his head cocked at the fountain, Spencer kept his eyes trained on the hallway.

Marv entered the cafeteria to begin cleaning up. But where was Walter Jamison? The head janitor had not emerged according to plan. Any minute, the angry, root-beer-soaked parents would flood the hallway in search of Spencer. He waited only a second longer before deciding it was time to improvise.

Spencer hoped that Daisy had all the doors open as he jogged toward the short stairway that led to the janitors' storage/office. He dug in his pocket for the flashlight and glove, maneuvering around the extra cans of root beer that jostled at his side. By the time he reached the top stair, Spencer was wearing the latex glove.

Spencer crouched on the steps, trying to see into the huge storage area. The dim stairway was the perfect place to use the flashlight. But Spencer needed to get Walter out of the basement first.

Shouts up the hallway confirmed that the parents were looking for him. He knew he didn't have much time. Taking both cans of root beer from his pockets, Spencer began to shake them vigorously. He felt the contents pressurizing, the aluminum cans turning as hard as the shell of an airplane.

Spencer cracked the top of the first can. The soda shot out, dousing his shoulder. Spencer quickly set the can on the top step, positioning it on its side so the fountain of brown liquid shot into the storage area. He set the second can beside the first one: dual guns.

With the bait set, Spencer edged around the corner. He was out of Walter Jamison's sight, but the parents up the hall spotted him instantly. Spencer held his position as the adults converged on him. If Jamison didn't take the bait in the next ten seconds, Spencer knew he would have to break cover and run.

Suddenly, Spencer saw a hand close over the root beer can, setting it upright and averting the stream. Spencer spun around the corner, the flashlight flicking on. An older man was on the stairs. At first it didn't look like the Walter Jamison from the picture. He was wearing khaki cargo pants and a red button-up shirt with a pressed collar. A big ring of keys dangled at his side. This man was totally bald and clean shaven, but the face was the same. Wrinkles around the tired green eyes, lean features well worn.

The flashlight's white beam erupted and found its mark instantly. In the dim stairwell, the light outlined the shape of a small hammer in a cargo pocket by Walter Jamison's left thigh.

Spencer didn't hesitate. He flung the flashlight into Jamison's face and leapt down the stairs at the man.

Spencer's hands grasped Walter's leg as the old man caught the boy by the neck. Spencer grunted in pain but didn't pull away as he managed to plunge a hand into the cargo pocket. He felt the hammer, cool and hard on his fingertips. As soon as Spencer had a firm grip on the hammer, he twisted away, turning to Jell-O in Jamison's hands.

The old janitor gasped as Spencer staggered up the steps. The parents were waiting for him, but no one seemed to be able to get a tight grip on the boy. He flowed through their fingers like a fish through water. He sprinted across the hall to the doors that sealed off the rest of the school. If Daisy had succeeded, the doors would be . . .

Open!

Spencer burst through, running wildly down the dark hallway. He held the bronze hammer before him like an Olympic torch. Behind him, the door opened and several figures dumped into the hallway. Spencer was running too hard to be sure, but he guessed that one of them would be Jamison.

Spencer passed through another set of should-be-locked doors, praising Daisy's name all the way to the boys' bathroom. He kicked open the boys' room door. The light was already on, and Spencer dashed toward the nail. Hitting the stall wall, Spencer reached up with the hammer.

For the first time, he hesitated, unsure how to pull the nail with such an antique tool. Unlike modern hammers, this one lacked the hooked prongs on the back. It was a primitive tool that seemed to have the capability only to pound nails.

Sounds of pursuit were catching up in the hallway. There was no more time for hesitation. In desperation, Spencer placed the hammer against the head of the bronze nail. A burst of golden light suddenly formed between the two objects. A pulse of power surged through Spencer's arm. Then, like a piece of metal picked up by a strong magnet, the little bronze nail popped out of the wall and fell with a tinkle to the tile floor.

CHAPTER 19

"HOLD MY HAND!"

Daisy burst outside into the fresh evening air. Behind her was a wake of unlocked doors in the school. She ran the length of the school, gasping for breath until she reentered through the front door. The scene in the entry hall was utter chaos, which meant, of course, that Spencer had done his job.

Daisy clutched her spelling review sheet in one hand, the corner wrinkled from the sweat of her grip. In the other hand, she jingled Mrs. Natcher's keys. Daisy's hair was matted with sweat from her short run. She was breathing hard and feeling awful about telling Mrs. Natcher a half-truth. The sooner Daisy returned the keys, the better.

The girl pushed open the cafeteria door. The place was a complete disaster. A collage of pink, tan, and brown syrups still decorated the center of the room. Everything else was laced with streaks of sticky root beer. Daisy spotted Marv in the corner, firing up a machine that squirted water and sucked up messes.

Mrs. Natcher stood nearby, gazing into the syrup splash with a mournful expression. Whether she was mourning over the ruined ice cream social or the wasted syrup, Daisy wasn't sure.

"Got my review sheet, Mrs. Natcher," Daisy said, snapping the teacher out of her reverie. "Thanks." Daisy held out the keys.

The teacher took the keys and dropped them into her purse. "You missed a real disaster," Mrs. Natcher said with a grave expression.

"Looks like it." Daisy turned toward the exit. She needed to get to the rendezvous spot to meet Mr. Hadley.

A firm hand suddenly gripped her arm. "Coincidence?" Mrs. Natcher said. "Coincidence that Spencer, your trouble-making friend, would be up to no good while you made off with my keys?"

Daisy suddenly looked paler than vanilla ice cream. A cold fear rushed all the way to the soles of her feet.

"You've got some explaining to do." Mrs. Natcher dragged her across the cafeteria, Daisy struggling uselessly to get away.

Then, out of nowhere, Dez Rylie appeared, a heaping bowl of mostly melted ice cream in his hand.

"Gullible Gates!" Dez's eyes narrowed to a glare of revenge. "I can't find your boyfriend, so I'll have to settle for you!" With one swift motion, the bully shoved the bowl of dripping ice cream into Daisy's face.

Shrapnel from the ice cream bomb splashed onto Mrs. Natcher's cheek, and the force of the impact knocked them both back. Mrs. Natcher took a step backward to steady herself, but the teacher's shoe came down in the syrup swamp. The slick mess tested Mrs. Natcher's ability to skate . . . and she failed. The boring woman went down, her gray hair bun acting like a mop for the strawberry topping. Daisy came loose in the process, but she staggered, blinded by the ice cream.

Daisy wiped her eyes. The rest of her face was still sticky and white, as if some kind of spa facial mask had gone wrong. She had to make it to the rendezvous spot with Garth Hadley before the janitors got her! Leaving Dez in shock and Mrs. Natcher in syrup, Daisy crossed the cafeteria and exited out the back door. There were kids in the bouncy castle, some giggling, some crying, all totally oblivious to the war inside.

Daisy leapt down the steps and ran past the castle. A huge form suddenly appeared around the edge of the bouncy building. Big hands reached for Daisy, but she turned sharply, running back up the steps.

"You're supposed to be cleaning the mess inside!" she screamed as Marv came after her.

"The mess isn't going anywhere," the janitor answered. "But it looks like the mess makers are."

Daisy flew back up the steps, her retreat totally cut off. She entered the cafeteria at the same time Spencer burst through the opposite door. The two kids ran toward one another, each pursued by a dangerous janitor, with Mrs. Natcher standing up in the middle.

"You got it?" Daisy shrieked.

"Got it!" Spencer answered.

Spencer and Daisy met in the center of the cafeteria. "This way!" Spencer retreated to a corner. Daisy followed, drops of melted ice cream still flinging off her face.

"What now?" Daisy asked. The two kids had their backs to a wall. The two janitors slowed, spreading into attack formation Alpha Beta and coming slowly toward the children.

"We're cornered," Daisy moaned.

"No!" Spencer gritted his teeth. In desperation, he pulled off the latex glove.

"Spencer Alan Zumbro!" his mother's voice pierced the cafeteria. "You come here this instant!" But Spencer wasn't listening. He couldn't, or his mom's voice would break his heart. *Focus on the secret mission.*

"Hold my hand," Spencer whispered to Daisy.

"Wha–?"

"Just do it!"

Daisy grabbed Spencer's hand. Walter and Marv pounced. Mrs. Natcher hung back in case the kids managed to break free.

And they *did* break free!

In the last possible instant, Spencer had shoved the latex glove over their clenched hands. The janitors' grasp held them for only a moment before Daisy and Spencer slid easily between their fingers.

It was awkward to run holding hands, trying to keep their palms close so the stretchy glove wouldn't slip off. The mob of parents had filed outside along the back cafeteria steps. It was difficult to navigate the crowd, even though no one could hold them. With the parents forming a barricade, there was only one place to run.

"You have to take off your shoes!" the bouncy castle worker screamed as Daisy and Spencer dove through the mesh flap into the air-filled arena. There were three first graders bouncing reluctantly, but they quickly vacated the castle as Spencer and Daisy leapt inside.

The big inflatable castle was square, with four blowup turrets, one on each corner. Mesh walls connected the corners, but the top was uncovered. Spencer glanced up. If they could get over the back wall, it would be an open field to the rendezvous site.

The inflated floor suddenly shifted. Spencer went down as Daisy went up. The motion caused their hands to release, and the latex glove fell to the floor.

The cause of the disruption was Marv's great bulk, leaping ungracefully through the castle entrance and displacing a lot of air as he landed. The entrance flap, designed for elementary-school-sized children, had proven to be tighter than Marv had apparently expected, and he was tangled up in it.

As the janitor struggled, Spencer handed the nail and hammer to Daisy. Interlocking his fingers, Spencer made a quick stirrup for her. She stepped into his cupped hands and, with a bounce, he sent her over the wall.

Daisy didn't fly too gracefully. On her way up, she screamed, dropping both items. Daisy landed hard on the grass outside, but the hammer and nail landed with a bounce on the castle's inflated floor.

Spencer caught the bronze hammer on the first bounce. But before he could recover the nail, Marv jumped.

It was like fighting on the moon. Spencer bounced out of reach. Marv came down, sending Spencer higher on his next bounce. Walter Jamison climbed through the castle flap, his gaunt face set with determination.

The bronze nail was like a single kernel of corn in a popcorn popper. Every time someone landed, the nail went in a new direction.

Spencer went for the glove, possibly his last chance of escape. Walter beat him to it, dive-bouncing across the castle floor. As Walter landed, Marv went up. The big janitor lost his balance and came down on his belly as the nail rolled under him. The sharp nail pierced the tarplike material of the bouncy castle with a tearing sound. Marv rolled away from the split and a gush of air went up. The castle turrets began to fold and tilt inward.

The irate bouncy-castle worker shouted and switched off the air machine that kept the castle upright. As the castle collapsed, Spencer made a final leap and vaulted over the sagging mesh wall.

Spencer ran so hard he felt sick. His legs pumped across the field till they were numb. He didn't look back to see if the janitors were pursuing him. He didn't want to imagine his family—his mom—so disappointed and upset. She

wouldn't understand what he was doing, why he had ruined the ice cream social and fled the premises.

The blue Toyota was idling at the rendezvous corner. As Spencer got close, Daisy threw open the door and he dove into the car. Garth Hadley was at the wheel. Even before the door was shut, the car was speeding down the street.

"Well?" Mr. Hadley asked. His clean, square face was anxious for the report.

Spencer held up the bronze hammer. It was one solid piece of metal, very plain, with no special designs or jewel-encrusted handle.

"We got the hammer," he said. "And here's the soap we borrowed." Spencer dug the little bottle from his pocket and handed it over.

"What about the nail?" Garth Hadley asked. "Did you get it?"

"Nope," said Spencer. "The bouncy castle did."

CHAPTER 20

"YOU'RE JUST LIKE YOUR FATHER SOMETIMES."

It was a quarter to midnight when the blue Toyota pulled into Hillside Estates and came to a gentle stop in front of Aunt Avril's house.

After their escape from the ice cream social, Garth Hadley had driven the kids out of Welcher to a small neighboring town. There, he bought them a late dinner at a twenty-four-hour dive. The bathroom was as dingy as they come, and Spencer held his breath the whole time as he washed his hands. The food was greasy, but as the adrenaline of the evening wore off, Spencer and Daisy found they were hungry.

Garth Hadley was pleased with their work and assured them that Walter Jamison had been stopped—at least momentarily. He still had the nail, but without the hammer there was no way for Walter to set up a link with the school again.

Hadley explained that the BEM would stay in town until they found a way to get the bronze nail, leaving Walter Jamison totally powerless.

"We could really use your help," Garth invited. "You two were great at the ice cream social."

"No, thanks," Spencer said quietly, poking at his last bite of country-fried steak. Daisy just shook her head.

"That's all right, kids," Hadley said. "The BEM is in your debt. You've been instrumental in crippling a criminal. Just let me know if you change your mind."

The drive back to Welcher was quiet and awkward. Daisy dozed in the backseat. Garth Hadley said nothing, his broad face studying the road ahead. Spencer watched the black night go by, wondering what kind of trouble he would be in with his mother, with the janitors, with the principal, with the angry, root-beer-stained parents . . . the list went on.

Had it been a mistake to help the BEM? It had gotten him in serious trouble, and he'd dragged Daisy down with him. Part of Spencer wished that he'd never spoken to Garth Hadley. But the world of the janitors was also fascinating and enticing: magical creatures roaming the halls, a latex glove that made the wearer slip through enemy fingers. . . . What other awesome tricks might exist that Spencer was completely unaware of?

Hadley dropped Daisy off first, the Gates's savage dog greeting them with a chorus of barking. Daisy, ashen-faced at the prospect of meeting her parents, jumped quickly out of the car. Light illuminated the windows of the little house. Daisy's parents were undoubtedly waiting up.

Aunt Avril's house, however, looked pitch-black from the street. For a hopeful minute, Spencer thought he might be able to slip upstairs to his bedroom and pretend like nothing had happened.

Spencer opened the car door and put his feet out.

"Hey." Garth Hadley reached over. "You've got a career in the Bureau of Educational Maintenance if you want one, kid."

Spencer looked back at Mr. Hadley, BEM regional representative. Spencer wanted to smile, but the things he'd done at the ice cream social pulled at the corners of his mouth. "I'm only twelve."

Hadley laughed, showing straight, white teeth. "I'm just saying . . ." He trailed off. His face resumed a more businesslike look. "As you've discovered, the BEM does a whole lot more than scrape gum. There's another world out there, Spencer. You've only tapped the surface, but you show real talent."

"Thanks," Spencer muttered, and he stood up. Garth Hadley was examining the bronze hammer again. Spencer thought he might say something more, but before Hadley had the chance, Spencer shut the car door.

Spencer stood alone on the dead grass as the blue Toyota drove out of Hillside Estates. The wealthy country neighborhood was alive with the chirrup of crickets. Somewhere in the distance, Spencer heard the *ch-ch-ch* of a large sprinkler. With a sigh, he walked up the steps, opened the front door, and locked it once he was inside.

"We have to talk."

Spencer's heart jumped, pulling his feet off the ground in surprise. His mother was seated on a scratched leather couch, enveloped in darkness.

"Mom! What are you doing in the dark? You totally freaked me out!"

"I freaked *you* out? Spencer, it's nearly midnight! Where have you been?"

Spencer didn't know what to do—ignore her and walk away, or spill everything and see what she believed. He needed time in his tidy bedroom. Time to sort everything out and decide what to do next.

"Can we talk about this tomorrow?" Spencer tried.

"Are you kidding? You're twelve years old, Spencer. I'm your mother and I have every right to know what's going on. You made a huge mess, left your little brother covered in ice cream toppings, popped the blow-up castle, and then ran away from—"

"I didn't pop the castle. It was that fat janitor guy."

"Don't make excuses for your poor actions! You're just like your father sometimes!"

Her words hit Spencer like a splash of icy water in the face. Comparing Spencer to Alan Zumbro evoked high emotion from both mother and son. Alice was trembling. Spencer didn't know whether he should feel insulted or proud.

They stared silently at one another, two dark silhouettes

in an oversized living room. Spencer had never felt so ashamed, so afraid of tomorrow. It was dark enough to cry, wasn't it? His mother was already doing it, so Spencer let a tear fall too.

"I'm afraid," he whispered. "I don't know what to do."

Alice held out her arms. Spencer shuffled toward her, uneasily at first, like a toddler learning to walk. Then he collapsed on the couch and felt his mother's arms wrap around his shoulders.

"It'll be all right," Alice whispered. "Just tell me what's going on."

Spencer swallowed hard. How much could he tell his mother before she decided that his childish imagination was out of control? Besides, Garth Hadley had told him not to talk about the creatures anymore. And Spencer's confession to the class had been met with laughter. Laughter that deeply hurt. If his mother didn't believe him, if she laughed . . .

But he had to tell her *something!* He needed to know what to do next and wanted someone else to decide it for him. Alice gave Spencer a comforting squeeze.

"Last Thursday," Spencer began. He wiped his eyes and took a deep breath. "After school, I met a guy from the Bureau of Educational Maintenance. Garth Hadley. He said the BEM needed my help to get something from the janitors. Something they . . . stole."

Spencer had to fib a little here. In the silent moments before he spoke, Spencer had already decided that telling the story would be much easier if he left out the *magic* altogether. There was no reason to mention the creatures. No reason to tempt his mother to laugh. After all, the janitors were the real problem. That was where he needed help.

"I did what Mr. Hadley said and took a bronze hammer from the janitor. I don't know what it was for. Maybe it was worth a lot of money or something."

Alice took a deep breath through her nose. One hand went to her forehead. "This isn't helping my headache at all," she muttered. "I'm worried, Spencer."

"I know." He bit his lip. "Me too. The janitors will probably be waiting for me tomorrow."

"It's not the janitors I'm worried about," Alice said. "It's Garth Hadley."

CHAPTER 21

"IS THIS TRUE, SPENCER?"

But Mom," whined Erica over breakfast, "I don't see why Spencer gets a ride to school while the rest of us have to take the bus."

"It's about last night," Holly guessed. "What Spencer did at the ice cream social."

Spencer stared at his soggy frosted flakes and tried to pretend that he wasn't in the room. His sister's words were painfully true. Mom was taking him to see the principal.

"We've got to go now or I'll be late for work," Alice said. It was, after all, her first day at Quick 'n' Speedy. "Just dump your cereal in the sink. I'll be waiting in the car."

Spencer climbed into the station wagon and tossed his backpack next to the car seat behind him. Max had already been dropped off at the day care, and all that was left of him were a few fragments of Cheerios on the seat.

They drove in silence. Spencer thought his mother seemed like a force to be reckoned with. She clearly wasn't happy about Spencer's involvement with the BEM. Now she gripped the steering wheel like it was Garth Hadley's neck.

Well before the morning busses arrived, Alice Zumbro pushed into Welcher Elementary's front office, Spencer in tow. Mrs. Hamp looked up from her desk, already planning a greeting that would test this woman's vocabulary.

"Do you require the immediate assistance of someone in an administrative position?" She feigned politeness, poorly.

"Listen," Alice said, clearly in no mood for prose, "we need to see the principal. I've only got five minutes."

"Principal Poach has not yet arrived," the secretary said. "His arrival is undoubtedly postponed by the traffic."

Alice rolled her eyes. "You've got to be kidding me. Traffic in Welcher is a contradiction. When will the principal be here?"

"He always arrives for morning announcements." Mrs. Hamp checked the clock on her computer. "Fifteen minutes, give or take."

"Shoot," Alice said. "I've got to be to work by then." She glanced at Spencer, but he was a statue.

"If you have a pressing concern, I could make a note and pass it to the principal when he arrives."

"My pressing concern," Alice said, leaning across the desk, "is for the safety of my children at Welcher Elementary School."

Mrs. Hamp leaned back defensively. "Has there been some betrayal of your trust in our school, Miss?"

"Don't *Miss* me, missy." Alice was getting worked up. Spencer couldn't decide if he should smile or not. It was kind of cool to hear how much his mom cared about his safety. Cool in an embarrassing sort of way.

"My son was approached by a stranger in this school. Whether the man was actually from the Bureau of Educational Maintenance or not does not excuse the fact that he enlisted my son's help to accomplish illegal acts."

Mrs. Hamp sat forward. Her eyes widened with the practice of someone with years of experience in meddling and gossip. "Illegal acts? Strangers in Welcher Elementary? Elaborate!"

Spencer shifted awkwardly as his mother gave the one-minute version of how Garth Hadley had asked him to steal something from the janitors. When Alice was finished, Mrs. Hamp sat back. Now the secretary's eyes narrowed and a smirk appeared.

"Children," Mrs. Hamp said knowingly, "have a way of leaving out important information."

Spencer slunk back as the secretary's accusatory gaze pierced him.

"Mr. Hadley is indeed a licensed member of the BEM," Mrs. Hamp said. "Last Thursday, he arrived at the school to perform a routine inspection *after* the school had been vacated. If your son did meet Mr. Hadley that day, it would have been due to his lack of obedience in exiting the school when the final bell rang."

Each word she spoke seemed to reduce Spencer. When she finished, he felt smaller than a toothpick.

"Is this true, Spencer?" his mother asked. "Were you in the school after you had been asked to leave?"

Wordlessly, Spencer nodded. Why hadn't he just told his mother the whole truth from the very start?

"But what about the other times he contacted you?" Alice asked. "Where did he meet you?"

Spencer wished it were another yes-or-no question so he could simply nod again. But now his mother had called on him to speak an answer. And oh, how that answer was bound to disappoint.

"I only met him once," said Spencer. "Last Thursday."

"You see!" Mrs. Hamp jumped in. "Welcher takes great pride in knowing every visitor that passes through these doors. Rest assured that Mr. Hadley will not come again, unless on official business for the BEM. And in such an instance, the school will be empty of children. As it *should* have been last Thursday."

Spencer glanced at the clock. His mother's time was spent if she wanted to be on time for her first day of work. But Spencer knew she wasn't done investigating yet. She put a hand on his shoulder.

"Did you contact this Hadley person on your own?"

Spencer nodded.

Then came the dreaded word. "How?"

Spencer looked at his feet as if hoping to find a different answer written there. "E-mail," he finally whispered.

"Spencer Alan Zumbro!" Her hand dropped from his

shoulder. "You know very well the rules of our family! That e-mail account is for contact with your friends in Washington. Anything else—*anything* else!—must be approved by me."

Alice put her hands on her hips. "I'm disappointed in you, Spencer." Mrs. Hamp was smiling at the family tension until Alice pointed a finger across the desk. "And I'm not happy with *you*, either. I don't care who Garth Hadley is. If the janitors stole something from him, it's the police he should contact, not my twelve-year-old son! I suggest a background search on school visitors."

Mrs. Hamp held up her hands in defense. "Don't look at me. Mr. Hadley's a government man. We don't interfere with them."

"Yeah? Well, I'm a *mother*. And you shouldn't interfere with me, either!"

CHAPTER 22

"RUINED BY CHILDISH RIFFRAFF!"

In the noisy moments just before class started, Spencer sat in his desk. A thin smile spread across his face when he recalled his mother chewing out Mrs. Hamp a few minutes ago. But the smile couldn't last, filled as he was with guilt and shame about disappointing his mom.

Daisy didn't look much better, sitting in the corner. She arrived at the classroom much later than usual, her eyes pink from sleeplessness and tears. They glanced at each other only briefly. Just long enough to make sure that they were both still alive.

Neither of them would look at Mrs. Natcher. They didn't want to see if she still had sticky strawberry syrup in her gray hair.

The only troublemaker who seemed unaffected by the events at the ice cream social was Dez. He belched in unison with the bell, trying to make his burp last longer. His expression quickly changed as Mrs. Hamp's crackly voice sounded over the intercom.

"Dezmond Rylie, Spencer Zumbro, and Daisy Gates. The principal has arrived and demands to see you— immediately."

Spencer stood on trembling legs. Daisy tried to get up twice, but seemed frozen in place. As Spencer passed her desk, she found the courage and stood at his side.

Dez moaned obnoxiously but jumped to his feet. Dez seemed to have no trouble walking, having gained his "principal's-office legs" through repeated trips to the front office.

"Take the hall pass," Mrs. Natcher said. She might have added, "You all get F's for the year," and Spencer wouldn't have been surprised.

At the door, Daisy shamefully lifted Baybee from its place on the bookshelf. The doll's diaper was modestly in place once more, but the plastic forehead looked a little scratched from the bathroom tile.

As they stepped into the hallway, Dez snatched the baby doll from Daisy's hand. "I don't trust you with that," he said, tucking the hall pass under his arm.

The three kids walked in silence for a while. But Dez, King of Unnecessary Noise, soon started making squishing sounds with his mouth every time he took a step.

"You know," Dez said, "the principal's not so bad if you know how to handle him." Spencer and Daisy didn't ac-knowledge, but Dez continued anyway. "He likes it if you call him respectful titles like 'Emperor Fatso,' or 'Honorable Senator Blimp.'"

"Be quiet, Dez," Daisy said.

"Huh?" cried the bully. "What happened to you, Gullible Gates? You used to believe *everything* I said."

"'Cause I used to think you might have something worth saying."

The kids were at the principal's office much sooner than they had hoped. But no amount of lollygagging could postpone the undesirable P-R-E-D-I-C-A-M-E-N-T they had gotten themselves into.

Mrs. Hamp had a pleased glint in her eye as she motioned for the three kids to wait on some benches until the principal was ready for them.

They waited about five minutes, Dez making Baybee dive-bomb off the bench onto her head over and over again while accompanying the scenario with gory sound effects.

Then the principal's door opened and Dez was summoned inside. The bully tossed Baybee onto the bench and went through the door as though he were going out to recess.

Daisy and Spencer waited nervously on the bench. Baybee sat between them, and Daisy held one of the doll's hands while Spencer held the other, feeling the uncontrollable need to hang on to something, even if it was only a lifeless, plastic doll.

Dez appeared a few minutes later, his face a storm cloud brewing with bolts of negative energy. "See you chumps in about a week," he grunted. "Emperor Fatso decided to spend me." Dez probably meant to say *suspend*, but the bully didn't look like he was in any mood to be corrected.

As Dez walked away, Spencer and Daisy's attention turned back to the principal's office. A man filled the doorway, almost as big around as he was tall.

Principal Poach wore a striped collared shirt and pink tie that looked miniature against his portly belly. He had a walrus face, complete with bristly brown mustache.

Principal Poach's eyes were squinty and small as he pointed at Spencer and Daisy with two fingers that looked like microwaved hot dogs. Then the hot-dog fingers wiggled, a gesture that Spencer interpreted to mean "get in my office now."

The two kids arose, Baybee dangling between them, and entered the office. Principal Poach shut the door and waddled to his desk chair. The principal was so round that the only way Spencer could tell he was walking, and not rolling, was by the stripes on his shirt. Once comfortably nestled into his padded chair, the principal stroked his mustache for a moment. Spencer looked for tusks, but didn't see any.

"An entire event—ruined!" Principal Poach said. His voice was high and whiny. It seemed biologically impossible for such a massive body to produce such a piercing voice. "Ruined by childish riffraff!" He slammed a hand onto the desk.

"Twenty-four years I have been principal of Welcher Elementary, and I have never—*never*—heard of such behavior. We do not tolerate it. We cannot abide it."

What Daisy and Spencer didn't know was that Principal

Poach was giving them his memorized speech for first-time offenders. Dez had made it to speech number eight before Principal Poach suspended him.

"During the Edo period of Japan, at the time of the Samurai, criminal punishment included such cruelties as imprisonment, exile, and penal labor. At any rate, the Samurai warriors of Japan saw the need for a corrective course of action to rectify one's misdoings."

The speech, aside from being really hard to understand, made Spencer and Daisy shift uncomfortably in their seats. The parts of Principal Poach's speech that Spencer understood were the bits about imprisonment, exile, and, although Spencer wasn't exactly sure about "penal," labor was never good.

"Thus it is with you, my young friends," Poach continued. "You are in need of guided correctional behavior. Due to the offense, I see fit to . . ."

At this point in the speech, the principal would generally insert a punishment; he had any number of them memorized. But that morning, Principal Poach did something extraordinary. He left the safety of his memorized speech, looked right at Spencer, and began to speak on his own.

"Mrs. Hamp told me of your mother's visit this morning. I find your claims about the BEM highly unlikely. However, safety of the children is our top priority, and we will monitor school visitors more closely in the future."

Great for the future, Spencer thought. *But what about the things that already happened?*

"We can never truly know if Mr. Hadley put you up to

the task of mess making, as you have declared. But *some-one* has to be punished. The ice cream social was a tragedy. I had more than a dozen e-mails from angry parents this morning. The janitors contacted me last night and I . . . I really *wanted* to suspend you." He sighed, his walrus cheeks jiggling.

Spencer and Daisy sat still as the principal rambled. They squeezed Baybee even tighter, feeling like they were barely balancing between suspension and the unknown.

"But I'm not going to," Poach went on. "Suspend you, that is." His hot-dog fingers were nervously interlaced. "I would have, but the janitors encouraged another punishment more appropriate to the offense."

Spencer and Daisy looked at each other, eyes wide. *Please, don't let it be what I'm thinking,* Spencer thought desperately.

The principal regained composure and picked up his speech at the "insert punishment here" line where he had departed. "You shall both spend time in detention with the janitors after school, every day for the rest of the week. I expect your full cooperation in this. Our head janitor, John Campbell, was very kind to dissuade me from suspending you. You might want to thank him."

Thank him? Yeah, right! Spencer felt sick. Daisy's tears finally leaked out. They were being turned over to the janitors. Marv and Walter would be furious about the theft of the hammer.

Spencer knew he would have preferred imprisonment or

exile. Heck, even a samurai execution might be less painful than what the janitors would do.

"In addition," Principal Poach went on, "you shall both write a nice letter of apology to the Parent-Teacher Association, who organized the ice cream social. The parents will be glad to see that you are paying for your wrong-doings. Unfortunately, I must forbid you from attending any PTA activities for the rest of this year."

With some effort, Principal Poach stood up and smiled a walrus smile. "That will be all, children. I expect that no further disciplinary action will be necessary. Do your home-work, eat your veggies, and don't go looking for any more trouble."

But Spencer and Daisy didn't have to look far to see trouble. Even as Principal Poach concluded his speech, one of Jamison's creatures, a vulture-bat, crawled out from be-hind a painting of George Washington and took flight. The little creature swooped down to Poach's desk and landed on the rim of an open can of peanuts. Both Daisy and Spencer had their eyes glued to the creature.

"What?" Poach huffed, following their gaze to his desk. Meanwhile, the vulture-bat folded its wings and dropped into the can, scavenging for nuts.

"Oh," the principal said. "I guess it's not professional to leave my snacks out, is it?" He picked up the can of peanuts. "But I just can't help myself. I *love* a good peanut."

In horror, Spencer and Daisy watched as the hot-dog fingers descended into the peanut can.

"Don't!" Spencer finally shouted. The last thing he

wanted was for the vulture-bat to get a good meal off the principal's fingers. The walrus-shaped man paused for a moment and glanced in the can. Apparently seeing nothing, he plunged in and withdrew a few peanuts. Poach stuffed the nuts into his mouth and crunched noisily.

"What's the matter with you?" the principal asked.

Spencer floundered for an excuse. Poach obviously hadn't seen *or* felt the creature in the can. "It's just that you . . . you forgot to wash your hands."

Principal Walrus chortled, his belly bouncing. "Pish posh," he said, pointing back at his desk. "I use instant hand sanitizer."

Spencer peered around the principal and saw the bottle of sanitizer. It was the kind that doctors claimed killed 99.99% of all germs.

Unfortunately, a slimy yellow salamander creature was wrapped around the bottle, wide mouth drooling all over the top.

CHAPTER 23

"SO FAR I'M GROUNDED FOR A WEEK."

Mrs. Natcher's classroom was relatively peaceful without Dez. At least, an artificial sense of peace could be felt if Spencer and Daisy avoided eye contact with Mrs. Natcher.

The rest of the school day passed normally. Spencer aced the spelling test and Daisy misspelled only *colonel*.

When the bell rang at the end of class, Spencer and Daisy hung back, wondering if it was worth trying to escape before detention. But what did it matter anyway? Sooner or later the janitors would catch them and punish them for stealing the bronze hammer.

The chance to run was shot down when Mrs. Natcher took Spencer and Daisy by the arms.

"The principal informed me of your detention with the

janitors," she said. "Perhaps I could help you find them, so you don't get *lost* along the way."

Mrs. Natcher escorted them down the hall to the waiting hulk of Marv Bills. With a formal head nod, Mrs. Natcher turned them over.

Marv glowered over the kids for a moment. "All right," he said once Mrs. Natcher was gone. "John Campbell isn't here right now, so you kids'll be scraping gum off the desks until he gets back."

"Don't you mean Walter Jamison?" Spencer said. He didn't mean for it to sound so defiant. Spencer just wanted Marv to know that he and Daisy were aware of the janitor's lies.

"Come on," Marv said and led the children to Mrs. Cleveland's sixth-grade classroom. Wordlessly, Marv withdrew two flat razor blades that retracted into a handle by sliding a button back and forth. From his other pocket, he took two pairs of latex gloves.

"You'll need these. I want you to get under each desk, use the blade to scrape off the gum, and then throw it in the trash. If you finish this room, move to the next. I'll come get you when Mr. Campbell arrives." Spencer and Daisy accepted the razor blades and Marv pushed them into the room.

It was a disgusting and intimidating assignment. The classroom had at least twenty-five desks. As Spencer crouched under the first desk and saw four hard, dried blobs, he silently vowed never to chew gum again. For Spencer, there could be no worse punishment than chipping off someone else's ABC gum.

Spencer pulled on his latex gloves. Last time he'd worn one, it had made him uncatchable. These gloves were plain and nonmagical, but at least they would keep the germs off his hands.

Daisy didn't seem to mind the task. She was already on her second desk, holding the fragments of stale gum in one gloved hand while working vigorously with the razor blade in the other. Taking a deep breath, Spencer followed her example and was surprised at how easily the old gum came free.

"I bet your parents weren't too happy last night," Spencer said.

"They were just worried sick. So far I'm grounded for a week. But it will probably be longer once Principal Poach calls to tell them what we did at the social."

"You didn't tell them?" Spencer dodged a piece of gum as it chipped off and fell toward him.

"What could I say? That we were on a secret mission for the BEM?" Daisy shook her head. "My parents have heard all kinds of stories from me. I know what they'd say: 'Daisy, dear, someone was trying to trick you.'"

"That's what my mom told me," Spencer said. "Minus the 'Daisy, dear' part."

"She thinks Garth Hadley was tricking us?" Daisy stopped scraping. "Could that be true?"

"I don't know. We just need to be careful."

They chipped rock-hard gum in silence.

"You sure made a mess in the cafeteria yesterday," Daisy reminisced, as though it were a pleasant memory. "Bet your parents were pretty mad about that. They were there, weren't they?"

"Just my mom," Spencer answered. "But yeah, she was pretty mad."

"What'd she say?"

"Said I was like my dad."

"Isn't that a good thing?" Daisy asked, halting her gum scraping.

"At *your* house it would be," answered Spencer. "But I haven't seen my dad since I was about ten."

"Where is he? On business somewhere?"

"His own business," said Spencer. It sounded too bitter, so Spencer explained. "My dad used to teach biology at a junior high school. His best friend was this scientist guy named Rod Grush. Sometimes they'd travel to do experiments and projects. It really made my mom mad because sometimes he'd be gone for days."

Spencer sat back. It was weird to tell this story. Like sharing a spoon with someone, which Spencer would never do for fear of germs. It seemed to link them together in an extra personal way.

"Got so bad," Spencer continued, "that Mom wouldn't even let us say Rod Grush's name around the house. About two years ago, my dad and Rod went to Texas for a project. He never came back."

"Must be a big project," Daisy said, turning back to her gum chipping.

Spencer felt his face go red. Gullible Gates didn't understand. How could she, with her funny, Ford-driving dad?

"No, Daisy," Spencer said. "You don't get it. He's not coming back. Nobody knows where he is. The junior high fired him. Mom says that his projects meant more to him than his family, and that's why he took off."

"What?" Daisy's voice was rich with disbelief. "I don't believe it," she said, a fresh piece of gum sticking to her razor blade.

"What do you mean, you don't believe it?" Spencer asked. He was getting angry, the way he always got when he thought too much about his dad.

"I mean, your dad's *got* to come back. Nobody loves their work more than their family."

Spencer slumped against the leg of a desk, his anger fleeing. His face was still hot and there were tears in his eyes. "I used to think that too. I miss him. He was the coolest guy."

"Did he say he'd come back?"

"Yeah," Spencer said, wiping a stray tear with his shoulder. He kept his head low so Daisy wouldn't see.

"Then you've got to believe him," answered Daisy.

"It's easy for you. You believe everyone."

"Not anymore. I only believe people that I trust."

"Do you trust *me?*"

"Duh," Daisy said. "I think you—"

Daisy stopped short and Spencer's tears dried instantly as the classroom door opened. Marv stepped inside. "John Campbell is ready to see you now. Follow me."

As Spencer tried to regain control of his emotions, the prospect of facing the head janitor made him weak. Daisy came to his side and they followed big Marv until they stood at the top of the janitorial steps. Spencer noticed a few spots of sticky, dried root beer that hadn't been mopped. The stains made polka dots on the stairs.

"Down," Marv pointed. The children obeyed, slowly descending the steps and feeling as if the janitors' storage/office would swallow them like a shark.

The basement room had been tidied since the last time Spencer and Daisy were down there. At the center desk, two chairs sat vacant, side by side. On the other side of the desk was the head janitor. Marv moved into position behind him like an ogre awaiting commands.

Walter Jamison gestured for the kids to be seated. Once they were in their chairs, the head janitor cleared his throat. "Did the principal tell you that I'd recommended detention with the janitors instead of suspension?"

"Yeah," Daisy answered.

"You should thank me," Walter replied. "You have become involved with a very dangerous organization. Being with us is the safest place for you right now."

"Why?" Spencer leaned forward. "So you can poison our brains with your magical experiments?"

Walter Jamison sighed and ran a hand across his bald head. "I need you to inform me of everything that Garth Hadley told you."

Spencer wanted to resist, but Daisy plunged in. Once she started, she seemed unable to stop. After pouring out

145

the whole story, she folded her arms and glanced at Spencer. He smiled briefly at her, grateful to have the truth out in the open.

"Spencer, Daisy," Walter Jamison began, his voice low. "I'm afraid you've been tricked."

CHAPTER 24

"A WARLOCK, ACTUALLY."

Tricked?" Daisy shouted, jumping to her feet. "That's what everyone keeps saying. But how do I know that *you're* not lying? The BEM is a government agency—"

"He's *not* lying," Marv said.

"You won't even tell us your real name!" Spencer said to the head janitor.

"We often use false names to protect ourselves from the enemy," Walter said. "I have been using the alias of John Campbell for several months now, but I assure you, my real name is Walter Jamison, as you've already discovered. Please," he continued, "allow us to explain."

He waited for the kids to calm down, then said, "Garth Hadley has filled you full of half-truths in order to make me into an enemy. He wants the hammer and nail for himself."

Walter held up his hand. "I should start at the beginning." He looked down to gather his thoughts.

"The United States was founded in 1776," Walter began. Spencer instantly hoped that this speech would have nothing to do with Samurai exile. "But even before the nation was formed, many colonists came from Great Britain."

"The pilgrims," Daisy said. "We know."

"All right. Once the American colonies were thriving and schools were established, a certain threat was discovered. Three types of creatures, or Toxites, began to reside in the schools. Pests of the worst kind. You've heard of termites, or dust mites? Well, Toxites are far worse. The winged one is called Rubbish, the furry one Filth, and the slimy one they named Grime.

"Three women spotted the creatures first. Their natural ability to see Toxites marked them as witches. They quickly discerned that, to everyone else, the little pests were invisible. These three witches discovered a correlation between the Toxite population and the learning curve. In other words, if there were more creatures in a school, students did poorly. Determined to fix the problem, the witches set about ridding the schools of Rubbish, Filth, and Grime."

"How'd they do that?" Daisy asked, her gullible side already absorbed by the story.

"Well," Walter said, "they tried sweeping them up, but the Toxites were resilient to ordinary brooms. So the witches developed new brooms that enabled them to crush the critters."

"And let me guess," Spencer said sarcastically. "Then the witches flew off on their brooms."

"Exactly. The magic in the Toxites is indestructible. For example, if a Filth is crushed by a witch's broom, the body turns to dust and the magic goes into the broom that destroyed it. When brooms are powered with Toxite magic, they gain the ability to defy gravity. Do you understand?"

"I understand," answered Spencer. "I just don't buy it yet."

"Let him finish," Daisy said.

"The witches knew they couldn't live forever, but they needed to keep the schools Toxite-free. They developed a way to expose other people to the Toxites' existence. The secret was carried on from generation to generation. When the United States was formed and the country began to expand, the need for Toxite-fighting janitors increased. The Bureau of Educational Maintenance was founded and the secret was kept between those of us in the BEM."

"Those of *us?*" Spencer asked. "You're part of the BEM too?"

"All school janitors are. But only about 50 percent know of the Toxites. You see, the creatures don't live in high schools. Even some junior high schools are bad environments for them."

"Why?"

"Many years after the witches, we discovered that the Toxites inhale active brain waves and exhale waves that interfere with the growing mind. They are most dangerous to younger students. In fact, by the time kids reach high school, the Toxites can't stand to be around them. To the creatures, it would be like breathing in really stinky air compared to the fresh air of the younger schools. It might even make some of them sick."

There was silence in the storage/office while Daisy and Spencer pondered the prospect of Toxites. Finally, Spencer said, "What does this have to do with Garth Hadley and the bronze hammer?"

"Right," Walter said. "You're very on task, Spencer. I like that." He held up three fingers. "There are actually three bronze hammers, each with a nail. Before dying, the witches transferred their knowledge and power into the hammers. I have Ninfa. *Had* Ninfa, I should say. Garth Hadley has her now."

"Why a hammer?" Spencer asked. "It's not like janitors use hammers for cleaning stuff."

"Janitors do more than clean things, kid," Marv said. "If something breaks in the school, who do you think fixes it?" Marv gestured at himself by jabbing a thumb into his chest. "Janitors use hammers all the time."

"Hammers represent the strength and hard work it takes to build something," Walter said. "The three witches were the builders and founders of everything magic. They left their legacy and power in the bronze hammers and nails."

"So, does having the hammer make you a witch?" Daisy asked.

"Well, in my case, a warlock, actually," Walter Jamison answered. "Witches are women. Currently all three hammers are held by men."

Daisy glanced at Spencer, her eyes wide. Gullible Gates had no problem accepting the idea that the school janitor was a magic warlock.

"It's like this." Marv took over. "Each warlock needs a place to do his experiments. He sets it up by pounding the nail into a building. Once the nail is secure, that building becomes the warlock's domain—the only place for him to experiment."

"What are these experiments?" Spencer asked.

"Well, the witches made special brooms to kill Toxites. In our day, the warlocks have developed many new tools to do the job—vacuums and mops, for instance. The three warlocks who hold the hammers receive small shipments of raw magic so they can continue experimenting."

"But you stole one of the hammers from a warlock and set up your own domain here! Didn't you?" Spencer stared into Walter Jamison's hard eyes.

"Yes, I did," the warlock answered. "I had to. Over a year ago, the BEM started withdrawing support from the schools. They instructed all Toxite-fighting janitors to step down and let the creatures take over. I felt strongly that we should continue our war against Toxites, and many other janitors shared my belief. I was able to steal Ninfa and establish myself as a warlock.

"I worked undercover at an elementary school in Arkansas. As a warlock, I received the shipments of raw magic. I began experimenting and creating equipment to kill Toxites. We started an underground operation, distributing Toxite-fighting supplies to janitors who still wanted to protect the kids.

"Unfortunately, our success betrays us. The harder we work, the more our schools excel. Toxite-free students typically do 75 percent better on tests than students that are exposed to the creatures. That's the whole reason the BEM is supposed to exist—to protect education."

"But the BEM's given up." Marv pulled a face, looking as if he wanted to spit. "It's up to us now. Up to the Rebel Janitors to save education."

Walter nodded. "We've been doing our best to keep Welcher Elementary Toxite-free. The best schools in this nation, the schools where kids can still learn, all have janitors from the Rebel Underground. The BEM is tracking us down and firing us one by one. But most of all, they've been looking for me."

Walter rubbed his forehead. "Now, without the hammer to drive the bronze nail, I can't set up my magical domain. I can't experiment. I can't create new Toxite-fighting equipment. I'm a sitting duck. Now all the BEM has to do is wait. It's only a matter of time before our equipment breaks down. Once it does, Toxites will run wild with no one to stop them."

"And if no one controls the Toxites," Daisy said, "all the kids will get stupid?"

"Education will take an irreversible dive." Walter leaned forward and lowered his voice. "Imagine a future without education. No one can do math. Businesses are crumbling. No one understands science and industry. Progression is halted, and then gradually gives way to digression. Things break and no one can mend them. The computer gives way to pen and paper, the automobile to the horse. No one can read. Laws are forgotten but weapons are not. No doctors, no police, no teachers. Terror and chaos reign. Disease, invasion, war. A base and futile fight for survival. That is the future the BEM is creating. That is the future without education."

The image was vivid in Spencer's mind. It didn't seem possible that the Bureau of Educational Maintenance could throw the nation into ruin.

"But," Spencer said, "Mrs. Natcher will teach us. She won't forget how to read."

"Teachers will teach," said Walter, "but the Toxites will be too strong for the kids to learn anything. Once the older generations die, this nation will fall into the hands of today's uneducated youth."

Spencer thought of little Max and shivered. By the time his brother was in school, the BEM's plan would be in full force.

"Why?" Daisy asked. "Why would they destroy the future?"

"We don't know why," Marv said. "Could be revenge. Maybe they're tired of cleaning up kids' messes, year after year, without so much as a thank you." Marv's face contorted in a disgusted expression. "Don't much care about their reasons. It just makes me sick. If the BEM won't give us equipment to kill the Toxites, then it's up to us."

"We have to fight back and maintain the ideals that the

Founding Witches believed in," said Walter. "These are corrupt times."

Spencer tilted his chair back on two legs. The janitors were either telling the truth or they had just fabricated the most elaborate lie in the history of lies. Spencer wanted to believe them, but it didn't seem possible that the Bureau of Educational Maintenance had gone evil and was letting kids' brains rot. Walter's picture of the uneducated future was frightening, but could it be trusted? One glance at Daisy revealed that she had fallen for the janitor's story, hook, line, and sinker.

"You're going to have to prove it," Spencer finally said.

Marv stepped forward. "Read the numbers, kid. Education is falling apart. What more do you want?"

Walter Jamison held up a hand. "Your concern is admirable, Spencer. You've been tricked once and you don't want to fall into another pit. I've told you everything and shown you all the proof I can. Just look at the evidence and trust in your feelings."

Silence filled the storage/office. Silence that became stifling and uncomfortable. After a moment, the warlock continued. "Hadley asked you to do some pretty extreme things: sneak out of class, create a giant mess, break into locked parts of the school, steal objects from the janitors. How did it make you feel to do those things, Spencer?"

Walter had hit a sensitive subject. Nothing about last week seemed right. Everything Garth Hadley had asked him to do had ended in disaster. Now he was in detention, nearly suspended. All on account of the BEM representative.

"All right," Spencer said, ending his guilt-wreaking chain of thoughts. "If I say I believe you, what do I have to do?"

"*Do?*" cried Walter, a grin spreading across his face. "You don't have to *do* anything. That would make me as bad as Hadley, recruiting kids to perform dangerous tasks. No, Spencer. We're here to help you, to keep you safe."

Walter stood, his hands clasped tightly. "The BEM has tried a forbidden tactic—exposing children to the existence of Toxites. There's no telling what else they might do, which is why I think you should prepare yourselves for the worst."

"What do you mean?" Daisy asked. Walter walked across the room. A high stack of boxes leaned against the back wall. Grabbing the boxes, he slid the stack sideways on a hidden metal runner and a door appeared. Painted on the door was the symbol of a large silver ring with at least a dozen keys dangling from it, splaying outward like rays from the sun.

"Boss," Marv whispered, his face nervous. But Walter merely smiled and unlocked the door. Spencer and Daisy stood up and came a few steps closer, trying to peer into the dark room beyond.

"The Toxites are real," Walter said. "And they're not going anywhere. You kids still have a lot of learning ahead of you. If you wish, we can teach you to fight the Toxites and keep yourselves safe from the BEM." Walter motioned for the kids to approach. "There's a whole world of skills to learn. But we'll just start with a closetful."

Walter Jamison flicked on the light.

CHAPTER 25

"TAKE A LOOK, BUT DON'T GET TOO CLOSE."

The room behind the hidden door was as large as the storage/office and had a low ceiling with exposed pipes and naked lightbulbs. The huge concealed closet smelled of sulfur and chili powder.

There were several long tables littered with pieces of janitorial equipment. Mops and brooms hung on one wall. The opposite wall was lined with vacuums: some upright, others little canister vacuums with long hoses. There were racks of spray bottles organized in rows of colors: pink, blue, green, yellow. And there was much more, but Spencer was distracted by a steaming vat in the center of the room.

Spencer took a step toward it, but suddenly, Marv's bearlike body moved to intercept.

"Get back," he grunted.

"Marv's right, Spencer," Walter said. "That container

holds a small amount of raw magic. We call it Glop. Take a look, but don't get too close."

Spencer and Daisy peered over the rim of the vat and saw gray goo, swirling and bubbling as though it were alive. The closet's unique smell definitely came from the Glop.

"That's the stuff?" Spencer said. It looked like someone had mixed pancake batter and concrete and then tried to carbonate it with dry ice.

"With the bronze nail in the wall, this entire school was my domain. Within the walls of Welcher Elementary, I was free to handle and experiment with the raw Glop. Since the nail was pulled, my domain has crumbled."

"What would happen if you touched the Glop now?"

"No one but an established warlock can handle the Glop. If any of us touched the raw magic now, we'd likely mutate into a Toxite."

"There is one exception," Marv said, shutting the closet door. "If Glop is diluted enough—one part Glop to five hundred parts of something else—it can be used to expose newcomers to the world of Toxites."

"So the pink soap was just super-diluted Glop?" Spencer asked. Walter nodded. "It sure made my face tingle."

"You're lucky it was a proper batch. A small error can be fatal when diluting Glop."

"I'm glad you did a good job," Spencer said.

The janitors looked at each other. Finally, Walter spoke. "The pink soap didn't come from us, Spencer. Someone else put it in the boy's bathroom that day. Who? We're not sure yet."

"Dez," Spencer suddenly whispered. "He was in the bathroom before me. Maybe he put it there."

"That's a possibility," Walter answered. "But he wouldn't have done it on his own. There must have been outside influence."

"Garth Hadley gave it to him," Spencer mused.

"If that's true," Marv said, "then we'd better get this Dez down here right now. Is he in your class?"

Spencer shook his head. "He just got suspended for the week."

"We'll check into it when he returns," Walter said. "Thanks for helping us figure that one out. We regret not contacting you two sooner, but things were hectic as we prepared for the BEM inspections. I was out of town for a few days. When I returned, Marv told me of his suspicions about you. By then it was too late. We found this message in the pocket of a recess aide's vest."

Walter took a small paper from a filing cabinet and handed it to Spencer.

> Get Spencer out of the boys' bathroom by the gym. Others may be with him. Take a vest and borrow keys from the janitors.
>
> —S.B.

The note was handwritten in black ink. Spencer studied the penmanship. There was something peculiar about it. Something that he couldn't quite put his finger on. He handed the note to Daisy so she could read it. When she was done, Walter placed it back in the filing cabinet.

"Who's S.B.?" Spencer asked.

"We were hoping you could tell us," Walter said. Spencer and Daisy glanced at each other, but the only BEM worker they knew was Garth Hadley.

"When we found that note, we knew you were really involved with the BEM," Marv said. "We wanted to find you on Monday, Spencer, but you didn't come to school. By the time we saw you at the ice cream social, the ball was already rolling."

"You caught us totally unprepared," Walter admitted. "The glove was a brilliant piece of wizardry, no doubt developed by one of the other warlocks."

"Hadley said you made it."

Walter shook his head. "Never seen anything like it. But we have one now," he said, gesturing toward the end table. Spencer saw the used latex glove in a limp pile. Seeing the glove reminded him of the destruction he'd caused the night before.

"I'm really sorry about yesterday," Spencer admitted.

"Me too," added Daisy.

"And *we're* sorry that we didn't get to you sooner. All of this could have been avoided."

Spencer took a deep breath. Knowing the janitor's side of the story made Garth Hadley look unquestionably guilty. Spencer couldn't believe he'd been tricked. He still felt the need to atone for his wrongdoings at the ice cream social.

"We'll help you get that hammer back, Mr. Jamison," Spencer said, his voice ringing with determination.

Walter Jamison smiled. "I can't let you do that, Spencer. Marv and I will do the best we can to recover Ninfa, but you kids need to stay away from the BEM. I'm afraid they might have more plans for you."

"What kind of plans?"

"I'm not sure. And we won't risk finding out." Walter glanced around the closet. He'd been using the room as a makeshift factory for several months now. Thanks to Spencer and Daisy, the entire Rebel Underground would die off and Toxites would destroy education.

"We have you in detention for three more days," the warlock said. "Will you let us teach you what we can?"

Spencer and Daisy nodded in unison. If they had to see Toxites for the rest of their lives, at least they could learn to kill the monsters.

"Good," Walter said, "because there is a war brewing."

CHAPTER 26

"TODAY WE'LL TRY OUT SOME BASICS."

Wednesday afternoon rolled around and Spencer and Daisy met at the top of the janitors' stairs. Unlike the previous day, they were anxious for detention. Marv met them as the school busses rolled away and led them down the stairs.

Grudgingly, Marv broke out two cans of soda and handed them to the kids.

"Walter's out scouting for Hadley's local hideout," Marv said. "He'll be back soon. And anyway, we've got to wait till the school clears out before we can give you an introduction to basic equipment."

Marv dug around in the desk and withdrew a paperback book with tattered edges. "Walter wanted me to show you this." He held it out so they could see the cover. It was drab brown. Embossed in the center was the symbol of a large metal ring with more than a dozen keys hanging from it. It was the same symbol that appeared on the Rebel Closet door.

"*The Janitor Handbook*," Marv said. "Fifth edition."

Spencer and Daisy almost forgot about their sodas as they thumbed through the contents of the *Handbook*. They skimmed through a chapter about the Founding Witches. There were several pages about the history and organization of the BEM. Much of the book was dedicated to the Toxites, including early and modern sketches of the creatures.

The kids were far from finished with the book by the time Walter arrived. The warlock reported that the school was finally clear, so he and Marv went into the hidden Rebel Closet. A moment later they emerged with a mop, two brooms, and a can of vacuum dust from an upright vacuum.

"So," Daisy told Spencer as they followed the janitors toward the gym. Daisy had *The Janitor Handbook* in one hand. "I'm pretty much grounded for life now."

"Poach called your parents yesterday?"

"I still can't believe what we did at the social."

"Don't remind me," Spencer said.

"What about your mom? Are you grounded too?"

Spencer nodded. "Grounded from the computer. My mom wasn't happy about me e-mailing without permission."

They entered the gym, and Walter locked the doors behind them.

"Today is just an introduction," Marv said. He didn't look overly pleased to be teaching the kids. Marv had been on the front lines, dealing with Spencer from the beginning. Unlike Walter, Marv seemed to be hanging onto a grudge.

"Today we'll try out some basics and let you go home. Tomorrow we'll observe some Toxites. Then, on Friday, hopefully you'll be ready to catch them. All right?" Marv took *The Janitor Handbook* from Daisy.

"Let's start with brooms," Walter said. "These particular sweepers carry a double-T charge. That means two Toxites have been crushed under the bristles."

Walter picked up a broom and held it firmly in both hands. "By hitting the bristles on the floor, some of the magic is activated, pushing the broom off the ground."

To demonstrate, Walter slammed the straw end of the broom against the gym floor. The broom jerked upward, Walter rising weightlessly as it lifted off the ground. He rose, hovered at the peak for a moment, then descended easily.

"For every action," he said, "there is an opposite and equal reaction. The harder I hit the broom on the floor, the higher I'll rise. You don't have to sit on the broom or ride it at all. As long as you're hanging onto the handle, your body will be as weightless as it would be in outer space. Let's practice."

Spencer and Daisy each took a broom. Spencer held onto the wooden handle and gently tapped the other end on the floor. The broom lifted and he drifted about two feet off the waxed wood floor. "That's awesome," he said, touching down again.

Daisy gave her broom a good whack and suddenly jetted into the air. She screamed as she reached her peak about halfway to the ceiling. Daisy drifted down and landed heavily, gasping for breath.

Spencer tried again, a little harder this time. "How do you steer?" he asked as he floated back to the three-point line on the gym floor.

"You don't, really," Marv said. "Whatever direction you take off in, that's where you're going to go."

Spencer and Daisy practiced with the brooms for about ten minutes. It was a rush every time their feet left the floor. Soon they were running, smacking their brooms down, and using their momentum to launch sideways.

"Brooms are helpful when trying to capture Toxites," Walter said. He took *The Janitor Handbook* from Marv and started thumbing through. "Let's see what the glossary says about brooms . . . ah, yes." Walter began reading aloud.

"Broom—swift and mobile, a broom can help you maneuver into tactical positions against which Toxites cannot defend. The strength of the bristles is usually such that a single blow will mete out immediate death to any Toxite. Highly effective in pursuit of winged Rubbish. Alternate uses include flying and sweeping floors." Walter looked up to see if there were any questions.

"Why don't you read 'Mops' while you're at it," Marv said, hefting a dirty white mop head on a long handle.

Walter turned a few pages. "Mop—accurate and constricting, a mop will deal instant death to any Toxite entangled therein. Highly effective in eliminating Filth and Grime. Alternate uses include ensnaring common objects and cleaning hard floors." Walter closed the book.

"Couldn't have said it better," Marv said.

Suddenly, Marv whipped the mop like he was casting a fishing line. To the kids' surprise, the strings of the mop extended, reaching out until they were nearly ten feet long. Spencer tried to step back, but the mop had wrapped around his arm. Quickly, the mop retracted, dragging Spencer forward until he stood only a foot away from Marv. The burly janitor grinned, showing yellow teeth. "Gotcha," he said as the mop unwound from Spencer's arm. "The range and strength will increase with every Toxite you destroy."

Walter set up a few close-range targets—an orange cone, a basketball, and one of Marv's shoes. Daisy went first and found it very difficult to aim the mop. She managed to entangle the basketball, but lost control as the mop reeled in.

Spencer was not much better, but he was determined to snag Marv's shoe. At last he succeeded, tangling the dirty sneaker in the mop strings and pulling it in.

"Last thing for today," Walter said, holding out the can. "Vacuum dust! When you use a vacuum to suck up a Filth or a Rubbish, the creature dies and its magic leaks into the vacuum. This charged dust is particularly helpful in immobilizing an escaping Toxite." He scooped up a small handful. "Run for it, Marv!" he shouted.

Instantly, the big janitor fell into a floor-shaking sprint. Walter made a funnel with his fingers and threw the dust like a Frisbee. The puff of gray shot through the air with the sound of a revving vacuum and struck Marv in the back. The big man stopped, his feet pasted to the ground and his knees almost buckling. His hair and beard were strained downward and the strangest suction sound filled the air.

After a moment, the sound subsided and Marv righted himself, his hair fluffier, like he'd been through a dryer cycle. The janitor scowled at Walter, but the warlock simply laughed.

"The harder you throw it, the more suction it creates on your opponent. Marv is strong, so I couldn't bring him down. But I've seen people with their faces flat on the floor from vac dust suction. Controlling the vacuum dust isn't as easy as it looks. Different hand positions change the distance and spread of your attack." Walter leafed through the pages of *The Janitor Handbook*. "Take a look at this diagram for the different throwing techniques and hand positions."

The Palm Blast (easy)
Wide spread of dust over
short distances.

The Funnel Throw (medium)
Accurate and dangerous over long distances.

The Thumb Shot (difficult)
Allows for hitting multiple
targets with one throw.

Spencer and Daisy practiced until the can was empty and the last bit of vacuum dust had been tossed across the gym. Marv grabbed a big dust mop and began sweeping up the thrown vacuum dust.

"Can we reuse it?" Daisy asked.

Walter shook his head. "The vac dust is spent. We'd have to get more from the bag before the vacuum maxes out."

"What do you mean by that?" Daisy asked.

"We can't use these things forever," Walter explained. "Glopified supplies have a Toxite kill limit of fifty."

"What happens if you max them out?" Spencer asked.

Marv gave him a look. "What do you think? They stop working. Once a Glopified broom hits fifty Toxites, the only thing you can do is throw that broom into a special dumpster. Someone will be around to collect it and dispose of it safely."

"Who collects the stuff from the magic-filled dumpster?"

"That information is classified," Marv said. "Time to go home."

Spencer didn't want to go home. All he could think about was the unbelievably cool equipment that Walter and Marv had just shown him. He couldn't help imagining Dez with a ten-foot mop wrapped around his face. Then Spencer thought of Mr. Hadley attacking, angry that Spencer and Daisy had betrayed him.

Could a broom lift them out of Hadley's reach?

CHAPTER 27

"FIRST THING YOU'VE GOT TO KNOW ABOUT TOXITES . . ."

Y ou should've put some Glop into a sports car or something," Daisy told Walter Jamison on Thursday afternoon. "That would be awesome. You could fly high, or drive over water. Who knows?"

Walter smiled, as Spencer found he often did. "It doesn't work quite like that. Good idea, though."

Spencer and Daisy were in the janitors' storage/office waiting for the school to vacate so they could train again.

"You see," Walter explained, "the Founding Witches were afraid that someone in the future would misuse Glop. They decided to put some limitations on the hammer and nail. One limitation is that Glop can only be handled by a warlock in an established domain. Another is that Glop can only be applied to certain objects that are useful in maintenance."

"So just vacuums and mops and stuff?"

"Those are the obvious ones," Walter said. "There are probably hundreds of possibilities—washers and dryers, keys, machines that wax the floor, buffers that shine it, lawn mowers, weed whackers—anything a janitor might use. I don't know. Exploration is dangerous. Penalties for misusing Glop usually keep warlocks from experimenting too far out of the ordinary. But the latex glove is new. Someone was daring enough to try that and it paid off."

"How'd they make the glove?" Spencer asked.

"Every time a warlock Glopifies something, he has to make a special formula. You start with a bit of raw Glop and carefully add other substances into it. Think of it like a witch's brew. I've seen warlocks add everything from a Rubbish wing to a drop of molten lead to a dash of paprika."

"Sounds like my dad's cooking," Daisy muttered.

"Once a successful Glop formula has been developed, the warlock can send a batch to other janitors. All they have to do is take a new latex glove and dip it into the Glop formula. After that, the glove is Glopified, and makes the wearer uncatchable. It would also make the glove strong enough to destroy Toxites, although I doubt that's its primary purpose. You see," Walter continued, "warlocks are only supposed to Glopify equipment that will aid them in catching Toxites."

"But that's not why they made the glove," Daisy said.

"That's what worries me," answered Walter. "By making the glove, the BEM has developed a Glopified object whose sole purpose seems aimed at attacking other humans. That is dangerous experimentation. I hate the thought, but the time may come when experimentation is all we'll be able to do to keep an upper hand."

"But you can't experiment unless you get the hammer back," Daisy reminded him.

Walter smiled. "Oh, we will get it back."

"We'll help," Spencer offered again. "We already have the BEM's trust; we could trick Hadley and . . ."

"No!" Walter snapped. His face suddenly looked extra weary. "We've already been over this. I don't want you two getting involved any deeper than you already are."

Spencer felt a pang of hurt. Didn't Walter trust them? Wasn't he impressed by their skills at the ice cream social? Spencer frowned. Jamison was just being stubborn, refusing to accept help from a kid.

Marv suddenly lumbered down the steps, slurping from a bottle of cream soda. "Coast is clear," he said. "All's quiet up there. I left several messes that are sure to attract some hungry Toxites."

Spencer and Daisy followed the two janitors up the stairs. They weren't training with equipment today. This was a day for observation.

"First thing you've got to know about Toxites," Marv said, keeping his voice very low and gravelly. "They hate being seen. Toxites thrive on being undetectable."

Spencer suddenly recalled how each time he'd seen a Toxite, the little creature had noticed him staring and scurried away.

"There," Walter hissed, dropping to a crouch in the

middle of the hall. The others followed his example. Spencer and Daisy peered ahead, straining to see what Walter had spotted.

"You see it?" The warlock pointed slowly. Halfway down the hall, a vulture-bat was perched on the edge of a garbage can. "That's a Rubbish. They feed on trash and litter. Those things can palate almost anything—scraps of food, paper, plastic, rubber . . . you name it."

"They don't fly straight, so they're hard to catch," Marv added. "Sometimes you can tangle them in a Glopified mop and that'll crush them. But brooms are best for Rubbishes."

Walter crept forward, staying close to the wall. The Rubbish had hopped into the trash can and was playing in the piled garbage like it was a birdbath. Walter, bent low, approached the can as the Rubbish dove deeper in search of an unseen treat.

Like a pouncing cat, Walter leapt up, grabbed the garbage sack that lined the can, and tied it closed. No sooner was the top sealed off, however, than the Rubbish tore through the plastic sack, wings pounding. A cold, limp French fry drooped from its hooked beak.

Spencer and Daisy reeled back, frightened by the sudden emergence. The Rubbish flapped down the hallway and around the corner.

Marv strode forward, grinning stupidly. "Thought that'd work?" he asked Walter.

"No," he answered. "But I wanted to prove something."

"What?" Marv asked.

"I wanted to show the kids how a skilled Toxite hunter can approach the creatures nearly undetected."

"You're lucky that thing didn't attack," Daisy said. "It barely missed your face when it came out of that bag."

Marv snorted. "Toxites don't attack people. That Rubbish is totally content in this environment. It inhales your brain waves and exhales apathy."

"Apathy?" Daisy asked. She'd heard that people exhaled carbon dioxide and plants exhaled oxygen. But what was apathy?

"Apathy is a lack of interest," Walter said. "When a Rubbish exhales, students nearby suddenly lose the desire to do any work. They become completely disinterested in whatever the teacher is saying. In short, they don't *want* to learn anything."

"Oh," Daisy said, grateful now that she only exhaled carbon dioxide.

"Other than that, Rubbishes don't attack physically," Walter said.

"Unless they're relocated," Marv said. "A few years back, Toxite scientists from the BEM did experiments to see how the creatures would fare in other environments. But the Toxites don't like to be moved out of schools. The scientists relocated some to restaurants, business buildings, and a few other locations. As soon as they were released, the Toxites went haywire and started attacking the scientists.

"An innocent bystander saw it. 'Course, she couldn't see the Toxites, so she thought the scientists were having some kind of spasm or seizure. Looked real creepy. She called an ambulance. Lucky thing, too, since four BEM workers were critically injured. The Toxites escaped, fighting a path all the way back to the school they were taken from. They're very territorial."

When Marv finished, Walter glanced disapprovingly at him. "I don't think that was necessary, Marv Bills," he said. "We're teaching the kids to *defend* against the Toxites, not to *fear* them."

"It's okay," Spencer said, but Daisy indeed looked frightened.

"Just thought they might like to know," Marv said defensively. He trudged down the hall, the other three falling in behind him.

When they reached the corner, Marv stopped, lifting a thick finger to his lips. Spencer and Daisy peered around the corner, eyes scanning the area.

Daisy saw them first—two Grimes relaxing in the drinking fountain. One pale body was curled around the spout where the water came out. The other had flattened its slimy body over the drain and was basking in a pool of stagnant water.

Spencer shuddered, feeling weak in his stomach. He would never, *ever* drink from a school fountain again. He swore to bring a personal water bottle from now on.

"Grimes," Marv whispered. "The only amphibious Toxite. They prefer moist areas like bathrooms and water fountains. But don't be surprised if they show up in a classroom. They can go anywhere."

"What do they eat?" Daisy asked, unable to take her eyes off their nasty little bodies.

"They can live on water alone," Walter said. "But they eat anything wet. The slimy buildup between tiles or around sinks is like candy to them."

"Yuck," Spencer said, trying not to gag. "Kill them already. I can't stand it." Could he ever wash his hands at school again? If the sinks were contaminated, what was the use? Even Principal Poach's instant hand sanitizer wasn't safe from the Grimes.

"They move fast," Marv said. "And they use the pipes like a subway system. Best way to sneak up is by coming directly at them. Their eyes are so far apart that Grimes have a small blind spot directly in front of them. That's why they turn their heads like that."

Spencer peeked around the corner again. Sure enough, both Grimes were lazily moving their heads back and forth, glazed white eyes half open in their relaxation.

"What are we doing here?" Daisy asked loudly. "Where's everybody else? Hey, look at that door, it's *so* cool!" She started walking down the hall toward a classroom door.

"Marv," Walter scolded. "We've waited too long."

Marv instantly jumped around the corner. The Grimes' bulbous eyes opened and the creatures scattered. Before Marv reached the drinking fountain, both Grimes had folded and stretched themselves to fit down the tiny holes of the drain.

"Whoa!" Daisy said. "Where am I going?" She turned around and rejoined the group.

"Sorry about that," Walter said. "Grimes exhale confusion and distraction. They stop kids from understanding simple instructions and often cause the sudden need to get out of your seat and move around. Teachers hate Grime breath. Don't know about it, but they hate what it makes kids do."

"I don't like it either," Daisy said. "How come Spencer didn't get confused?"

"Certain Toxites work better on certain students," Marv answered. "By the time you reach high school, Toxite toxins probably won't affect you at all. That's why the critters love younger schools."

"Sorry we waited so long to chase off the Grimes," Walter apologized. "We thought we were far enough away that you wouldn't feel the effects. Apparently not."

"What I want to know," Spencer said, "is what would have happened if I wanted a drink?"

"You saw," said Marv. "They run away."

Spencer shook his head. "What if I couldn't see them? What if I was an ordinary student? Would they still scatter?" He was thinking of all the times he'd sipped from a school fountain, wondering if he'd sucked up Grime germs in the process.

"If you can't see them, they aren't there," Walter said.

"No," Spencer said. "That doesn't make sense."

"You'll see," Walter replied. "If a Toxite knows it can't be seen, it'll stay right where it is, breathing in brain waves."

Spencer suddenly remembered Principal Poach's

hot-dog fingers reaching through the Rubbish in the peanut can. "What if someone touches them?"

"If they don't see them, they won't feel them, either. But now that you two can see them, Toxites will probably stay farther away from you."

Marv bent down and took a swig from the drinking fountain. Spencer almost hurled. The big man stood up tall again, water in his black beard. "There's one more kind of Toxite we'd like to show you," he said.

They walked up by Mrs. Natcher's class, then down by the gyms. Marv started to grow impatient as they looped back, the four figures moving stealthily through the hallway. They passed through a set of doors and found themselves in the school library. Using the bookshelves as a shield, the janitors and the kids crawled forward until, at last, they saw what they were searching for.

"Filth," Walter whispered.

Spencer and Daisy took turns looking around the corner of the shelf. A dust gopher was sniffing the floor nearby. It was the size of a guinea pig but, on closer inspection, looked more like a porcupine. Along the creature's back were spiky, dust-covered quills, almost unseen below its long, dusty hair. The rodent face was downturned, and long woodchuck teeth tilled the carpet in search of fresh dust.

The Filth waddled a few steps, found a particularly rich spot, and began scratching at the carpet with its clawed feet. A cloud of dust arose and the Filth snapped and licked at the carpet.

"Can you guess what they eat?" Marv whispered, but Spencer wasn't listening. He was curled on the carpet, his breathing deep and regular.

He was asleep.

CHAPTER 28

"IT DOESN'T SEEM FAIR."

S hoo!" Walter cried, rolling out from his hiding place behind the bookshelf. The Filth's quills bristled, an act that sent up a puff of gray dust. If Walter had brought a Glopified vacuum, the creature would have been a goner. But since he was unarmed, the Filth scuttled away, ducking out of sight beneath the historical fiction shelf.

Spencer revived quickly, distantly aware of Daisy calling his name. He quickly shrugged off the fatigue and sat up, his face reddening with embarrassment.

"What happened?" he asked.

"The Filth got you," Marv said. "That was a big one. Had potent breath."

The four of them stood, Spencer leaning against the bookshelf and yawning.

"Filth breath will plunge you into such a deep sleep, you won't hear a word the teacher says."

A light clicked on in Spencer's mind. All the times he'd been drowsy in class . . . especially during Miss Sharmelle's lecture on algebra. Maybe it hadn't actually been so boring. There must have been a Filth in the room. But why did the Filth breath attack Spencer so hard, while kids like Dez didn't even blink a heavy eye?

"It doesn't seem fair," Spencer said. "Some other kids in my class, like Dez, for example—he doesn't seem affected by *any* of the Toxites. Is he just strong enough to resist their breath?"

Walter gave a half smile, a reminiscent look on his old face. "I was eighteen when I got my first job as a janitor. My mentor was a wise Toxite hunter who answered that same question for me." Walter folded his arms.

"One day, I was observing the Toxites during school lunch. There were two particular boys that I noticed— complete opposites. The first sat in the corner. His table was swarmed with Toxites. The poor fellow was caught between bouts of distraction and fatigue so severe he could hardly eat.

"The second boy sat across the room. He ate his food quickly, and I noticed that not a single Toxite lingered near him."

Spencer could imagine himself in the story, surrounded by Toxites.

"After observing the scene, I commented to my mentor, 'That first boy must be very bad, all surrounded by Toxites as he is. And I'll bet that second child is well-behaved, strong, and smart.'

"My mentor chuckled. 'Walter,' he said, 'how little you understand. The truth is rather the opposite. The first boy is trying very hard. His mind is active and he wants to learn. Those are rich brain waves, and the Toxites swarm around him to feed. That second boy is a ruffian with no desire to be in school. Even in a school that was Toxite-free, that child wouldn't learn a thing.'"

Walter nodded at Spencer and Daisy. "I hope you understand. We're not fighting for the Dezmonds of the school. The Toxites don't waste their breath on kids like him. We're fighting the Toxites for *you*. You are the ones in danger, because you have a great desire to learn and to grow." He sighed. "It may not seem fair. But it's true. Take it as a compliment from the Toxites. Take it as a challenge. There're only two ways to get rid of the creatures. Either you give up and quit learning so they leave you alone . . . or you *fight* for your education." Walter clapped them on the shoulders. "What's it going to be?"

Spencer and Daisy shared a glance. "We fight."

"Good." Walter smiled. "Let's head back to the office. I need to get on with my search for the local BEM hideout."

As they walked down the hallway, Spencer thought back to the time he was employed by Garth Hadley. With the janitors, he felt so positive and confident. Something he'd never felt with the BEM. Walter and Marv never asked Spencer to do things he didn't want to do. They were teaching him, helping him to protect himself. It wasn't something

Spencer could explain with words. It was more of a feeling. A feeling of trust in the janitors.

"I can't believe we saw so many Toxites today," Daisy said, as they rounded a corner.

"That's nothing," said Marv. "The few schools that are staffed by the Rebel janitors are keeping the Toxite population very low. In schools where the BEM has taken over, the hallways are crawling with Toxites. Hundreds of them. Disgusts me. For more than three hundred years, the BEM has kept schools creature-free. Now they're tracking down all Toxite-fighting janitors and firing them. What's this world coming to?"

Hundreds of Toxites? Spencer couldn't imagine what that would be like. What, Spencer wondered, could possibly have motivated the Bureau of Educational Maintenance to withdraw support from the schools? Why did they want the creatures to ruin education? A single Filth had sent him snoring. A single Grime had caused Daisy to take special interest in a door. What would happen to Welcher Elementary if the BEM fired Walter and Marv?

Spencer felt a wave of guilt wash over him. *He* had crippled the Rebel janitors by turning the hammer over to Garth Hadley. Now all the BEM needed was the nail. Hadley was powerful and determined. If he got it, all hope for the Rebel janitors would be shattered.

The seed of an idea rooted in Spencer's mind. It grew as he and Daisy left the school and walked to the Gates home. It probably wasn't a safe idea. It meant doing things he shouldn't do. But it might make all the difference.

The idea was almost fully grown by the time Mr. Gates dropped Spencer at Hillside Estates. He had talked himself out of it two or three times, but it kept coming back. The need to help the janitors, to save education, outweighed all risks.

A quick search of the house assured Spencer that his mother wasn't home yet. She was probably picking up his siblings from day care, so he'd have to be fast. It would be a short message; he already had the words planned out.

Spencer sat down at the computer and swallowed hard. The thought of disobeying his mother caused his heart to sink into his stomach, as if someone had suctioned it with a strong puff of vac dust. Spencer wiped his sweating palms on his pants and tried to overcome the guilty feeling that threatened to undermine his plan.

"For the good of education," he whispered, almost inaudibly. "For the future."

With a cautious glance over his shoulder, Spencer logged into his e-mail and typed as fast as he could.

To: ghadley@bem.gov
From: SpenceZ@wahoo.com
Subject: None

Dear Mr. Hadley,

I changed my mind. Daisy and I can get the nail from Walter Jamison tomorrow after school. People are suspicious of you at the school. Why don't we meet at your local hideout to hand it over?

Let me know where and when.

Spencer

CHAPTER 29

"LET'S HUNT."

Friday dragged on and on. Even though it was the last Dez-free day of class, Spencer couldn't wait for the bell to ring and their final training with the janitors to start. In his backpack, Spencer had the key to their success. It was the printed e-mail, including his original message and Garth Hadley's response.

Spencer had kept it a secret from everyone, even Daisy. At the end of training with the janitors today, Spencer would present the information to Walter Jamison. Garth Hadley's local hideout.

So much anticipation made it hard to sit still.

At last, the bell rang and he and Daisy rushed down to the janitors' storage/office. Walter was seated at the desk, nervously rubbing his bald scalp. Marv was straightening a rack of spray bottles on the wall. The entrance to the Rebel Closet was hidden behind the sliding tower of boxes.

Greetings were short and terse, totally unlike the last few days. Something had happened—Spencer could almost taste it in the air.

"What's up?" Spencer asked, trying to play it cool.

"Things are getting tight without Ninfa," Walter said. "Supplies are running out. The BEM shut down a Rebel school in Colorado last night. Two of our janitors were fired. And Garth Hadley attacked Welcher Elementary at one o'clock this morning."

"What?"

"We were here late, shampooing carpets and brainstorming possible BEM hideouts. Luckily we saw them coming," Marv said. "I stalled them with vac dust while Walter got safely outside with the bronze nail."

"It was too close," Walter said.

"Any idea where they're hiding?" Spencer asked. He couldn't help it, but he was setting himself up to look like a real hero.

"None," Walter said. "My lead last night was a dead end. Welcher's not that big. I've checked everywhere. Garth Hadley must be using an alias."

"We should get started," Marv said. "Time's running out. We need to get these kids prepared."

"Right," Walter agreed as Marv pulled aside the boxes to expose the Rebel Closet. Light glinted on the painted emblem of the janitor key ring as the warlock unlocked the door and strode into the secret closet.

The room looked undisturbed since the last time they entered. Without the hammer to drive the bronze nail, Walter was still unable to touch the swirling vat of Glop in the center of the room.

"Everyone should take a baggie of vacuum dust," Walter said. From the table, Marv retrieved four Ziploc bags, each with a premeasured amount of gray dust.

"And everyone should take a Glopified weapon," said Marv. "I'm taking a vacuum." He wheeled an upright vacuum with a white cord out of the closet. Walter reached for a pushbroom.

Spencer and Daisy walked around the closet like kids in a candy shop. There were so many Glopified, Toxite-killing weapons that the kids had never seen before. Spencer wondered at each one, hoping he could have detention the following week to be trained with more.

"What's this?" Daisy asked, picking up a bulging vacuum bag.

"Careful," Walter warned. "That thing's got more charge than any other object in this room. It really belongs in the dumpster."

"Can't you get some vac dust out of it?" Spencer asked. "It would probably be super powerful."

"That bag's been overcharged. It contains the power of nearly three hundred Toxites. For some unknown reason, it didn't max out at fifty like all the other supplies. We call that bag the Vortex."

"So it has different powers than vac dust?" Daisy asked, examining the thick, papery bag.

"The Vortex is unstable," said Walter. "The dust inside is extremely powerful, but by the time the bag is pierced, it would be too late. Everything in this room would get sucked into the bag. BEM journals account for one other Vortex that was created somehow in the 1980s. When the bag was punctured, the suction was so strong that it pulled the paint off the walls and the carpet rolled up like a burrito. Only the person holding it didn't get sucked inside. Think of it like a black hole inside a vacuum bag."

Daisy set the Vortex gently back on the shelf where she'd gotten it, saying, "I don't think I want to use that today." Instead, Daisy chose a mop with a splintery wooden handle.

Spencer looked at the brooms hanging on the rack before him. Above each broom was a number written in marker.

"Is this the Toxite charge?" Spencer asked.

"Exactly," Walter said, hefting his pushbroom. "This one has a 6T charge. That means I've crushed six Toxites with this pushbroom. Every Toxite I destroy with it will increase the speed and strength of my pushbroom until I max it out at fifty."

"Is a pushbroom different from a normal broom?" Spencer asked.

"Quite opposites, actually," Walter answered. "Instead of lifting me off the ground, my pushbroom will send the Toxites flying, if I hit them right."

Daisy looked back at the spot where her mop had hung.

It had a 1T charge. She quickly put it back on the rack in exchange for a 12T mop.

Spencer picked out a 4T broom with straw bristles. Checking his baggie of vac dust, he followed Daisy and Walter out of the Rebel Closet.

"We'll stick to our usual daily maintenance routes," Walter explained. "I'll take Daisy with me to do the center hallway and the library. Marv, you take Spencer to the north hallway and the gym. Whoever finishes first will come back to work the entry hallway and cafeteria. But be careful—I think Principal Poach is still in the building." Walter checked his watch. "Meet back here in forty-five minutes. Try to catch one of each kind—for instructional purposes." He hefted his pushbroom like a rifle. "Let's hunt."

Spencer waved to Daisy and followed Marv down the hallway. The "out of order" sign was gone from the boys' bathroom. The nail wasn't in the wall anymore, so there was no reason to keep the bathroom closed. Marv plugged his vacuum into an outlet next to the door.

"We'll start here," Marv said. "I'll kick open the door and you run inside. If there's a Grime in there, it'll probably bolt, so you've got to be fast." Spencer nodded to show that he understood.

Marv fired up his vacuum and tilted it so he could race it forward on the back wheels like a chariot. Then he stepped forward and gave the bathroom door a big kick. The door swung inward, testing the strength of its hinges.

In a flash, Spencer was inside. Just as Marv had suspected, there was a Grime perched on the edge of the sink.

Spencer swiped for the slimy creature with his broom. The pokey bristles raked down the Grime's back and the salamander creature fell to the floor. Spencer wielded the broom around like an axe and came down for a fatal chop. His broom hit the floor hard.

But the Grime was gone.

The force of impact sent the broom rocketing to the ceiling, Spencer flying alongside. Below, the Grime slithered toward the floor drain. But escape was blocked, as Marv's upright vacuum dropped over the drain, eagerly sucking.

Without stopping, the Grime redirected. Spencer was pinned to the ceiling, the broom still straining upward. Taking a deep breath, Spencer let go of the broom. Gravity returned instantly and he dropped heavily and crumpled to his knees on the tile.

"The toilet!" Marv shouted, pulling a suction hose from the side of his vacuum.

Spencer recovered and leapt for the open stall door. The Grime was climbing the side of the toilet bowl, bulbous fingertips like suction cups on the slick surface.

Spencer's broom had dislodged from the bathroom ceiling and was floating down. But there was no time to go for it. Hastily, the boy opened his Ziploc bag and gathered a small fistful of charged vac dust.

The Grime was on the toilet seat when Spencer's dust hit from behind. The suction sound filled the resonant bathroom and the force of the vac dust sucked the creature off the rim. The Grime fell with a splash into the water, the force pinning it below the surface.

"Grab it!" Marv shouted, leaving his vacuum and racing toward the stall.

Spencer stared into the toilet at the immobile Grime. Maybe with a long pair of gloves, Spencer would brave reaching into the toilet . . . but bare-handed?

The vacuum dust wouldn't hold much longer. Spencer reached out his hand and then drew back, unable.

The Grime recovered in a moment and took one stroke toward the back of the toilet. The moment before it vanished down the hole, Marv's bare hand plunged into the depths. He seized the Grime by the tail and flung it to the floor.

The Grime bounced and flopped like a fish on dry land. In a moment it was on its feet again, but a moment was all Marv needed. The vacuum wheels raced forward and the churning, spinning underpinnings of the vacuum closed down on the Grime.

There was a splattering of pale yellow slime. The vacuum sucked harder, seeming to choke on something. Then the machine swallowed and there was nothing.

Marv turned the vacuum off and silence filled the bathroom. Spencer slowly picked up his broom, aware that Marv was glaring at him.

"Why didn't you grab it?" the big janitor asked as they exited the bathroom. "Almost got away."

"I just . . . froze," Spencer answered apologetically. "Maybe the Grime breath confused me." *Or maybe*, thought Spencer, *I just couldn't stick my hand into the toilet.*

They walked silently into the hall. Marv unlocked a set of gym doors. "I set a full garbage bin in the corner of the gym after lunch. It should have attracted a Rubbish or two by now."

And sure enough, two Rubbishes were frolicking in the trash. Their beaks snipped at each other playfully and they dove deeper into the bin to see who could surface with the greatest treasure.

Marv slowly worked his way to an outlet on the wall. He plugged in his vacuum but didn't turn it on. Spencer crept up beside him.

"The best way," Marv whispered, "is for you to stay up in the air. If you can make a ruckus above them, chances are they'll come low where I can get them with my vacuum."

"You ready?" Spencer asked. Marv nodded, his finger hovering above the vacuum's *on* switch. Spencer moved away from the wall. He took two running steps in the direction of the garbage and dropped his broom bristles heavily to the floor.

Spencer lifted off at an angle, racing through the air. The Rubbishes spotted him, and the garbage-bin fun stopped immediately. Their vulture-like heads perked up and their leathery bat wings flexed.

Hanging tight to the broom handle, Spencer slammed into the wall above the garbage bin. The proximity made the Rubbishes skittish; one took off, flying low. Marv sprinted in that direction, vacuum wheels turning at maximum speed.

Spencer descended slowly along the wall. In a moment, the Rubbish hiding in the garbage would have a free path upward. Twisting his body around, Spencer tapped the broom bristles against the wall. The opposite reaction sent him gliding sideways across the gym. The Rubbish waited, ruffled its wings, and took flight as Spencer drifted away.

In a moment, Spencer seized an exit sign above the door and pulled himself back to the wall, still clinging to the broom with one hand.

"Got one!" Marv shouted from the center of the gym.

Seeing the last Rubbish escaping higher, Spencer kicked off the exit sign, slamming his broom against the wall at the last minute. The new burst of energy sent him shooting toward the flying Rubbish. One-handed, Spencer scrambled with the little bag of vac dust. Mimicking the widespread palm blast that Walter had taught them, Spencer hurled the dust.

A puff of dark dust billowed out of his hand like a mushroom cloud. The Rubbish was caught in the burst, its wings buckling under the suction. Marv was in position as the creature plummeted to the gym floor.

Spencer, still dangling one-handed from the broom, suddenly realized his mistake. Unable to change his broom's course, Spencer flew straight into the residual dust cloud. The deafening sound of rushing air filled his ears as the vacuum dust fought to bring down the broom. The gravity-defying broom strained upward while Spencer's body was caught in the suction of the vac dust.

Spencer's fingers slipped and he plummeted toward the gym floor. He tried to brace for impact, deaf to all noise except the rushing vac dust. Then, to Spencer's great surprise, he landed on something soft.

Marv.

The bulky janitor wrapped his arms around Spencer, but the downward force was too strong. Marv was flattened on his back with Spencer pinned to his chest. They were stuck for only a moment before the suction from the vac dust suddenly ended.

Spencer rolled aside, moaning. The sound of rushing air was replaced by Marv's idling vacuum.

"You get him?" Spencer gasped, still lying on the floor. Overhead, he watched his broom descend.

"Got you instead." Marv grunted, standing up. "The second Rubbish got away."

"Sorry," Spencer apologized. "I guess I'm not too good at Toxite hunting."

Marv turned off the vacuum and jerked on the cord to unplug his machine. "Look, you're just a beginner." But Marv's tone agreed with Spencer's failure.

"What now?" Spencer stood up and retrieved his broom from the air.

"Quiet!" Marv hissed. A dusty Filth had just waddled under the door and entered the gym.

"All right," Marv said, "here's what we'll do. You go around the side and come at it from the left. I'll get my vacuum plugged in and—" Marv never got to finish.

The gym door flew open and the Filth scurried out of sight. Spencer clutched his broom like a weapon as two figures raced into the gym.

One of them was Garth Hadley.

CHAPTER 30

"GET AWAY FROM HIM!"

As soon as the intruders burst into the room, Marv acted. Tearing open the papery bag on his vacuum, the burly janitor grabbed two fistfuls of charged vac dust, doubling the amount in his Ziploc bag. Marv abandoned the upright vacuum and sprinted to Spencer's side in two floor-shaking steps.

Suddenly, the power went out, plunging the gym into darkness. Two flashlights flicked on. One cast a normal beam that swept across the gym in search of Spencer and Marv. But the flashlight in Garth Hadley's hand cast a white beam that shifted erratically from Spencer's broom to Marv's fistfuls of vac dust and over to the abandoned vacuum.

No doubt about it. Hadley was looking for the bronze nail.

Spencer's eyes adjusted quickly to the darkness. Garth Hadley and his companion, a skinny man with a pointy nose, fanned out to block the gym exits as they moved steadily forward. Each wore a latex glove that Spencer knew was charged. Aside from the flashlight, Garth was toting a mop with a long handle. He held it behind his flashlight so it wouldn't attract the beam.

"Back up," Marv whispered. "Keep heading for the back wall. There is an emergency exit in the northeast corner. Go!"

Marv leapt forward, growling like a grizzly. The two intruders were too far apart for him to attack them both simultaneously, so Marv went for Hadley.

The BEM rep saw him coming, pulled back his mop, and cast the dirty white mop strings flinging in Marv's direction. Just before the mop reached its target, Marv released a puff of vacuum dust. Suction filled the room. The vac dust had just enough strength to knock Hadley's mop off target.

The mop strings dropped and Marv hurdled them like an overweight track star. The second fistful of vac dust, expertly delivered with a funnel throw, struck Hadley in the chest. The strong man shouted and crumpled to his knees. Hadley's clothes were stretched tight against his skin from the downward suction.

Spencer kicked open the emergency exit, flooding the gym with late afternoon sunlight. But the exit was suddenly blocked by a fat man with a broom in his hands. Spencer reeled backward into the gym, noticing the skinny man setting an intercept course. There was nowhere to go but up.

Spencer hit the bristles of his broom against the gym floor, feeling the jerk of the wood in his hands and the unique weightlessness as he lifted. Then the broom shuddered under new weight. The skinny man had seized Spencer's rising ankle, and the broom was struggling to lift them both. The other man charged inside from the emergency exit, pulling a handful of dust from his pocket.

"Ghhhaaaar!" Marv bellowed, pounding into the rising skinny man and sending him sprawling across the gym floor. Spencer shot upward like a helium balloon with its string cut. Glancing down, he saw the fat man from the emergency exit immobilizing Marv with a taste of his own medicine. Across the room, Garth Hadley was recovering. All eyes went upward to the floating boy.

Spencer made contact with the high gym ceiling a little harder than he'd hoped. Below, the three men gathered like vultures to await his inevitable descent. But what if he didn't descend?

Not far away was a basketball hoop hooked into the ceiling with cables. During P.E., the teacher lowered the hoop so the kids could play. The rest of the time, it was folded up against the ceiling. The perfect place.

Still plastered against the ceiling and holding tight to the broom, Spencer used his feet to scrape along, sliding in the direction of the hoop. He was almost there when he felt the broom begin to descend. Kicking off the ceiling, Spencer drifted the last few feet and caught the edge of the backboard. He positioned his legs through the hoop like a very uncomfortable chair, still holding tight to his broom as it became heavy in his hands again.

Below, the BEM workers began mumbling and cursing. The skinny man had his flashlight trained on Spencer. Garth Hadley cast with his mop, the strings lengthening and stretching upward. The cast fell short . . . but not by much. Hadley flicked the mop again. This time, Spencer had to pull his feet up as the hungry mop strings threatened to entangle him and drag him from his perch.

"Get away from him!" Marv cried from behind. In their hopes to reach Spencer, they had left the big janitor unguarded. Marv had recovered from the suction dust and had a trick of his own.

Before anyone could move, Marv used the thumb shot, flicking out tufts of dust like a professional marbles player. The well-aimed dust struck the fat man and the skinny man, bringing them to their faces on the gym floor. The third puff missed Garth Hadley, who countered with an attack from his mop. The strings wrapped around Marv's big belly, tying both arms to his sides and tipping him off balance. The mop retracted, dragging Marv to rest at Hadley's feet.

Spencer knew he had to get away while commotion reigned below. Positioning himself to kick off the hoop, Spencer tapped his broom against the backboard. The boy leapt from his perch, using the gentle tap from the broom to cross the room and descend at the gym door. He touched the floor, his broom still floating beside him. Without looking back for Marv, Spencer ran into the hall.

He dashed toward the middle hallway. The most

important thing was to warn Walter so the warlock could get away with the bronze nail. Spencer stopped at an intersection in the hallway.

To his right were the library's double doors, closed tight. To his left was the middle hallway, with Mrs. Natcher's classroom at the end. Daylight was shining through the exit doors by Mrs. Natcher's room, and Spencer saw the silhouettes of four fighting figures. Grunts and shouts echoed down the middle hallway.

Spencer saw Walter pressing hard to get past three new BEM workers blocking the way. His pushbroom was broken, the handle snapped in half. Spencer scanned the area. Where was Daisy? Wasn't she supposed to be with Walter?

At the sound of running footfalls, Spencer whirled around. Garth Hadley was charging down the hall. Spencer seemed frozen to the carpet. There were too many BEM workers. They'd never get away!

With a shout, Walter leapt for the doorway, but mop strings tangled him just like they had Marv. The warlock slammed against the wall and slumped to the carpet.

Spencer dropped his broom and ran—not left or right, but straight ahead. He needed to find Daisy. He needed to find a hiding spot in the dark school. He needed to run . . . faster!

CHAPTER 31

"I WISH YOU'D JUST CALL ME SARAH."

Spencer rounded the corner and sprinted toward the front doors of the school. But what good was escaping? Marv and Walter had fallen and Spencer needed to help before the BEM hauled them away.

Spencer reeled back as he passed the principal's office. There was a light on—a flashlight or a candle, maybe, since the power was still out.

Spencer had sworn he would never enter Principal Poach's office again. But this was different. Poach could call the cops and they could stop the janitornapping that was happening in the middle hall. Besides, it was a great hiding spot since Garth Hadley wouldn't follow him into the oc-cupied office.

Ducking quickly through the first doorway, Spencer found himself in the waiting area where he and Daisy had

199

once sat on a bench with Baybee. He was reaching for the principal's doorknob when he heard voices floating out of the office.

"Not a problem at all," Poach's nasal voice squeaked. "I'm just sorry about this power outage."

"I don't mind," answered a feminine voice. "I know it wasn't a convenient time for an interview, but thanks for letting me in."

Spencer stopped. *Letting me in?* Through the wavy glass of the office door, he could see only vague outlines and flickering shadows. But whoever was inside the office was about to come out.

It was time to hide.

Spencer crossed the waiting area and threw himself under a computer desk. Pressing his face against the ground, he could see only shoes as the principal's door opened.

A pair of high heels clicked across the floor and paused. A waft of flowery perfume drifted under the desk, reminding Spencer of someone. He just couldn't think who.

Poach's walrus shoes waddled forward. "You are an excellent candidate. Unfortunately, we're not looking to hire right now."

"I understand," the woman said.

"Mrs. Bently—" he started.

"Please," the woman interrupted, "I wish you'd just call me Sarah."

"Sarah," Poach restarted. "You'll be the first to know if anything opens up. I was very . . . impressed."

"Thanks for your time," the sultry voice answered. Then the high heels clicked away.

Spencer didn't dare move. He watched Poach's brown shoes shuffle back into the office. The heavy man sighed, and Spencer heard him gathering papers. Just then, the power returned. Overhead, Spencer felt the computer shudder back to life on the desk. The walrus principal made a contented sound, followed by a little chuckle.

Five minutes later, the principal's shoes reappeared. The office door pulled closed and the man waddled away.

Spencer waited another painstakingly long five minutes before crawling out of his hiding spot. Cautiously, he peeked into the entry hallway. There was no one in sight. The front of the school appeared totally deserted.

Just in case, Spencer opened his Ziploc bag and pinched out the remaining vac dust. His hand was sweaty and the dirty fibers clung to his palm. He wondered how that might affect his toss.

Spencer checked the cafeteria. Empty. He walked down to the middle hall. Empty. The library. Empty. The north hall and gym. Empty. Empty.

Spencer was alone. Garth Hadley had taken the janitors. Why? Why did Hadley attack? Spencer felt his face go red. He had a deal with Garth! They were supposed to meet at the hideout in a half hour, at six o'clock. Spencer thought he had it all mapped out—he would go to the BEM hideout with Walter and Marv, take Hadley by surprise, and steal the hammer back.

Everything was ruined now. Garth Hadley had Walter,

the hammer, and the nail. There was only one thing left for Spencer to do.

Find Daisy.

Spencer wandered back to the janitors' storage/office. It was about the only place he hadn't looked. Spencer jogged down the steps, jumping the last three and landing in the dim office area. No sooner did his feet touch the floor than the sound of a revving vacuum hit him from the side.

Spencer felt a handful of vac dust strike his face. The suction force dragged him to the ground. He writhed on his side, twisting to see his attacker. Why hadn't he been more careful? Of course the janitors' storage/office would be a trap!

Daisy stepped out from behind a stack of boxes, a horrified look on her face. "Oops! Sorry, Spencer!" she cried, running to him. He heard her voice through the rushing sound of the vac dust. "I heard someone coming and panicked." Daisy knelt down by his side. "Gee, I'm glad it's you."

The two kids could do nothing but wait until the suction wore off. At last, Spencer stood up. His brown hair was tousled and he felt like he'd just been chucked out of a typhoon. He sighed wearily. There was no sense in getting mad at Daisy. She'd only been trying to protect herself.

"They took the janitors," Spencer said.

"Walter?" she asked.

"Yeah, they got them both." Spencer dropped his head. "That means they have the bronze nail. Garth Hadley will be long gone by now."

"They didn't get the nail," Daisy said, reaching into her pocket. Triumphantly, she pinched the bronze nail between her thumb and finger, holding it out for Spencer to admire.

"Wh–?" Spencer stammered. "How did you get that?"

"Walter gave it to me. We were in the cafeteria, going for a Grime, when we heard someone coming down the hallway. Walter gave me the nail and his keys and told me to hide. He went out to face them. When the coast was clear, I ran down here."

Spencer felt like hugging Daisy. If Hadley didn't have the nail, he wouldn't leave town. That meant there was a chance to rescue the janitors! And Spencer knew right where Garth Hadley was hiding.

Nearly tearing off his backpack's zipper with excitement, Spencer dug through his pack until he found the paper he was looking for. Pulling it out, he thrust it at Daisy. She took the paper and read quickly, her eyebrows crinkled in concentration.

To: ghadley@bem.gov
From: SpenceZ@wahoo.com
Subject: None

Dear Mr. Hadley,

I changed my mind. Daisy and I can get the nail from Walter Jamison tomorrow after school. People are suspicious of you at the school. Why don't we meet at your local hideout to hand it over?

Let me know where and when.

Spencer

To: SpenceZ@wahoo.com
From: ghadley@bem.gov
Subject: RE None

Spencer,

Good for you. I want you to know you're making the right choice. I knew the BEM could count on you. If you get the nail tomorrow, I'll be waiting for you at six o'clock. Bring the nail to 542 East Maple Street, Apt. 2, right across from Maple Park. If I'm not there, you'll find a spare key under a clay pot on the front porch.

Sincerely grateful,

Garth Hadley
BEM regional representative

Daisy looked up from the printed e-mail, an expression of severe disapproval on her face. She handed the paper back to Spencer and folded her arms.

"You weren't supposed to e-mail him again," she said. "Walter told you not to. So did your mom. Weren't you grounded from e-mail?"

"Who cares right now?" Spencer said. "All that matters is—we know where Hadley's staying."

"What makes you think he'll still be there?" Daisy asked.

"I don't know," answered Spencer. "Maybe he'll already be gone, but I can't think of a better plan right now. Can you?"

Daisy remained silent for a few moments, racking her brain for a better idea. Finally, she shook her head.

"Hadley's not going anywhere without that nail,"

Spencer reasoned. "He might relocate since he knows we're working with the janitors and I found out where his hideout is. But if we hurry, we might be able to catch him unaware."

Spencer pushed aside the secret tower of boxes. "You said you have Walter's keys?" In response, Daisy withdrew the massive ring laden with jingling keys. "Then let's get this open and grab some equipment."

"You really think this is a good idea?" Daisy asked, reluctantly handing Spencer the keys.

"All I know," Spencer said, opening the Rebel Closet, "is that Marv got taken so I could get away. If *we* had been captured, don't you think Walter would come after us?"

"That's different. They're adults."

"We can't trust any other adults. Who do you want to tell? Principal Poach? He's the one who let the BEM in!" Spencer was rambling, anger controlling him. Garth Hadley had tricked him and now the janitors were gone.

Daisy sighed. "You're right, of course. We have to save them. Or try, at least."

"Good," Spencer said. "I couldn't do it without you." He dumped out his backpack on the floor. "Let's gear up and go."

"What should we take?" Daisy asked, studying the room. "There's a lot of stuff in here." She picked up a squirt bottle with blue cleaning solution inside. "What about this?" Daisy set it back on the shelf and lifted a toilet plunger. "Or this?"

"I don't think this is the time to experiment with new equipment. Let's just stick to what we know." Spencer filled his backpack full of vac dust and grabbed a 7T broom and a

14T mop from the rack on the wall. He picked up the discarded latex glove from the table.

"Where's your backpack?" Spencer asked.

Daisy ducked out of the closet and reappeared a few moments later. To Daisy's protests, Spencer dumped everything from her backpack onto the floor. Hastily, he began stuffing it full of vac dust while Daisy picked out a broom and a mop for herself. The backpack was half full when Spencer spotted the overcharged Vortex vacuum bag on the shelf. He quickly placed it in the partially loaded backpack.

"But that's the overcharged bag!" Daisy said. "Walter said that was dangerous."

"I know," answered Spencer. "That's why we're taking it."

CHAPTER 32

"HE'S JUST GOING INSIDE."

Daisy, having lived all of her eleven years in Welcher, knew exactly where Maple Park was located. She often picnicked there with her parents. It was a long walk from the elementary school, and the urgency of their mission made it seem even longer.

They were an odd sight—two kids half jogging down the street with bulging backpacks, each carrying a mop and a broom.

After Spencer had loaded the volatile Vortex vacuum bag into Daisy's backpack, she refused to carry it. Unwilling to give it up, Spencer shouldered her backpack and gave his to Daisy. That was fine for Daisy but unfortunate for Spencer, since Daisy still used the pink princess backpack she had gotten in third grade.

Dez would have had a thing or two to say if he could

have seen them. But then again, had Dez seen them, the bully probably would have ended up pinned to the sidewalk with a mouthful of vac dust.

At last, Spencer and Daisy jogged into Maple Park, careful not to let the bristles of their brooms brush the ground.

"Those are the apartments," Daisy said, pointing across the street. Her forehead was sweaty and she wiped it with her forearm. They moved slowly across the park, passing a young couple who were having a picnic, getting laughs from other kids on the playground equipment. But Spencer and Daisy went forward with determination.

Soon they were close enough to see the numbers on the apartment doors. Number 2 was on the ground level, a small concrete pad making up the front porch.

"Okay," Spencer said, pulling on the latex glove. In addition to the princess backpack, Spencer had pockets full of vac dust. "If it gets bad, you run for it. If I call for help, come fast."

They had solidified their plan during the long walk from the school to the park. Daisy would keep the bronze nail and stay in the park. Spencer would enter through the apartment's front door and rescue the captive janitors . . . if anyone was still there.

"Be careful," Daisy urged, a nervous whine in her voice.

Wordlessly, Spencer jogged across Maple Street and approached apartment 2. He crouched, hoping no one could see him through the apartment windows. Holding his mop and broom like weapons, Spencer felt like an army man running from trench to trench.

Spencer dropped to his knees on the concrete porch

and lifted the clay pot. He felt a rush of relief when he saw the spare key. With his gloved hand, Spencer picked it up. Holding mop and broom in one hand, Spencer stayed on his knees and slowly, silently, inserted the key into the lock.

There were voices inside.

•   •   •

Across the street, Daisy bit her lower lip and tensed her muscles nervously. When someone spoke at her side, she nearly whacked the stranger with her broom.

"What's your friend doing there?" the man asked suspiciously. He had nicely combed hair and a yellow polo shirt. Daisy had seen him pushing a child on the swings.

"What?" asked Daisy tensely.

The stranger pointed. "What's he doing?"

"He's just going inside."

"But why's he being so sneaky about it?" The stranger looked annoyed. "And what's with the brooms and stuff?"

•   •   •

Spencer turned the doorknob. He took a deep breath, his hand sweating profusely under the latex glove. With one swift motion, he shoved the door open and sprang into the living room.

A suede couch and recliner sat on his left. On the right he saw a dining table and a small kitchen area. A dark hallway angled past the kitchen.

Spencer whirled around, his gloved hand full of vac

dust and his left hand wielding the mop and broom. He surveyed the whole area in a moment and determined that it was empty. The voices he'd heard from the porch turned out to be the Three Stooges yelling at each other in black-and-white on an old TV channel.

There was one place left to look. Spencer strode down the little hallway, past an empty bathroom on one side. Tacked onto a closed door at the end of the hall was a torn sheet of paper. Silently, Spencer read the handwritten note.

Spencer,

This will probably be our last personal communication. I knew you were working with the janitors and I didn't appreciate you lying to me about getting the nail. Since you were waiting until six o'clock, I decided to strike early—when you were least expecting it.

Walter didn't have the nail, so I won't be leaving town yet. Feel free to take what you want from this apartment. This was only our secondary hideout. Did you really think I'd tell you where I've been staying? Anyway, your friends from Welcher Elementary are just beyond this door.

Sincerely,

Garth Hadley

Spencer could barely finish reading. Walter and Marv! Just beyond the door! Anxiously, Spencer grabbed the knob and threw it open.

Spencer suddenly yawned, his mind cloudy with fatigue. He was looking for a comfortable place to lie down when he saw them.

Toxites.

Everywhere.

The nasty little creatures were crawling all over the apartment bedroom. Whatever had prevented them from leaving the room lost effect when Spencer opened the door. The Toxites all turned, baring tooth and claw. Only one thing stood between them and the school to which they desperately wanted to return.

And that one thing was just a boy.

Any hint of fatigue left Spencer immediately as the Toxites rushed forward. He staggered backward, scrambling to get out of the hallway. Behind him, two dozen Toxites were swarming the walls, floor, and ceiling.

When Spencer reached the living room, he spun around, swiping his broom through the air. The bristles struck a flying Rubbish with bone-shattering force. The vulture-bat exploded in a flash of light and Spencer felt a fresh surge of power flow up the broom's handle.

Spencer flicked the mop forward, sending the strings like a net down the hallway. At the same time, he struck the broom on the floor, lifting off the ground as half a dozen Filths scuttled beneath him, dusty quills raised aggressively.

Spencer hit the ceiling as the mop retracted, dragging

a Grime and a Filth to their death. Entangled in the mop strings, the Grime popped with a splat of slime and the Filth vanished in a puff of dust.

Spencer was helplessly pinned next to the ceiling fan, watching three Rubbishes wing a jagged pattern toward him. He felt pain sear through his leg as one sharp beak nipped a bit of flesh from above his knee. The other Rubbish was swarming for his face.

With no other option, Spencer let go of the broom. His weight returned instantly and he plummeted onto the suede couch, hoping that the landing wouldn't puncture the unstable Vortex bag in his backpack.

A Filth jumped onto the couch and snarled. Spencer rolled away, waving his mop clumsily. On the television, the Three Stooges were in the act of bonking each other on the head with a two-by-four when Spencer's mop handle went into the screen. The TV shattered, glass flying across the living room.

Spencer dove forward, emptying a pocketful of vac dust on the way. Two Grimes and a Filth were immobilized. Spencer's broom slowly descended from the ceiling.

A slimy Grime sprang from the back of the recliner and landed on Spencer's right forearm, its suction-cup finger pads latching onto the skin. Spencer screamed and jerked with the pain. He tried to wrench the thing free, but it held with a tarlike grip, slurping and burning. The mop fell to the floor and the Toxites began picking it apart.

Spencer tried to crush the Grime against the wall.

Nothing was strong enough to kill the monster. Only a Glopified object would have the strength to destroy it.

Quickly, Spencer stripped the latex glove from his right hand and stuffed it onto his left. His left hand closed tightly around the Grime. He felt the strength of the Glopified glove . . . and the Grime felt it too. Squeezing for all he was worth, Spencer ripped the monster off his arm and felt the Grime explode in his hand, its energy flowing into the glove.

There was no time for Spencer to be grossed out by the yellowish gunk dripping down his arm. The Grime had left painful purple welts where it had held him.

Spencer went for the mop, tripped, and landed painfully on a bristling Filth. The dusty quills stuck into his side as if he'd fallen on a cactus. Grunting from the pain, Spencer tossed his second pocketful of vac dust, suctioning two more Toxites to the floor. He grabbed the mop and swung it like a club, entangling three more as a Rubbish swooped down and raked a claw along his cheek.

There were too many! He had to get out of the apartment—out of the angry, relocated Toxites' way! Spencer cleared a path across the room with his mop. He needed to reach the broom before the Toxites tore it apart.

Lunging, he caught the handle of the broom in one hand. Two Rubbishes were diving from above, and a Filth bared its sharp, rodent teeth. Kicking off the couch, Spencer slammed the broom against the floor. The door was too far away. But the window . . .

• • •

Across the street, Daisy was doing all she could to keep the stranger from calling the police.

"It's a game we like to play," she lied. "Ya put your right broom in, ya put your right broom out, ya put your right broom in and you shake it all about," Daisy trailed off, wagging her broom in the man's face. "It's kind of weird, I know. But it's actually fun if you give it a chance."

"Seems a little rowdy in there," the stranger said, not willing to put his cell phone away just yet.

"Yeah," Daisy said. "Sometimes it gets a little out of hand. You know, when somebody wants to put the mop in . . ."

Suddenly, there was a shower of glass and Spencer burst through the front window, gripping his broom tightly. He shot across the apartment yard, barely missed a tree, and continued flying across the street.

Daisy and the stranger were both speechless: the stranger, because a boy appeared to be flying across the street, and Daisy, because a dozen Toxites were flooding out of the broken window behind Spencer.

Spencer's feet touched down just yards from Daisy. The boy hit the ground running to keep pace with his descending broom. "Come on!" he shouted at Daisy without missing a beat.

"Now, wait a minute," the man with the polo shirt demanded. He whipped up his phone, apparently deciding to involve the police. But before he could dial the number, a puff of dark dust struck his phone and sent it clattering to the sidewalk, vibrating with the force of suction.

It was a good shot and the stranger stood dumbfounded. Daisy blew on her sweaty fingers, causing a few dusty particles to billow like smoke from a gun.

CHAPTER 33

"YOU'RE A GENIUS."

Spencer drifted over Aunt Avril's dead lawn toward his second-story bedroom window. It was risky to use the broom where anyone might be watching, but it might be far worse trying to explain to his mother why he and his friend had come home with mops, brooms, and backpacks full of vacuum dust.

As the two kids had fled Maple Park, Spencer instinctively turned toward home. Daisy's house was closer, but the savage Toxites were carving a path of destruction to get back to Welcher Elementary and the Gates home was right along the way. It would be safer if they got to Hillside Estates where they could make new plans in peace.

Spencer braced his feet on the windowsill and popped off the screen. He always left his window open an inch so the air in his room wouldn't get stuffy. Spencer waited for his broom's gravity to return before climbing through. He quietly dropped to the floor and waved for Daisy to follow him. She glanced around the neighborhood nervously, then struck her broom on the ground and started to rise.

Spencer propped his mop and broom in the corner and slipped Daisy's pink princess backpack off his tired shoulders. It was good to be back in his sanctuary, where everything had its place. But as Spencer surveyed the room, he noticed several major irregularities. His closet door was open, the hamper overturned, and dirty clothes strewn across the floor. The pillows were off the bed and his checkered bedspread was wrinkled.

Spencer's first reaction was defensive. What if the BEM had somehow sabotaged his room, planting more angry Toxites in case the beasts in the apartment didn't do the job? But upon closer inspection, Spencer realized that the wrinkle pattern on the bedspread was all too familiar— jumping little Max feet.

Suddenly, a head of brown hair popped out from under the bed. Max screamed with delight when he saw Spencer standing by the closet door.

"How you get in?" Max shrieked. "I wanna scare you."

"You *did*, for a minute," Spencer said angrily. "Get out, right now. Did you forget that my room is off-limits to you?"

Max crawled out from his hiding place, lip trembling. "I . . . I just wanna play."

"Out!" Spencer ordered unsympathetically. He stood rigid, his arm pointing to the door. Little Max bowed his head and walked out of the room.

"That was a nice older brother," Daisy said from the windowsill once Max was gone.

"What do you know about it, *only child?*" Spencer retorted, shutting the door and moving to straighten his bedspread.

"I just think you're being kind of rude right now."

"Look," Spencer said, throwing his pillows angrily onto the bed. "*You* didn't get attacked by killer Toxites. *You* didn't get a lying note from the BEM. I have a right to be upset now, okay?"

Daisy nodded patiently. "All right. You did have it rough today. I'll just get out of your way." She leaned out the window, ready to use her broom.

"Wait," Spencer said. "I get it. Don't go."

"Will you be nice to me and apologize to your brother?"

"He should apologize to *me*. Look at the mess he made!" Daisy folded her arms stubbornly.

Spencer sighed. "Fine. Next time I see him, I'll apologize."

"Good," Daisy said, resuming her usual countenance. She stepped off the window seat, crossed the room, and sat down on Spencer's wrinkle-free bedspread. "How's your cut?"

Spencer lifted a hand to his cheek. He could feel a line of hard, dried blood. "I'm fine," Spencer assured. "What we really need to do is find out where Garth Hadley is holding the janitors."

"I don't know," Daisy said. "Walter searched for a week

and couldn't find him. What makes you think we'll do any better?"

Spencer grunted. "We *have* to find them. It won't be long before the BEM figures out that we have the nail. They'll track us down as easy as pie. What then?" Spencer started gathering the dirty clothes that Max had spread across the room. He hoped that Daisy wouldn't notice his underwear. Angrily, he flung the clothes back into the closet, one piece at a time.

Garth had tricked him—tried to hurt him! Spencer had thought he had everything under control, but the Maple Street apartment was nothing but a setup. Garth Hadley would be laughing. Laughing hard. He'd tricked a twelve-year-old—wow. Would Hadley keep laughing if the twelve-year-old tricked him back?

"Spencer!" Daisy scolded. Without realizing it, Spencer had twisted a shirt in his hands until the fabric began to tear.

"We have to find them!" Spencer shouted, hurling the shirt into the closet.

"Calm down," she said coolly. "Let's sort out what we know."

Spencer stopped straightening his room and rubbed his forehead in thought. "Well, there's like, five or six BEM workers in town. And they could each have a couple of fake names; that seems to be the trend right now."

"But even if they were using real names," Daisy said, "the only one we know is Garth Hadley."

"Oh, good. We're back to where we started." Spencer

reached down, snatched a pair of shorts by the hem, and
gave them a good flick into the closet. As he did so, a small
piece of crumpled paper fell to the floor. Momentarily intrigued, Spencer straightened it out. When he saw what was
written on it, he sighed and crumpled it again.

"What was that?" Daisy asked.

"Nothing," Spencer said, tossing the scrap into the
wastebasket by his dresser. "Just some stupid note that
Nancy wrote."

"Love note?" Daisy asked, jumping off the bed and
reaching into the trash basket. Daisy opened the paper and,
to Spencer's annoyance, read aloud:

Spencer is so out. Draw something on his face.
—Nancy

"Yeah," Spencer said, shutting his closet door at last.
"Remember the day that Dez drew on my face? I guess
Nancy thought it would be funny."

"Nancy Pepperton?" Daisy asked, staring hard at the
paper.

"The *only* Nancy in our class."

"Yeah, but . . ." Daisy stammered. "This sure isn't
Nancy's handwriting. I know because she's way sloppy and
hard to read. Not like this."

Spencer stole the scrap from Daisy's hands, scrutinizing the penmanship with the eye of a detective. It was true.
The handwriting was far nicer than anything a sixth grader

221

could conjure. And wait a minute . . . there was something familiar about the way his name was written.

"Yes!" Spencer suddenly shouted, tossing the paper in the air like a single piece of confetti. "This is the same handwriting on the paper that Walter found in the recess aide's vest!"

"Wait. I don't think Nancy Pepperton is working for the BEM," Daisy said.

"Of course not." Spencer rubbed his hands together. All of his anger and energy flowed into this new clue.

Daisy watched him pace for several minutes. Finally she burst out, "Well, who wrote it, then?"

"I don't know," Spencer shouted back. "I'm trying to sort it all out." In that moment, something clicked. It was so obvious! How could he possibly have overlooked it?

"Daisy," he cried, crossing the room till they were only a foot apart. "All this time we were trying to figure out who could have put that little bottle of pink soap in the bathroom."

"Who?"

"It was obviously the same person who wrote the note for Dez to draw on my face."

"Who?"

"Leslie Sharmelle! Our substitute when Mrs. Natcher was sick last week."

"Whoa," mumbled Daisy, her eyes bulging as she tried to sort that one out. "But Miss Sharmelle's a girl. She can't go in the boys' bathroom!"

"Oh, please, Daisy!" Spencer slapped a hand to his

forehead. "That's not going to stop her. Even *you* have been in the boys' bathroom."

"What if it was Dez?" said Daisy. "What if Miss Sharmelle gave the soap to Dez and he put it in the bathroom? He had some weird crush on her, remember? Dez would have done anything for her."

But Spencer wasn't really listening. He didn't care exactly *who* had put the soap in the boy's bathroom. He had enough evidence against the substitute teacher anyway.

"Think about it, Daisy," Spencer said. "Leslie Sharmelle was a BEM spy from day one. They needed a kid to work for them inside the school. It was the only way to get close enough to Walter and steal the bronze hammer. The BEM must have poisoned Mrs. Natcher so we would have a substitute. Then Leslie planted a Filth in my desk. That's why I fell asleep after recess that day.

"Once I was out, Miss Sharmelle used Nancy's name and somehow dropped the note on Dez's desk so he would draw on my face. Then she planted the soap—or maybe she gave it to Dez—and the next day she was gone. Miss Sharmelle did her part. The rest was up to Garth Hadley."

"Wait a minute," Daisy said. "The note that the janitors found in the recess vest was signed by S.B. If Leslie Sharmelle wrote it, shouldn't it be L.S.?"

"Fake name," Spencer explained. "While I was hiding out under the desk by Principal Poach's office, a woman came out of an interview. He called her Mrs. Bently, but she said, 'I wish you'd just call me Sarah.' Get it? Sarah Bently! S.B."

"What does that have to do with Leslie?"

"It *was* Leslie! Same clicky high heels and everything. She even wore the same flowery perfume. Leslie staged an interview with the principal so he would open the doors. That's how everybody got inside to capture the janitors."

Daisy thought about it for several minutes. The evening sunlight angled through the bedroom window and a breeze played in the leaves of a nearby tree.

Daisy nodded, finally adding, "Spencer. You're a genius."

"Thanks," Spencer said, grinning. The rage he'd been feeling earlier was totally replaced by hope.

"At least we have three names to work with now," Daisy said. Listing them on her fingers, she stated, "Garth Hadley, Leslie Sharmelle, and Sarah Bently."

"Let's hope that's enough," Spencer said, crossing the room. He shouldered the princess backpack and hefted his mop and broom. "Come on."

"Where are we going now?" Daisy asked.

"To rescue the janitors."

"But where?" She followed him onto the windowsill.

"The Best Western Hotel."

CHAPTER 34

"THERE'S ALWAYS A TURNING POINT."

A shampoo bottle.

Spencer was basing his whole hypothesis on a shampoo bottle. Leslie Sharmelle's little container of pink soap had come from a Best Western Hotel. Daisy reminded him that there were probably hundreds of Best Westerns, any one of which could have provided the bottle. Maybe Spencer was grasping at straws—but it was worth a shot.

They drifted down to the dry grass of Aunt Avril's house.

"Do you have any idea how far away the Best Western is from here?" Daisy asked. She answered without giving him time to speak. "It's, like, a lot of miles. Clear out by the highway, Spencer. I don't think I can walk that far."

"Maybe we can ride bikes," Spencer said. "I think there's an extra in the garage."

Daisy grabbed his sleeve. "You have to remember," she said, "we're only kids. No one trusted Garth Hadley because he relied on kids to do his work when he should have gone to the police. There's always a turning point, Spencer, when we have to hand it over to adults we can trust."

"But the police will never believe us!" he cried.

"I'm not talking about the police," said Daisy. "I'm talking about your mom."

"Mom?"

"She stood up for you in the office. She believed every bit about Garth Hadley."

"That's just 'cause I didn't tell her everything. Only the believable parts."

"So you're a chameleon," Daisy said.

"I'm not a—" Spencer moaned.

"You can't keep changing colors, Spencer. If you tell your mom the whole truth, she'll believe you."

"My mom's not . . . argh!" Spencer grabbed his head. They didn't have time for this. "She really doesn't like *magical* things."

"This isn't about magic. It's about telling the truth so someone will help us save Walter and Marv."

Spencer sighed. She was right, as usual. If his mother was inside, they needed her help. Spencer left Daisy standing on the crispy grass. He entered the house, screaming for his mother.

Alice came around the corner. "What's wrong, Spence? What's the matter?" There was no time to explain everything, such as why he was wearing a princess backpack and holding a mop and broom. She gasped. "My word, you're hurt!" Alice gently touched the scratch on his cheek.

"I'm fine." Spencer pulled away. "But other people are in danger. Garth Hadley broke into the school and kidnapped the janitors. I'm pretty sure he took them to the Best Western Hotel, so we've got to rescue them."

"Hold on," Alice said. "Garth Hadley?"

Daisy suddenly appeared in the doorway, lending credence to Spencer's story. "Saw it with our own eyes, while we were training . . . I mean, in detention."

Alice fumbled for the phone. "This is bad," she muttered. "We need to call the police."

Spencer slumped to the couch, defeated. "Not the police. I knew this would happen."

"Hello," Alice said into the telephone. "I'm calling to report an abduction. Two janitors from Welcher Elementary School."

Pause.

"Yes, janitors."

Pause.

"No, but my son saw it."

Pause.

"Twelve years old. He thinks they're being held at the Best Western Hotel."

"We've got names for a search," Daisy whispered. "Garth Hadley, Leslie Sharmelle, and Sarah Bently."

Alice repeated the names to the dispatcher.

Pause.

"Okay, thank you. 'Bye." The phone went dead in Alice's hand.

"Did they believe you?" Daisy asked.

"They said they'd send someone over. But who's going to believe a twelve-year-old witness?" Alice clapped her hands. "I've got to run to the neighbor's."

"Why?"

"We need a babysitter. Go get in the car."

CHAPTER 35

"THEY'RE HERE, I KNOW IT."

The Best Western stood at the far edge of town, beside the highway that came from Pocatello and went on to Boise. Praised as Welcher's finest hotel, it sported a nice pool and spa along with a continental breakfast for guests. It was a lofty two stories with the lobby entrance under a covered driveway. The parking lot had only a few cars in it. Spencer was disappointed not to see the white BEM van or Garth Hadley's blue Toyota.

It was dusk as the Zumbro station wagon pulled into the hotel parking lot. The front bumper was sagging, crooked from an old accident. One of the headlights had burned out. The car, in its own way, seemed to imitate the expression of its surprised driver.

Alice's mouth was sagging open, crooked in disbelief.

229

One eye was squinted shut as she tried to process what her son had just explained on the drive from Hillside Estates.

"And you've seen these . . . *creatures* every day?" she verified.

"Yes," Spencer said. "The janitors were teaching us to defend against them when the BEM broke in and kidnapped them."

"And those brooms and mops in the backseat? Those are *magical* weapons?"

Alice pulled into an empty stall near the entrance to the hotel. The car rocked back as she parked it, and she too leaned back against her headrest, running fingers through her hair. "This is absolutely crazy, Spencer. I . . . I don't know what to say."

"We'll show you, Mom," he replied. "But first, we have to rescue the janitors. They're here, I know it."

Daisy leaned forward from the backseat. "And we can't let them get this." She held out her hand, showing Alice the little bronze nail in her palm. "No matter what."

Before Alice had any more time to digest their story, headlights flashed. A police car pulled under the covered awning and two officers casually climbed out.

"Let's go check this out," came the muffled voice of the female officer as they strode into the building.

Spencer glanced at Daisy, who quickly closed her fist around the nail. When he looked at his mom, her expression was determined.

"You two stay here," Alice said. She opened the car door. "I'm just going to be a fly on the wall. Be right back."

Spencer and Daisy watched her vanish through the hotel entrance.

"I knew she would trust you," Daisy said. "It makes a difference when you tell the *whole* truth. No one can trust a chameleon."

Spencer grinned and popped his door open.

"What are you doing?" asked Daisy.

"Preparing for an ambush. I have a feeling that the police won't find anything. When they leave, I want to be ready."

Daisy helped him pull the equipment from the backseat. They stashed the mops and brooms behind a trimmed landscape bush near the entrance. In the fading daylight, the janitorial equipment was hardly visible.

A moment later, Alice emerged from the building. Spencer called quietly from his hiding spot in the bushes.

"They're here," Alice said. Spencer pumped a victorious fist into the air. "They have a room in Sarah Bently's name: 211. Been here for about two weeks." Alice shook her head. "The officers told the receptionist not to worry. The call about kidnapped janitors was most likely a prank."

"No way," Daisy said. "Somebody prank-called about kidnapping janitors? What a coincidence!"

Spencer shared a look with his mom. There was no point in trying to explain it to Daisy. She was obviously in a gullible mood. A mood that Spencer suddenly understood.

Seeing Daisy anxiously chew her lip, leaning against the wall of a hotel full of dangerous enemies, it clicked. Daisy

Gates was most gullible when she was nervous. That's why Dez brought it out in her so often.

Spencer's pity for Daisy melted into understanding. Daisy couldn't help being gullible any more than Spencer could help washing his hands before lunch. It was instinct.

"What do we do now?" Daisy asked.

"We wait for the police to finish their *investigation*," Spencer said.

Spencer glanced at the row of hotel windows. Room 211 would be on the second floor. If this one was like most hotels Spencer had visited, the even rooms would be on one side and odd rooms on the other.

"I've got an idea," Spencer said. "Count by odds for me."

Alice looked puzzled, but Daisy was used to doing what she was told, unquestioningly. She counted odds, and Spencer held up a finger for each number she said. When Daisy reached eleven, Spencer was showing six fingers.

"So," Spencer said, walking around the side of the building. He counted six windows from the end on the second story. The drapes were open wide and the flashing, bluish light of a television could be seen in the oncoming darkness.

"I need a broom."

Daisy dug in the bush, accidentally handed him a mop, then traded it for the broom.

"Spencer?" his mother said. But this was beyond her now.

Spencer jogged to the wall, estimated the distance to the window, and tapped his broom on the ground. He floated up slowly, using one hand to guide himself along the wall. Staying clear of the window, he peeked sideways into the hotel room.

An old man was lying on his back under the covers, his fat stomach rising and falling with the rhythm of his snores. The TV blared a rerun of *Wheel of Fortune*.

Spencer descended to the ground next to Daisy, shaking his head. "Not it. Must be on the other side," he said.

Suddenly, Alice snatched the broom from Spencer's hand. "What is . . ." She shook it, like she was strangling the broom handle. "Spencer! This is . . . dangerous, crazy—I don't know! Where did you get this?"

"This," Spencer took the broom from his mother, "is just the beginning. We're up against worse things than this, Mom. I told you it was real."

"You shouldn't be . . . you can't . . ."

Just then the officers emerged from the hotel. Spencer, Daisy, and Alice ducked into the concealment of the bushes.

" . . . the lady's son was probably confused," said the woman officer.

"Yeah," chuckled the other. "Who's going to abduct a school janitor?"

"Probably a high ransom. Didn't you know that janitors make millions?"

They both burst into laughter, climbing into the police car. The automobile pulled out of the parking lot and disappeared down the highway.

"Did you hear that?" Daisy whispered. "I had no idea Walter was a millionaire!"

"Yep," said Spencer. "And Marv's a brain surgeon." He tightened the straps on his pink backpack and dug into the bush for the other supplies.

"So, what does *that* do?" Alice pointed to the mop. "Does it fly, too?"

Spencer grinned. It was weird to know so much about something that his mom had never even imagined possible. "There's no time to explain it all, Mom. The BEM knows we're coming. I'm sure the police gave us away. The longer we wait, the better chance for them to get away."

"Hold on, son," Alice said. "You are *not* going in there to take them by force. Do you remember that you're only twelve years old?"

Spencer didn't want to argue with his mother. This was the risk of bringing her along. She had been supportive so far, but no mother would knowingly let her son go into a fight.

"What should we do, then?" Spencer asked. "If the police won't get involved, who will?"

"Oh, the police are getting involved, so help me." Alice slapped her pockets. "Shoot, I left my phone in the car." She turned to Spencer. "You two—*stay*."

Spencer fidgeted as his mom jogged across the parking lot. "Daisy," Spencer said without breaking his gaze toward his mom, "I need you to follow me."

"But we can't. Your mom said *stay*."

Stay was a dog command, meant for animals. But dogs didn't plot or plan. Dogs didn't have the weight of the world on their shoulders, the future of education hanging over their heads. *Stay* was fine for a dog . . . but not for Spencer.

Alice had just looked up from the station wagon, cell phone in hand, when Spencer and Daisy bolted into the hotel. The kids sprinted through the lobby, mops and brooms in hand, backpacks jangling. They saw the stairs, but that wasn't the plan.

Spencer and Daisy exited the hotel as quickly as they'd entered. But now they were on the other side of the building, the side that Spencer was sure had a window to room 211.

"This has got to be it," Spencer said, counting six windows again. "You still got the nail?" Daisy patted her pocket, face grim and nervous.

"I need you to stay down here," Spencer explained. "In about a minute, my mom is going to show up. Try to calm her down, convince her that I know what I'm doing." As he talked, Spencer slipped the latex glove onto his right hand and hastily stocked both pockets with quick-access vac dust. "Okay. I'm going up."

It was almost fully dark outside and a narrow strip of light leaked out where the curtains didn't seal together. That gap was all Spencer needed.

He floated up to the window and pulled himself close until he was almost standing on the narrow brick ledge. All Spencer could see was a dim corner of the hotel room. But tied in that corner was big Marv Bills.

Spencer strained around, trying to locate Walter and see how many BEM workers were in the room. He didn't have much time to decide how to attack. His broom was already trying to descend. The window was wide open, so only the screen and the curtain kept him out.

"Is that someone at the door? *Again?*" Garth Hadley's voice drifted out the window.

Someone at the door? But who? For a moment, Spencer wondered if the police had returned.

"I'll get it," answered a woman. It was Leslie Sharmelle, or Sarah Bently, or whoever she was. "Put the Rebels in the bathroom again."

Spencer pressed his ear to the screen. He heard the door open. "My son!" shouted a frantic voice. "Where is he?"

Spencer nearly toppled from the windowsill. It was his mother at the door! Alice must have thought he and Daisy had gone upstairs . . .

There was no time to lose! His mother was in danger and the opportunity for a surprise attack was dwindling. He acted—impulsively, instinctively, but not without surprise. A twelve-year-old boy flying through a second-story window was always going to be a surprise.

CHAPTER 36

"THANKS, KID."

Spencer used the mop, flicking it at the screen as hard as he could. The Glopified strings ripped off the screen and entangled the curtains, stripping them from the curtain rod.

Spencer didn't have time to wait for the mop to retract, so he threw it down. At the same moment, he lunged through the open window, striking his broom against the sill to give him an extra boost.

Spencer's mother was standing in the doorway, fear and surprise flashing across her face. Only a few feet before her stood Leslie Sharmelle wearing a baggy sweatshirt and stretch pants. The pink streaks were gone from her spunky hair and now she was platinum blonde. Leslie barely had time to turn away from the doorway before Spencer hit her with a palm blast of vac dust, suctioning her to the floor.

Garth Hadley was in a much more strategic position. As Spencer shot across the room, the strong BEM worker seized the boy's foot . . . only to find that it slipped through his hands like Jell-O.

Spencer noticed an adjoining door that linked rooms 211 and 209. In the corner, Marv was struggling to his feet, hands still bound. Walter was nowhere to be seen. Perhaps the warlock was in the next room.

"Gloves!" Garth shouted as he scrambled toward Marv. But Spencer was already there. The broom clattered against the wall as Spencer ducked behind the big janitor, checking the knots at his wrists. He tugged at them for a moment, but the ropes were too tight.

Garth leapt forward and grabbed Marv by the front of his shirt, Spencer cowering behind. Garth would have punched the big janitor square in the nose, but Marv suddenly slipped through his grasp.

"Ha ha!" Marv exclaimed, feeling Spencer shove the sweaty latex glove onto his bound hand. Marv flexed, but the ropes still held.

"What the . . . ?" Hadley said. Marv threw his full weight forward and checked Garth Hadley to the floor.

Out of the corner of his eye, Spencer saw his mom lunge forward, tackling Leslie as she recovered from the vac dust. "Mom!" he shouted.

Alice had Leslie's arms pinned. She blew at an errant strand of hair in her face. "Don't worry about me, Spence." She drove an elbow into the middle of Leslie's back. "Get out of here and find Daisy!"

Spencer gave a half grin. If Alice was anything, she was independent. Spencer ducked behind Marv. "Go!" he shouted, using the big janitor as a shield to cross the room.

With his hands tied behind his back, Marv lowered his head like a charging ram and burst into the adjoining room, Spencer close behind.

Walter was strapped to a chair, a lamp illuminating his face as in a professional interrogation. Five angry BEM workers were scrambling around the room, gathering supplies to fight the intruders. Among them, Spencer recognized the skinny man with the pointy nose, the pimply recess aide, and the fat guy from the gym's emergency exit. The other two were strangers.

Marv and Spencer paused in the doorway, surveying the area. The room was set up like Walter's Rebel Closet, minus the vat of gurgling gray Glop. Vacuums, mops, brooms, and a myriad of other Glopified tools were ready for use. But Spencer was only searching for something sharp to cut the janitors free.

"Chaaaarge!" Spencer shouted when he spotted an open pocketknife on top of the little refrigerator. Like a faithful warhorse, Marv galloped forward. He head-butted the skinny dude and sent him sprawling on the floor. The pimply guy bounced from the bed and grasped a handful of Marv's shaggy black hair, but it was impossible to hang on while Marv wore the glove.

One of the strangers tossed a well-aimed fistful of vac dust, and Spencer's shield finally went down. At the same time, the fat BEM worker donned his own latex glove and grabbed Marv by the throat.

Spencer dove aside, springing from one queen bed to the next. On his way, he grabbed a pushbroom from the wall. If he remembered correctly from Walter's training, the pushbroom should send his enemies flying. Spencer struck the nearest man once . . . twice.

Yes! The pushbroom flung the BEM worker helplessly toward the ceiling. Another man was charging, but Spencer hurled the pushbroom like a javelin and the man floated backward over the bed.

Marv was thrashing on the floor, his face turning beet red as the fat BEM worker continued to choke. Spencer reached the fridge, grabbed the pocketknife, and ran to Walter. With two cuts from the sharp blade, the warlock was free.

Walter Jamison leapt to his feet, snatched a mop from the rack, and dealt a painful blow to the back of the fat man's head. Marv gasped for breath, veins still bulging across his forehead.

Walter grabbed a second mop, stepped over Marv's body, and began casting an impenetrable network of elongated mop strings. Spencer rolled Marv onto his side and cut the ropes around his wrists.

"Thanks, kid," Marv huffed. "That was brave of you to come alone."

"I didn't come alone," Spencer said. Suddenly he remembered his mom, wrestling with Leslie in the other room, and Daisy waiting nervously outside.

"My mom's over there," he said. "She was supposed to stay with Daisy outside. We've got to help her! She doesn't know what she's up against." Spencer stepped forward, but Walter cut him off.

"Marv," Walter said, still spinning a defensive net with the mops, "take Spencer to help Daisy. I'll hold off these three and get Mrs. Zumbro."

"Come on." Marv grabbed Spencer's shoulder and steered him toward the window. In the lighted parking lot below, Spencer saw Daisy sprinting away from the hotel. Close behind, and gaining fast, Garth Hadley and Leslie Sharmelle descended on brooms.

"Oh, no!" Spencer cried. "Daisy has the nail. If they catch her . . ."

"Get a broom." Marv jerked open the window and pulled off the screen. With a broom in hand, the big man clambered onto the sill just as two BEM workers launched from the next window.

"Hey!" Marv shouted, striking his bristles on the ground and jumping into a collision course. Spencer followed, leaving his mother tied in the next room and Walter to rescue her.

Once in the air, the broom's course was unalterable. Marv sped forward and smashed into the skinny guy. Marv's bulk won out and the BEM worker's broom was knocked askew.

Spencer's launch had set him higher than all the others. From his bird's-eye view, he saw Garth Hadley and Leslie Sharmelle close the gap on Daisy.

Spencer heard the faint suction of vac dust and saw Daisy topple to the blacktop. Her broom dropped and shot off on its own. The mop tumbled from her grasp.

"No!" Spencer shouted, anger flooding through him. Garth picked up the mop and stood guard while Leslie pried open Daisy's clenched hand. Spencer floated, trying uselessly to make his broom descend.

"Got it!" he heard Leslie shout. Spencer felt his stomach sink. The Barbie woman stood up and tossed the tiny object to Garth Hadley. They had found the bronze nail!

Too far away to do anything, Marv was fistfighting the two BEM workers in the parking lot. Spencer finally touched ground as Leslie and Garth reached a silver Lexus sports car.

Spencer had a chance to reach them if he stayed low and kicked off with enough force. The boy sprinted a few steps, angled his body forward, and whacked the broom bristles on the blacktop. The broom streaked forward, Spencer swinging a leg over the handle and riding it like a stick horse.

Leslie was in the driver's seat and the motor revved as she turned on the car. Given his current angle and speed, Spencer guessed he would hit the car's windshield in about a second and a half. Whether he had enough thrust to break through, Spencer never got to find out.

In the split second before impact, Garth Hadley leaned out the passenger window and cast the mop he'd stolen from Daisy. The strings wrangled Spencer from the broom and the mop retracted as Leslie peeled out. Spencer was caught like a bug in a butterfly net as the car sped for the exit.

Suddenly, big hands snatched him out of the mop strings, and Spencer felt totally disoriented. Marv held Spencer like he'd caught a touchdown pass. Momentum and gravity pulled the two of them over. They collapsed in the parking lot as the silver sports car took the corner too sharply and scraped the exhaust pipe on the curb.

"Daisy?" Spencer whispered, sitting up painfully. The girl was walking toward them. Her face was tear-streaked and her hands and knees were scraped from her fall.

"You all right?" Spencer asked, stumbling to his feet.

"They got the nail," she sobbed. "I tried to get away, but they came too fast."

"It's okay," Spencer tried to comfort. He clenched his fists in frustration. He never should have left her alone. She really could have been hurt.

Marv stood up, dusting his big belly. The burly janitor was equally scraped and bleeding, and he already had a black eye and loose tooth from his fistfight with the BEM workers. Spencer glanced across the parking lot. The skinny guy and the pimply guy were collapsed on the grass nearby. Apparently, Marv had won.

Suddenly, the side door of the Best Western burst open. The last three BEM workers charged forward, arms laden with Glopified weapons. Spencer felt a surge of fear. What had they done to Walter and his mom?

Weaponless, Marv stepped forward, clenching his beefy fists. Marv was never truly weaponless as long as he had hands. But the BEM workers were coming fast, the first one almost within mop range.

The screech of tires caused Spencer, Daisy, and Marv to whirl around. The Zumbro station wagon rounded the corner of the Best Western, single headlight shining on them. The BEM worker struck at Marv with his mop, but the car intercepted, brakes squealing to a halt in front of Spencer.

Walter rolled down the passenger's window.

"Get in!"

CHAPTER 37

"THE SCHOOL BOARD."

L ooks like we got to you just in time," Walter Jamison said as the station wagon pulled onto the highway. "Those three BEM workers weren't going to show you any mercy. Mrs. Zumbro and I barely got away."

Alice hadn't said a word. She gripped the steering wheel, unblinking. Spencer noticed the ash-white color of her face. *Welcome to my world, Mom.*

Spencer and Daisy were squeezed in by Max's crumb-filled car seat while Marv sprawled out in the back. There weren't many cars on the two-lane highway, and Spencer could see the Lexus's taillights far ahead.

"We'll never catch them," Spencer whispered. "They're driving a sports car."

This seemed to snap Alice out of her trance. "Hey!" she said. "This baby's never let us down." She patted the dashboard. "And she's been with us as long as you have, Spencer. Is your seat belt buckled, young man?"

Peering over his mom's shoulder, Spencer saw the speedometer's needle rising past 70. The whole car was shaking like a jackhammer. He quickly sat back and snapped the seat belt securely across him.

"Your mom gave an impressive show back there," Walter said. "Knocked two of those guys over with a mop. And she didn't even use the Glopified end."

Spencer tried to imagine his mom swinging a mop like a club. It was a stretch of his imagination.

"Turn here," Walter pointed. "We'll take the back roads through Welcher. Cut them off at the intersection by Maple Park."

"You know where they're going?" Spencer asked anxiously.

"Welcher Elementary School," Marv said. "It's a sure bet."

"But why? If they got the hammer and nail, why would they go back to the school?"

"The School Board," Walter explained. "Hadley needs it to replace me as the next warlock."

"What's the School Board?" Daisy asked.

"When the Founding Witches placed their power into the bronze hammers, they recognized the need for a transfer of power for someone to become a witch or warlock—a rite of passage that would complicate the procedure and discourage thieves from stealing the hammers.

"The Witches formed the School Board—a plank of

magical wood that would transfer the power from one warlock to his successor. After the Witches died, the Board was cut into thirteen square pieces. The idea was that each American colony would safeguard one piece. In order for Garth Hadley to take my power, he must pound the nail into the School Board. That resets the nail—kind of like wiping a computer hard drive.

"If Garth manages to do that, he'll be cloaked in a magical Aura and no one will be able to touch him until he sets his domain. The Aura will provide him a safe walk. All he'll have to do is choose a building for his domain, pound the nail, and he'll be the new warlock."

"But why would he risk going for the Board in Welcher?" Spencer asked. "Why not drive it into one of the other twelve pieces?"

"Welcher is the most accessible," said Walter. "With time, eight of the pieces were destroyed. Four of the five remaining have been appraised as antique hardwood and fashioned into items that are now safeguarded in museums: picture frames, a historic plaque, an antique clock. Nearly impossible to reach. That leaves one."

"At our school," Spencer mused. "But how'd it get there?"

"I brought it with me." Walter grinned at an old memory. "A year ago, when the BEM withdrew support from the schools, I stole Ninfa from a factory in Florida. With a little help from some Rebel spies, I managed to drive the nail into the remaining School Board. From there, I was protected by the Aura, so I took the Board and established my first domain in Arkansas. The BEM tracked me down, so I moved to Welcher. You know the rest."

Walter pointed. "Turn left." Alice spun the wheel and the station wagon squealed around a corner.

"What'll we do once we reach the school?" asked Spencer.

"Mrs. Zumbro will drop me and Marv in the parking lot and take you two out of harm's way."

"But we can help!"

"NO!" Alice and Walter shouted in unison.

"I need to make sure you kids are safe," the warlock said. "You've become too involved already. Marv and I can handle this. If we beat Garth to the School Board, we should be able to defend it."

"That should be no problem, right?" Spencer said. "Garth will have to search every room to find the School Board, but you guys already know where it is."

Walter grimaced. "I'm afraid the BEM already did the searching. Why do you think Miss Leslie Sharmelle came to your classroom as a substitute?"

Daisy and Spencer shared an astonished glance.

"The School Board is in Mrs. Natcher's room?" Spencer couldn't believe what he was hearing.

"And if you haven't guessed it yet," Walter said. "It's actually *your* desk."

CHAPTER 38

"INTO THE SCHOOL!"

Wait a minute," Spencer muttered. It took a second to process what Walter just said. His desk? It seemed so ordinary. "My desk is the School Board?"

"Part of it, anyway," said Walter. "About a square foot. In an attempt to disguise the magic wood, we inlaid the School Board into your desktop."

Spencer tried to imagine his battered desk, wondering which part was the crucial magical wood. Was it the part with that funny message about Mrs. Natcher smelling like cabbage?

The station wagon rounded the last corner and Alice gunned it down the straight road into Welcher Elementary School. As he craned his neck to see out the windshield, Spencer's heart sank.

The blue Toyota Garth had once driven was parked askew, the doors wide open.

"Couldn't be," Spencer whispered. "Garth was in that silver car with Leslie."

"More BEM workers," Marv guessed. "Preparing the way so Garth will have an easy entry once he arrives."

They didn't see the worst part until Alice swung the station wagon into the parking lot and its single headlight flashed across the school. The double doors that led into the middle hallway were smashed open. Glass lay in glinting shards, leaving a jagged, dark opening into the school.

"Drop us here." Walter's voice was an urgent whisper. Alice screeched to a stop.

"We're unarmed," Marv said from the backseat.

"Thanks for mentioning that." Walter gripped the car door, ready to spring out.

"Take this." Daisy swung Spencer's backpack over to Marv. "It's got vac dust."

"We'll need it."

"Let's go!" Marv flung open the door and shouldered the backpack. Spencer watched the two janitors cautiously approach the broken school door.

Headlights suddenly flooded the parking lot. Spencer and Daisy whirled around to see a big vehicle speeding toward the station wagon. Squinting against the lights, Spencer saw what it was.

The white BEM van.

Alice threw the car in gear and slammed on the gas. But the acceleration on the old station wagon made a tortoise look fast. Before the tires had made a complete revolution, the BEM van slammed into the side of the Zumbro station wagon.

Metal folded and glass crunched. Airbags deployed in the front, slamming Alice against the seat. Daisy flew into Spencer and he knocked his head against the window.

"Mom!" Spencer cried. "You okay?" He didn't have to ask about Daisy. She was clinging to his sleeve, whimpering but unharmed.

"I don't know who these people think they are!" his mother shouted from the front seat. "But somebody's going to pay for that!" She was twisting the key in the ignition, but the attempt was futile. The station wagon was parked forever.

"We gotta get out," Daisy said. Marv and Walter were racing back toward the station wagon.

Spencer tested the door. It was stiff, but with some pressure from his shoulder, it popped open. Daisy followed him out as Alice climbed across the passenger seat. Marv ripped open the door and helped her to her feet.

"Into the school!" Walter cried as the BEM van doors opened and several angry workers leapt out. Daisy led the group through the shattered opening in the door, Marv bringing up the rear.

The first BEM worker tried to follow them in, but Marv was ready for him. A fistful of vac dust struck the enemy, suctioning him onto the shards of broken glass.

"They're trying to get in!" Daisy pointed down the hallway where two BEM workers knelt at the lock to Mrs.

Natcher's door. One held a flashlight while the other fiddled with slender lock-picking tools.

Walter knocked them both back with a palm blast of vacuum dust. Marv stepped over the pinned bodies and inserted his key into Mrs. Natcher's doorknob.

"Inside! Quickly!" Walter ushered the others into the classroom. Just as the BEM workers poured into the hallway, the warlock slammed the door and twisted the lock.

Marv started shoving desks against the door for a barricade. Walter retreated to the center of the room. He exhaled a sigh of relief and briefly touched Spencer's desk. Then he crossed to the window, pulling things along to block it.

Spencer glanced at his mom. She didn't look so good. It looked as if the evening was turning out to be more than she could digest. As soon as she saw Spencer staring, Alice grabbed a desk and shoved it toward the door.

That was Mom. Strong and independent, if not a little frazzled. She clearly couldn't let her son see a weakness. Especially not now, when courage was being stretched like taffy.

"What now?" Daisy pushed her own desk and Marv picked it up to make a stack.

"We hold out," Walter said. "The BEM will have to retreat before school starts in the morning. That should buy us at least eight hours to smuggle the School Board safely away. All we need to do is survive tonight."

Mrs. Natcher's room seemed foreign in the darkness of night. Alice reached for the lights, but Walter stopped her.

It was better if the enemy couldn't see them. Spencer strode over to his desk, the object of so much attention. It was funny. He'd been so close to the School Board for weeks.

"Hadley already has Ninfa and the nail. If he gets into this room, all could be lost." Walter dumped over a table and propped it against the window. "The most important thing is to keep Garth Hadley away from Spencer's desk."

"I think we have a problem." Spencer looked up. "This isn't my desk."

CHAPTER 39

"ACTUALLY . . . THAT WAS ME."

Everyone stopped. Marv dropped the desk he'd been holding. All eyes were on Spencer, begging for him to be mistaken so they could ignore his last statement.

"This desk isn't mine," Spencer repeated.

"What do you mean? It's got your name on it." Marv stomped forward.

"This is my name tag, but it isn't my desk."

The others gathered closer, abandoning their efforts to fortify the room. Spencer felt his stomach sinking.

"Are you sure?" Walter asked.

"Positive," said Spencer. "I know, because some dummy wrote *Mrs. N smells like cabbige* on mine. Some dummy who couldn't even spell *cabbage*."

"Um," Marv grunted. "Actually . . . that was me. *I* scratched that into the School Board."

"You?" Daisy said. "Why?"

"Well, she *does* smell." Marv shrugged.

"But why'd you write it?"

"Walter told me to add some subtle marks to make it look more like a normal desk instead of a magic board."

"Very subtle," Spencer said.

"Enough!" The warlock waved his hands. "If this desktop doesn't have the School Board, then we've got major trouble."

"They switched it," Spencer said. "They switched my desk for a fake."

Walter nodded. "They knew we would stop at nothing to get in this classroom. All our attention was focused here."

"But what about the guys picking the lock?" Alice asked.

"A decoy."

Marv grabbed the stack of desks and threw them away from the door, breaking down the barrier that he'd so desperately built.

"And now," Walter muttered. "Now they have us right where they want us—trapped in a classroom."

Marv uncovered the door and threw himself against it. He shouted with rage as Walter's prediction became reality. The door to Mrs. Natcher's classroom was blocked. Alice ran to the window, but shadowed faces of BEM workers already clogged the escape.

"We're surrounded," she said. Marv slammed against the door again. The big janitor was determined, and Spencer was surprised to see the blockade hold against such a force as Marv.

"We need to find out where they've taken the real School Board," Walter said.

Daisy suddenly dropped to her knees and started emptying Spencer's fake desk. "If they really switched them, then all we need to do is find out whose desk this really is." She pulled out a notebook. On the cover was a label: *Haley Rasmussen's writing notebook*.

"Haley Rasmussen," Daisy muttered. "She's in Mrs. Cleveland's class. That's only two rooms down!"

Marv threw his bulk against the door, but it still didn't budge. Alice ducked out of sight by the window.

"We need another way out," said Walter, as though no one else were thinking it. "Every moment we wait brings Garth Hadley closer to the school. Once he's here, nothing will stop him from becoming a warlock."

"Let me just open this door and we'll stroll on down to Mrs. Cleveland's room," Marv said sarcastically. He threw his shoulder against it once more, but it was still solid.

Spencer glanced at Daisy, who was staring at the ceiling. "The vent!" she said. "We could climb into the air vent and escape."

Spencer sized up the vent. It was small, but they would be able to fit. "Nice one, Daisy!"

In no time, Walter was standing atop two stacked desks, straining on the vent cover. "Marv!" he said, jumping down. "I need you."

Marv lumbered over and climbed up. He was a frightening sight, gingerly balancing on two desks, like a circus elephant standing on a tiny ball. With one meaty hand, Marv seized the vent cover and ripped it from the ceiling. White dust snowed down on the shaggy man as he looked up.

"No way I'm fitting," Marv quickly determined. He and Walter traded places on the desks.

The warlock grasped both sides of the open vent and tried to pull himself in. His bald head disappeared into the ceiling. But, to everyone below, it was obvious that Walter's shoulders were too broad to fit.

"Useless," he said when his head reappeared.

"Wait." Spencer stepped forward. "What about us?"

Before Walter could answer, Alice was climbing up next to him. "Fine," she muttered. "I guess *I'll* go."

Spencer knew that his offer had prodded his mother into action. Her motherly instinct would be too strong to let her son enter into potential danger.

"This isn't going to be good," Spencer whispered to Daisy. He had to avert his eyes from the scene. His mother was atop the desks now, clinging to Walter Jamison. "My mom's terrified of heights."

"I got you, I got you," Walter assured. He helped her grasp the vent. With his hands, Walter made a cradle for her foot. Her head disappeared into the vent.

Spencer covered his ears. Any moment now, his mother would start screaming.

And she did. "Get me down! Down right now! NOW!"

It was something Spencer had learned on a family vacation three years ago. They'd gone to Mesa Verde to tour the Native American ruins. Mom had gotten halfway through one of the cliff dwellings when she just froze. It had taken two park rangers to get her back on level ground.

It wasn't just the twelve-foot height of Mrs. Natcher's classroom ceiling that got Alice Zumbro screaming. It was a deadly combination of . . .

"Heights *and* tight spaces," Spencer whispered.

Normally, Spencer would have been embarrassed by his mother's outburst. But there was no time for that now. As Walter and Marv got Alice back on flat ground, Spencer volunteered again.

"You've got to let us try. Garth Hadley could be here by now."

Walter glanced at Alice for parental approval.

"Please, Mom. I can do this. I'll be careful."

Still flushed and out of breath, Alice nodded wordlessly. Spencer scampered up the desks and stepped into Walter's cupped hands.

"I don't know what you have planned," the warlock said, "but you better be careful. Your mother will never forgive me if something happens to you." Without waiting for a response, Walter boosted Spencer into the metal air vent.

It was a tight fit with the princess backpack. Movement was limited to something between a crawl and a slither. Daisy's face suddenly appeared behind him. Spencer reached back and took her hand.

She was still pulling her legs into the vent when a loud crash filled the classroom below. Shouts drifted up, filling the vent.

"What's happening?" Spencer hissed.

Daisy twisted around, peering over her shoulder. "They've come into the classroom!" she whispered back.

"Must have seen us escaping and tried to stop it," said Spencer.

"Walter's down," narrated Daisy. "He looks hurt. Your mom's all tangled up in a mop. They got Marv, too. No, wait. He's breaking free. He's heading to the door!"

Suddenly, Glopified mop strings shot up from below and filled the vent opening.

"Spencer!" Daisy cried as the strings twisted around her leg. He reached back desperately, grabbing for anything. His hands found something and he pulled . . . on her braid!

Daisy yelped from the pain as she became the victim of a human tug-of-war. At last, the mop strings retracted and Spencer let go.

"Ow," Daisy whimpered, grabbing the top of her head. "Who do you think I am, Rapunzel?" She stroked her thick braid. "This isn't a rope, you know."

"Sorry," Spencer said. "Let's get out of here before they attack again."

CHAPTER 40

"STOP SINGING!"

Spencer and Daisy snaked their way forward through the vent system of Welcher Elementary School.

"If we go two rooms over," Spencer whispered, "we'll come out right in Mrs. Cleveland's room. They won't expect us to pop out of the ceiling."

Spencer sounded much more confident than he felt. A million things could go wrong between here and there. He had no idea what they would do once they dropped into Mrs. Cleveland's room. How could they get the desk safely away when all they had was a pink backpack full of vacuum dust? Besides, Garth might already be in there, pounding the nail into the School Board.

I've still got the Vortex, Spencer reminded himself.

"I think this is it," Spencer whispered. The vent shaft branched, leading to a downward drop into a classroom.

"Have you ever noticed how shiny this vent is?" Daisy asked. Spencer glanced over his shoulder to see that she'd fallen behind. "And it's kind of cool how they hook all the different pieces of metal together. I really like this vent."

What was Daisy *talking* about? How could she pay attention to the vent when they were so close to Mrs. Cleveland's room?

Then he saw it, and everything made sense.

A pale Grime was only inches behind her. Bulbous fingertips clung to the metallic vent shaft. The Toxite was enjoying Daisy's brain waves while sending out strong waves of distraction to confuse the girl.

"Behind you, Daisy!" Spencer hissed. "There's a Grime right above you."

"Come back here, Spencer," she said calmly. "You've got to see this."

"No!" Spencer said. "You have to listen to me." But it was too late. The Grime breath was doing its trick. Daisy wasn't hearing anything else.

"I *love* this vent! I think this is the coolest place I've ever been."

Spencer was torn. He needed Daisy's help, but if he went back to vac dust the Grime, he'd waste precious time in reaching the School Board.

Daisy was beyond reason. Now she was singing a lullaby to the vent, her voice getting a little too loud. If the BEM workers below heard the noise, Spencer's surprise attack would be ruined.

"Quiet!" Spencer urged. "Stop singing! You've got to be quiet!"

Suddenly, the Grime scuttled away, aware of its detection. Before Spencer could breathe a sigh of relief, before Daisy could come to her senses, a hand clamped over the girl's mouth from behind.

Daisy tried to scream, but the sound was muffled. Someone had followed them into the vent! But who? It had to be someone small enough . . .

A blast of flowery perfume hit Spencer as a face appeared behind Daisy. It was Leslie Sharmelle. And if Leslie was here, that meant Garth would be . . .

"I found them!" the thin woman shouted. Her voice echoed down the resonant vent, sounding in every nearby classroom. "They're up in the—"

Spencer hit Leslie with a fistful of vac dust from the backpack. Her voice cut short as the suction dragged. Daisy was trapped helplessly beneath the BEM woman, but Spencer had no choice.

Spencer reached the branch in the vent shaft and entered feet first. He wriggled backward until he arrived at the drop into the classroom. Reaching down with a palm blast of vac dust, Spencer hit the vent cover. Suction ripped the bolts out of the ceiling and sent the slotted cover crashing into Mrs. Cleveland's room. He pushed his legs through the blown-out opening and peered into the classroom.

There were at least half a dozen BEM workers prowling the room with a myriad of Glopified weapons in hand. The door was barricaded by a few stacked desks, just as Marv had done in Mrs. Natcher's room. The window, too, was blocked and under watchful eye.

Garth Hadley was at the center of the room. The bronze hammer flashed in his hand. His other hand was in a fist, undoubtedly clenching the nail. Garth was bent over one of the desks, scrutinizing the wooden surface. But the clattering vent cover caused him to look up.

A pair of sneakers emerged from the ceiling. Garth set the point of the nail against the desk, but before he could swing the hammer, Spencer jumped.

In midair, Spencer hurled a dose of vacuum dust. The controlled funnel throw struck Garth in the chest and suctioned him to the floor. A split second later, Spencer landed painfully on the teacher's desk. He bounced and crumpled to the floor.

The pain was intense and throbbing. Spencer felt blackness clouding his vision. If he passed out, all would be lost. Garth would recover from the vac dust and drive the nail while Daisy was trapped with Leslie in the vent above.

Spencer blinked hard. The BEM workers were converging on him. A mop lashed out. Spencer was immediately wrapped and turned upside down. The mop dragged him across the classroom floor. He tried to scream Daisy's name, but couldn't muster the strength.

The barricaded door suddenly shuddered. Spencer craned his neck to see. Something struck the door again. This time the stacked desks tumbled and the door slammed on its hinges. A shaggy form filled the doorway, a sawed-off pushbroom in his hands.

"Marv!" Seeing the burly janitor infused Spencer with an unknown strength. His painful fall was numbed by adrenaline.

The BEM workers swarmed at Marv, desperate to repel the intruder and give their boss time to drive the nail. A handful of vac dust struck his side, but Marv groaned like a Titan and resisted the suction. He was immobile, but still on his feet.

Spencer wormed his way out of the tight mop strings. Marv was going to need his help. The boy was reaching for the mop when something jerked him off his feet and threw him onto the nearest desk. Garth Hadley had him pinned, holding tight to the pink straps of Daisy's backpack.

"Fighting us is the wrong choice, Spencer," he said. "You showed promise. You could have been one of us."

"Help rot kids' brains?" Spencer shouted. "Never!"

"It's for the good of all. If only you'd believe me."

"You lied about the janitors!"

"Not *everything* was a lie, Spencer. Some of it was true. And I can explain the rest if you'll give me a chance."

"I'm not letting you change colors again!"

"Change colors?" Garth asked.

"You're a chameleon! And them's the worst kind of folks!" Spencer kicked savagely, landing his foot in Garth Hadley's stomach. Then, fumbling in the side compartment of the desk beneath him, Spencer grabbed a textbook. With all his strength, he swung the book like a baseball bat, clobbering Garth on the side of the head.

Garth Hadley staggered, momentarily stunned. Spencer

glanced at the weapon in his hands. A math book. That had to hurt—433 pages of mathematical pain.

Let's times that by two! he thought.

Spencer swung again, dealing a blow to the other side of Garth's head. Then he threw the textbook and lunged past the dazed man.

Spencer reached his desk, the School Board. Atop the wooden surface, the bronze nail had toppled. It spun lazily next to Marv's misspelled inscription about Mrs. N. Spencer snatched the nail and found the hammer on the carpet nearby.

There was a great deal of thumping and banging resonating from the open vent. No doubt Daisy was putting up a fight.

Marv was still battling the other BEM workers. Some had collapsed on the floor; others were sent spiraling upward as Marv wielded his short-handled pushbroom like a knight's sword.

Spencer turned as Garth Hadley charged. The boy started to brandish the bronze hammer like a weapon. Then a better idea came.

At his feet was a broom. Kicking it up, Spencer struck the bristles and launched to the ceiling. Garth cursed as Spencer rose out of reach with Ninfa and the nail.

He hit the ceiling only a foot from the open vent. Spencer carefully reached out and shoved the bronze hammer into the air vent. Leslie might reach it before Daisy, but at least it was momentarily out of Garth's grasp.

Daisy's face suddenly appeared in the hole. "Spencer!"

she shouted. His broom was starting to descend. Desperately, he reached out with the bronze nail. Daisy's hand closed around the item as Spencer slipped out of reach.

"Yes!" Daisy cried. But her celebration was followed by a scream. Daisy's face disappeared into the vent again, Leslie Sharmelle dragging her backward.

Garth was waiting for him when Spencer touched down. The boy felt the air whoosh out of his lungs as Hadley tackled him to the floor.

Marv bellowed as mop strings tangled around his arm. He shook free and somersaulted across the classroom, his weight and momentum making him unstoppable.

Marv struck the School Board desk and bowled it over. All of Spencer's school supplies tumbled across the carpet.

"This is the right one?" Marv asked.

"Yes!" Spencer shouted.

With a roar, the big janitor hefted the desk above his head and threw it. The desk tumbled across the room with a tremendous clamor. The metal legs bent and the wooden desktop cracked. Which was exactly what Marv wanted.

Marv leapt into the air and body-slammed the desk. The desktop splintered violently and came totally free. Marv picked up the wood and stripped away loose slivers. At last, he was holding a fragment of wood about a square foot in size—the School Board.

Marv quickly tucked the magic wood under one arm for a quick escape. Garth Hadley saw the plan and abandoned Spencer.

"Look out, Marv!" Spencer screamed. The janitor turned to face the oncoming BEM rep.

Garth swung a fist. Marv caught it and threw him back as more workers came at him. Others had turned to the classroom door, blocking it again to complicate Marv's escape.

Spencer grimaced at the noise coming from the overhead vent. The shaft was probably too narrow for Leslie to get past. Daisy seemed to be holding her own, but it was only a matter of time before Leslie overpowered her. If that happened, Daisy would need a fast way out of the air vent.

Searching quickly, Spencer found the broom he'd used before. He aimed the broom, struck the bristles, and let it go. The broom shot out of his hands and entered the vent's dark opening in the ceiling.

Marv was surrounded, Daisy was trapped. Spencer felt hope slipping away. Where were his mother and Walter? Daisy had last seen them mop-tied in Mrs. Natcher's room. Spencer could only assume they were still there, powerless to escape. Wherever they were, Spencer couldn't count on them for help.

Marv was still fighting like a giant, holding the School Board securely under his arm. He had taken several blows to the head, and dark blood streamed down his face into his shaggy black beard. The bearlike man was grunting and groaning. Struck from the side by a puff of vacuum dust, Marv dropped to his knees.

"The vent, Marv!" Spencer shouted. It was their only chance. The janitor met his stare across the room.

Straining against the vac dust, Marv grabbed his sawed-off pushbroom. Pulling the School Board from under his arm, Marv took careful aim and hit the wooden board with the Glopified pushbroom.

The School Board rocketed upward and clattered noisily into the metal vent shaft. Everyone watched it sail out of reach.

All hope was on Daisy now. She had everything that Garth needed to become a warlock. But Leslie was still up there too.

"No!" shouted Garth Hadley, thrusting his mop at Marv. The strings elongated, wrapping multiple times around the big janitor's pained face and pulling him to his stomach. The pushbroom fell from Marv's hands and another worker grabbed it. He swung, hitting Marv across the back and sending him into the air.

Garth Hadley laughed cruelly, dragging Marv through the air with his mop like a clumsy, injured bird on a leash. At last, Garth threw Marv against the chalkboard, where the big man collapsed in a motionless heap, suffocating from the strings around his face.

Spencer watched the torture in stunned silence from across the classroom. He remembered the first time Garth Hadley had put a hand on his shoulder, enlisting his help to catch the "criminal" head janitor.

Lies! Garth Hadley was a liar. A cruel, mean liar.

"Give me a broom," Garth demanded. "I'm going up." One of the BEM workers stepped forward with a charged broom. Daisy would never survive an attack from both sides.

Garth would claim Ninfa and the School Board. He'd become a warlock.

But Spencer couldn't let that happen—no matter what!

Spencer pulled the pink princess backpack from his shoulders and ripped open the zipper. Vacuum dust was useless now. Spencer stared at the other object in the backpack, a wild thought forming in his head. It was too risky. He couldn't possibly . . . but his hands were already moving.

The spilled contents of his desk were all around him. He snatched a sharp pencil from the floor and lifted out the overcharged Vortex vacuum bag. Spencer was breathing hard, wishing there were some other way. Walter had warned about the Vortex; it was unstable, unpredictable.

Overhead, Spencer heard Daisy scream. It reverberated in the metal vent, amplifying the sound of her terror. Garth Hadley took aim and struck the bristles of his broom against the floor.

Without another thought, Spencer stabbed the sharp pencil into the vacuum bag.

CHAPTER 41

"SOMEONE HAS TO END THIS!"

As soon as the tip of the pencil pierced the papery fabric of the vacuum bag, a deafening suction sound filled the classroom—three hundred times louder than any puff of vac dust.

Spencer held onto the pencil, clenching the bag with all his might. Everything around him went black and he struggled to maintain consciousness.

On his knees, Spencer saw a funnel of dark dust issuing out of the bag. It grew, twisting and pitching like a giant tornado with Spencer at its root.

At the opposite end of the shifting tornado, Spencer saw dim visions of the classroom: Marv's limp body, a mangled desk, Garth Hadley rising on his broom. But these scenes seemed miles away, frozen in time.

Then something crashed down the dust funnel, spiraling

toward him. Spencer flinched, seeing a math book and a chair come hurtling at his face. At the last moment, both objects were sucked into the vacuum bag in Spencer's hand, passing the boy without so much as a scrape.

But that was just the beginning.

The Vortex was soon tearing everything inward. There were so many objects twisting toward him that Spencer could see only glimpses. The teacher's computer, an overhead projector, desks, cabinets, fragments of chalkboard . . . everything!

But the worst part was the bodies. Spencer saw human figures, indistinguishable among the rubble. He tried to count them, but it was impossible to see anything clearly at the base of the tornado.

Spencer cried out, screaming against the deafening squall. His own voice seemed to get caught in the dust funnel and sucked into the Vortex. Spencer felt tears flinging off his face. The sharp pencil slipped from his hand and disappeared into the vacuum bag. He felt the pink straps of the princess backpack snap. It swirled above his head and then vanished.

It took everything Spencer had not to let go of the dangerous bag. Still, his grip was slipping. Spencer had no doubt that he would end up inside the bag just like everything else unless he could hang on . . . just hang on!

Whoosh!

The tornado suddenly folded in on itself, crackling and hissing as it was sucked into the Vortex bag. Spencer felt the vacuum bag shudder in his hand. It felt no different from how it had been before—no heavier, no bigger. But as moonlight angled through the classroom's blown-out window, Spencer saw that *everything* was gone.

The classroom was utterly destroyed. He was kneeling on bare concrete. The force of the suction had imploded the walls, tearing the sheetrock like paper. The sink in the back of the classroom had been pulled into the bag. A surge of water shot from the broken pipe, running across the floor like a river.

He was alone in the desolation.

Glancing up, Spencer saw that the ceiling tiles were gone. The insulation, too, had been sucked away. Sparking wires hung where the lights had been. Cracks angled across the bare ceiling, almost wide enough to expose the night sky.

But among the crooked roof trusses, a twisted, metal vent shaft remained, bent askew and dangling precariously.

"Daisy!" Spencer whispered hopefully. Through some stroke of fate, the vent had survived, held in place by the metal roof supports. And if the vent had survived, then Daisy might have, too!

Then, as if the vent had sensed his optimism and wanted to dispel it, the damaged shaft slid from the metal roof truss with a groan. The vent fell in slow motion, Spencer wishing he could intervene. But what more could he do than watch helplessly and hope for the best?

The vent made a mighty crash as it hit the concrete floor of the skeleton classroom. Overhead, the weakened roof creaked.

Spencer raced forward. Water from the busted pipe was already forming a puddle, so he carefully set the Vortex on top of the twisted vent.

Please, he silently hoped. *Let her be in there!* Falling to his knees, Spencer peered into the narrow chute.

An arm stretched out of the dark vent, barely visible. In desperation, Spencer grasped the hand. To his relief, the hand grasped back.

The roof rasped as something fell from above and crashed onto the floor behind him. Spencer risked a glance upward. A patch of starlit sky winked through a new hole in the roof.

It's coming down, he thought, his throat tightening. *This whole room is going to collapse!*

Spencer glanced at the door, mentally preparing his escape. But the doorway had been sucked into the Vortex, and rubble blocked the exit. Gasping, Spencer turned to the window. The glass was gone, but he might be able to climb out with Daisy before the roof caved.

"Come on," Spencer whispered. He pulled on the hand and felt Daisy trying to work free. The flooding water, the groaning roof . . . it was enough to make his head spin.

Another portion of the roof caved in. Plumes of dust rose from the rubble like swirling, pale ghosts. A foreshadowing of death and a tomb of rubble if they didn't get out soon.

"Come on, Daisy!" Spencer called into the vent. He could see her head and shoulders now.

"Spencer," the girl moaned, an eerie sound that

resonated in the metal shaft. Sliding her other arm forward, Daisy opened her hand. The bronze nail was clutched so tightly that it left a red mark on her white palm.

Her dedication was admirable. Through all the danger and commotion, even as the vent plummeted twelve feet to the hard floor, Daisy had kept an iron grip on the nail. She knew what was at stake if Garth took Ninfa and the nail.

"It's okay," Spencer called into the vent. "It's over now."

Right then, something slammed into him from behind. Spencer's head clanged against the metal vent shaft. In a dazed stupor, he saw Leslie Sharmelle reach down and pluck the bronze nail from Daisy's open palm.

"How . . . ?" Spencer tried. Leslie must have also survived inside the vent. Then, as he was distracted with rescuing Daisy, Leslie had slipped out the other end of the metal shaft. The thin woman, covered with cuts and bruises, glanced around the gutted classroom. In one hand, Ninfa glistened, wet from the rising water. Under her arm was the splintery School Board. And now she had the nail . . .

"Devil knows what happened to Garth Hadley," she screamed, her face contorted with madness. "But *someone* has to end this!"

Leslie placed the School Board on the vent and set the sharp tip of the nail against the wood. With a wicked shriek, Leslie raised Ninfa to drive the nail home.

Rubble crashed down from above. The roof gave the most terrifying groan yet, causing Leslie to glance up. In that crucial moment of distraction, Spencer leapt forward.

Slipping the wet hammer from her hand, he lunged at the School Board.

Leslie was still holding the bronze nail to the wood when Spencer struck with the hammer. Once—twice. She cursed as the hammer smashed her fingers. But, with a third strike from Ninfa, the head of the bronze nail was smooth against the School Board.

The room was dreadfully silent. Even the roof stopped its creaking—the calm before the storm.

Leslie backed away from the Board in shock. Spencer gripped the hammer, his eyes wide in disbelief at his own actions. *He* had driven the nail! But Leslie had been right; *someone* had to end this.

Then the roof cracked violently, as if to make up for its moment of silence.

"Daisy," Spencer cried. "You've got to get up!"

Leslie had fallen to her knees, hands outstretched, as if the world had just slipped through her fingers. With such a dazed, blank stare, Spencer would have thought her a mannequin if it hadn't been for the slight tremble of her chin.

Dropping Ninfa, Spencer grabbed both of Daisy's hands and jerked the girl out of the bent air shaft. Beside her tumbled the broom that Spencer had launched into the vent.

"Hang on!" Spencer shouted. Her arms feebly clung to his neck and Spencer helped her straddle the broom handle. He picked up Ninfa and shoved the hammer into Daisy's hand. Turning back for the School Board, Spencer saw that Leslie Sharmelle was holding it tightly.

As the roof sloughed inward, Spencer leapt sideways,

slamming the broom bristles against the floor as hard as he could. Spencer's left hand reached out, grasping the papery Vortex bag from the broken air vent. The two kids shot sideways, sailing toward the blown-out classroom window and into the dark sky.

Behind them, the room crumpled like a cardboard box. The sound was sickening—the kind of crunching and crashing that the kids would never forget.

Spencer and Daisy drifted into the parking lot as the weak broom struggled to keep them both aloft. The landing was awkward and they both tumbled to the blacktop.

"What happened?" Daisy said. She had found the strength to rise on her own feet.

Spencer looked at the crumbled, moonlit wreckage of Mrs. Cleveland's classroom. "I think we won."

"No," Daisy whispered. "What happened to *you*?"

Spencer stepped away from her, wondering what she meant. He looked down and gasped.

"You're glowing."

CHAPTER 42

"WHAT HAPPENED TO ME?"

The classroom accident made the news. A janitor by the name of John Campbell was the first responder. He'd been at the school late, shampooing carpets, when a violent crash led him to discover the ruined classroom and call 911.

Not only was the accident newsworthy, but several mysterious events surrounding the collapse of the classroom also gained the media's attention. Police were still investigating.

Only one person was found in the rubble of the broken room. She was quickly taken by Life Flight to the hospital. The young woman was in critical condition, having suffered broken bones and a concussion to the head. Police scoured the area, but no other individuals were found.

News reporters commented that, as the debris was cleared, the classroom was found to be completely stripped.

Desks, computer, carpet, even the classroom sink was gone. Authorities believe the operation was some kind of massive classroom theft.

To make things worse, the woman had stolen a vehicle from Hillside Estates. Fortunately, John Campbell was able to cripple her escape by driving a BEM van into the stolen station wagon.

Police were waiting until the unnamed blonde recovered before interrogating her about the alleged station wagon theft and total destruction of school property.

There was much hearsay and speculation as to the cause of the classroom cave-in. Answers to these questions would be resolved only when the victim regained stability.

But there were many things, of course, that the news would never know. The true story went more like this:

Spencer and Daisy raced into Mrs. Natcher's classroom. Walter and Alice were on the floor, tightly mop-tied. The kids untangled them, and Alice fell on her son with hugs and worried exclamations. But it was Walter's reaction that really frightened him.

"Spencer," the warlock hissed. He put a hand to his bald head. "The Aura."

"What do you mean?" Alice asked, pushing Spencer back for inspection. "What happened?"

"You drove the nail, didn't you," stated Walter.

Spencer stared down at his body, cloaked in a warm, gold glow. "What happened to me?"

"Since you drove the nail," Walter explained, "you're protected by the magical Aura until you set up a domain."

"Set up a domain . . . ?" Spencer mumbled in disbelief. The consequences of his actions were uncomfortably starting to set in.

"Aura? What Aura?" Alice started combing over Spencer like something was hidden in his hair.

"You can't see it because it exists on the same plane as the Toxites and you haven't been exposed yet," the warlock explained.

Daisy handed Ninfa to Walter.

"Where's the School Board?" he asked.

"It's under the rubble in Mrs. Cleveland's room," Spencer said. "There wasn't time to get it away from Leslie."

Then Walter noticed the vacuum bag cradled in Spencer's arm. The boy clung to it, the only tangible evidence of what he'd done. A memorial to utter destruction.

"You did what you had to, Spencer," Walter said.

"Marv," Spencer whispered. "I killed him." He remembered the burly janitor rolling across the classroom, fighting like a dragon. The Vortex had claimed Marv just as it had the other BEM workers and Garth Hadley. Spencer felt his eyes welling with tears.

"I didn't mean to," he mumbled. "He saved my life . . ." His mom put an arm across his shoulders. Daisy stared unblinking at the bag.

"Marv knew the dangers involved in this kind of janitorial work," Walter said. "There was nothing else you could have done. Marv would be proud of you—and your decision to use the Vortex."

Spencer swallowed hard. He held out the Vortex, begging

Walter to take it. The janitor held up his hands. "He may not be dead," Walter said. "The Vortex is a mystery to us all. Keep the bag. If there's a way to recover him, we'll find it."

Walter strode purposefully out of Mrs. Natcher's room and disappeared down the hallway. The others stood in reverent silence for a moment. When Spencer finally moved, his feet seemed heavy and sluggish.

By the time they caught up to Walter, he'd been to the Rebel closet and stood before the wreckage of Mrs. Cleveland's room with a pushbroom.

"Stand back," he cautioned. The janitor struck the rubble of the collapsed doorway and sent it floating.

"Be careful," Daisy said as he tunneled out of sight, bits of brick and twisted shards of metal flying out of his way.

A moment later, Walter returned with the School Board, the nail set firmly in the magical desktop. He handed the board to Alice and glanced back at the crumpled classroom.

"I've got to get back in there. Leslie's still alive, but she's going to need first aid." He dug in his pocket and pulled out a car key. "Mrs. Zumbro, I need you to get the children out of here before the police arrive. Please go. Take my car." Walter handed her the key. "Red Pontiac Grand Am."

"What about you?" Daisy asked.

"I'm calling 911. I need to get Leslie out of there." The warlock looked once more at Spencer and gave him a stoic nod. Then he sent the rubble flying again as he burrowed into the wreckage to rescue the enemy.

The two kids followed Alice through the school's

broken doors and into the parking lot. Spencer couldn't help but notice how Daisy stared at him while they walked. The Aura illuminated the whole hallway, powerful and frightening. Spencer bit back the urge to cry.

What had he done?

CHAPTER 43

"IT'S A BIG DECISION."

Thanks for coming," Spencer said, clearing a spot on the leather couch for Walter to sit down. "Sorry about the mess," he added. "My family's not the cleanest."

"Don't worry about it," Walter answered with a smile, sliding one of Max's toy dump trucks aside with his foot. "I'm a janitor. I'm used to messes."

It was Saturday afternoon, cool and rainy. A quick phone call had brought Walter Jamison to the house.

"I saw you on the news this morning," Spencer said.

"Oh, no. Did my hair look all right?" Walter asked sarcastically, running a hand over his bald head.

"How's Leslie Sharmelle, or Sarah Bently . . . or whoever she is?"

"She'll survive," Walter said. "But when she wakes up, she'll wish she hadn't. Everyone thinks she stole your station wagon and emptied Mrs. Cleveland's classroom. By the time I was finished talking to the police, I even had her blamed for the mysterious cave-in. I don't suspect we'll be seeing much more of Leslie Sharmelle."

Alice Zumbro entered from the kitchen, a few store-bought cookies on a plate. "It was all I could find," she said. "Wish they were homemade."

The janitor took a cookie and sat back. "I'm really proud of you," he said. "Both of you." His eyes looked exceptionally tired and weary. "Insurance will cover the station wagon," Walter said. "Once they prove Leslie guilty, you should get a new car."

"The old station wagon suited us fine." Alice shook her head. "Twelve years of safe driving, and then—*wham!*" Alice clapped her hands. "Some jerk totals it in a parking lot."

"How is Daisy holding up?" Walter asked. "She showed such courage."

"She was pretty shaken up last night," Alice said. "Luckily, I was able to calm her parents when we dropped her off."

"Everyone that discovers the truth will be in danger of the BEM," Walter said. "Poor Daisy's involved, whether she likes it or not. But I'm counting on you to keep her safe, Mrs. Zumbro. We really mustn't bring Mr. and Mrs. Gates into this."

"I'll watch Daisy," Alice promised. "And it shouldn't be a problem to keep her folks innocent. They're quite clueless about a lot. Surprisingly gullible."

They chewed the dry cookies in awkward silence.

"Oh." Spencer reached over to the coffee table. "Here's the School Board and Ninfa." He picked up the hammer and the heavy piece of antique wood. "I'm ready to get rid of this Aura." Spencer glanced down at his shimmering arms. "You don't know how hard it was to fall asleep last night. I was like a walking nightlight."

"You seem the same to me," Alice said. It was a simple statement, but she had no idea how much that meant to Spencer. He felt so foreign, so alien. It was comforting to know that his mom couldn't see anything different about him.

Walter chuckled. "Regretfully, Mrs. Zumbro, we don't keep a stock of revealing soap at the school. Too risky. Spencer will have to create a new batch if he chooses to expose you. It might take some time, but he'll get it." Walter nodded at Spencer. "There's a lot you have to learn about being a warlock. I don't claim to be an expert, but I'll help you as much as I can."

He took another cookie from the plate. "Where will you drive the nail? Give it some thought. It's a big decision."

"Not for me." Spencer held out the objects to Walter. "I don't think the Rebel Underground should have to rely on a twelve-year-old warlock," Spencer explained. "You can keep supplying the Rebels, and maybe the Toxites won't take over *every* school."

Walter reverently took the bronze hammer and School Board from Spencer's outstretched hands. "I'm honored."

"Now will I stop glowing?" Spencer glanced at his arms.

Walter placed the tip of Ninfa against the head of the bronze nail. A magic bond formed instantly and started lifting the nail free of the wood. The small bronze nail fell tinkling onto the coffee table.

Instantly, the protective Aura around Spencer began to fade. He closed his eyes and sighed. When he opened them again, the glow was completely extinguished.

Spencer retrieved the fallen nail and handed it to Walter. "Just promise me that you'll Glopify some really cool stuff."

Walter grinned. "I told you once that I feared a war might be brewing. The BEM's new experiments will redefine the world of Glopified equipment. They're not out to fight Toxites anymore. They're fighting *us*."

"Well, I hope they know what they're up against," Alice said. "Because *nobody* messes with my kids."

Spencer had taken that for granted until he had seen his mom tackle Leslie Sharmelle at the hotel. It was nice to have a mom who cared.

"There's one more thing," Spencer said. He stepped into the other room and returned with the Vortex. He had debated giving it up. The vacuum bag represented painful memories, true. But to Spencer it was also an icon of sacrifice and friendship. "I want you to have this." He handed it to Walter.

The janitor accepted the bag with a sad smile. "Spencer," he said, "Marv would want—"

"I don't . . ." Spencer held up his hands. "I don't want to talk about it."

Walter sighed and pulled on a baseball cap. "Thank you for the cookies, Mrs. Zumbro." He pocketed Ninfa and the nail and tucked the School Board under one arm.

At the door, Walter Jamison turned. He stared hard at the boy. "Thank you, Spencer. For everything." Then he disappeared into the rain, sidestepping a puddle on the sidewalk.

"Until Monday," the boy whispered. So why did Spencer feel like that was good-bye?

CHAPTER 44

"A VAN?"

Daisy Gates reached her goal of being the first student to enter the school on Monday morning. Close behind was Spencer.

Bright and early, the two kids had met on the playground and entered Welcher Elementary, anxious to see how Walter had reestablished his domain. The kids walked briskly to the janitor stairwell only to stop short, their hearts beating fast.

Boxes.

Cardboard boxes were taped shut and piled on the stairs. Spencer and Daisy waded past a stack and were starting down the stairwell when they came face-to-face with a somber Walter Jamison.

"What is this?" Spencer asked, pointing at the stuff piling up.

Walter set down the box he was carrying and rubbed a hand along his bald head. "Ah, glad you're here. I need some extra helpers to carry things out to the van."

"Van? What are you talking about?" Daisy cried.

Walter nodded. "I'm done here," he said quietly.

"What?" Spencer and Daisy shouted in unison.

"I've been fired," Walter explained. "We knew it would happen. The BEM is still in charge."

"I don't care!" Spencer said angrily. "We beat the BEM!"

Walter shook his head. "We beat Garth Hadley and stumped the BEM's plans to make him the next warlock. But one doesn't *beat* the Bureau of Educational Maintenance."

"But," said Spencer, looking for an excuse. "But the nail and the hammer . . ."

"They are safe," Walter said. "I re-drove the bronze nail into the School Board yesterday. Then I chose my new domain. I'm a full-fledged warlock again, ready to experiment—thanks to you two."

"But where will you go?" Daisy asked.

Walter lowered his voice. "The BEM will track me down wherever I set up. But if I can remain in motion . . ." He grinned to himself. "I have established my new domain in a van."

"A van?" Daisy asked.

"A fifteen-passenger vehicle," he replied. "It should be large enough to experiment with Glop. And since the van will already have wheels, I'll be able to make deliveries to the Rebel schools without ever leaving my domain."

"No," Spencer interrupted. "I won't let you leave. Who's going to replace you?"

"The Bureau has hired two new janitors," said the warlock. "They'll arrive at Welcher in a few days."

"BEM workers? Here?" Spencer stomped his foot. "But they'll let the Toxites take over. Without you, I'll be sleeping through every lesson!"

"Haven't we taught you anything?" Walter asked. "The Toxites will multiply, true. But as long as you can see them, *you* can fight them." He picked up the box. "I'll be around to give you new supplies as often as I can manage. As long as you two are here, I'll consider Welcher Elementary part of the Underground."

Spencer clenched his fists. It couldn't be true. Soon he would wake up and know that this whole scene was nothing but a nightmare. Walter couldn't leave now! Not after Marv had died. Not after all they'd been through together.

"Look," Walter said, "I know it's hard to accept. It isn't like I *want* to go. There's nothing I'd rather do than stay here and watch out for you kids. But I won't leave you totally friendless."

"What do you mean?" Daisy asked.

"Principal Poach just hired a new lunch lady." Walter lowered his voice. "Her name is Meredith List. She's an old friend of mine. She knows about Toxites and she's loyal to the Rebel Underground. If you ever need to contact me, just tell Meredith."

Spencer slumped down onto a nearby box. A lunch lady

wasn't the best trade for a warlock, but at least there would be an adult in Welcher who knew about Toxites.

"Ten minutes till the bell rings," Walter said. "Do you kids mind giving me a hand with some of this stuff?"

Spencer, Daisy, and Walter waddled out to the parking lot, their arms laden with boxes, janitorial equipment, and half-completed warlock experiments. A brown fifteen-passenger van was parked in the nearest stall, the back open. It was stripped of its rear seats, much like Garth Hadley's BEM van. But Walter's brown van seemed a hundred times friendlier.

The three of them piled their armloads into the back of the van. Walter dusted off his hands and smiled. "I'll go back for the last load," he said. "You two run along to class before the bell rings."

"Where are you going after this?" Spencer asked, stalling—anything to avoid saying good-bye.

"Oh, I don't know," Walter said, looking up into the bright blue sky like he could see forever into space. "First thing I need is an assistant. My niece has volunteered to go with me. She's young, but she's worked as a janitor since she was seventeen, so she knows a few tricks. She should make a good replacement for . . . um . . ."

"For Marv," Spencer said. But he knew that wasn't true. Nobody could really replace Marv Bills.

"We'll head over to some Rebel schools in Wyoming and Colorado, keep moving south." Walter shrugged. "There's endless work to be done, and when we're finished with that, there'll still be gum to scrape. You kids can't seem to keep it in your mouths." Walter smiled, a transparent attempt to lighten the mood. Spencer stared back gloomily and Daisy gazed down at her shoelaces.

The three of them stood awkwardly in the September morning, Spencer having a stare-off with Walter Jamison.

"Listen, Spencer," the warlock said, rubbing his forehead. "There's something I should probably tell you. I was going to tell you sooner, but then I thought maybe I should wait. Now, since I don't know when I'll see you again, well . . ." Walter sighed.

"What?"

"I just wanted to let you know . . . I think your father would be proud of you."

Spencer heard his heartbeat in his ears, growing steadily faster. Was that supposed to be a compliment? Didn't Walter know that Spencer's dad had disappeared years ago?

He's got to come back, Daisy had said when they were scraping gum. *Nobody loves their work more than their family.*

As if reading Spencer's mind, Walter said, "He meant to come home, Spencer. Alan Zumbro was a good man."

"You knew him?" Spencer asked in utter disbelief.

"Your father was an excellent Toxite biologist. He was part of the BEM before the Bureau went haywire. Smart man. Once I sat in on a lecture he gave at a Bureau conference. The topic was Filth anatomy—way over my head. The BEM really valued the experiments that Alan did to understand the anatomy and physiology behind Toxites."

Spencer almost had to gasp for breath. His father! A Toxite scientist? It was almost impossible to believe. Yet it made perfect sense. Spencer's mother was always annoyed by Alan's secretive behavior—his mediocre explanations of where he'd been and why he'd been out so late.

"You're just like your father sometimes!" Spencer's mother had told him. Suddenly, he realized how right she'd been.

"I'm sorry, Spencer," Walter said with a curt nod.

Sorry? Sorry for what? Spencer had never felt better in his whole life! But the solemn expression on the janitor's face quickly killed his joy. At last, Spencer asked the unanswerable question.

"Why hasn't he come home yet?"

Walter exhaled slowly. He made eye contact, then broke it before answering. "Your father went to Texas for an experiment with the Toxites . . ."

"Yes, I know," Spencer interrupted. "He went with Rod Grush two years ago—"

Walter silenced the boy by raising his hand. "The experiment was very dangerous; lots of unstable variables—"

"What was he doing?" Spencer cut him off again. "What *was* the project?"

"Alan was attempting to trace Glop back to its very source. He was on the cusp of discovery when it happened."

"What happened?" shouted Spencer. "What?"

"Your father disappeared."

Silence.

Spencer felt it starting in his stomach. A sick rejection of the truth, pulling at his insides. This was unacceptable.

"Poof? Gone?" Spencer cried. "That's not good enough! What happened to him?"

"I'm telling you," Walter said, "no one knows what happened down there."

Spencer felt like all his bones had turned to jelly. So close to learning the truth about his dad . . . nobody just *disappeared*. His dad had to be *somewhere*.

"Tell you what," Walter said, changing his tone of voice. "Since I'm headed south, I'll do my best to pick up some new clues. In my opinion, the case was never investigated as much as it should have been." The warlock smiled. "I promise, Spencer. I'll do as much as I can."

The bell rang, shrill and obnoxious. Daisy tugged at Spencer's sleeve. "We'd better go," she said.

"Yeah," said Spencer, taking a deep breath. Walter extended a hand and Spencer shook it.

"Get going," Walter urged them.

Daisy and Spencer turned to face Welcher Elementary School. With Dez back from suspension and a school full of toxin-breathing Toxites, who could tell what new adventures the day might hold?

1. Spencer knows he saw some creatures in the school, but he denies it when Dez threatens him after lunch. Have you ever had trouble standing up for something you know is right? What made it hard?

2. Mr. Gates says that a chameleon is someone whose story changes depending on who he's talking to. Is it important to always tell the whole story? Why, or why not?

3. Daisy tells Spencer that he needs to believe that his dad will come back. Why is it important to have hope? What kinds of things should we hope for?

4. Garth Hadley tricks Spencer and Daisy into doing things for him. How can you know when someone is asking you to do the wrong thing? What should you say if that happens?

5. Spencer waits till after the ice cream social to tell his mom what is going on. By then, he has already caused a lot of problems. How could Spencer have handled that situation differently? What kind of things should we talk to our parents about?

6. Garth Hadley communicates with Spencer via e-mail. Spencer continues to e-mail even after he's been told not to. Why was that a dangerous choice? How can you be safe on the Internet?

7. If you could have one Glopified cleaning supply, which would it be? Why?

8. For unknown reasons, the BEM has stopped fighting Toxites. The Rebel janitors continue to fight the creatures so that kids can keep learning. Would you join the BEM or the Rebel janitors? Why is it important to get a good education?

9. Spencer and Daisy discover that the Toxites stop kids from learning by creating sleepiness, apathy, and distraction. What are some things in school that make it hard for you to learn? How can you overcome them?

10. Walter tells Spencer that Toxites work harder on kids who really try to learn. Why don't Toxites "waste their breath" on kids like Dez? How hard would the Toxites have to work to get you?

11. If you could Glopify a new cleaning supply, what would it be? What magical power would it have?

12. At the end of the book, Spencer temporarily becomes a warlock. If you had that power, would you give it back to Walter Jamison? Why, or why not?

ACKNOWLEDGMENTS

It seems like every time I turn around, I meet someone new to thank. So many awesome people have helped me transform *Janitors* into what it needed to be.

Thanks to everyone at Shadow Mountain for doing so much to help launch this series—especially Chris Schoebinger for believing in the story and having the vision of where this could go. I'm also grateful to Heidi Taylor for patiently working through the rough spots with me, and to Emily Watts for her excellent editorial work.

Another big thanks goes to my wise agent, Rubin Pfeffer, for starting me off on the right foot. Thanks to Brandon Dorman for bringing the story to life with his amazing artwork and illustrations.

I want to acknowledge and thank my good parents for always fostering my creativity and supporting my hobbies.

Now, for the team of family and friends who read the early manuscript and gave me feedback: Mom, Dad, Jess and Dave, Laura (for countless drafts) and Martin, Molly and Mike, C and Hil, the Dykstras, Lance, and two of my youngest readers, Anna and Maren. Thank you all so much.

A shout-out also goes to the dark hallways of Mount Logan Middle School for inspiring me, and to the mysterious custodians who wandered those halls: Ray, Glenn, Mike, and Paige.

Of course, I owe a special thanks to my wonderful, patient wife, Connie, for supporting me along the road to publication.

And thanks to you, reader, for picking up this book! Now, grab your mop and get back to work. There are lots of Toxites out there, and someone's got to stop them!

Enjoy this sneak peek of
Book Two of *Janitors*

TYLER WHITESIDES

JANITORS

SECRETS OF NEW FOREST ACADEMY

COMING
FALL 2012

Visit www.tylerwhitesides.com

SHADOW
MOUNTAIN

CHAPTER I

"WE'VE GOT TROUBLE!"

Dez Rylie belched. It wasn't a long belch by his standards, but it was certainly enough to get him in trouble again. It would have been nothing new in Mrs. Natcher's classroom. But this was the library, a sanctuary of research and silence.

Well, usually. Today was different, and not just because it was a Friday.

"That's enough!"

Spencer blinked the sleepiness out of his eyes and shook his head. Had the librarian just shouted?

"It's over!" Sure enough, Mr. Fields, the balding librarian, was losing his cool. And rightfully so.

Spencer's sixth-grade classmates were behaving ridiculously. Several students were slouched hopelessly at the study tables, books abandoned and research topics forgotten. They stared at the librarian, lazily chewing gum like they didn't care a thing about consequences. Other kids wandered between bookshelves, laughing and smiling, happily distracted from their work. A few students were sound asleep, drooling on expensive library books.

"I'm not going to deal with this behavior anymore. Your teacher's coming to fetch you! Gather your things." He shooed the students with the backs of his hands.

Spencer used his knuckles to rub the sleepiness from his eyes. When he opened them again, he noticed that the seat next to him was empty. Where was Daisy? Spencer glanced around the library and spotted the girl a few bookshelves away. Daisy was on her hands and knees in front of the picture books—laughing.

Oh, no. Something was very wrong.

Spencer had fallen asleep during research and Daisy was hopelessly distracted. That could only mean one thing . . .

Spencer stood up, anxiously scanning the library for movement. Instinctively, his hand reached into his backpack to grip a small Ziploc bag of vacuum dust. Spencer turned a slow circle, eyes flicking from bookshelf to bookshelf. The students were showing all the signs—so where were the Toxites?

The library door opened, and the air seemed to grow old and stuffy with Mrs. Natcher's arrival. One look at her unruly class sent a new streak of gray through her tightly pinned hair bun.

"Class!" she called in her usual manner. "Class! You will be silent in three, two, one." Mrs. Natcher clapped her hands, but this usual method did little against the potent breath of the Toxites that pervaded the library.

Spencer yawned big enough to make his eyes water. Then, with blurry vision, he saw a flash of movement. Spencer blinked away the tears to see a pale, slimy creature leap from the History section and land on a nearby table. Half a dozen kids were staring in that direction, but the monster scuttled invisibly across their notebooks.

Spencer snapped the seal on his Ziploc bag and pinched out a bit of vacuum dust. If the creature turned toward him, Spencer would have to stop it, no matter how crazy he might look throwing vac dust at invisible monsters.

Across the table, Dez stood up, his backpack gaping open like a dirty mouth. Before Spencer could move, the yellow, lizard-like creature leapt into the backpack's dark opening. Dez casually picked up his notebook, the pages discolored and crinkly from an old apple juice spill, and dropped it into his pack. With another belch, he zipped his backpack and turned.

Of all the kids in the class, Dez was probably the least affected by Toxite breath. The rich brainwaves that the Toxites enjoyed didn't often come wafting out of Dez's head. The creatures mostly left him alone, saving their potent anti-learning breath for other, more sincere students. But, affected or not, Dez was about to unknowingly transport a Grime back to the classroom.

Dez was wandering halfheartedly toward the doorway where Mrs. Natcher stood with her nose turned up at her class. Spencer gritted his teeth and stepped into Dez's path, eyes locked on the big kid's backpack.

"What are you staring at, Doofus?" Dez asked. "Never seen a backpack before?"

Spencer glanced sideways at Daisy, but she was too far away and much too distracted to help. The slimy Grimes were toughest on Daisy. Their distracting breath didn't bother Spencer much at all, but seeing Daisy like that reminded him why he couldn't let Dez get past. If the backpack made it into Mrs. Natcher's classroom, then the Toxite would emerge. Spencer and Daisy had worked too hard to keep their classroom Toxite-free. And Dez was about to spoil it by giving this creature a free ride.

"Listen, Dez," Spencer said, "you've got to leave your backpack here."

"Huh?" Dez pulled a face. Then he narrowed his eyes. "You trying to steal from me? I'll break your fingers if you touch my Empty 3 Player."

"Your what?"

"My Empty 3 Player. Don't you ever listen to music?"

Spencer rolled his eyes. "This isn't about your *mp3*, Dez. Just leave your backpack here."

"Why don't you make me?" Dez smirked.

Spencer took a deep breath and gripped his vac dust even harder. He was losing time. Mrs. Natcher and the librarian were rounding up the students one by one. It wouldn't be long before they got to Dez.

Spencer stepped away, letting the bully think he'd won another fight. Dez threw back his head and started laughing.

It was an obnoxious, fake laugh, and Dez dragged it out so long that it lost any intimidation effect he might have been hoping for.

Just as Dez stepped forward, Spencer flicked his right hand, releasing the pinch of vacuum dust. With a sound like a suctioning vacuum, the backpack jerked out of Dez's hands and hit the floor.

"Hey!" Dez swung a fist, but Spencer jumped back and retreated across the library, fighting waves of Toxite fatigue along the way.

Dez stooped to retrieve his backpack. He pulled on the shoulder straps, but the backpack was suctioned tightly to the floor, rattling slightly.

"Huh?" Dez grunted and pulled harder.

A few bookshelves away, Spencer grabbed Daisy by the shoulders and yanked the girl to her feet. "We've got trouble, Daisy."

"Hi, Spencer!" Daisy said, like she was meeting him for the first time. "There's a really funny piece of carpet right here, did you see it?" She chuckled. "Oh, it makes me laugh."

"Snap out of it, Daisy! There are Toxites in here. Lots of them! I can't seem to find them, but they're affecting everyone."

Spencer glanced back at Dez. The bully had managed to get the backpack off the floor for a moment, but the suction pulled it down again.

"Dez has one in his backpack," Spencer said. "If we don't stop him, he'll take it back to the classroom!"

Daisy squinted. Spencer could tell she was fighting against the distracting Toxite breath. She glanced over at Dez. The sight of the bully with the backpack managed to break through her distractions.

"The suction won't last," Daisy said. "Maybe we could . . . Hey! What's that over there?"

Spencer's shoulders slumped as Daisy trundled away to inspect another patch of carpet. But there was no time to go after her. Mrs. Natcher was making a beeline right for the spot where Dez was thrashing with the backpack.

"Dezmond Rylie! What on earth are you doing to that poor backpack?" the teacher called.

Spencer backed against the wall, a sudden yawn overtaking him. Why not give up? He was out of options anyway. Why not lie down and take a rest? After all, he *was* exhausted.

Spencer leaned heavily against the wall. He was just sliding down to the comfort of the carpet when a gray lump fell from a bookshelf and landed in a quivering heap at his feet.

It was another Toxite: a Filth this time. This was the most dangerous type of Toxite for Spencer. Being close to the spiky dust gophers always made him sluggish and tired. But this particular Filth was suctioned to the floor, gopher teeth chattering and sharp quills clicking.

The Filth's breath was instantly stolen away by the puff of vacuum dust holding it down. But who had thrown the blast? The sleepiness vanished, and, with renewed energy,

Spencer looked up. Daisy stood a few feet away, a sandwich bag of vac dust in her hand.

"Get up, sleepyhead," Daisy said. Somehow she had managed to stave off the distracting Grime breath—at least momentarily. "We've got to stop Dez."

Spencer jumped up. Dez and Mrs. Natcher were conversing. At their feet, the backpack lay still. Spencer could tell that the suction had worn off. Any minute now, Dez would pick it up and take it back to infest the classroom.

How could Spencer possibly get Dez to leave his backpack in the library? Spencer leaned against the wall and felt the answer right at his fingertips.

"Careful," Daisy said. "That's the fire alarm."

Spencer nodded grimly. Then, with sweaty hands, he pulled down on the red handle.

ABOUT THE AUTHOR

TYLER WHITESIDES worked as a janitor at a middle school to put himself through college. It was there that he discovered the many secrets and mysteries that can be hidden in a dusty school. Tyler graduated from Utah State University with a degree in music. He enjoys spending time in the mountains, cooking on the barbecue, and vacuuming. Tyler lives in Logan, Utah, with his wife, Connie, a third-grade teacher. *Janitors* is his first novel.

PARKING
THE
MOOSE

PARKING
THE
MOOSE

ONE AMERICAN'S EPIC QUEST TO UNCOVER
HIS INCREDIBLE CANADIAN ROOTS

Dave Hill

ANCHOR CANADA

Library and Archives Canada Cataloguing in Publication

Title: Parking the moose / Dave Hill.
Names: Hill, Dave, 1974- author.
Identifiers: Canadiana 20190051469 | ISBN 9780385690065 (softcover)
Subjects: LCSH: Hill, Dave, 1974—Travel—Canada. | LCSH: Comedians—Travel—
Canada. | LCSH: Comedians—United States—Biography. | LCSH: National characteristics,
Canadian—Humor. | LCSH: Canada—Description and travel—Humor.
Classification: LCC PN2287.H498 A3 2020 | DDC 792.702/8092—dc23

Cover design: David Gee
Cover image: © jeff roques / Getty Images

Printed and bound in Canada

Published in Canada by Anchor Canada,
a division of Penguin Random House Canada Limited,
a Penguin Random House Company

www.penguinrandomhouse.ca

10 9 8 7 6 5 4 3 2

Penguin
Random House
ANCHOR CANADA

For my father, Robert W. Hill Sr., who isn't from Canada
but took me there twice, which is awesome.

Dedicated to the memories of my grandfather Clarence Vincent Blake Sr.,
who was from Canada, Bob Kato, who always wanted to live there,
and Trudy Stewart, my friend and Saskatchewan tour guide.

CONTENTS

"Canada—will we ever really understand it? Probably not. But one thing I can tell you for sure is that I, for one, intend to at least try."

—DAVE HILL, NOVEMBER 24, 2017

INTRODUCTION

A Brief Message to You, the Attractive Canadian Reader

THERE'S AN IDEA most of us Americans tend to learn when we are children. I'm guessing you've heard about it. It's that our country is the "greatest nation on Earth," the "land of the free and the home of the brave" and all that. We're spoon-fed the belief that absolutely no one outside of the United States could possibly have it as good as we do; not only that, but almost anywhere else on the planet, we'd probably be thrown in some damp, dimly lit, poorly decorated dungeon, flogged with an expired sausage and subjected to an endless round of mother jokes—or worse—for even thinking about enjoying life the way we do, each and every day, without even really trying. It's a notion that's reinforced in school, at home, on late-night TV commercials for used-car dealerships of exceptionally dubious integrity, and just about everywhere else until it's pretty much burned on the brain.

While it would seem most Americans swallow this idea whole, some never questioning it for even a nanosecond their whole lives, it never really took with me. You see, while I was born and raised in Cleveland, Ohio,* my grandfather was from Canada—Clinton, Ontario, to be exact. And practically every Sunday at dinner, he'd remind my siblings and me and anyone else within earshot that it

---

* The Paris of Northeastern Ohio. Ask anyone.

was not America, but Canada, this magical and mysterious land just across the mighty Lake Erie, that was, in fact, the best.

I can't remember what reasons my grandfather gave to back up his claim. He might not have even had any. But just saying that Canada was the best would have been enough, considering he was the patriarch and, therefore—according to general unwritten rules of the patriarchy at the time and/or unwritten rules regarding who gets to sit at the head of the table without a fight—was usually allowed to be right about everything. Regardless, I bought it hook, line and sinker. I suppose to my young mind it was just a package deal—if I loved my grandfather, then I must also love Canada and accept my grandfather's view that I'd been living in a relative shithole this whole time. Or maybe I just figured it was a surefire way to make it into his will. Either way, it wasn't long before I began to accept the reality that I was a guy living in a land that was both literally and figuratively beneath Canada. I bit my tongue as I said the Pledge of Allegiance before class each day in elementary school, and throughout my formative years I would mumble politely at best during the national anthem before sporting events.

The notion of Canadian superiority quickly spread throughout most areas of my young life. "Alex Trebek," I'd think as a child basking in the pale glow of the family room television set. "Now *there's* a guy who really gets it."

Similarly, while my peers kept busy with football, basketball, baseball and other decidedly inferior—and non-Canadian—sports, ice hockey became the only sport for me. I signed up to play in the local youth league and watched every game our local cable television provider dared to broadcast.* For me, Don Cherry's voice was the voice of God, and his sportcoats were totally reasonable. And my working knowledge of all the obscure Canadian towns my

---

* At the time, the American Midwest was a relative hockey wasteland compared to the east coast and whatever states bordered Canada, so broadcasting hockey games in that part of the country was pretty much ratings suicide.

favourite NHL players came from was impeccable. You could bring up Flin Flon, Manitoba, for example, and I wouldn't even flinch.

"You gotta love the Bombers' chances," I'd respond. It could have easily been considered a form of autism by modern medical standards.

It didn't end there, either.

Whenever bacon was served at home, I'd be sure to mention my preference for the far more delicious Canadian variety, which to the untrained American eye simply registered as a form of ham. Likewise, if a song by Triumph* came on the radio, I'd be the first to tell you to crank it as loud as it would go so I could feel the prog-tinged hard rock in my chest the way the almighty trio of Rik Emmett, Mike Levine and Gil Moore** had no doubt intended. And whenever the subject of health care was brought up, I was more vocal about the vast merits of the Canadian system than per-haps any other nine-year-old you'd ever want to meet. Okay, I'm lying about that last part, but hopefully you see my point—I was so into Canada that it was actually kind of weird.

All of this began to fade, however, when, sadly, my grandfather died shortly after my twelfth birthday, and I suddenly found myself with no real Canadian advocate in my life. Sure, there was a kid from outside of Toronto who had transferred into my elementary school around that same time, but seeing as how he wanted nothing more than to quietly blend in with all the other kids in suburban Cleveland, my attempts at engaging him in a conversation about,

---

* I know what you're thinking: "What about Rush, Dave?" But Rush was already huge in America and, as a result, no longer Canadian enough for my refined tastes.

** I suppose it is at this point that I should point out that, while Gil Moore is no slouch, I do prefer the Triumph numbers on which Rik Emmett handled lead vocals. Better to be clear on this now than to wait for the question to be innocently posed in the middle of a book tour Q&A—something I envision to be a mostly family-friendly event—and have a full-on brawl break out as the result of my potentially controversial stance on this power trio–based matter.

say, the goings-on in nearby Crotch Lake, Ontario, or the unseemly side of the southcentral-Quebec poutine industry, for example, were either met with resistance or ignored entirely. Before long, I became just like most other Americans and allowed myself to drift into a state of wilful Canadian ignorance. Suddenly, my grandfather's homeland, which I had until this point in my life considered to be a vast, culturally diverse, largely moose-friendly utopia only a few hours away by station wagon, was no longer something to be celebrated, but something to be feared or, perhaps even worse, dismissed altogether.

"After all," I figured, "we've already got Alan Thicke and Pamela Anderson down here—what the hell else could those Canucks possibly have left to offer?"

Over time, however, my Canadian roots could no longer be denied, slowly bubbling to the surface of my very being the way I'm guessing maple syrup does if you try to boil it or something. And questions also began to arise.

"Who are the Tragically Hip, and what exactly do they want from us?"

"What is curling—and, perhaps more importantly, *why* is curling?"

And, last but not least, "How could a country so close to the United States manage to be so very different from us?"

As I barrel into middle age, probably the last years of my life in which daily moisturizing will produce any results whatsoever, my desire to reconnect with my Canadian heritage and answer these and other distinctly Canadian questions only grows stronger. And, let's face it, if Canada and I are gonna dance, it should probably be now; because, in just a few short decades, a day trip to some sad casino outside of Niagara Falls with the other diapered and heavily medicated residents of whatever retirement facility I wind up getting dropped off at in the middle of the night might be as good as it gets. If I want to make things right with my grandfather's homeland, it's time to get cracking. And while, sure, it would be well within my rights as a typical American to just stick with the plan and remain blissfully unaware of the many nuances of your fair country until my death, don't I owe it to my grandfather to at least try to get some sense of what he was so proud of all those years ago around the dinner table—and, who knows, maybe even get to know who he was a little better in the process? I tend to think so.

I suppose, as long as we're on the topic, it might also worth be mentioning that, as I sit here writing this, there is a hate-spewing game show host in the White House, and the idea of living, you know, literally anywhere else on Earth but America grows with each passing tweet. I'd be lying if I said I wasn't one of the millions of Americans who, on the night of the 2016 US presidential election— in an effort fuelled both by a desire for self-preservation and Scotch—helped crash the website that tells you how to move to Canada. And while I promise you that the focus of this book won't be on how America is on fire and I and a lot of other Americans just think it might be nice to, you know, maybe take a little trip across your border and talk things out with you guys over a peameal bacon sandwich, a case of Molson and a carton or two of Canadian Classics, it would be impossible not to have the T-word creep into mind at least occasionally as I write. My apologies in advance.

Lest you be worried that things are definitely about to get a whole lot cozier up there, however, fear not—as much as I ask myself whether it might be the perfect time to move to Canada, this great land my grandfather wouldn't shut the hell up about, I'll try to ask myself (and whomever else might listen) how America, and perhaps even the rest of the world, might try to be at least a little more Canadian every once in a while. As best I can tell, it certainly couldn't hurt.

It suddenly occurs to me at this point that you might be wondering exactly who I am. I'm glad you asked. My name is Dave Hill and, as hinted at previously, I am an American person. I should probably also mention that I am a comedian, author, musician, actor and radio host, and that, together, all of these things have garnered me a measure of fame in the United States that has made it nearly impossible for me to walk down the street, shop for groceries or even stop off at the plasma donation centre without imagining that at least someone I encounter is probably wondering whether they have, in fact, seen me late, late at night on basic cable television, for a few seconds at one point or another. My fame in Canada, however, does not even begin to approach this level, which is exactly why I'm the perfect guy to write this book about your country. My Canadian anonymity (or "CA," as I shall refer to it in the pages that follow should it happen to come up again)* allows me to slip into your country almost completely undetected, just a regular guy with off-beat good looks, flawless hair and a light yet intriguing fragrance that keeps you coming back for more, going about his business like it's no big deal at all. Keep a-moving, everybody—nothing to see here.

Anyway, I guess what I'm trying to say that is what you are about to read is, from where I'm sitting, the definitive book on Canada written by a non-Canadian.** I have travelled your land extensively, rambling north, south and other directions as I drink in its endless wonders and, more importantly, see things in a way that you, the Canadian, will never, ever in a million, trillion years be able to, no matter how hard you try.

However, in case you're now under the impression that you can go ahead and set all your other books on Canada on fire, perhaps as part of some bizarre late-night ritual involving airy garments, wayward livestock and a complete disregard for the neighbours, I must stress that, while I certainly won't stop you from doing that—and, in fact, would very much like to be around for that sort of thing should you decide to do so—this book is by no means exhaustive, comprehensive or complete in its inquisition or analysis of your fine nation. In fact, if I'm being completely honest, when I agreed to write the thing, my publisher just gave me five hundred

---

* I don't think this is a spoiler or anything, but in rereading everything, I realize it actually doesn't, in case you were about to write a note in the margin or something reminding yourself what CA means.

** As far as citizenship goes, anyway. However, I maintain that I am, in fact, ¼ Canadian by blood and most certainly in my heart.

bucks (Canadian) in cash and told me to have at it. To my credit, however, I know how to stretch a dollar, so I have managed to cover a lot of ground, both literally and figuratively,* and in the pages that follow, I'll tell you as honestly as I can exactly what I have found.

And now, before you turn the page and dive right into what I am confident will be the greatest Canada-based literary thrill ride of your lifetime,** I'd like to get a couple last things out of the way.

While I realize that you are probably expecting me, as a typical American who grew up in the eighties, to come out guns blazing with all sorts of Bob and Doug McKenzie-isms in the very first chapter, I, as a proud quarter Canadian, am quite simply better than that. I am also well aware that—despite the fact that those guys are awesome, hilarious and exactly what the typical American assumes you guys are all exactly like, 24/7—you are probably as sick of all that as I am of hearing people quote the "Hello, Cleveland" line from *This Is Spinal Tap* at this point. So, fear not—while there will be plenty of name-calling in the pages that follow, *hoser* will not be among them (very much).***

Furthermore, while my original plan for this book was to simply wax philosophical about why Canadians say "sorry" (pronounced— well, you know) all the time until I hit my contractually agreed-upon word count and call it a day, I realize you guys have probably had it

---

* I suppose I should also mention that, while my original plan was to just hop on a motorcycle, or maybe into the back of a windowless cargo van driven by a man with time on his hands and a penchant for mischief, and explore Canada in one long and rambling adventure that would have made Kerouac look like a shut-in, my dog would have killed me, so instead, I broke my ongoing Canadian exploration into several short trips that had me passing in and out of the Toronto airport more often than Geddy Lee. I need you to be cool with this.

** And anyone else's, the more I sit here thinking about it.

*** Also, if I were to start quoting a Canadian TV show, it would be *Letterkenny*, one of Canada's other great exports.

with that by now, too. Also, as best I can tell, Canadians say "sorry" kind of like us Americans say "excuse me"—sure, on the rare occasion, it can actually be used as an apology, but more often, it seems to be used to convey all sorts of other things, even something along the lines of "fuck you" if you say it just right.*

And finally, I realize that you, and perhaps even other readers of this book, may not, in fact, be even slightly Canadian and are now paralyzed with the fear that what follows is simply not for your eyes. Rest assured, however, that I have been careful to write this book in a manner in which any and all connoisseurs of fine literature, regardless of their nationality or geographical coordinates, will be able to enjoy again and again until their sudden and mysterious death.

And with that, I now ask you to kindly turn the page.

I stand on guard for thee,
Dave Hill

---

* Especially if you're in Toronto. Am I right or am I right? Who's with me? What's with those pricks, anyway?

TORONTO, ONTARIO

Hard Lessons in the Big Smoke

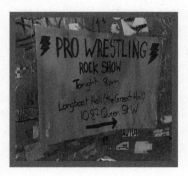

I HAVE TO admit, the idea of attacking Canada* for the purposes of this book was a bit daunting. For starters, it's much bigger than anyone expected. And I'll bet even Justin Trudeau himself would struggle to tell you with any certainty where it ends and whatever is above Canada begins. Furthermore, I'm embarrassed to admit that, while I've visited roughly two dozen countries in my time on Earth, some of them again and again, I had somehow only managed to make it to Canada a handful of times prior to the beginning of my research on this book—a sad reality, considering the fact that I swear you can see it from the shores of my native Cleveland, despite a lot of people telling me I was actually just staring at a breakwall at the time.

Making matters even worse, as I prepared for the first of my expeditions to Canada as a guy about to write what I consider to be

---

* Not literally, of course. You are under almost no real threat from me as of this writing.

a reasonably thick book about it, it occurred to me just how little of your country's history I actually knew—which is to say I knew pretty much nothing. With America, it's easy—a bunch of English people got tired of being told how to practise their religion and decided to come over here, where they then killed a bunch of Native Americans so they'd eventually have enough room for their above-ground swimming pools, vape shops and other indisputable must-haves, and now, just a few hundred years later, we have a Cheeto-hued president who won the office on a platform of, among other things, giving people a hard time about how they practise their religion.

The story of Canada, however, is far more complicated. For example, did you know that the first attempt by Europeans to colonize Canada dates back to around 1000 AD, when Norsemen settled at a place called L'Anse aux Meadows in Newfoundland? And that it took another nine hundred years or so for Canadian reggae-tinged rapper Snow to unlease his "Informer" single on an unsuspecting public?* I know—I couldn't believe it, either. And, needless to say, a lot of stuff happened in between and since.

But before I could dive into any of that, I had other business to attend to, so I scheduled a trip to Toronto. I know what you're thinking—going to Toronto in an effort to learn about Canada is a little obvious or "on the nose,"** and I couldn't agree more. In fact, if you ask the average American to name a Canadian city,***

---

* And now, a quarter century later, we are not one bit closer to understanding what the song's most prominent lyric—"a licky boom boom down"— might possibly mean. However, please know that my inevitable follow-up to this book will tackle the subject head on and talk about little else.

** Or is it? In my tireless research for this book, I have learned that nearly half of Toronto's population was not born in Canada—which, of course, begs the question: Is Toronto, in fact, Canada's least Canadian city? Signs point to yes.

*** A popular American parlour game.

he or she will say Toronto nine times out of ten,* so to just hop on a plane bound for "Tdot" might seem just plain lazy to you, the Canadian reader, who can probably name eight or ten other Canadian cities without even really trying. And while I would have preferred to kick things off in, say, Moose Jaw, Saskatchewan, Medicine Hat, Alberta, or perhaps even Dildo, Newfoundland,** the fact is that my publisher is located in Toronto. And since it was my aim to write the definitive book about Canada by a non-Canadian, to show up and knock back a few cold ones with them on their home turf was my way of letting them know I meant business.

To be fair, I was no stranger to Toronto. In fact, most the times I had previously visited Canada, it was to go to Toronto. I've played in bands at the legendary El Mocambo rock club a few times, attended the Toronto International Film Festival twice, and have eaten at Gretzky's*** at least once more than anyone living independently probably should.

My first visit to Toronto, however, was with my family—all nine of us crammed into the family station wagon, Canadian grandfather included—in the late seventies, a simpler time for everyone. I could be getting this wrong, but as I recall, we were going as some sort of reward to my grandfather for putting up with our American bullshit for so long. This would be his chance to return to his roots and go fully feral as far as being Canadian was concerned, if only for a couple of days. We were all pretty pumped

---

* Montreal and Vancouver are also popular answers. I, of course, always say Regina, Saskatchewan. But that's because I realize that, when pronounced correctly, that answer is funny every single time, and always will be, and no one will ever change my mind about this in a million, trillion years.

** Okay, *especially* Dildo, Newfoundland.

*** The popular, family-friendly Wayne Gretzky–themed restaurant where, if you like eating nachos while surrounded by old hockey equipment, you have just hit a street called Easy.

about the trip, but especially him—so much, in fact, that as soon as we crossed the border into Ontario on the drive in, my grandfather began frantically waving and yelling "Hello!" out the car window to whoever had the misfortune of just so happening to be walking down the street, minding his or her own Canadian business, as we pulled into your country.

"Stop it, Clare!"* my grandmother yelled at him as she did her best to disappear in the back seat, which admittedly wasn't that hard since, this being the 1970s and all, our station wagon was more like a hearse with benches. "They're gonna think you're some kind of weirdo."

"They're Canadian, Bernie,"** my grandfather replied. "It would be weird if I *didn't* say hello." Then he went back to waving and yelling some more. For what it's worth, at least a couple people did manage a faint wave back at him, so I guess he won that round.

The only other thing I remember is that, at some point, my grandfather ditched my entire family to go knock back a few at the bar in the CN Tower, an episode that was significant in that it it showed me at an early age that good times were yours for the taking in Canada if you just set your mind to it. I tried to remember that as my girlfriend and I flew into town one Friday afternoon in

---

* My grandfather's name was Clarence Blake, but he was known to my grandmother and others of his generation as Clare. And as long as we're on the topic, my middle name is also Clare, partly in tribute to my grandfather, but also because the majority of my Irish ancestors were from County Clare, so my parents figured they'd kill two birds with one stone. On the rare occasion that anyone asks, however, I usually tell them my middle name is Clarence. It makes it sound like I've got a better chance of winning a fight, or perhaps help you install that new deck, than Clare does.

** My grandmother's given name was actually Agnes, but for some reason or another she was known to most as Bernie, short for Bernadette, her middle name.

May on an Air Canada flight from LaGuardia to Toronto Pearson International Airport.*

It wasn't my plan to bring my girlfriend on all of my upcoming trips to Canada, but since I knew this one probably wouldn't involve dogsledding, knuckle hopping with Inuit, listening to that one song by Len,** or any of the other awesome Canadian stuff I planned to get up to on the regular on future visits, I figured it was probably safe enough to drag her along this time.

I was already getting excited about things before the plane had even left the tarmac. Not only had the TSA agent at LaGuardia insisted upon a pat-down of my jeans that made me feel dangerous, but the concession stand near our gate sold Canadian beer for those of us who could not wait to quite literally begin drinking in the wonders of the True North any longer. Also, I'd never flown on Air Canada—or, for that matter, any Canadian airline—before, and the fact that the announcements were all given in both English *and* French was thrilling. At first.

"Again with the French!" I thought, cursing the entire province of Quebec after about the third or fourth time the flight attendant came over the PA system to blather on and on in two different languages. "*Assez!*"***

---

* As a Canadian, you are probably already required by law to know this, but the popular Canadian rock band Rush (or simply "Rush," as they are known to Canadians) wrote an instrumental track called "YYZ," named after the airport code for Toronto Pearson International Airport. How many airports have a song by a Canadian progressive rock trio named after them? Not many, I bet. Also, as that sort of thing goes, I would argue "YYZ" is the best one.

** I realize, of course, that the Toronto-based brother-sister alternative rock duo Len indeed had many wonderful songs, but in this case I am referring to their international hit "Steal My Sunshine," perhaps one of the catchiest songs of all time, and if you disagree, we both know you're lying, and that's just sad.

*** Please note that while I do find it annoying to hear English announcements repeated in French over and over again, the fact that all Canadian products have everything printed on them in both English and French is something I don't think I'll ever tire of. It just looks cooler, and everyone knows it.

Still, I had bigger fish to fry—a fish called the Entire Nation of Canada, so I tried not to let it get to me too much.

I had arranged for us to stay at an Airbnb apartment in Queen West, an area of Toronto that internet research had suggested was "hip," which I usually find is code for "you can buy mid-century modern furniture there." We took a cab from the airport and, as I was a guy looking to reconnect with my roots in this magical land to the north where, just ninety or so years earlier, my grandfather had apparently woken up one day and thought, "Screw it—I'm moving to Cleveland," I tried to be on the lookout for any and all Canadianness that might come my way at any given moment. It was admittedly hard to pick up on at first, but I knew if I was patient, I would be rewarded tenfold.

A short, rainy drive later, we arrived at the Drake Hotel, where my editors Tim and Scott had already begun toasting what would eventually become the very pages you hold in your hand right now.

"An important thing to know about Toronto is that the rest of Canada absolutely hates it," Scott told me as I began grilling them both on all matters Canadian over a pint of Mill Street beer.* "Even more than non–New Yorkers hate New York."

Having lived in New York for the past fourteen years, I kind of understood what he meant, but I was also a bit confused. After all, what's not to like about Toronto? Everyone seems really friendly, Anne Murray is from there and, as mentioned just a few short paragraphs ago, hockey's Wayne Gretzky** has his very own restaurant right there in town.***

---

* As part of my research, I tried to only drink beverages made in Canada. It's a commitment, but not a hard one because, let's face it, your beer is better than the American stuff, something I mention both to curry favour and also because it's true.

** Or simply "Wayne Gretzky," as he is known to the Canadian people.

*** Did I mention that, at Gretzky's, there is a hamburger called the 99 Burger that has Gretzky's jersey number branded into the bun? I've been called "easily entertained" before, but I still think that's pretty awesome.

"Why do they hate Toronto?" I asked. "It seems great here."

"They just do," Scott said. "They just do."

It was then that I declared it my mission over the next forty-eight hours to figure out exactly what was so awful about Toronto, a city I'd associated up until this point with nothing but good times and a surprising variety of condiment options when it came time to buy a hot dog on the street.*

With that in mind, I excused myself to go to the restroom just long enough for Scott and Tim to pick up the tab, after which my girlfriend and I headed over to my friend Gregg's restaurant, the Ace, over on Roncesvalles Avenue, a street whose name I struggle to pronounce. Gregg is actually from New Jersey, but had ditched America for Toronto without warning a decade earlier.** I hadn't seen him since, and hoped to reconnect and get some further insight into Canada and why he decided to move there. But despite—or perhaps because of—all this, Gregg ended up leaving town at the last minute, which left me with no choice but try to get to the bottom of things myself.

"Gregg sent me," I told the waitress as soon as we walked through the door. She was impressed to the point of remaining largely speechless and gave us a table.

As for the Ace itself, it's a former diner turned cozy, candlelit bistro where—in my experience, anyway—your friend Gregg will end up paying for all your drinks by way of a text message to your waitress if you just keeping bringing up the fact that you're Gregg's friend and you can't believe he left town the one time you came to visit him, even though you haven't seen each other in over ten years. I can't recommend it enough.

As my girlfriend and I sat there, knocking back those delicious free drinks, however, it occurred to us that—at least so far, anyway—Toronto didn't seem that different from America at all.

---

* For example, corn. Who knew?

** To be fair, he probably did tell some people, the more I think about it.

"It kind of feels like we're in Brooklyn right now," my girlfriend said as she looked around the room at the assorted tattooed and bearded patrons knocking back drinks with presumably at least one unexpected ingredient.

"Maybe *that's* why everyone else in Canada hates Toronto," I replied. "You know, because it's awesome like New York."

We really weren't sure. Either way, we decided to hit the town with guns blazing the next day in hopes of discovering both what makes Toronto distinctly Canadian and why the nearly thirty million other people living in Canada think it sucks so much.

Back at our apartment that night, we were woken shortly after 1 a.m. by the sound of a party going on down the hall, where techno music and the annoying, presumably drunken screams of the kind of people who listen to techno music could be heard so loudly through our bedroom wall, I would have sworn the bash was at our place.

"Oh no," my girlfriend moaned. "Canada has assholes, too."

I didn't see it coming, either—at least, not the techno part. Sure, April Wine or Chilliwack, maybe, but not techno—that's some next-level bullshit, the kind of crap that would happen in America or something.

Despite having had our sleep interrupted by Canadian revelry, we managed an early start exploring the city the next day. To be fair, Queen West wasn't that much different than a residential neighbourhood in any other major city in the Western world, full of adorable cafés, boutiques hawking throw pillows with something or another reasonably clever stitched onto them, and the occasional drifter. But what caught our attention more than any of those things was a crude, fluorescent-pink cardboard sign tacked to a telephone pole that advertised both "pro wrestling" and a "rock show" happening that night—preferably simultaneously, as far as we were concerned—just down the street from where we were staying. We couldn't believe our good fortune.

"Two of our favourite things, together at last," I said while pointing frantically at the sign.

I took my girlfriend's silence to mean that she was just as excited about the combination wrestling match/rock show that we would definitely, without question be attending together later that night as I was. It almost seemed too good to be true. In fact, as anyone who knows me will tell you, if you were planning some sort of sting operation designed to lure me in without any resistance whatsoever, this would be exactly the way to do it. The challenge now, of course, would be to make the time between then and the wrestling match/rock show go as quickly as possible.

We walked farther down the block and discovered a Rolling Stones–themed establishment called Stones Place.* I had a great idea to walk in and order something they couldn't possibly have on the menu—like circus peanuts or thumb tacks, maybe—and then, when the bartender said they didn't have that there, I'd respond with a humorous line about how "you can't always get what you want" at Stones Place. Since it was still morning and the place was closed, though, we continued on, and I just assumed I'd figure out some other way to brighten someone's day later on.

A couple blocks later, we stumbled upon a shop that sold vintage clothes and other random knick-knackery. I took the fact that a giant poster of Rush, at the peak of their powers, was prominently displayed near the entrance as a good and very Canadian omen. And I wasn't wrong, either; moments later, I found a satin Montreal Canadiens jacket, priced to move at just thirty-five dollars (Canadian).** It was my size and everything.

---

* I did some research and learned that the owner of the place just so happens to be named Stone. So while, on the face of it, there are arguably way better names for Rolling Stones–themed bars than this one, in this particular case, they've really nailed it.

** As my friend the Canadian musician and author Paul Myers later pointed out to me when I showed him my cool new purchase, perhaps the reason the Canadiens jacket was so cheap was that we were in Toronto, home of the Maple Leafs, of course. I was embarrassed my detective skills hadn't kicked in to help me figure that one out for myself.

"Check it out!" I called out to my girlfriend on the other side of the store as I modelled the jacket. "Now no one will know I'm not from here."*

I couldn't part with your weirdly see-through money fast enough. And while I definitely would have worn—and maybe even slept in— my new Canadiens jacket for the rest of the trip under most other circumstances, between the fact that it was nearly 70 degrees** outside and my not wanting to run into any friction with whatever Toronto Maple Leafs–loving street toughs might have been prowling the area, I ended up dropping it back at the apartment before we continued on our Canadian mission.

Our next stop was the Hockey Hall of Fame, a place I'd been twice before already, but I told my girlfriend I'd never been for fear that she might say twice is enough, which it definitely isn't. There's not a lot to say about the Hockey Hall of Fame, other than it's perfect to me, and if it were big enough to consume all of Ontario, I would still suggest adding a couple more rooms of whatever hockey jerseys and equipment you could find. Also, the fact that the guy charging people to take their picture in front of the Stanley Cup would also happily agree to take their picture with their phone for free instead might be the most Canadian thing I have seen thus far. In America, he would have already been sent to jail, released and be starring in his own reality show by now.

With the Hockey Hall of Fame out of my system for this trip, next up was Kensington Market. My friend, the comedian and Toronto resident Nick Flanagan, told me it would be a good place to go, both for fun times and to observe the people of Toronto in their natural habitat. There I had hoped to stumble upon some distinctly Canadian happening, like a log-rolling contest, or maybe even Randy Bachman buying maple syrup–scented candles. But while it was an absolutely pleasant excursion, it just wasn't to be. I did buy a pair of sunglasses on the street after the old Chinese lady selling them managed to convince me they made me look "really

---

* Except for everybody, my friend Paul Myers seemed to be pointing out.

** Roughly 21 degrees Celsius.

cool." I figured they'd come in handy when I was rocking out and watching pro wrestling at the exact same time later that night.

"Whaddya think?" I asked my girlfriend as I modelled them in the afternoon sun.

"It's probably too late to return them," she replied, giving me that extra vote of confidence I was looking for.

Reasonably satisfied with our Kensington Market experience, my girlfriend and I headed back to Queen West to plot our next move and rest up a bit for the hot Canadian night ahead. On the recommendation of my editor Scott, we decided to have an early dinner at a place called Boralia, not far from where we were staying.

According to its website, Boralia "celebrates the historic origins of Canadian cuisine," a phrase that reminded me of a night out in Chicago I'd had way back in the nineties. A friend of a friend told us she knew a great place for late-night Saskatchewan food.

"That sounds amazing," I told her. "What kind of dishes do they serve?"

"I think it's like Chinese food," she explained.

I was admittedly confused, but also thrilled at the prospect of what I imagined would be burly lumberjacks serving platters of chicken with broccoli and shrimp lo mein to our hammered party of seven. After further prodding, however, it was discovered that my friend's friend was simply mispronouncing the word *Szechuan*, and we wouldn't be sampling the weirdly Chinese delicacies of Saskatoon after all. My point, of course, is that the wonders of Canadian food and drink* remained largely a mystery to me, and I was hoping all of that was about to change.

---

* The one exception is the Bloody Caesar, which I was introduced to on that same trip to Toronto back in the nineties. If you're a Canadian who enjoys a drink from time to time, you definitely already know this, but the Bloody Caesar is like a Bloody Mary except that it incorporates Clamato (tomato juice and clam juice—together at last!) instead of just regular, bullshitty tomato juice, and the rim of the glass is dipped in celery salt instead of being left bare like some goddamn animal might. In my expert opinion, if, God forbid, the Bloody Caesar and Bloody Mary were to wind up in a maximum-security correctional facility together, the Bloody Mary would unquestionably be the Bloody Caesar's bitch. Well done, Canada!

We arrived at Boralia right when it opened for dinner at 5:30 p.m. and were promptly seated in a booth.

"Have you dined with us before?" our waitress asked.

"No," I explained. "We're visiting from America."

I'm not sure why I instantly went against my secret plan of trying to blend in as much as possible while in Canada, but seeing as how we were the only two customers in the place at this early hour, it was a safe bet we wouldn't be running into any other native Clevelanders there, so I guess I just let my guard down.

"Can you recommend any distinctly Canadian dishes we might try?" I asked her, no doubt sounding like someone who had just studied one of those Canadian-as-a-second-language books I am confident exists.

The waitress explained that it was noted on the menu which dishes were "distinctly Canadian dishes" (my words, not hers, as much as I hoped she would start calling them that too). And while the food we ended up having was absolutely delicious, it seemed more modern and artisanal, and not what I imagined my grandfather, for example, might have dined on all those years ago, when he and his family of ten all lived together in a tiny little barn in Ontario—much less what a tired lumberjack might help himself to a plate of after a long night of serving up Chinese food to famished drunkards in Saskatchewan.

We had a little time to kill before the awesome professional wrestling match/rock show we'd definitely be attending later, so we stopped off at a bar called Sweaty Betty's, another recommendation from my buddy Nick. I didn't expect to gain much Canadian insight while we were there, because at first it just seemed like a typical New York hipster bar. But as my girlfriend and I sat there, nursing our drinks, we began to notice something peculiar: every few minutes or so, a handful of millennial types would wander in, order shots, knock them back and immediately walk out the door.

"Is this a Canadian thing?" my girlfriend wondered aloud after the third or fourth group of party people came and went, at least slightly drunker than when they had arrived.

"I'm not sure," I replied. "But definitely watch where you step on the sidewalk when we leave."

I thought to ask the bartender about the mysterious shot-and-leave manoeuvre, but she was one of those tattooed, stern-looking rock 'n' roll types, the kind of girl who works at a place called Sweaty Betty's, and I've never had the gumption to look bartenders like that in the eye, with my soft, soft skin and all.

Speaking of feeling inadequate, another distinctly Canadian drinking hazard I discovered at Sweaty Betty's was the fact that you guys have one-dollar and two-dollar coins, neither of which is possible to leave as a tip with any sort of dramatic effect, even if left together, which I'm told would be quite the power move.

"Check me out," I'd hoped the look on my face would suggest as I laid a coin down on the bar. "Look who's laying down an extra dollar for you like it's no big deal at all; like I've done it before and I'll do it again because I have."

But it was dark and loud and the bartender I was terrified of didn't notice, so I found myself pulling the tip back toward me like one of those old monkey coin banks and then pushing it forward, over and over again, in hopes of, at long last, making some sort of connection with a girl who just couldn't be reached.

Sufficiently drunk both to really enjoy myself and be pretty sure I was really fun to be around, it was finally time to head on over to the main event. The professional wrestling/rock show was just a few blocks away, so we sprinted over to the building at the address listed on the cardboard sign we'd seen earlier. As we walked in, we noticed women in fancy gowns and men in tailored suits milling around, seemingly well into their evening of fun. The sounds of a live jazz band could be heard coming down from the floor above. We began ascending the stairs and, after just a few steps, an official-looking woman in a pantsuit suddenly appeared on the landing.

"I'm sorry—this is a private event," she said to us, looking us up and down in our casual attire, the kind one might wear to a combination wrestling match and rock show, for example.

"But we're here for the combination wrestling match and rock show," I told her, hoping to clear up what was obviously some sort of misunderstanding.

"We're having a *wedding* here right now," she replied, clearly annoyed and not nearly as excited about the prospect of rock music and wrestling happening at the same time as I was.

"Okay, we'll come back," I said. "What time does the wrestling match/rock show start?"

"There *isn't* one," she responded.

Then she looked at me like I was the crazy one, even though I had seen a handwritten cardboard sign advertising a combination rock show/wrestling match happening at this very address and had the pictures to prove it. Who knows—maybe it was a sting operation after all.

Dejected, we called it an early night, headed back to the apartment and hoped our neighbours had gotten the techno out of their systems as we drifted into slumber.

As for the next day, as luck would have it, the Toronto Blue Jays were scheduled to play the Texas Rangers that afternoon. And while I am well aware of the irony of trying to have a uniquely Canadian experience by attending a Major League Baseball game, my girlfriend and I decided to head over to the Rogers Centre to see if we might score tickets to the game anyway. So there.

By the time we got to the stadium, it was already swarming with Blue Jays fans, most of whom wore team jerseys and assorted other Blue Jays paraphernalia, our favourite of which by a mile* was a blue T-shirt with I LOVE B.J.'s printed across the chest. I couldn't stop giggling. And I wondered how it had never, in all these years, occurred to me that the Blue Jays' initials were so endlessly entertaining. There it was, hiding in plain sight. I kicked myself for having never thought of it myself. And I felt happy for whoever *had* thought of it and had the good sense to print up T-shirts that will never not be funny, no matter how many times I see them, or how old I get.

---

* 1.609344 kilometres.

"We *have* to get a couple of those T-shirts!" I said to my girlfriend while pointing at a guy who understandably seemed pretty pleased with himself for wearing his that day.

"*You* can get one," my girlfriend replied.

"But it says I LOVE B.J.'S," I said, barely able to contain myself. "Don't you get it?"

"Yeah, I get it," my girlfriend said, growing weirdly impatient. "Now let's get some tickets before it sells out."

In the end, we were able to snag a couple tickets on the upper level along the third base line. Since the weather was nice that day, the retractable roof of Rogers Centre remained open, which was a bonus.

As soon as we got inside, I grabbed a beer and went in search of a souvenir stand so I could enjoy the game to its fullest in what I'm confident is the greatest T-shirt in Major League Baseball history. Still, I looked high and low, stopping off at pretty much every souvenir stand in the place, only to discover that not a single one of them sold I LOVE B.J.'S shirts.

"Yeah, we don't have those for sale inside the stadium," the lady at the very last souvenir stand I tried told me with a look on her face that suggested she was tired of having to explain this to guys just like me at every single home game.

"Why?" I asked. "Do you hate money or something?"

The lady just kind of looked at me after that, and my girlfriend ended up buying a not-nearly-as-entertaining Blue Jays shirt, seemingly in an attempt to smooth things over. Slightly deflated, we decided to go find our seats and check out the game.

As it turned out, the Texas Rangers had managed to score a run and were up 1–0 already.

"Go, Blue Jays!" my girlfriend screamed, trying to fit in as we settled into our seats.

"Fuck you, Texas!" I screamed, just doing my part.

"No foul language," my girlfriend said, elbowing me.

To me, it just stood to reason that baseball fans who walk around wearing T-shirts that make reference to "B.J.'s" could probably handle an F-bomb or two from a guy who just wants their team to win at least half as much they do. But between my girlfriend being upset with me and the increasingly uncomfortable-looking family of four seated directly in front of us, I tried to keep things PG-13 at worst for the rest of the game.

Having had my profanity wings clipped, things got boring pretty quickly in our seats, since neither my girlfriend nor I is admittedly that into baseball, aside from it being a fun thing to have happening in front of you while drinking, so after an inning or two, we figured we'd stretch our legs a bit and see what other kinds of action might be available at Rogers Centre. Along the way, we found a crowded, standing-room-only area on the upper level. It was there that my girlfriend spotted a group of guys decked out in Cleveland Indians attire.

"Cleveland!" my girlfriend squealed before making a beeline for them.

As for me, I stayed put while a guy in a Blue Jays jersey who seemed to be easily the drunkest guy in the entire stadium—and perhaps even in Major League Baseball—entertained everyone around him, myself included, by flailing around indiscriminately and occasionally making high-pitched noises in a manner that suggested support for the Blue Jays organization. A few minutes later, my girlfriend reappeared.

"Those guys are from Cleveland," she excitedly informed me.

"Oh," I replied.

"I told them we're from Cleveland too," she said. "You should say hi!"

"Why would I want to do that?" I asked.

"Because they're from Cleveland and we're from Cleveland and we're all in Toronto," she replied.

"Who cares?" I said as I turned my attention back to the guy making high-pitched noises as though he thought it might directly affect the Blue Jays' chances of making it to the World Series.

My girlfriend seemed kind of annoyed with me at this point, but my whole plan while researching this book was to try and blend in, to appear to the average Canadian person that I was totally one of them, not some yokel who wasn't even from Canada and, worse, spent his time at Rogers Centre trying to bond with whatever other non-Canadian yokels managed to slip past security. Plus, the feeling I was getting from pretending we were the only two people out of the 46,188* people in attendance not from the Greater Toronto Area was nothing short of intoxicating.

After the Rangers managed to get a couple more runs, my girlfriend and I decided to continue exploring the place. As we walked along the upper level, it appeared that we had suddenly hit the jackpot in terms of fun at Rogers Centre. There, just outside of the restrooms, was an exceptionally large Blue Jays logo, in front of which what appeared to be families were taking turns getting their photos taken to, I guess, commemorate the time they went to see the Blue Jays square off against the Rangers at Rogers Centre on the exact same day that intrepid American journalist Dave Hill happened to be in attendance.

As you can probably imagine, the line to get your picture taken in front of the exceptionally large Blue Jays logo was pretty long because yeah, right, like you're not gonna get your picture in front of a giant blue jay should the opportunity arise, but my girlfriend and I wasted no time joining it.

"I can't wait to get our picture taken in front of that giant Blue Jays logo," I told her. "It's gonna be awesome."

"Yeah," she said, though it was hard to say whether she really meant it.

After what felt like an eternity, my girlfriend and I had advanced far enough in the line to get to the point where the picture-taking people expect you to fork over some cash for the privilege.

"How much to get our picture taken in front of the exceptionally large Blue Jay?" I asked the lady who looked like she was in charge.

"I'm sorry, sir," she said, frowning in that way one sometimes does when delivering bad news to a wide-eyed grown man. "This is just for children."

---

* I checked.

"What if you're in your forties?" I asked her.

"Then you have to have a child with you to get your picture taken," she explained.

I took a look around the general area to see if there might be any children looking to make a quick buck before deciding I should probably abandon that idea for all sorts of reasons. Then I just turned back to the lady and told her how I didn't have legal access to a child that day.

"Then I'm sorry—you can't get your picture taken," she replied before trying to make eye contact with the father and son standing behind us.

As the father and son awkwardly stepped around the two of us, I thought once more about that thing my editor Scott had said about how everyone else in Canada hates Toronto.

And it was in that moment that I totally, totally got it.

2

CLINTON, ONTARIO

Farm Living

MY GRANDFATHER'S NAME was Clarence Vincent Blake Sr. He was a husband to my grandmother Agnes Blake, a father to my mother, Bernadette, and her five siblings, and a grandfather to me, my four siblings and my eleven cousins. He was also a haberdasher and the undisputed* menswear authority of the east side of Cleveland. His specialty was golf attire, and to prove it, I have more than one photo of him and golf legend Jack Nicklaus at least pretending to be really excited about a pile of golf sweaters.

"My job will always be secure," my grandfather supposedly once told my dad, "because no matter what happens with the economy, people will always need clothes to wear golfing."

It was flawed logic, perhaps, but it's hard not to admire the winning attitude. And for what it's worth, I still have a couple of those sweaters, and they are really, really nice—stylish, breathable,

---

* At least I never heard anyone dispute it. Then again, he died when I was twelve, and who would argue about that sort of thing in front of a child?

the whole deal. And I say that as a guy who doesn't even own clubs.

Before any of the above, however, my grandfather was a guy from Clinton, Ontario, the town where his grandparents Timothy Blake and Ellen Leydan settled after emigrating from Ireland to Canada with their sons, Thomas and Richard (my great-grandfather), around 1850, shortly before Canada was founded in 1867, a date I just looked up on the internet. I'm still not entirely sure how or why my great-great-grandparents wound up in Canada instead of, say, simply making a beeline for the glitz and glamour of nearby Cleveland, Ohio, the city where my grandfather would eventually wind up in the first half of the twentieth century after a brief stint in Detroit, get into the golf sweater game and start a family. I'd heard it said that any Irish with a criminal record, a penchant for mischief or even just a mild case of resting bitch face would, when trying to gain entry into the United States in the 1800s, be automatically shipped up north to Canada instead to have a good, hard think about what they'd done. And while I'm not exactly sure which, if any, of these categories my great-great-grandparents might have fit into, for whatever reason, they found themselves together in Clinton many years ago, eager to start a new life for themselves as homesteaders in this mysterious new land that would eventually give birth to the snowblower,* Bachman-Turner Overdrive,** the wildly popular board game Trivial Pursuit*** and a bunch of other stuff I will do my best to mention at least once in the pages that follow.

As the story goes, Timothy and Ellen were given a few acres of land by the Canadian government and were told to have at it. And have at it they did, working the soil and raising a family in a

---

* Invented in Quebec in 1927 by Arthur Sicard, a man who clearly knew a good time when he saw it.

** Formed in 1973 after Randy Bachman left the Guess Who in an effort to let all of us know that we, in fact, had not seen anything yet.

*** Invented in Quebec in 1979 by a photographer named Chris Haney, who, after discovering pieces of his Scrabble game were missing, apparently just said, "Screw it!" and decided to come up with a whole new game altogether.

tiny farmhouse no bigger than an unfathomably large postage stamp. Their son Richard later inherited the farm, continued to work the land and—faced with the kind of downtime that was common in that pre–basic cable and internet age—also went on to raise a daughter and eight sons (including my grandfather Clarence Blake) with his wife, Catherine Phelan, a big city girl* seventeen years his junior, who was born in Toronto in 1857.

By all accounts, it was hard living in those days. One winter, my grandfather's brother Frank just up and died without warning. It is an incident that, as best I can tell, is still chalked up after all these years to just the cost of doing business at the time.

By the turn of the twentieth century, however, the Blakes found their groove, handed the tiny farmhouse over to the chickens and built themselves a much bigger home elsewhere on their land. While farming remained the family business, one year during his teens, my grandfather and two of his brothers had bigger ideas and decided to ship off to Winnipeg to work for a few years at a shirt factory, a metaphor for something that will likely occur to me a few pages from now, when it's too late for either of us to turn back.

I'm not sure what would inspire a teenage boy to move to a whole other province to work in a shirt factory, but the important thing is that, as a result, my grandfather learned the ins and outs of what makes for a quality garment, the kind that you can even one day talk a six-time Masters Tournament champion into wearing. In fact, as I sit here, it's hard not to wish my grandfather could see me now, and maybe even rifle through my closets, to see the man that I've become, one who owns all sorts of nice shirts—and you can ask anyone.

"Quality fabric, flawless stitching, unfused collars—these shirts really do have it all," my grandfather would say, clutching a few at once by their sleeves. "I'm proud of you."

---

* I can't say for sure whether Catherine was literally big. However, I was delighted to hear from my uncle Joe that his father once told a story about Catherine's aunt telling her, "Eat up, Catherine, or Richard will think you are delicate," a line Morrissey would have no doubt killed to have written.

Anyway, I had heard stories about my grandfather's family farm my whole life. When I was growing up, in fact, among the knick-knackery in our TV room was the massive wooden bludgeon of sorts that my great-grandmother reportedly used to make mashed potatoes—and other things that required mashing in their preparation for her large family. While a great conversation piece, the potato masher was also occasionally employed as an instrument of defence during the sibling altercations of my youth—for example, when we couldn't all agree on what television program to watch, or when someone was just being kind of annoying. I can't remember whether anyone ever really wound up the victim of its business end, but I remember that to even threaten another family member with it filled my siblings and me with some form of pride, the pride of knowing that we were living history and that our grandfather's family's Canadian struggle wasn't for naught.

When it came time to actually make my inaugural pilgrimage to Clinton, however, I had some real research to do. For starters, I didn't even know the name of the town my grandfather was from, which felt like a key bit of information. For most of my life, I had described the location of my grandfather's boyhood home to anyone who might ask as simply being "outside of Guelph." But this is only because, back when I was a kid, I saw an ad in the back of a hockey magazine for a youth hockey school located in Guelph and somehow became convinced that attending it would guarantee me an electrifying career in the NHL.

"Was Grandpa's farm near Guelph?" I remember asking my mother during the same conversation in which I'd hoped to convince her and my dad to fork over the cash to send me to hockey school there.*

"No," my mother replied. "It's outside of Guelph."

---

* Something, it's worth nothing, that never happened, which is why I now do stuff like write books instead of, say, regaling young and old alike with tales of my illustrious career with the New York Rangers and how it's important to get as many shots on goal as possible and always give 110 percent, both on and off the ice, no matter where you are in life.

But then again, aren't all of us, Guelphites aside, "outside of Guelph" if you really think about it?

Sorry—I didn't mean to blow your mind.

Getting back to Clinton, however, the reality is that it is not only 134 kilometres from Guelph, but, more importantly, a mere 503 kilometres from my native Cleveland, so I decided the best time to make the trip would be the next time I was back in Ohio.

I finally found myself back in Cleveland for the Fourth of July* holiday and my dad's birthday, which is the next day, so I knew it was finally time to strike. I had considered making the trip to Clinton by myself, but then I figured it might be slightly less creepy to show up on the doorstep of my grandfather's old house with a reasonably pleasant-looking friend in tow instead of all alone like some sort of drifter, so I asked my buddy Joe to make the trip with me. I'd admittedly only become friends with Joe a few months prior, but I gathered that he had the makings of a solid road trip companion. My girlfriend, however, is a bit more cautious than I am and wasn't entirely convinced.

"How do you know he won't kill you, defile your corpse and dump your body in the woods along the way, leaving it to be devoured by woodland creatures with especially low standards, thereby making it impossible for Canadian and American authorities alike to piece together the grisly crime that happened as a result of your apparent willingness to get into a car with just about anybody?" my girlfriend asked just minutes before Joe, who had so kindly offered to drive, pulled into her parents' driveway to pick me up.

By now, I was accustomed to my girlfriend speculating on various people's capacity for committing brutal crimes and didn't think much of it. Still, I tried to comfort her by telling her how

---

* You probably already know this, but the Fourth of July, or Independence Day, as it is also known, is the day Americans celebrate being free of British rule by getting really drunk and playing with explosives. It is a day on which many an American goes to bed with fewer fingers than they woke up with.

Joe's dad had been a play-by-play announcer for the Cleveland Cavaliers basketball team* and that doing even one of those things she mentioned would undoubtedly bring way too much negative attention to his family to make it worth it, so there was no real reason to be concerned. Just to be safe, though, she coyly snapped a photo of Joe's licence plate as we pulled away so that the authorities might have something to go on on the off chance I was wrong.

Clinton is located in Huron County, Ontario, just across Lake Huron from the thumb on the geographic boxing glove that I maintain the state of Michigan has always been. The drive to Clinton from Cleveland takes about five hours as you travel west along Lake Erie and dip through Toledo, Ann Arbor and Detroit before finally reaching Canada. I tried to conserve my energy along the way and not allow myself to get too worked up until we were actually in Canada proper, something that's admittedly not that hard to do when driving through Ohio and Michigan. We did try and stop off for coffee at a McDonald's in Detroit, the clientele of which mostly seemed liked extras from an especially low-key episode of the *The Walking Dead*, but otherwise, things didn't heat up much until we got to the Canadian border, which was when I was officially no longer able to contain myself.

"Where you guys headed?" the Canadian border patrol officer asked as he scanned our passports.

"Clinton, Ontario!" I stated in a manner that I hoped would suggest the gravity of our journey, but probably didn't.

"Do either of you have any guns or drugs on you?" he then asked, seemingly not nearly as excited about the Clinton thing as I was.

"No," we answered while shaking our heads like we meant it.

"Okay," the officer said, handing our passports back to Joe. "Enjoy your visit."

---

* Sorry, Joe, if you're reading this—I just can't help mentioning this whenever possible.

I was admittedly expecting a bit more of a shakedown before being waved into your country like that, and I was even a bit disappointed we didn't get one. After all, Joe and I were both inadvertently wearing green army jackets—Joe because he was actually in the army for a while, and me because the colour goes nicely with my eyes—and, historically speaking, anyway, it's a look not unpopular with nutjobs, riff-raff and street toughs alike. Still, I guess it was nice that the border patrol guy gave us the benefit of the doubt.

Now that we were in Canada and all, Joe and I figured we should start Canada-ing it up as soon as possible, so we pulled into the first Tim Hortons* we saw for some coffee and a snack. We have Tim Hortons in the United States now—there's one just a few blocks from my apartment in New York City, in fact—but this would be the first Tim Hortons I had been to in Canada, so I was understandably pumped.

"Did you know Tim Horton was a professional hockey player before becoming a donut magnate?" I asked Joe as we waited for our order.

"Yeah," Joe replied. "Pretty cool."

"And did you know that Tim Horton had a hamburger restaurant before he got into the donut game?" I asked, trying to make it seem like I hadn't literally just been reading the Tim Horton Wikipedia page in the car as we pulled in.

"I think I heard that, actually," Joe said, seemingly unimpressed with my strong working knowledge of both Tim Horton and the Horton donut empire.

"And did you know that Tim Horton died tragically in a car accident at the age of forty-four?" I then asked him.

"No," Joe said, grabbing his order from the counter and heading for the car. "I didn't."

---

* The lack of an apostrophe here drives me insane, but think of the millions my publisher will save on ink as this literary classic is no doubt reprinted again and again over time.

Things went quiet for a moment after that, and I was worried my death talk might have dampened the mood. But as soon as we pulled back onto the highway, our piping-hot Tim Hortons coffees in hand, the excitement was back in full force.

"So, have you ever been to your grandfather's farm before?" Joe asked as we pushed north along Lake Huron toward Clinton.

"No," I told him. "I've only seen pictures."

"Cool."

"Yeah."

As we continued on to Clinton, I tried to soak up any and all Canadianness I could while gazing out the window. It was admittedly slow going at first.

"When do you think we'll hit some action?" I wondered to Joe.

"I'm not sure," Joe said, keeping his eyes on the road ahead. "Just keep your eyes peeled."

Then, as if on cue, I spotted an extremely large inflatable slice of pizza for sale at the side of the road alongside some other, not nearly as cool inflatable items, all of which I eventually surmised were rafts intended to be enjoyed on the unforgiving* waters of nearby Lake Huron.

"I think we just found it," I said, directing Joe's attention to the pizza raft.

"Yep," Joe said, nodding.

"In fact, if the rest of this trip ends up being even half as cool as that extremely large inflatable slice of pizza, I think we've got a pretty good time ahead of us," I speculated.

"Definitely," Joe replied.

As it turned out, the intensity died down almost immediately after we passed the inflatable pizza, picking up momentarily a few minutes later, when we passed a bunch of Adirondack chairs for sale that had been painted to look like the Canadian flag,

---

* Apparently, more than a thousand shipwrecks have been recorded on Lake Huron. What the hell do I know but it seems to me you wanna be around next Christmas, you do your boating on Lake Erie instead!

complete with maple leaf–shaped back,* before quickly dying down again for the rest of the drive. But it didn't matter, because before long, Joe and I found ourselves in Clinton proper, which was nothing short of exhilarating.

Downtown Clinton, the part of Clinton where we assumed all the hot Clintonian action must be, isn't much more than one intersection lined with shops and a restaurant or two. And while I originally figured we'd mill around there for a bit, get a taste of things and perhaps even have a few meaningful interactions with the locals before driving to my grandfather's farm and walking right up to the front door just to see what might happen, the anticipation was just too much to resist.

"What the hell are you wasting your time kicking around town for?" I imagined my grandfather calling to me from Valhalla** as Joe was about to pull into a parking spot. "My boyhood home is just down the goddamn road!"***

With that in mind, I instead told Joe to keep driving. We continued down the main road for about a mile before we hit Summerhill Road, where my grandfather's old place was located. I was surprised at how excited I was to finally see it. I suppose it was a combination of things. First, of course, was the anticipation of seeing this place I'd heard about and seen old photos of my

---

* I'd like to think it was the official chair of the vacationing Canadian, as he or she kicks back with a fresh Bloody Caesar on each armrest as a Sloan or Chilliwack album plays softly in the background, but it's hard to really know for sure.

** Norse mythology enthusiasts will recognize Valhalla as the place Vikings go after being slain in battle. And while my grandfather wasn't technically a Viking, the menswear industry is no walk in the park either, so that seems like as a good a place as any for him to spend the afterlife.

*** I don't remember my grandfather swearing that much in real life, but then again, I was a kid then, and I imagine he used profanity more freely around grown men like me and Joe.

whole life. But there was also the knowledge of how thrilled my grandfather would have been to know I had actually bothered to make the trip, and that my friend Joe had even talked his wife into letting him borrow her car for the drive so that we might show up with slightly less-empty Big Gulp cups in tow when we did it. And, of course, I just felt good about the fact that, after so much talking about it with my editors, my uncle Joe and even you, dear reader, for the past several thousand words, I was finally showing up to have a look around.

Summerhill Road itself is a gravel road lined with cornfields and other crops. When they inevitably make the movie of this book, there's no way they'll be able to oversell it. The sun was shining and there wasn't a cloud in the sky as we drove along. In fact, I wouldn't have been surprised if Kevin Costner himself stepped out into the middle of the road wearing a flannel shirt and clutching a baseball mitt, a reference to the popular film *Field of Dreams* that I am hoping works here, though it's admittedly been a while since I watched part of that movie one day on cable at my sister's house.

Anyway, we continued down the road until suddenly there it was, an old brick house I felt I'd known my whole life. I half expected my grandfather as a very young man to step out the front door and wonder aloud who had stopped a car in front of his house, and also what the hell a Toyota is.

"Now what do we do?" I asked Joe as he idled the car in the middle of the road.

"You wanna knock on the door?" Joe asked.

"I guess so," I said.

With that, Joe pulled the car onto the grass directly in front of my grandfather's old place.

"Don't park directly in front of the house," I told him. "Park down the road a bit so they don't immediately assume we've come to kill them or ask them to accept the Lord or anything."

After Joe parked the car a less-threatening distance from the house, we got out and began slowly walking up the driveway. There were no cars in the driveway, which gave off a "We're not home" vibe that only made me more paranoid as I naturally assumed the current residents would pull in just as I was standing on their front porch, looking like I was up to no good, like one of those burglars from those home security system commercials. Even so, I continued walking. Joe, however, hung back a bit in that way you do when it's not your own grandfather's former house, anyway.

I climbed the front stairs and looked through the glass of the front door. As I looked inside, I imagined my grandfather, his parents and eight siblings inside, presumably waiting for my great-grandmother to finish mashing something with that big hunk of wood we used to have at our house. And I imagined, clanging in the distance, the massive cowbell from my grandfather's farm that we also used to have in our TV room, which we would even occasionally force the family dog to wear. Then I knocked a couple times in that gentle manner you use when you're not entirely sure you want someone to answer. When that yielded no results, I dug deep and knocked again, this time at a volume that suggested I might very well be there to arrest someone. Still nothing.

Assuming no one was home, I began peering into the windows along the porch with the confidence of a person who isn't expecting to get shot. It was a beautiful home. My aunt Kay had visited some years earlier with my uncle John, and they'd been invited inside by the current owner. Kay told me that apparently some renovations had been made, but the original woodwork and flooring were intact. Aside from some modern amenities, the interior looked much like it must have way back when my grandfather and his family lived here. It was at this point that I imagined what it might be like to somehow buy the place myself, load it up with all sorts of snacks and never, ever leave again as long as I lived, in an actual physical manifestation of man's tendency to live in the past. And it was immediately at that point that Joe snapped me back into reality.

"Looks like no one's home, huh?" Joe said. "Should we head into town or something?"

"Sure," I replied, quickly transitioning back to the now.

Prior to the trip, my aunt Kay had also given me directions to a nearby cemetery where a bunch of my relatives were buried. I'm not really a "cemetery guy," per se, but she assured me it was close to the house, so we decided to swing by there next, as long as we were in the area.

"You can spot the Blake plots pretty easily because the ground around them has been cemented over," my uncle Joe had told me.

Supposedly, one of my relatives had decided to do this so that there'd be no grass to cut around the Blake plots, a move that strikes me as both considerate and weird. Regardless, it did make the graves easy to find, as it was a small cemetery and the big block of cement in the middle of it really stuck out.

We parked the car and began walking toward the Blake graves. And as we did, it occurred to me that I'd never really visited a cemetery before, aside from attending a burial. Part of me figured we'd be chased out immediately by some guy we'd later find out had been dead for fifty years, but it didn't happen. Instead, Joe and I just climbed onto the big cement block and stared at the Blake tombstones as I did my best to remember exactly how I was related to each of the people buried beneath us. For his part, Joe took a few pictures of me in front of the tombstones.

As I stood there, trying to figure out how to pose appropriately* in front of the graves of relatives I'd never known, I began to think of my grandfather, and I again wondered what he might think if he could see me now. Would he be proud of me, or think I was just plain nuts? And what would be his take on the whole cemented-over graves thing? Would he, like me, want to go back in time and tell his relatives about Astroturf and how someone was probably going to invent it any day now? Or that whoever is tasked with cutting the grass at the cemetery now probably thinks the cemented-over graves are totally weird too? I wasn't entirely sure, so I figured we should probably just head into town and see what might happen next.

---

* It's important to look like you're happy to be there but still not having a ton of fun or anything.

"Well, that was fun," I said to Joe, nodding toward the cemetery as we pulled away.

"Yeah," Joe replied, though I'm not sure he really meant it.

On the drive back toward Clinton's main drag, we passed a sign along the road for Clinton Raceway, where they apparently have harness racing. I pulled up their website on my phone and saw that it was billed as "Huron County's Entertainment Destination," a sure sign that the inflatable pizza we had seen on the drive in was about to be left in the dust in terms of excitement on this trip. I made a mental note to swing by once it was officially time to cut loose.

A few minutes later, we found ourselves back in town again, where Joe parked along the street directly in front of a charity thrift shop whose window display celebrated the Canadian sesquicentennial that just so happened to be taking place during our visit. It was an attractive display, mostly comprising hockey sticks and various old shirts and jerseys with the word *Canada* on them, but tucked in the corner, I spotted a cast-iron moose roughly the size of a small cat.

"I got dibs on the moose," I said to Joe in case he had spotted it, too, and thought maybe he was going to buy it instead, something I wasn't about to let happen even after he drove and everything.

Joe didn't put up a fight, but unfortunately the store was closed anyway, so I told him we needed to come back the next day and buy that damn moose as soon as the place opened.

"Not so fast," Joe said. I assumed he was suggesting that he intended to buy the moose himself after all, but it turned out there was a sign in the window saying that none of the objects would be for sale until July 11, which was days away, by which time we'd be long gone from Clinton in particular and Huron County in general, at least physically if not emotionally.

"I'm sure they'll let me buy it after I tell them we're just visiting from America and won't be here on the eleventh," I said to Joe, who seemed to think that sounded perfectly reasonable, too.

Confident in the knowledge that I would soon be the proud owner of a cat-sized cast-iron moose, Joe and I continued down the block and headed into a diner on the corner for some coffee. There, in the dessert case, I spotted a cream-filled cookie in the shape of a maple leaf. I'm not technically a detective, but it was at this point that I was pretty sure I was hot on the trail of a distinctly Canadian dessert-based experience.

"Excuse me," I said, getting the attention of the woman behind the counter. "What are these cookies in the shape of a maple leaf?"

"Those are maple leaf cookies," she replied.

A less confident man might have been swallowed whole by the brief silence that followed, the silence where the woman behind the counter thinks I might be an idiot and I, for my part, am sure of it, but instead I just plowed ahead and ordered two of the cookies I had really been counting on to have an at least slightly less obvious name. You might also be questioning my mental capacities at this point so it's probably worth noting that I've since learned that maple-leaf cookies are pretty much everywhere in Canada. But, for what it's worth, these were not your everyday boxed maple leaf cookies like the ones you get at the airport; they were *homemade* maple leaf cookies, which is to say they were even more disgusting than the store-bought kind. Unless, of course, you like maple leaf cookies, in which case I suggest you get on the next bus to Clinton posthaste, because these things were incredible, even better than the fancy store-bought kind if you can believe it

After knocking back a couple rounds of coffee and eating a respectable portion of our maple leaf cookies, Joe and I decided to ask the only other people in the diner if they had any tips on what else we might do for fun while we were in town. Since Joe is more of an outgoing type than I am, he approached an older couple finishing their lunch at a table in the back as I stood creepily a few feet behind him.

"We're visiting from the United States," Joe told them. "Can you recommend anything we might do while we're in Clinton?"

"There's the Clinton Raceway," the man at the table said, "but it's the off-season, so they're closed for a few more weeks."

The older couple didn't have any other hot tips besides maybe sticking in town a few more weeks until the raceway opened, an admittedly bold yet unfortunately unrealistic move since Joe's wife needed the car back, so we nodded politely and headed outside for some air and to let it fully sink in that a visit to "Huron County's Entertainment Destination" just wasn't in the cards for us, which is when we spotted a "sporting goods" store across the street. I figured this meant they sold hockey equipment mostly, what with us being in Canada and all, but when we walked inside, I realized that by "sporting goods," they meant "hunting equipment." I'm not much for guns or crossbows, but I do like the outfits people tend to wear when using those things, so I figured it was at least worth a look around. As for Joe, as I mentioned, he used to be in the army and still goes to a shooting range on occasion, so I figured he'd be our ticket to "fitting in" with the other two guys in the store—even though, as I also mentioned, we were both wearing army jackets, which probably should have been enough to seal the deal already. I thought to maybe loudly say something or another to Joe about how we'd "lost a lot of men that day" as a bit of an icebreaker as we walked in to the shop, but he had another idea.

Joe knew enough about guns to ask to see an old Russian rifle hanging behind the counter by name, which, in the end, turned out to be even more effective than our cool jackets, if you can believe it.

"You shoot?" the twentysomething store employee behind the counter asked Joe as he stood there, holding the Russian rifle in a manner that suggested he had done that sort of thing before.

"Yeah, I go to a range every once in a while back in Cleveland, where I live," Joe replied.

They said a few gun-related things to each other that I didn't understand at all after that, but then the conversation turned to the fact that we were visiting from the United States.

"Did I hear you're visiting from the United States?" asked a fiftysomething man in medical scrubs standing nearby in that casual manner one tends to employ when killing a bit of time in a gun shop.

"Yeah, we drove up from Cleveland," I told him.

We exchanged a few pleasantries after that, and then, seeing as we were standing in a gun store and all, the conversation quickly turned to the differences in gun laws between the United States and Canada.

"We have more restrictions here," said the guy in the medical scrubs—who we soon learned was actually a dentist with a practice across the street, above the diner where we almost finished two whole maple leaf cookies—stating the obvious.

"You can only get a magazine with five rounds here," the guy behind the counter said, offering just one example of Canada's entirely reasonable gun laws that, for some reason, we don't have in the United States.*

"Yeah," the dentist chimed in, "some guy here tried to shoot a bunch of people a few years ago, so now they wire them so you can't fit any more bullets."

While the two men agreed that it would be "more fun" to be able to shoot more than five rounds at a time, they seemed only mildly annoyed that they had to stop and load another magazine so that they could start shooting their guns again.

"Seems to me that if you need more than five bullets at a time, you either suck at shooting or you've got something really negative planned," I said, just making conversation.

The two men mostly just nodded after that before bringing up the subject of handguns.

"There are so many rules for handguns here," the guy behind the counter said.

"It would be fun to own one, but the rules just make it too much of a hassle," the dentist agreed before rattling off a bunch of the aforementioned rules.

"That's so annoying," I said, totally one of the guys at this point.

---

* Actually, I'm pretty sure I know the reason, but that's a whole other book.

"We can't even sell them in our store," the guy behind the counter said, shaking his head. "We'd have to get a whole other licence."

I've admittedly never hung out at a gun store in America, but something tells me this conversation wouldn't have been so laid-back had it happened there. As much as I gathered that the dentist and the guy behind the counter were seriously into guns, they seemed about as annoyed with the gun control laws in Canada as a twelve-year-old might be if you told him he'd have to wait a half hour after eating before going swimming.

As I find is usually the case lately when you're in a foreign country and people find out you're from the United States, before long the conversation inevitably turned to the orange game show host currently residing in the White House.

"I should warn you," the dentist said, "I am a bit of a fan of his."

"We should warn you," Joe replied, "we don't like him at all."

"Oh, that's fine," the dentist said, seemingly a bit apologetic. "You two are clearly enlightened, so I can certainly respect your difference of opinion."

It was hard to keep myself from giggling at this point because, while I can only assume our gun conversation wouldn't have gone as calmly had it happened in the States, I can absolutely guarantee you that no conversation between pro- and anti-Trump people back home has ever been even close to this cordial.

We continued our Trump conversation for a couple more minutes and were relieved to discover that, while Joe and I completely disagreed with everything the dentist had to say about him, he only liked the Orange One because of some of his trade policies and not, for example, because he thinks Mexicans are rapists or all Haitians have AIDS* or anything like that. And then, as the conversation wound down, the guy behind the counter suddenly disappeared to the back of the store, only to reappear moments later with an English bulldog puppy in tow. It was at this point that

---

* Part of me thinks that I should try to reference a more contemporary Trump statement than these old chestnuts, but who can possibly keep up?

all four of us were finally and unquestionably in 100 percent agreement about something: he was the bestest dog!

Having ended things on a high note, Joe and I decided to walk across the street and take a few pictures in front of a giant radar antenna. I'm sure at least a few people will accuse me of totally burying the lede on this one, and reasonably so, but Clinton, aside from being the hometown of my late grandfather, is also Canada's home of radar.* I know—I couldn't believe it, either. Apparently the Royal Canadian Air Force had a base in Clinton during World War II that was used primarily for training in radar, which at the time was a top-secret device, kind of like how fax machines or hand sanitizer used to be when they first came out. The base is gone, but the massive radar antenna remains, dazzling any and all who happen to pass through the main intersection of downtown Clinton, myself included.

Joe and I got our radar excitement out of our systems after a couple of minutes and briefly toyed with stopping into a burger joint across the street because I'd read an online review of the place that said the owner yells at customers, something I was curious to witness in a Canadian setting. In the end, though, I figured I could probably get someone to yell at me somewhere else that night if I really set my mind to it, so we instead decided to go dump our bags at the Airbnb I had rented for us just down the road in Huron East.

Huron East turned out to be almost identical to Clinton, which is to say it was delightful and seemed to consist mostly of just one intersection. The apartment we rented for the night was above some shops and was oddly sprawling, given the price and the fact that just two dudes from Cleveland would be staying there. In the event that we ended up making a ton of friends later that night, something I was most certainly counting on, I made a mental note that the party should definitely be at our place. There were barstools around an island in the kitchen and everything.

---

* Fun fact: the local men's senior hockey team is called the Clinton Radars. You're never gonna guess what their logo is.

"You ever been to Kitchener?" I imagined asking a local beauty who would most likely be hanging at our place with us and thirty-eight of her friends later that night as we knocked back so many cases of Labatt's, we'd undoubtedly be saddled with an additional cleaning fee. It was going to be really, really cool.

We had asked the guy at the gun store where we might go for hot, distinctly Canadian times later that night, and he suggested we head over to nearby Bayfield, Ontario. So, after changing out of army jackets and into some other jackets that were different but still pretty cool, Joe and I made the short drive over.

Bayfield sits right on the shore of Lake Huron, so close to Michigan that we could practically give it the finger from where we parked the car. From the looks of it, I gathered it's a place where people have summer homes, and the bit of Googling I just did confirms it. There's a main drag there, with a few bars and restaurants. Naturally, we chose the one with the most action, which in this case meant there were about nine people inside. The guy at the gun store had also told us that the 150th-anniversary celebrations would begin to take place the following night, so the electricity in both the bar and the seating area was palpable. Drinks were flowing, and at least a couple of tables had ordered the artichoke dip.

Joe and I bellied up to the bar and ordered some drinks. I did my best to pick up on any Canadianness that might be happening before my eyes, but I can't imagine things were that much different than in a similar location across Lake Huron, in whatever town in Michigan the locals head to when they want to get loose during the summertime. Eventually, I decided to abandon my quest altogether for the night, even going so far as to order a Belgian ale. Naturally it was around this time that the Canadianness of the place made itself known. Since Joe and I had had just enough to drink to convince ourselves that we had extremely intelligent and important things to say about any number of topics, we ended up rambling to each other long into the night. At one point, we looked up to discover we were the only ones left in the restaurant and, as the place had been almost entirely cleaned up by this point, presumably had been for a while already.

"I feel like in America they would have booted our asses a while ago," I said to Joe.

"Definitely," Joe agreed.

We knocked back what was left of our drinks and headed for the door. On the way out, I muttered "Sorry!" to the handful of staff members—who, I imagine, couldn't wait for us to leave—doing my best to sound like I was born and raised in the next town over at the very farthest. It felt good.

Joe and I woke early the next morning as a light rain sprinkled down on scenic East Huron. Our first plan of action besides break-fast was to return to the charity shop we'd passed the day before so I could secure the cast-iron moose. To that end, we made the short drive back to Clinton and parked the car across the street from the diner where we'd had the maple-leaf cookie encounter. And it was as we crossed the street that I noticed something else that struck me as strange and, presumably, very, very Canadian: the cars stopped for us. This wasn't because we were in a crosswalk at a stoplight, or an intersection with a stop sign. The cars weren't required to stop for us, but they did anyway.

"Should we test this?" I asked Joe after it happened the first time.

"Yes," Joe replied. "Yes, we should."

With that, Joe and I crossed the street again, this time back toward his car. The cars all stopped again. And when we did it three or four more times, they did it then, too. It was exhilarating—two American idiots jaywalking to their heart's content in celebration of Canadian courtesy. In America, I bet we'd have been roadkill by the second attempt, at the very latest.*

---

* It has been suggested to me that the real reason the cars stopped for us was simply because we were in a small town and not because we were in Canada. However, shortly after my return stateside, I decided to test this theory in a small hamlet outside of Akron, Ohio and nearly got run over by a Geo Tracker.

"This is paradise," I said to Joe as we crossed the street one last time and headed inside the diner, where I'd at least like to think that they treated us like regulars because we'd been there once already. There, we quickly devoured some eggs and toast and paid our tab before setting our sights on acquiring the moose next door.

I assumed the moose transaction would be a quick one, but I couldn't have been more wrong.

"I'd like to buy the moose in the window," I told a woman of about sixty, wearing an embroidered sweatshirt, who held things down at the register.

"Items in window aren't for sale until the eleventh," the woman said, pretty much quoting the sign in the window verbatim. "Oh, I know," I said with a shrug that suggested a full charm assault was just around the corner for this woman. "It's just that I'm visiting from the United States and we're leaving town today, so I was hoping I could just buy it today, you know, since we're standing here in the store right now and all."

"He wants to buy the moose," the woman said, calling over to another woman in her fifties who was tidying a nearby housewares display. "No," the housewares lady said. "It's not for sale until the eleventh."

"Are you sure you can't just sell it to me anyway?" I asked her. "My grandfather grew up here in Clinton and I'm just in town for the day to see his farm and have a look around. As you do."

"That's nice," the lady at the register told me, before pointing out to me for a third time that they weren't going to sell me the damn moose today. "You can buy the moose on the eleventh."

"But we're leaving today," I replied. "Is there any way you could just sell it to me now?"

"You'd have to have someone come in on the eleventh and buy it for you," the housewares lady chimed in.

"But the nearest person I know lives in Toronto," I explained. "I don't know anyone in Clinton."

"What about your grandfather?" the woman behind the counter asked. "Can't he pick it up for you?"

"I don't know, Grandpa, can you?" I said, looking to the ceiling while hoping to break the two women entirely.

"Oh, I'm sorry," the woman behind the counter said.

"That's okay," I told her. "He's been gone over thirty years now, and it doesn't make sense to blame you, really."

It was at this point that I figured they'd just start wrapping up the moose for me, maybe even in some fancy, moose-themed crepe paper they'd been saving in the back for just such an occasion, but it wasn't the case, so I tried another plan of attack.

"I'm actually in town researching a book that I'm writing," I told the ladies.

"What's your book about?" the lady behind the counter asked.

"Canada," I replied. "I'm travelling all over and writing my observations about your country, like how everyone is really nice and accommodating and, you know, not afraid to bend the rules a little bit when a guy just wants to pick up a used moose for himself."

They giggled a bit at this, which felt like progress, so I pressed on.

"I'm writing the book for Penguin Random House, actually," I continued, before looking away in a manner to suggest that the fact I was writing a book for a major publisher and not just writing it by hand onto used napkins in my basement or in the back of a van wasn't really a big deal at all, and not something I'd brought up in hopes of impressing them and ultimately forcing them to finally give in and sell me the damn moose already.

"That's nice," the housewares lady said.

"Yeah," I said, agreeing with her. "In fact, I was thinking I could maybe even put that moose on the cover, give you guys full credit and everything . . . if you let me buy it, of course."

"My dad is writing a book," the housewares lady said, seemingly not hearing that last part.

"Oh yeah?" I replied, trying not to sound competitive. "Who's his publisher?"

"He's just writing it in a notebook at his house," the housewares lady said. "It's about how he had to flee his country because of the war."

"That's so great," I said, trying to sound interested. "So, you gonna sell me the moose or not?"

"I'll tell you what," the lady behind the counter interjected, most likely because she was trying to get rid of me at this point. "Give me a call on the eleventh, and maybe we can figure something out."

"Thank you, I guess," I said, reluctantly taking her card.

Joe and I then took a lap around the store on the off chance that there was another moose for sale that wasn't subject to some bizarre rule that I will never understand in a million, trillion years.

"You know, I could probably make you a moose just like that," Joe, who just so happens to also be a sculptor, mentioned to me as we admired the various offerings in the menswear section.

"That would be great," I said. "I can't believe they won't sell me the moose today."

"Me neither," Joe replied. "I should point out, though, that I can't make a *cast-iron* moose like that—it would have be made out of plaster or something."

For a split second, I hated Joe for getting my hopes up before immediately dashing them like that with promises of a moose that had pretty much zero chance of being as awesome as the one in the store window the ladies seemed hellbent on not letting me buy. But then I remembered that he was driving, and I should probably let go of any much-deserved anger so I wouldn't get stranded in Clinton with still weeks to go before the town's fabled raceway was set to open for the season.

"Let's get out of here," I said to Joe before heading for the door.

We had originally planned on heading home the same way we'd driven up the day before, but the map on my phone said traffic was bad in that direction and it would take an hour less to get back to Cleveland by heading west and dipping through Buffalo, so we decided to drive that way instead, a thrill as we'd get an unexpected taste of Buffalo—as if this trip hadn't been enough of a thrill ride already.

We were about to pull out of Clinton when I suddenly felt compelled to swing by my grandfather's old place once more on the off chance that its current resident was home.

"Do you mind?" I asked Joe.

"Not at all," he said as he pointed the car back in the direction of Summerhill Road.

We arrived back a couple minutes later, and were immediately confronted by a Doberman pinscher barking loudly in the driveway, just like in those movies where a bunch of people are about to get shot. I figured the dog's presence might be the result of the current occupants of the house hearing about two guys in army jackets lingering on their property the day before and deciding to bone up on security, but when the dog ran behind the house in fear after I took a couple non-threatening steps toward it, I dismissed this notion.

The dog reappeared a moment later, accompanied by a shih tzu and an attractive woman in a dress who appeared to be in her forties.

"Can I help you?" she asked.

"My name is Dave," I said. "My grandfather Clarence Blake grew up in this house, and I was just swinging by to have a look."

"We've had a few Blakes swing by the house over the years," she said with a smile, presumably referring to my Aunt Kay and Uncle John and whoever else might have showed up unannounced, a "thing" for my bloodline, it would seem, over the years.

I hoped that the woman might then invite us into the house to have a look around, but I certainly understood when she didn't, what with my and Joe's rock look and all. But she was kind enough to take us around back for a look at the endless acres behind the house, where I can only assume my grandfather and his siblings chased each around for hours on end—who knows, maybe even with that massive potato masher in hand on those occasions when they wanted to heat things up a bit.

As it turned out, the woman and her husband had been living in the house for over twenty years and were only the second owners since my grandfather's family vacated the place.

"The owners before us were friends with Liberace," the woman casually mentioned at one point during our conversation. "Apparently, he used to pop by the house and play for them whenever he was in the area."

If you're anything like me, this news should come as quite the bombshell. Did the fact that Liberace hung out in my grandfather's house after he and his family had long since moved out suggest family greatness? Probably not. But damned if it isn't greatness-adjacent, and I'll take it.

It was hard to imagine anything topping the Liberace news, so after a couple more minutes of chitchat, Joe and I decided to let the woman get back to her day and we headed to the car, still buzzing with delight about the whole Liberace thing.

"Liberace," I said. "He was right there playing piano in my grandfather's house."

"After he and his family had moved out though," Joe said.

"It still counts," I told him, "especially when you don't believe in time and space like me. Anyway, we should probably hit the road."

Since the drive back took us through much more of Canada than we'd seen on the way in, there was something peculiar that I noticed about Canada on this portion of the trip, specifically the mostly rural areas we passed through: there was almost no unnecessary signage or billboards. And nothing in front of any of the homes gave much if any indication as to what sort of person might live inside. Even the cars had almost no additional ornamentation, whether it be an old political bumper sticker someone hadn't bothered to remove once the election in question had passed, a rear-view mirror ornament suggesting an affinity for some sports team or another, or even a set of truck nuts* hanging from a

---

* In the event that truck nuts have not yet reached a level of global, or at least Canadian, awareness, they are a set of synthetic testicles that sophisticated types like to attach to the back bumpers of their cars to let people know they are not exactly opposed to the idea of good times all the time.

bumper so as to say to me as I passed, "Hey, Dave, the guy behind the wheel of this Chevy pickup totally, totally gets you." This was all further underscored by the fact that, as soon as we got back stateside, the assault of billboards advertising ambulance-chasing lawyers, adult superstores and fireworks priced to move was almost immediate. How had I never noticed them before?

Even more obnoxious than all those billboards, however, was the US border patrol officer welcoming us back home.

"What were you doing in Canada?" he asked us in a tone that suggested he hoped he'd have us doing hard labour by sundown at the very latest.

I explained to the officer how we had driven up to Clinton from Cleveland for the night to see my grandfather's farm and have a look around town.

"You drove all that way just to see a farm?" he then asked in a manner that suggested he was officially turning the screws. "Seems like a long way to drive just to see some farm."

It was at this point that I wanted to mention that thing about how I was also writing the most definitive book about Canada ever written by a non-Canadian and that our trip was part of my research for that aforementioned and very important book and that, as long as we were on the topic, Liberace himself used to visit my grandfather's old farm whenever he was in the area, but it all seemed like it would be wasted on him, this damn rube who probably wouldn't know a legendary, classically trained Vegas showman like Liberace if he got slapped around by him. Instead, I just said yes, the border patrol officer handed our passports back as though he was completely disgusted, and Joe and I continued on our way and finished the remainder of our journey without incident unless you count when Joe turned off that one Third Eye Blind song with the "do-do-do-dos" that I maintain is still pretty catchy no matter what anyone else says.

Within a few days of our trip, I found myself back in New York and decided to give the charity shop in Clinton a ring to check on the status of the moose I was still determined to make my own despite their damn rules.

"I remember you," the lady on the phone said after I explained myself. "You were the tall guy with long hair."

"Long*ish*, maybe, but yeah," I replied. "I actually wore it longer in the nineties if you can believe that."

"Right," she said, presumably enthralled. "Anyway, send me an email with your address and I'll calculate how much it'll cost to ship the moose to you."

I was thrilled she'd decided to bend the rules enough to ship the moose to me rather than, for example, having my grandfather come back from the dead to pick it up in person for me, much as I would like to have seen that. And I was even more thrilled when the cost of the moose and shipping combined was less than $50 Canadian.

"The moose is on its way to you now," the charity shop lady wrote in response to the email I'd sent her with my address. "Send me a cheque when you can."

Suddenly, I was more shocked than I was even after the Liberace news. After all, the chances of anyone in America sending a complete stranger something in the mail before they'd been paid in full for it are less than zero. And, after spending every second in Canada on the lookout for distinctly Canadian experiences, something that I have to assume is the most Canadian thing ever happened to me as I was sitting on my couch with my dog in New York City. It was a lot to take in, even for the dog.

As for the moose, it showed up a few days later in a cardboard box that looked like it had been thrown down at least a couple flights of stairs. One of its legs was poking through a hole in the side as if it had perhaps been trying to escape. When I opened the box, I discovered the moose had not been packed in Styrofoam peanuts or old newspaper like one might expect, but had instead simply been wrapped in what appeared to be leftover plastic wrap from the dry cleaners, which I guess allowed it to stay dry, at least, as it bounced all over the inside of the box, presumably holding on for dear life. One of the moose antlers had broken off entirely, and at least a couple tines from the other had snapped off as well. As far as scenarios involving cat-sized, cast-iron moose go, this one was nothing short of horrifying, not unlike that scene in the *The Godfather* when the guy wakes up with a severed horse head in his bed, something that seems pretty hard to sleep through but whatever—it was a different time.

Anyway, with a bit of super glue and more patience than I'll ever have, my girlfriend was eventually able to piece the moose back together after a few attempts. And if you step back from it enough and squint just a little, it looks just as good as it did in the window display of that charity shop back in Clinton one sunny July afternoon.

But when you look at it up close and see what it's been through, and recognize that even the slightest nudge would undo every last bit of my girlfriend's hard work, it's hard not to at least consider the possibility that maybe, just maybe, those ladies back at the charity shop were somehow also trying to send me a message when they sent me that moose, a message that said, loud and clear, "Don't mess with Canada, bitch."

3

QUEBEC CITY, QUEBEC

Je Ne Peux Pas Sentir Mon Visage*

I'D LONG HEARD that the people of Quebec hate the rest of Canada—so much, in fact, that they've been trying to leave the country altogether since just a few minutes after becoming a part of it. Keeping this in mind, I figured it only stood to reason that the people of Quebec weren't exactly crazy about Americans, either, and in fact, probably hated them even more than they do non-Quebecois Canadians. Given my unflagging desire to win over the people who seem to like me least, I couldn't wait to go there. I guess it's kind of like how cats, somehow sensing the fact that I'm so allergic that I practically require a tracheotomy if I even think about them, insist on at least trying to take a nap on my face whenever the opportunity presents itself.

Since my friend Carl is a bit of a masochist, too, as evidenced in part by the fact that he recently and willingly moved to Indiana, I figured he would be the perfect wingman for my Quebec invasion.

---

* I can't feel my face.

In fact, when I suggested he join me for a "guys' weekend within reason,"* where we'd have almost no idea what anyone else was saying the whole time, his response was an enthusiastic "*Oui!*"

As for the province of Quebec, I'd been to Montreal twice— once with my family as a kid, a trip from which I only remember that Montreal seemed different from Cleveland, and again a couple years ago to promote my second book,** a trip marked by an unfortunate first encounter with poutine bought from a vendor I have since learned had no business being in the curd game.

When it came time to visit Quebec for the purposes of this book, however, I wanted to dig deeper and go even more French-Canadian than Montreal, so I decided Carl and I should make a beeline for Quebec City, a place I knew next to nothing about other than that it's so Canadian, it's hard to even find direct flights there from New York City and that the sadly now-defunct Quebec Nordiques hockey team had quite possibly the greatest logo of all time—even though, all these years later, I still can't say with confidence what it's supposed to represent.***

Speaking of non-direct flights, I had a layover in Toronto on the way to Quebec City, which meant going through customs before I could catch the final leg of my flight.

"Where are you going in Canada?" the customs agent asked in that manner (equal parts bored and annoyed) that customs agents tend to speak in—at least when talking to me.

"Quebec City," I said.

---

* No one dies, no one gets arrested, no one catches anything and, perhaps most importantly, all body hair remains intact. The more I think about it, it's really just about getting together for a beer or two and maybe some light snacks.

** It is called *Dave Hill Doesn't Live Here Anymore*. And while I do recommend that you seek it out, I should warn you that, aside from the fact that I wrote it, it is an almost entirely non-Canadian work of literature.

*** Actually, I just Googled it and learned that the Nordiques logo is supposed to depict an igloo holding a hockey stick, which just confuses me. I mean, yeah, that's exactly what it always looked like to me all those years, but I just didn't think it was possible that that's what they really decided to go with.

"Why?!" he then asked with more than a bit of disdain in his voice. I'm not entirely sure what the disdainful tone was about. I figured he either didn't like me,* didn't like Quebec City, or perhaps hated both equally. But all three of those options only made me want to visit Quebec City that much more, so I guess I won that round, especially after I told him I "just wanted to see it," which only seemed to upset him even more, something that warmed my heart no end.

After another short flight, I arrived at Jean Lesage airport in Quebec City, where Carl was already waiting for me, raring to go, with Indiana both physically and emotionally in the distance, if only for a few days. We picked up our rental car, a go-cart of an automobile I assumed we'd probably die in at some point over the next few days, given all the ice and snow covering the roads, and headed toward an Airbnb I'd arranged for us, located in the Quebec City neighbourhood of Limoilou, which the listing promised was "hip" and "up and coming"—Airbnb-speak for "not as conveniently located as you'd probably hoped, but still technically in town, so calm down—you're getting a pretty good deal on this one."

Once we hit the road, I turned on the radio and began scanning the stations. I knew French was the predominant language in all of Quebec, but I was surprised—delighted, even—to find not a single English-language station. These people weren't messing around. In fact, aside from a French-speaking DJ on one station who went from speaking French to excitedly blurting out the phrase "That's my testicles!" in English before immediately reverting to French, we heard no one speaking English whatsoever at any point during our three-day visit, unless they were speaking directly to us. I'll admit it would have been nice to at least know the context under which the DJ inexplicably decided to reference

---

* To be fair, this is more likely related to my nagging self-esteem issues, which somehow persist even after multiple basic cable appearances and this one time I got a free black coffee at a coffee shop near my house because the barista liked one of my YouTube videos.

his balls in English like that, but there's also something really nice, even magical, about having no idea at all. It is something I shall keep with me for the rest of my life, a little gift I can think of in the small hours of the night to remind myself that life is indeed beautiful if you just know where to look.

Anyway, it's worth noting at this point that much of the east coast of North America was experiencing a brutal cold front at the time of our visit. In New York City, for example, temperatures were hovering around zero degrees Fahrenheit. But that seemed like nothing compared to the cold Carl and I felt after finally stepping out of the car once we pulled into Quebec City proper. It was a ruthless cold, a sinister cold, a cold that said, "Fuck you, you fucking American fucks!"—in French, of course, which just sounds cooler and—let's be honest—much classier.

"With the wind chill it's minus-19* right now," Carl told me, looking at his phone—which, for the record, would die from the cold moments later.

I became instantly convinced that the likelihood of both of us returning to the United States without at least a few fingers and toes amputated as a result of frostbite wasn't very high at all. It also suddenly occurred to me that maybe the disdainful customs agent knew the weather situation here, and *that* was why he gave me the attitude when I told him where I was headed—not because he hated me, or Quebec City, or perhaps some carefully considered combination of both.

"Who knows," I thought as I wrapped a scarf across my face and did my best to hold back the tears, "maybe we could have become friends."

Our apartment wasn't quite ready yet, so Carl and I decided to kill some time by stopping into a coffee shop at the end of the block.

"*Bonjour!*" the young woman behind the counter said to me when I approached. She said something else in French immediately after that, which is, of course, when I froze. It's a problem I

---

* Fahrenheit, or roughly minus-357 degrees Celsius.

seem to have developed in recent years when encountering people who address me in a language other than English and presumably expect me to answer in that same language. In some rare cases, I know enough of the other language to respond with some equivalent to "Hello!" But the problem with that is it usually makes the other person think you might know how to say other stuff in their language, so they keep talking in that language, seemingly eager to find out what you might come up with to say next, which in turn only frightens me even more. It's a vicious cycle. Making matters worse is the fact that, while the French language is indeed beautiful, whenever someone speaks it to me, I immediately and almost always wrongly assume they are either mad at me or are trying to talk me into having sex, which in nine out of ten cases only adds to my nervousness.

Fortunately, however, Carl speaks French at least as well as a Parisian three-year-old, so when I just stood there, speechless, after the woman behind the counter addressed me in French, he decided to take over and say something that ultimately succeeded in getting her to bring us each a coffee and croissant. Also, for what it's worth, a new trick I learned after a day or so of being in Quebec City is that if I simply say "*Bonjour!*" to someone as soon as I encounter them, they almost immediately reply in English, having noted my complete inability to say even the simplest of French words properly.

"We have a real idiot on our hands here," I imagine them thinking, except, you know, in French. It works every time, and I feel great about it. My technique is even more effective when I say "*Bonjour!*" to someone at night, something that usually causes them to look at my wrist to see if I'm wearing a medical bracelet.

After getting settled in our rental apartment and waiting for night to fall so we might have a chance of moving undetected, Carl and I decided to take to the frigid streets once more, heading first to a bar Carl had read was known for having good beer. There, our plan was to blend in with the locals and really jump into Quebec City–living headfirst. That plan fell apart quickly, however, when I boldly decided to order what I thought said "cheese and crackers" in French on the menu, only to be informed it was actually an extremely salty cheese that came in a brine-filled jar in a tone that suggested that if I made this sort of mistake again, I would be asked to leave. As for the cheese, it looked like cooked spaghetti that had been braided like some sort of particularly advanced sailor's knot and was absolutely delicious.*

"This cheese is incredible," I said loudly to Carl, hoping to win over the locals with my enthusiasm for their cheese—and cheese talk in general.

"We should get some of this cheese before we leave town," Carl agreed.

"Indeed we should," I replied. "It is the best cheese."

I expected this to be a real conversation starter, the kind that would see us chatting long into the night with locals eager to adopt us—a couple of guys who know quality cheese when they taste it— as their own, but it didn't do much other than get the bartender to begrudgingly suggest we might be able to find this mysterious salty cheese at a grocery store or "somewhere else that sells cheese." We thanked her for this helpful tip, finished our beers and headed back into the night, which had somehow managed to become even colder in the short time we had spent inside the place with the exceptional cheese. It was a cold that forced me to tell myself that I indeed wanted to live with every horrible step. It also reminded me of my childhood, when, after a few hours of playing outside in the not-nearly-as-cold Cleveland winter, my mother would send one of my older siblings out to check on me and make sure I was still breathing and not in the process of being mummified in a snow-drift somewhere. I decided I owed it to her to not die on the streets of Quebec City that night. It was the least I could do, what with her having raised me into a mostly functioning adult.

---

* I'm hoping this description will make sense to any Quebec natives reading this right now and that, in turn, you will get in touch and let me know what this cheese is called, since the bartender would only tell us that it was indeed "salty," even though you and I both know there has got to be an official name for that sort of thing, dammit.

I had looked on the internet to see what bar in town specialized in heavy metal, and told Carl I wanted to go there next. My love for heavy metal aside, I find that going to the local heavy metal bar in any city is usually a good way to meet outgoing folks who are eager to enhance your stay in their town. Since Carl tends to lead a largely heavy metal–free lifestyle, something I will never understand, I left out the heavy metal part and just told him it was another place that had good beer, just like the one he had picked out, something I'd also read and was aware was an entirely reasonable thing to say in the midst of a "guys' weekend."* It was only about half a mile away in the Saint Roch area of town, but we only made it a few hellish blocks before we found ourselves trying to get into the first place we passed along the way that had its lights on in hopes of warming up. That turned out to be a nail salon.

"Please d-do our n-n-nails!" I begged no one in particular as we tried to figure out if anyone was still inside. "We're d-d-d-dying!"

But it turned out the place was closed, so we had no choice but to trudge onward as visions of some local finding our frozen bodies in a snowdrift a few hours later danced in my head.

"Poor Americans—they're frozen solid," they'd think as they poked us with a hockey stick or some other object that allowed them to keep their distance. "And what horribly unmanicured nails they have—that may very well be the saddest part of all this."

Eventually, though, we found the place we were looking for, and I was delighted to find that not only were they playing heavy metal inside, but they were playing *Canadian* heavy metal. And it wasn't just any Canadian heavy metal, either—it was Voivod, a Canadian heavy metal band that is actually from Quebec—Jonquière, to be exact, wherever that is. In short, things couldn't possibly have been going better as far as I was concerned.

"Voivod," I said to the bartender as we took a seat, letting him know that—despite my affinity for bright colours and patterns— I know Quebecois heavy metal when I hear it. "Nice."

---

* Within reason.

My plan worked, as he instantly began chatting with us about the beer menu and heavy metal in general. To be fair, there was only one other person in the bar at the time, but I'd like to think the effect would have been exactly the same had the place been absolutely packed.

"Are Voivod from around here?" I asked the bartender, since I hadn't yet looked up exactly where Voivod were from on Wikipedia, like I did just a couple paragraphs ago.

"No, I think they might live in Montreal," he said with a hint of contempt. "Most Quebec bands move to Montreal at some point when they're trying to make it."

"I hate when they do that," I replied, shaking my head in an attempt to bond further and, who knows, maybe even get a free drink out of the guy while I was at it.

"Yeah," the bartender agreed. "It's kinda lame."

"I'll say," I replied, suddenly realizing that feigning a disdain for Montreal may very well be the most Quebec thing I could possibly do in that moment. "Montreal—I'm so tired of their bullshit."

As for the other customer in the place, he looked to be about seventy, and we soon learned that he had moved to Quebec City from France fifty years earlier. I liked the idea that a guy could move here from a whole other country and wind up drinking all by himself in a heavy metal bar on an absolutely freezing Friday evening.

"If everything goes as planned," I said to Carl, nodding in the Frenchman's direction, "that will be me someday."

"You got this," the always-supportive Carl replied. "I just know it."

Since it was so ridiculously cold outside, the conversation eventually turned to the weather.

"A lot of people—zey die," the Frenchman said in summation at one point. "From ze cold."

Because of his French accent, it still sounded like he was trying to have sex with me, but I realized that's not where his head was at and he was just trying to remind us to bundle up when we left.

We had been in Quebec for several hours and had yet to eat any poutine whatsoever, so on the recommendation of the bartender, we headed down the block to a place that had that sort of thing. As I mentioned earlier, this wasn't going to be my first dance with poutine, and I was more than a little skeptical of jumping back in. Based on everything I'd heard, poutine was the Canadian equivalent of what Americans other than me tend to call disco fries, which is to say French fries covered in gravy and melted cheese. It is a sad dish intended to mask the almost entirely unavoidable pain of human existence if only for a few minutes, usually at 3 a.m. while completely hammered and very much alone, even in a crowded room.

As I understood it, poutine was pretty much the same thing, except the melted cheese is replaced with cheese curds—which, at least on paper anyway, are much grosser, mostly because of the word *curds*, which should have been reconsidered long before it made its way into widespread use. That said, however, I'm not a monster, so on my previous trip to Montreal, I'd decided to keep an open mind and take the plunge, even if it did happen to be 11 a.m. on a Sunday when I was completely sober. I picked up an order to go from a poutine stand and began digging in as I headed back to my hotel. It tasted of equal parts French fries and dumpster in the hot summer sun, which is to say pretty good and pretty awful at the same time. I had a few bites and then, while none of the locals were looking, threw what was left in the trash before any real shame managed to set in and while I could still feel my limbs.

All of the above said, however, Carl this night was fired up to eat some poutine and I was at least a little bit drunk at this point, so it seemed like the perfect time to give poutine another go. We got a couple orders and I was delighted to find that, when prepared properly—and/or not the way the place I'd had it in Montreal went about it—poutine is absolutely delicious and is quite possibly the perfect food, in fact, even after you go to the trouble of actually finding out what cheese curds are and learn that they are solid pieces of curdled milk also sometimes known as "squeaky cheese," which is even more disgusting than when I had no idea what I was talking about. It's hard to imagine how nihilistic the first person to pop a hunk of cheese curd in to his mouth, presumably just to break up the day a little bit and see what happened, must have been, but I'm glad he did. It seems to have worked out great for everybody, including me and especially Carl, who pledged right then and there to eat poutine whenever possible the rest of his visit—and in life in general moving forward.

Fortified by poutine and at least a couple more beers, Carl and I then headed off into the Quebec City night in the direction of our rental apartment. And if, God forbid, we died along the way, we didn't really care; on this night, we had lived—at least in terms of eating poutine, anyway. For the record, though, we made it, and as soon as I crawled into bed, I fell into a deep and satisfying sleep, the kind that can only be had after eating an entire order of poutine, finishing what was left of Carl's while he was in the restroom, and even polishing off the chicken wings I had ordered in the event that the whole poutine thing didn't work out in the first place.

Carl and I awoke early the next morning, him because he's used to waking up at 6:30 a.m. because he has kids, and me because I was tired of waking up every half hour to use the bathroom after a night of drinking beer. The plan that day was to go dogsledding, something I chose to believe that every Quebec native did whenever possible, even though in reality, I'm guessing it exists at this point mostly to occupy tourists so that the locals can more easily go about their day without interference. I found a kennel about a half hour outside of the city that not only offered dogsledding, but also snowmobiling, snowshoeing, overnight stays in a yurt, and any number of other activities I was fairly certain would end in our deaths. Since Carl had a family to go home to and I had a rental car to return, we decided to just commit to a one-hour dogsledding excursion, which seemed long enough that we could say we did it, yet still short enough to minimize the odds of either of us having to make a difficult phone call to the other's loved ones afterward.

Probably the greatest challenge in getting to the dogsledding place—other than deciding which of us would be in charge of navigating and which one of us would be in charge of finding that radio station where the guy had been talking about his testicles—was to make sense of the speed-limit signs. Aside from a wild afternoon spent studying the metric system back in the third grade or so, I'm not intimately familiar with the system of measurement the vast majority of the world tends to use. And while the speedometer of our car featured both kilometres and miles per hour, it felt like too much effort to try to make sense of it all while also keeping an eye on the road, so I instead decided to go with what I like to call the "vibe of the road," which is kind of like "going with the flow," only a lot more French Canadians end up honking at you for driving too slow. When we finally turned down a country road a short while later to discover a three-storey-high sculpture of a Siberian husky, I was pretty sure we had found the place. I also made a mental note to get one of those giant Siberian huskies for myself if it's the last thing I ever did.

"*Bonjour!*" I said to the guy sitting behind the counter in the portable trailer that comprised the office of the dogsledding place.

"You are here to sled with ze dogs?" he asked in a thick French-Canadian accent.

"Yez," I replied. "We are here to sled with ze dogs."

The guy then explained that we should come back in ten minutes, when our instructor was ready. In the meantime, we could have a look around, he explained. Carl and I headed out back to find a variety of dogs, almost all of which appeared to be either Siberian huskies, Alaskan malamutes or some perhaps combination of both. I knew these dogs were bred to survive in extremely cold temperatures, but I was surprised to find many of them actually napping in the snow. It was almost like they were showing off.

"Look at us!" their faces seemed to say. "It's absolutely freezing out, and the ground is covered in ice and snow, but we're just gonna take a catnap real quick before we have to get chained to a sled and drag some assholes through the woods for the fifth time today."

I thought to tell them how there was a chocolate Lab and a golden retriever sleeping in front of a massive heater inside the trailer, but I didn't want to be a dick about it, so instead I just said,

"Hi, I'm Dave" to all of the dogs outside—as I am inexplicably inclined to do whenever left alone with animals. Even with that, though, the sled dogs mostly ignored us, so we kept looking around and, moments later, discovered a small shed with a sign that said PUPPIES on the door. What with me being a puppy fanatic from way back and all, it seemed too good to be true, almost like a trap where, as soon as I opened the door, I'd find Royal Canadian Mounted Police inside who had been waiting there all morning to arrest me for some impropriety or another.

"Looks like someone's about to be shipped back to New York City," one of them would say before slapping some cuffs on me and asking me to hop on the back of his horse—which, for the record, would have been kind of fun, the more I think about it. Instead, though, we found four Siberian husky puppies in a small pen with a heat lamp, which was admittedly adorable, but not the scenario I had hoped for, one straight out of *101 Dalmatians*, only instead of Dalmatian puppies, there are Siberian husky puppies getting up to all sorts of mischief and, who knows, maybe even solving a few crimes while they're at it. Even so, it was pretty cool—including the signs on the wall telling the puppies' stories in the first person, something I always get a kick out of.

"When I get a little bigger, I will start learning how to pull a sled!" one of the signs read. It was fun imagining what sort of voice each of the puppies might have had and which ones, for example, might struggle to properly pronounce the letter *R*, as most puppies tend to do, and stuff like that. But then I thought about the fact that even these puppies probably knew more French than I did at that point, and I was momentarily overcome with a profound sadness. It didn't matter, though, because it was time to go back to the trailer to meet our dogsledding instructor, anyway, so I couldn't let any of that get to my head.

We returned to the trailer to find our instructor for the day, a young woman named Cathérine, waiting for us. She instructed us to slip into one of the snowsuits they provided so we wouldn't die—at least not today—and meet her outside.

Once outside, Cathérine began showing us the dogsledding basics on a sled that had no dogs attached to it. As best I could tell, the idea was to just stand there and let the dogs do all the work while occasionally hitting the brakes to keep things from getting too nuts out there on the trail, but it's hard to say. There's just something about standing in the middle of the woods in a snowsuit while listening to a beautiful young woman with a French-Canadian accent explain to me how to work a dogsled that causes me to drift off and fantasize about a whole new life for myself, one where I'm living in a log cabin in the middle of the woods in Quebec, possibly chopping wood all day, but more likely just baking pies or something as I wait for my beautiful young dogsledding bride to return home from a long day of keeping her dogs in line while tolerating tourists looking to get back to frigid nature.

"*Bonjour*, Cathérine!" I'd say as she walked into the front door, covered in some adorable mixture of snow and dog spit. "Today I made blueberry!"

I ended up focusing on that mostly, while I hoped Carl was picking up on any finer details that might come in handy once we were out on the trail with actual dogs pulling us, probably wherever the hell they felt like.

Usually, there are a few sleds on the trail with each instructor, but as it turned out, Carl and I were the only ones who had signed up for our time slot. And while I'd hoped we'd each get our own dogsleds, we were instead told to share one—a potentially emasculating situation, as far as I was concerned, as only one of us would be allowed to "drive" the sled at a time, while the other one sat in front in a scenario I choose to believe is called "riding bitch," even though it probably isn't. To his credit, Carl let me drive first, since he knew I would probably say that's what happened when it came time to write this book, anyway.

I hate to keep bringing up the fact that it was ridiculously cold out, but considering the fact that we had just signed up to be dragged through the woods by dogs for an hour straight while it was well below freezing outside, it simply cannot be overstated. And like an idiot, I had neglected to pack a decent scarf, instead opting for one that had the insulating qualities of a strip of used gauze but that I thought would look good in photographs.

"I've heard of people getting fingers and toes cut off from frostbite," I thought, "but what do they do when your face gets frostbitten? Do they cut that off too? I mean, I need that!"

I'm sure the above scenario is easily Googled, but I was too horrified to even think about it, and rather than starting to calculate the odds of returning home with parts of my face missing, I just did my best to shield my face from the cold with the bullshitty, yet ultimately flattering scarf I'd brought along for the trip.

"Just follow me!" our instructor Cathérine told us in that lovely accent that had me wondering whether our kids—and who knows, maybe even our kids' kids—would have the same accent, my accent, or maybe some weird mix of both. "When I slow down, you slow down! When I speed up, you speed up!"

The truth is, Cathérine was so far ahead of us that I couldn't really tell what she was saying at all most of the time. Usually, I just gave her a thumbs-up sign while Carl and I quietly debated what she may or may not have just said and which one of us she liked better, even though, to be fair, she probably hadn't given it much thought if any at all.

There were five dogs attached to our sled, not exactly an Iditarod-ready number as best I could tell, but still enough to get us moving at a pretty good clip. In grade school, I'd read a book whose title I can't remember in which children had loaded their sleds with bars of gold and ridden them through the forest past Nazis who were none the wiser, so it was fun to pretend that that's what Carl and I were up to as we sped through the woods, our dogs barking and yipping all the way in front of us, as I stood at the back of the sled and Carl sat bundled up in front of me like a goddamn schoolgirl. This didn't last long, though, because after just a few minutes on the trail, Cathérine signalled for us to bring things to a halt as there was another sled stopped on the trail ahead of us. It was hard to see exactly what was going on—the dogs attached to

the sled in front of Cathérine's appeared to be entangled somehow as the instructor in charge crawled along the ground, trying
in vain to separate them.

"They are—how you say—making babies!" Cathérine explained
after a few moments. I'd like to think she winked at me as she said
this, but she was honestly too far ahead of us for me to tell one way
or another. God, I loved that girl.

Anyway, I thought it was bad a little earlier, when one of Cathérine's
dogs stopped in its tracks to take a crap right in the middle of the
trail, but dogs screwing on the job? This was some next-level shit.
Then again, the more I thought about it, I could totally see it. You're
a handsome young male Siberian husky, she's an attractive young
Alaskan malamute. Sure, you've seen each other around the yard a
few times, but the timing just never felt right. Then, suddenly, you
find yourselves out in the middle of the woods, running as fast as
you can while a sled loaded with tourists trying to take selfies drags
behind you, threatening to run you right over should you decide to
stop, since the tourists in question aren't exactly great with the
brakes. Emotions run high, and suddenly, there's only one thing left
to do: stop in your tracks, wayward-tourist-sled threat be damned,
and just start pumping away like there's no tomorrow while a father
tries to explain to his small child of indeterminate gender exactly
what the fluffy black-and-white dog is doing to the fluffy brown and
white dog. We've all been there. It's a story as old as time itself.

As is often the case when dogs get romantic, whether it's in the
dead of winter or not, the two dogs became stuck together from
all that red-hot lovemaking.* And after a few tries, the instructor
who had been trying to separate them eventually gave up and
instead just removed them from the sled they'd been pulling

---

* As you can probably imagine, I couldn't resist doing a bit of research
on the subject, and as it turns out, once inside the female dog's vagina,
the male dog's penis swells up so large that the male is unable to remove
it, sometimes for as long as thirty minutes, during which time the male
continuously ejaculates into the female. Seems like showing off, if you
ask me, but there you have it.

and tied them to a nearby tree, presumably to have a good, long think about what they had done before being picked up later, as the father looked on in horror and his small child began sobbing uncontrollably as one sometimes does when suddenly confronted with the complexities of life. Then, whatever dogs had managed to resist the urge to just start porking in the middle of the woods right in front of everybody pulled the rest of us down the trail, whatever was left of our innocence gone forever.

As we pulled away, it was hard not to feel sorry for the two canine lovers. Sex can be plenty awkward as it is. But imagine finishing up and then being dragged into a snowdrift and chained to a pine tree together in the dead of the winter. That's just weird. And, not to get too judgmental toward the dogs in question, more than just a little bit unprofessional, I might add, especially in these increasingly sensitive times. Then again, it's hard not to admire their *joie de vivre*. In fact, the more I think about it, we could all learn a lot from those two dogs who, for all I know, are still out there, pumping away like a couple of champs.

With the furry young couple behind us, we continued through the woods a while longer before we stopped and I let Carl have a turn standing at the back of the sled while I curled into the fetal position in the front, an experience that, it turned out, is admittedly only slightly less exciting than standing at the back of the sled as you are still racing through the woods behind five dogs and a woman whom, in an alternate reality, I am treating like gold right now somewhere in the wilds of rural Quebec. And if you take into account the possibility that any combination of the dogs pulling her sled and the dogs pulling you might put on the brakes without any notice whatsoever and just start making sweet, sweet doggy love right there on trail without even the slightest inkling of shame, the whole experience is plain electrifying. It made Carl and me feel like a slightly more giggly Lewis and Clark the whole way—and for at least a couple more hours after our dogsled journey had concluded.

"*Merci*," I said to Cathérine as I tipped her a twenty and Carl and I headed back to the car. "I will never, ever forget this day."

——

At the heavy metal bar the night before, I had made a casual inquiry of our bartender as to the whereabouts of Peter, Marian and Anton Stastny, three legendary brothers who defected from Czechoslovakia to Canada to play for the Quebec Nordiques hockey team in the 1980s. It was my hope that at least one of them was still in town and couldn't wait to hang out with me. Our bartender said he thought at least the first part of that last sentence was true, and after a bit of light internet research, I learned that Marian, the oldest of the three Stastny brothers, in fact owned and operated a golf course and hotel in Saint-Nicolas, which is located on the south shore of the St. Lawrence River near Quebec City and just so happened to be not far off our route back to town after our dogsledding excursion. Carl didn't know or care who the Stastny brothers were, but, sensing I would completely lose it if he didn't agree to take a detour to Marian Stastny's golf course on the way back to town, agreed to our next highly important mission.

We were able to find Marian Stastny's golf course and hotel pretty easily, but had somehow failed to take into account the fact that it was a freezing-cold January afternoon and the entire landscape as far the eye could see was covered in ice and snow. Or that maybe, just maybe, a golf course might not be open at that time of year. That didn't stop us from pulling into the parking lot anyway and getting a good look at the place, which consisted mostly of a yellow Victorian-style building that sort of looked like the Overlook Hotel if Wes Anderson had decided to do a remake of *The Shining*. With the car idling in the parking lot, I decided to give the place a ring.

"Stastny Golf Course and Hotel, former hockey great speaking," I imagined Marian Stastny himself would say as soon as he picked up.

"Oh hey, Marian," I'd reply. "It's Dave Hill, from America."

"Dave! Of course!" Marian would scream excitedly into the phone in what I am hoping is a bizarre Czech-meets-French-Canadian accent. "I was hoping you'd swing by! Hey—why don't you come on in and I'll regale with you tales of my time with the Nordiques over a cup of hot cocoa? Oh, and if I happen to have any old jerseys or whatever somewhere in here, you are more than welcome to them! You'd actually be doing me a favour by taking them! Hahahaha!"

We'd both laugh for a bit after that last sentence. It was going to be so, so great.

Instead, however, I got the answering machine, and we immediately decided to get the hell out of there before anyone discovered two Americans just sitting in the parking lot of a golf course and hotel during the off-season like a couple of Marian Stastny–stalking creeps.

After reconstituting ourselves back at the rental apartment, Carl and I took to the frigid streets of Quebec City once more. I probably should have mentioned this earlier, but just a few weeks before this trip, I'd taken a cruise up the coast of Norway, which in winter, of course, is freezing and sunlight-free twenty-two hours of the day. During those other two hours, it's still freezing and there is still not much sunlight—just enough to make it seem like someone might have left the refrigerator door open in middle of the night or something. All of that being said, however, Quebec City on this visit was worse. In fact, as we headed out into the night once more, I remembered how my editor Tim had warned me that it might be like "Siberia with fries" if I were to come at this time of year, and it occurred to me that he was being far too generous. That still didn't stop us from trudging a mile* in the snow to some place we'd been told had good oysters.

At the oyster place, Carl and I knocked back a few dozen oysters with beer and spoke English loudly enough to alert everyone around us to the fact that we were from out of town. It paid off nicely, however, as our bartender insisted we do a shot of gin mixed with maple syrup with him before we headed back out into the snow. I don't think I'd normally agree to do a shot of gin, and

---

* 1.609344 kilometres. But you knew that.

I can't imagine I'd do a shot of maple syrup willingly, either, but somehow the combination of the two was something I couldn't get enough of. Was it disgusting? you ask. Absolutely, maybe the worst thing I've ever had in my mouth, and that's saying something. But the fact that the bartender wanted to commemorate our Quebec City visit by doing a shot of it with us made us feel welcome and, indeed, alive.

"Gin and maple syrup—together at last!" I said before knocking back my required dosage.

"Remind me to pick up a bottle of this before we leave town," Carl said to me as we both waited for the taste to leave our mouths.

"Yeah," I nodded. "We should probably only drink this stuff from now on."

On the recommendation of our bartender at the oyster/gin-with-maple-syrup place, we headed over to the bar across the street for a drink, where Carl ordered what would amount to his third order of poutine during our visit. When did he have the second order of poutine? you ask. That was before we went dogsledding. I wasn't going to mention it, but I'm tired of covering for him. The man has a problem, and it's time the world, especially the fine people of Canada, knew.

I waited in disgust as Carl finished his poutine. Then, sated by what is technically a poutine hat trick* if you want to get technical about it, I convinced Carl to head back out into the ridiculously cold night as soon as he finished. And it was at this point that it finally occurred to me that maybe were weren't seeing Quebec City for what it really is, but instead in a rare moment when its citizens, like us, were too busy trying not to freeze to death to get up to much else. For starters, where was the anti-American animosity I had pretty much counted on at the start of the trip? I mean, sure, the more I think about it, that thing about getting me and Carl to drink a shot of gin mixed with maple syrup arguably might have

---

* In hockey, when a single player scores three goals, it is called a hat trick. But you knew that too, right?

been part of a cruel joke, but other than that and the fact that the bartender who served us salty cheese played it close to the vest when it came to letting us know where we might acquire some more for personal use, we were met with kindness at every turn. It was honestly a bit disappointing. Even so, we continued into the night for a nightcap at the heavy metal bar we'd gone to the night before in hopes that someone somewhere might somehow mistreat us before our evening was through.

Since this was our second visit to the heavy metal bar, Carl and I nodded to the bartender like we were regulars as soon as we arrived. He appeared to be a bit confused, as, to be fair, it was the not the same bartender who had been working the night before. And for what it's worth, the lone Frenchman was nowhere in sight, either. That didn't stop us from settling around the one free table in the joint like we owned the place, a feeling solidified by the fact that the bartender the night before had given us each a free sticker with the bar's logo.

The heavy metal bar was packed, which I'd hoped meant that I would be able to really gain some keen insights into the people of Quebec City. But aside from the fact that everyone was speaking French, we could have just as easily been somewhere in Cleveland, for example. But then I started paying a bit closer attention. And it was at this point that I noticed the music playing in the background: the Michael Schenker Group, a remarkably curious choice. What's the significance? you ask. Let me explain.

The Michael Schenker Group is the long-time vehicle of the German guitarist Michael Schenker, estranged brother of Rudolf Schenker, guitarist for the multiplatinum-selling German hard rock and heavy metal group the Scorpions. Michael, the younger of the two Schenker brothers, was himself a member of the Scorpions for a short time before moving on to a brief and turbulent tenure as lead guitarist for the British hard rock band UFO, no slouches when it comes to arena-ready rock themselves. In 1979, Michael formed the Michael Schenker Group in an effort to unleash his singular brand of neoclassically-inspired guitar riffs (mostly played on his trademark black-and-white Flying V guitar) on an unsuspecting public. It is dynamic, uncompromising music that is arguably not very popular at all. In fact, to play it in a public setting that is not an actual concert by the Michael Schenker Group is in itself a form of rebellion—which, in turn, is why I found it to be the most distinctly French-Canadian thing I had witnessed during our visit. Here we were in a crowded bar in Quebec City with—Carl and me aside— attractive young people enjoying themselves as far as the eye could see. Certainly, this would be the time to play music with some sort of broad appeal, or at the very least, stick to the hits of Quebec's own progressive metal masters Voivod. But no—instead, whoever was in charge of the music at the heavy metal bar that night decided to go with the obscure works of a man who walks alone: one Michael Schenker, a guy who could totally still be in the Scorpions right now if he felt like it but instead chooses otherwise. And to me, that is perhaps the most Quebec thing that has ever happened. Because what is Quebec, if not a city that doesn't care what you or the rest of Canada or even the world thinks or wants, that doesn't care what everyone else is doing? On this night, Quebec said loud and clear, "You will listen to the Michael Schenker Group and *like* it!" And that alone is reason enough for me to never stop loving that town.

(Before we go any further, I just wanted to take a moment to thank you for indulging me by at least skimming over what is surely one of the more Michael Schenker–heavy paragraphs you will come across in modern Canadacentric literature. Your patience shall be rewarded tenfold—maybe not in these pages, but some- where, I am confident.)

Emboldened by what I maintain was a profoundly Quebecois experience that just so happened to involve a German neoclassical guitarist, Carl and I finished our beers and returned to Limoilou to rest up for the adventures awaiting us the following morning.

I had set aside our last day in Quebec City for historical research, which is to say this would be the day when we'd visit some of those places that perhaps didn't sound particularly fun but which we fig- ured we should probably see anyway, so that it didn't sound like we just ended up drinking the whole time we were here. To that end, our first stop was the Plains of Abraham, located in the heart of Quebec City. To the untrained eye, the Plains of Abraham appear to be just a large park where the locals go jogging and sort of wander aimlessly until they are finally asked to leave. And while it is definitely that, it is also the historic site of the Battle of the Plains of Abraham, a decisive battle of the Seven Years' War in which the British went toe to toe against the French just outside the walls of Quebec City— or the Old City as it is now called, and, for the record, where Carl and I enjoyed a delicious and traditional French-Canadian break-fast* before we decided to get serious about our visit.

As the story goes, the battle itself lasted only an hour or so and took place on the land of a farmer named Abraham Martin, a man it's safe to assume must have been seriously annoyed by the whole thing. Anyway, shots were fired, blood was lost, and at least a couple guys wound up on the wrong end of a cannon. And while it and the events surrounding it are a complicated affair, the long and short of it is that the English took control of the nation and Tim Hortons donuts are more popular than croissants in Canada by an extremely wide margin to this day.

On the day of our visit, there was little sign of the bloodshed referenced above. There was, however, an ice rink—more of an ice track, really—located in the centre of the park, where a brave few ignored the threat of frostbite and pneumonia and circled gamely in the morning sunlight. As I watched them slowly glide along, it occurred to me that to join them would, in fact, be the most Canadian thing I could do right then and there.

"We should probably get out there and do a few laps," I said to Carl as we watched them from the comfort of our toasty rental car. "My grandfather would be so, so proud."

"Sure," Carl reluctantly agreed. "I mean, I guess technically we could get out there if you want."

---

* You're probably wondering at this point if Carl ordered poutine for break-fast. Yes, yes he did.

"Yup," I said, nodding. "We probably could."

And we almost did. But then I remembered for the umpteenth time how absurdly cold it was outside, and my desire to not die and to maybe hear that French-Canadian DJ say, "That's my testicles!" at least once more in my lifetime eventually won over. To be fair, though, I'd be lying if I said at least some small part of me didn't die as we slowly pulled away. I tried to comfort myself by recalling that no self-respecting Canadian—or even a one-quarter-Canadian person—hits the ice in rented skates, at least according to my grandfather, who insisted that we all be fitted with our very own skates just shortly after having the placenta rinsed off of us. But deep down inside, I knew that the French weren't the only ones who had been defeated on the Plains of Abraham. I, Dave Hill, had suffered a loss there, too, one that I wouldn't recover from for several blocks at least.

Next on our list of Quebec City–area must-sees was the Basilica of Sainte-Anne-de-Beaupré, located about thirty kilometres away along the St. Lawrence River. As anyone who knows me will tell you, I love a nice church—they smell nice, and sometimes there are even free donuts to be had. With both of those things in mind, we drove there as quickly as we could.

By the looks of the map on my phone, the Basilica of Sainte-Anne-de-Beaupré was surrounded by fields of greenery where it was my hope that deer, bunnies and other woodland creatures scampered about as beautiful examples of God's bold and vast creations. Instead, however, as we got closer to the church, we mostly just found convenience stores, cheap motels and even cheaper gift shops at every turn. But as much of a letdown as that was, my excitement instantly returned when Carl brought to my attention an attraction called the Cyclorama of Jerusalem, a panoramic painting (with adjoining gift shop, of course) designed to give its visitors the sensation of visiting Jerusalem at the time of the crucifixion of Jesus.

"Wasn't I literally just saying how much I'd always wished I could visit Jerusalem at the time of the crucifixion of Jesus?" I asked Carl.

"Sure," he replied unconvincingly. "I guess so."

As excited as we both were, however, our hopes were quickly dashed when we learned that, against all odds, the Cyclorama was closed on Sundays. You'd think a business located directly across the street from a church, that just so happens to live and die on the fact that it offers its visitors the sensation of visiting Jerusalem at the time of the crucifixion of Jesus, might be open on Sundays, a.k.a. "The Lord's Day." In fact, you'd think they might be open *only* on Sundays. But no, they were closed. And as a result, Carl and I were left to wonder what it might have been like to visit Jerusalem at the time of the crucifixion of Jesus and, who knows, maybe even drop some cash on a T-shirt commemorating what had just happened. Suddenly, the fact that we wimped out on going ice skating at the Plains of Abraham was only the second-saddest thing that happened to me that day.

Undeterred, however, I parked the car and Carl and I headed across the street to the Basilica of Sainte-Anne-de-Beaupré. To be fair, it's an impressive structure full of gold, marble, stained glass, elaborate woodwork and all the other usual stuff one expects from an old-ass church. But what really stood out to me was the array of crutches, arm slings, leg braces and other trappings of the injured, infirmed and disabled that hung from the pillars at the front entrance of the church. As the story goes, the basilica's namesake, St. Anne, is believed by religious types to be responsible for miracles. As a result, people apparently come from all over the world to be healed there. And while that's all well and good and no one hopes more than I do that a person can be healed of just about anything once inside, it just seems to me that if St. Anne heals, say, your messed-up leg, the least you could do is take your damn crutch with you when you're leaving, whether you need the thing or not, instead of forcing whoever is in charge of maintaining the place into putting together the hands-down-weirdest lost and found I've ever seen in my whole life at a church entrance.

As I stared up at the bizarre tangle of medical supplies mounted to the front of each pillar, I also wondered about those whose enthusiasm might have gotten the best of them after travelling all that way in hopes of being healed.

"Who wants a leg brace?" the afflicted might ask as he hastily removes the unwieldy contraption from his leg and tosses it on the cold marble floor, confident he won't be wearing it on the trip back to Regina, Saskatoon or wherever else he might have limped in from. "I sure won't be needing this anymore!"

Then, once the excitement wears off and pride gets the best of him, the guy whose leg is still absolutely killing him is forced to lurch out of the place with a smile on his face, at least until he can get back to the car, make sure the windows are rolled up, and scream bloody murder in relative privacy.

Fortunately for both Carl and me, our problems were largely mental, so the healing powers of the basilica were of little use to us in the end. Even so, we threw whatever loose change we had into the donations till before heading back to the car. I figured it couldn't hurt.

Confident we had done our due diligence in terms of taking in a bit of culture and history during our visit, Carl and I grabbed a few donuts to go from Tim Hortons and headed back to the apartment to steel ourselves for the night ahead. Word on the street—and also the news—had it that a bad snowstorm was headed Quebec City's way that night, and I figured we could perhaps double down on our Canadian experience by seeking out a "traditional Quebec restaurant" to dine at on our last night in town. I did a bit of research and found a restaurant in the Old City that specialized in "old-fashioned Quebec cuisine" and was supposedly located in the oldest house in all of Quebec. More importantly, the waitresses featured on the restaurant's website were all what, were I not an absolute gentleman, I would describe as totally smoking hot.

"We have to go to this restaurant," I said to Carl, pointing at my computer screen. "The waitresses are all superfoxes."

"What kind of food do they serve?" Carl asked.

"It's not important," I replied, shutting my laptop. "Be ready in fifteen or I'm leaving without you."

For the record, Carl was ready in ten, and a short cab ride later, we arrived at our destination. The joke was on us, however—or at least me, anyway—as, once inside, we quickly learned that we were the victims of a classic bait and switch. The fresh-faced Quebecois beauties featured on the website were nowhere in sight. Instead, the entire waitstaff appeared to be comprised of members of a progressive rock band—or, at the very least, guys who hang out with members of a progressive rock band, ponytails and inadequate mustaches and all.

As Carl attempted to stifle his laughter at me, I tried to comfort myself with the fact that we would be enjoying "old-fashioned Quebec cuisine" any minute now, even if it was going to be served to us by dudes who looked like they lived in their parents' basements. In the end, however, while the food was perfectly delicious, it mostly consisted of the fairly conventional and seemingly not-very-Canadian-at-all meat and fish offerings paired with equally conventional soups and sides consisting of steamed vegetables, rice and other trappings of homestyle Sunday dinners. In fact, it kind of felt like we were an old married couple out for a quiet dinner. The fact that we both opted for the prix fixe menu and I had the salmon only further aggravated the situation.

"How is your potato soup?" I asked Carl.

"Pretty good," Carl answered. "Yours?"

"Pretty good," I replied. "Did you try the rolls?"

"Yes. Not bad."

"Not bad at all."

It went on just like that for about forty-five minutes until Carl and I decided to grab the cheque and head to the heavy metal bar in hopes that we might end our Quebec City visit with as much of a bang as could be mustered.

When we got there, however, we found just one lone bartender and not a single other customer, not even the lone Frenchman, in sight. And instead of the soothing sounds of heavy metal coming from the sound system, there was *reggae* playing quietly in the background, which made for the most disturbing juxtaposition of

Canada and reggae since Bryan Adams unleashed "Reggae Christmas" on an unsuspecting public in 1984. Don't get me wrong: I've got no beef with reggae. But this simply wasn't the time for it, not when there are no fewer than thirteen excellent Voivod albums we could have just as easily been listening to at that point.

Carl and I downed our beers and headed back to Limoilou, where city workers were busy clearing the thick blanket of snow that had fallen since we'd stepped out for the evening. Once back inside the apartment, Carl and I heard a distant rumble approaching from down the block, and we both raced to the window to see what it might be. We looked outside to discover a massive snow blower—the largest I'd even seen, in fact—hurling snow into the back of a dump truck that followed it down the street.

"I think the truck takes all the snow and dumps it in the St. Lawrence River," Carl said as we both stared giddily out the window.

"What does the snow blower do in the meantime?" I asked.

"Another dump truck comes along, and then the snow blower fills that one up with snow too," he explained.

"Sweet."

"Totally."

As we stood marvelling at the teamwork of man and machine at work in the street outside, it was hard not to think of one Arthur Sicard, the bold Quebec native who, as mentioned previously in these pages, yes, invented the snow blower way back in 1927. I wondered what he would have thought of the majesty of what unfolded in front of me and Carl on that blustery evening, and how proud he would surely have been as he watched what was once his simple little invention toss the hell out of that snow into a massive truck that would eventually slip into the night and dump it in the mighty St. Lawrence so that maybe, just maybe, Carl and I, two weary travellers from a quiet country to the south, might be able to get in our puny rental car and make our way to the airport the next morning without incident. And it was in that moment that I realized I was finally witnessing the real Quebec, the awesome Quebec, the one

I had been looking for all along. The only thing left to do now was take a step back and give that massive snow blower a big salute, so that's exactly what I did. Carl thought it was weird, but whatever—it's not like he's even the least bit Canadian anyway, so screw that guy.

4

MERRICKVILLE, ONTARIO

Encounter with a Northern God

WHETHER YOU'VE BEEN following my career from the very beginning or you just happened to inadvertently glance at the flap of this book, you might be aware that I until recently hosted an obscure radio program called *The Goddamn Dave Hill Show* on WFMU in Jersey City, New Jersey. It was a three-hour program, most of which was dedicated to technical difficulties and dead air, but I also managed to take a few phone calls from listeners. Also, thanks to the magic of the internet, people could listen and call in from all over the world, even Canada.

In fact, one night I received a phone call from a curious fellow from Merrickville, Ontario, named Nils. He spoke with an unmistakable Canadian accent as he explained that he listened to the show every week while drinking alone in his garage. Naturally, my listeners and I fell in love with him instantly, hanging on his every word, even when he seemed to have set the phone down as he got up to do something else entirely in his garage. Nils quickly became a regular caller, and before long I realized I needed to see his garage at least once for myself before I died lest my time on this earth be entirely for naught. And with that, I made a plan with him to broadcast live from his garage one cold and damp Monday night in February.

When my friend Joe, whom you no doubt remember from our trip to my grandfather's farm in Clinton, Ontario (you know, the one during which he promised to make me a moose exactly like the one I'd found in a charity thrift shop, but the record will show that he still hasn't as of this writing*), heard I was going to visit Nils, he asked if he could come, too. I was a little worried Nils might feel overwhelmed by having two boorish-within-reason Americans just show up in his garage like that, but on the off chance that Nils was some sort of crazed serial killer,** I figured I'd have a better chance of survival—or at the very least, wouldn't die alone—if Joe was there with me, so I said, "Sure. Why not?"

Merrickville is located about an hour outside of Ottawa, so I figured, what with me writing the definitive book about Canada by a non-Canadian, I might try and schedule a one-on-one meeting with Prime Minister Justin Trudeau as long as I was in the area.

"He seems like a nice enough guy," I thought. "How hard could it possibly be? In fact, he'd probably welcome the opportunity to break up the day a little bit."

---

* I realize you may be wondering why I would still want Joe to make me a replica of the moose I found in the charity shop in Clinton when I ended up being able to get the charity-shop moose shipped to me in New York City. This is because, if I had two separate moose, I would be able to more easily enjoy a moose in cast-iron form in more than one room of my apartment— I would no longer need to carry the one moose I now have from room to room to prolong my moose enjoyment. I could leave the living room where the moose from the charity shop is on display and move straight into the bedroom, where there would be a bedroom moose on display, just waiting for me to take in its mighty moose majesty. Ultimately, it would be nice to have a moose for each room of my home. But then again, who do I think I am—Jennifer Aniston?

** Then again, now that I think about it, are there any other kind?

You'll be shocked, however, to hear that the email I sent to Justin through his website went unreturned, as did the second, admittedly more profanity-laced one. So much for him being the "Prime Minister of the people," or a "regular guy," or any of that other stuff his obviously highly skilled PR team would have us believe. In fact, please let the record show that, as of this writing, I am interpreting Justin's lack of response on this matter as his way of officially telling me to go screw myself. And yes, I was surprised to learn that he would use such language, too. But I guess we can just take everything we ever thought we knew about Justin Trudeau and throw it out the window. In my experience, at least, he will let you down at every turn.

Anyway, the upside of Justin Trudeau basically telling me to go screw myself this go-round was that I was able to take a more leisurely approach to my trip, flying into Ottawa late in the morning on the day of my radio show rather than getting there first thing to have breakfast with Justin at his favourite diner, play a game of racquetball together, or whatever. Since I still needed to eat, however, prior to boarding my Air Canada flight in Newark, I bought a three-bean salad at the airport that turned out to also have corn in it, something I took as an omen to expect the unexpected, at least as far as this particular Canadian adventure went, anyway. And in the interest of getting into the proper mindset for my trip, I listened to Ottawa's own New Swears,* an extremely catchy rock quartet, on my headphones throughout the flight, even when announcements were being made in French, something I normally don't like to miss out on because, as I may have mentioned previously, it makes me feel more sophisticated.

---

* In the likelihood that the entire lineup of New Swears are reading this book right now, ideally together, there is no need to thank me for the plug I just gave you. And, no, you don't owe me anything in return either. Unless, of course, you want to prove that you're no Justin Trudeau and would be up for a quality hang next time I roll through town. Whatever, just putting it out there. It's nothing you need to think about right now as you enjoy this book.

It's a quick jaunt from Newark to Ottawa, but as the plane touched down into the land of ice and snow,* I already felt like I was a world away from my comparatively balmy homeland. That distance felt even greater after I stopped in the restroom at the Ottawa airport to discover a man relieving himself while somehow keeping his legs pressed flush against the sides of the urinal, a perplexing and especially dicey technique for reasons I don't have time to get into in these pages. As I stared at him for much longer than I assume he was comfortable with, I realized the omen of the three-bean salad was already proving itself to be true.

In an effort to blend in a bit more than usual on this trip, I wore a Quebec Nordiques winter hat I had seen during my trip to Quebec City, resisted the urge to buy, and subsequently paid twice as much for online once I realized my life would be a mess without it. And it couldn't have worked better, as the customs agent at the Ottawa airport seemed to be under the impression that I was just visiting from the next province over.

"*Bonjour!*" she said.

"Oh no," I said with a laugh. "I'm actually from Cleveland. I'm guessing my hat threw you for a major loop."

"What?" she asked.

"My hat—it's from the now-defunct Quebec Nordiques hockey team," I explained. "In fact, did you know that former Quebec Nordiques great Marian Stastny owns a golf club just outside of Quebec City and my friend Carl and I actually—"

"Passport, please," she said.

Anyway, it was pretty cool. For both of us.

I got through customs without a hitch and continued to the arrivals area, where Nils had kindly offered to pick me up. The pessimist in me figured this might be the point where I was tossed into

---

* I think we both know this isn't a common nickname for Ottawa or even Canada in general and that I simply lifted a line from "Immigrant Song" by Led Zeppelin just now. My point is just that it was just really icy and snowy when I landed. Also, Zeppelin rules!

the back of an unmarked cargo van with Northwest Territories plates* that would immediately speed off and take me to some remote destination where I would be subjected to some bizarre and distinctly Canadian medical experiments—or at least get my feelings hurt—and the part of me that craves adventure was counting on it. In the end, though, Nils arrived in a minivan with seemingly no intent to harm me in any way whatsoever.

"Hey there," Nils said, displaying a similar affection for defunct Canadian sports teams by way of a Montreal Expos baseball cap.

"Hey," I replied, before exchanging a handshake that morphed into the kind of tentative hug that men who have up until now only spoken to each other over the airwaves can't help but share.

"Nice Nordiques hat," Nils said as I got in the passenger seat.

"You sure it doesn't make it seem like I'm trying too hard to blend in?" I asked, immediately letting my guard down.

"It kind of does," Nils admitted. "But it's still a pretty cool hat."

Since I didn't want to seem overly impressionable, and the hat was indeed pretty cool, I left it on another couple minutes before removing it when Nils wasn't looking and sheepishly stuffing it into my messenger bag.

"We can just drive straight to Merrickville, or did you want to see a bit of Ottawa first?" Nils asked as we pulled out of the airport. I was inclined to say no at first, as, given my beef with Justin Trudeau mentioned earlier, I didn't want to give him the satisfaction of somehow getting word that I had agreed to a minivan tour of his stomping grounds. But in the interest of drinking in as much of Canada as humanly possible, I reluctantly said yes in the end.

A short drive later, Nils and I found ourselves in Ottawa proper.

"This is the Glebe," Nils said, nodding out the window as we headed down the main drag of the weirdly named area he'd just mentioned.

---

* As long as I'm on the topic, kudos to whoever had the idea to make the Northwest Territories licence plate in the shape of a polar bear. This is the greatest thing that has ever happened, at least in terms of licence plates anyway.

"The Glebe," I replied. "It sounds like the kind of place where wizards and trolls hang out."

"They kind of do," Nils said. "In fact, I used to get hammered around here a lot when I was younger."

As it turned out, Nils had lived in Ottawa in his twenties before heading north to work in the oil industry.

"You could always spot the oil workers when they'd come back to town because they wore brand-new jeans and always blew their money on the latest electronic gadgets and stuff," Nils explained. "I worked in oil until I had my first kid and realized I didn't want to be away from home anymore."

Nils and I continued our minivan tour of Ottawa, eventually rolling up to Parliament Hill, which was beautiful.

"Is that where Justin Trudeau works?" I asked.

"I think he has an office somewhere in there," Nils replied.

"That prick," I said under my breath.

"What was that?" Nils asked.

"Well, let's just say Justin Trudeau isn't exactly great with responding to email and leave it at that," I said, trying to get back to admiring the architecture.

Things got quiet for a couple blocks after that, until we passed by a hotel where Nils's wife Jen used to work.

"She was working at the front desk and used to take bookings for the spa they have in there," Nils began. "One day, Wayne Gretzky tried to make an appointment."

"Awesome," I said, brightening up as I usually do when Gretzky talk comes into play.

"They were fully booked, and Jen didn't know who Wayne Gretzky was, so she said no," Nils continued.

"No way!" I replied.

"Way," Nils continued. "And then, I guess, he tried to politely ask if she might be able to make an exception, what with him being the greatest hockey player ever and all."

"I thought Wayne Gretzky always says that Gordie Howe was the greatest hockey player of all time," I said.

"Well, he didn't actually come out and say he was the greatest hockey player ever or anything," Nils clarified. "He just hinted that he wasn't bad* at it and maybe she could make an exception for him."

"Then what did she say?" I asked eagerly.

"She still said no," Nils said.

I had yet to meet Jen, but I liked her already—not because I want to live in a world where Wayne Gretzky doesn't get exactly what he wants whenever he wants, but because I liked the idea that not even one of the most famous Canadians in history was going to get special treatment on Jen's watch. I couldn't wait to meet her.

As Nils pointed his minivan in the direction of home, we soon found ourselves driving along the Rideau Canal, which was packed with folks of all ages, some skating along its frozen waters, some standing closer to the shore, just taking in the majesty of it all while drinking what I choose to believe was hot cocoa spiked with Crown Royal—which admittedly might be disgusting in practice, but whatever, this is my book.

"Wow," I said. "That's a lot of people out there for a Monday, huh?"

"It's Family Day," Nils explained.

"What does that mean?" I asked.

"It's a national holiday," Nils told me. "Everyone gets work and school off, and most businesses are closed, too."

"And then what?" I asked.

"People do stuff like go skating on the Rideau Canal," he said. "You know, family stuff."

"Because it's Family Day," I said in an effort to let Nils know I was really getting it.

"Right," Nils said. "Because it's Family Day."

It was a nice concept that admittedly confused me at first, given the fact that, what with me being an American living in the current era and all, anything with the word *family* in it tends to conjure

---

* For example, did you know that Wayne Gretzky is the leading scorer in NHL history with more combined goals and assists than any other player ever? That alone would probably be enough to get me through the day most days. It is my sincere hope that it also brings Wayne some form of solace.

images of the US Congress trying to pass laws against the LGBT community or women's reproductive rights—that's a long way from families simply getting out and enjoying the day together. But this admittedly might just be my own hang-up. I did, however, do a bit of research and learned that Canadian federal employees *don't* get Family Day off work, which likely meant that my nemesis Justin Trudeau, whimsical socks and all, was still slaving away somewhere at that very moment, no matter what everyone else in the country was doing, an image that heartened me.

Getting back to the Rideau Canal, it is at this point that I would love more than anything to tell you that I insisted that Nils pull the minivan over immediately as I slipped on a pair of skates and began gliding effortlessly down the mighty Rideau like Oksana Baiul in her prime.* But the fact is, I just didn't see this whole frozen canal thing coming, so I neglected to pack my skates. It's a real shame, too, as nothing would have honoured my Canadian grandfather more than to have his grandson Dave show up in Ontario, more than thirty years after his death, and school mofos up and down the Rideau Canal without even really trying. Instead, I just grabbed a handful of peanuts from the bag Nils had sitting there on the dashboard and we continued in the direction of Merrickville, my head hanging in shame for at least a few blocks until Nils pointed out a couple people actually riding snowmobiles along the canal, an image that understandably caused me to perk right up again.

"Whoa!" I said, having never seen someone riding a snowmobile in person before, what with the fact that I'm from the suburbs of Cleveland, Ohio, and the only other place I've ever lived for an

---

* Figure skating buffs will no doubt remember Oksana as the Ukrainian winner of the gold medal at the 1994 Winter Olympics in Lillehammer, Norway. It was a wild time, to be sure. All eyes were on US figure skating darling Nancy Kerrigan, who had recently been clubbed in the knee by a thug sent her way by arch-rival and fellow US figure skating darling (within reason) Tonya Harding, no slouch on the ice herself. But then Oksana just showed up and said, "Oh, is that the gold medal? Why don't I just take that?" Hardly a day goes by when I don't bring it up in conversation, no matter what else is being talked about at the time.

extended period is New York City. "Don't they worry about falling through the ice?"

"It's pretty frozen out there, so it doesn't happen all that much," Nils explained.

"But sometimes?" I asked.

"Sure, once in a while, I guess."

"Cool."

Sensing my enthusiasm for distinctly Canadian winter activities, Nils mentioned he knew of a curling place not far from his house.

"Think we could actually go curling?" I asked.

"We could try," Nils replied.

It seemed like a solid plan, since, from what I already knew about curling, you just need a broom and a six-pack or two and you're off to the races. Also, it's worth noting that this trip occurred at least a few weeks before the people of America were absolutely consumed with curling fever as a result of the US men's curling team beating the Canadian team to win the gold medal at the 2018 Winter Olympics in PyeongChang, South Korea. Indeed, it was a wild time in our nation's history, during which Americans simply could not and would not shut up about curling for a solid four hours or so, something I bring up simply to point out that I am not some sort of bandwagon jumper, but someone who has held an at-least-vague interest in curling for pretty much as long as I can remember—and who knows, maybe even longer.

We pulled up to the curling facility a few minutes later. I couldn't wait to get out there and do whatever those guys are doing when they're playing curling, a sport I was pretty much sure I was going to be incredible at.

"This place used to be a hockey rink when I was a kid, but they converted it into a curling place," Nils said as we got out of his minivan.

"Really?" I asked. "Didn't the hockey players revolt?"

"No—I think they just made another hockey rink somewhere else."

"Oh," I replied, slightly disappointed that the standoff between curling players and hockey players I had been excitedly picturing in my mind had apparently never taken place.

We headed inside to find a handful of sixtysomething men kicking back with a few beers, presumably coming down from yet another round of hot curling action.

"Can I help you?" asked one of the men, whom I took to be the leader—though I admittedly only thought that because he had a hat on—as he set his beer down and began walking toward us like he wasn't ruling out the possibility of a fight.

"My friend is visiting from the United States and wanted to try curling," Nils explained while nodding in my direction.

"We're done curling today," the man said. "Besides, even if we weren't, he still couldn't play with us."

"Why?" I asked, trying to sound as non-aggressive as possible even though he was clearly asking for it.

"Well, for starters, do you own curling shoes?" the man asked.

"No," I replied.

"Well, you can't curl without curling shoes," the man said, seemingly pretty pleased with himself for laying down the law like that.

"Where can I get those?" I asked.

"We sell them here," he answered.

"Great," I replied. "I'd like one pair of curling shoes, please."

"Sorry, we can't sell you those," he said with a smile, "but I'll show you guys around if you like."

Nils and I weren't looking for any curling trouble, so rather than bothering to get up in the guy's business about why they weren't willing to sell me a damn pair of curling shoes, a type of footwear I imagine I could buy and sell ten times over, we just accepted his offer to show us around and followed him out to the curling rink or court or whatever the hell it's called.*

"This is it," the man said proudly as he gestured to the ice. "Five sheets of ice to curl on."

---

* Also, as long as I'm on the topic, imagine how much more attitude I would have gotten from this guy had we visited after the Canadian team lost to the American team at the Olympics. We both probably would have been bleeding at this point.

"But only if you've got proper curling shoes," I said.

"But only if you've got proper curling shoes," he said right back.

"How does curling work?" I asked. "Is it pretty much like bocce ball, only on ice?"

"Not exactly," the man replied.

"But similar?" I asked.

"It's similar, sure," he explained, "but curling is ultimately its own thing."

I could tell he was getting defensive, so, rather than getting him further riled up, I decided to change the topic to something more agreeable.

"Is it okay if I walk out on the ice?" I asked.

"No," the man said.

"Is it because I don't have those curling shoes you won't sell me for reasons I will never understand?" I asked.

He didn't answer me after that. Instead, he just started talking to Nils mostly, but I'd like to think that had more to do with the fact that Nils was wearing a hat, too, and not because I'd said anything wrong.

"We've had teams from all over the world come here to play," the man said, gesturing to a variety of flags hanging on the wall from countries as far away as Japan.

"Sounds like you guys have a lot of fun curling," Nils replied.

"Yup," the man, seemingly thrilled with himself for denying me the opportunity of totally dominating him at curling that afternoon, said with a smile. "And we drink a lot of beer while we do it!"

It was nice to be right about one thing, at least.

Our tour concluded, Nils and I thanked the guy for letting us stare at sheets of ice for a few minutes and headed back out to the minivan. A short drive later, we found ourselves in Merrickville proper.

"Merrickville is pretty popular with tourists," Nils told me as we rolled into town.

Since it was a cold, damp day in February, the tourists weren't out in full force—or at all, really. And the fact that it was Family Day wasn't helping matters.

"Some of the stores will still be open here, though, because this is the kind of place people like to come to on their day off," Nils said. "But generally speaking the stores are closed on Family Day."

Given my penchant for entirely useless knick-knacks, I suggested we have a look inside an antique shop that appeared to be one of the few shops open for business that day. Nils parked out front and we began to have a look around, first at all the stuff lined up in front of the shop, and then heading inside to see what treasures awaited us. To be fair, most antique shops I've encountered, unless they are of the super-expensive, high-end variety, mostly traffic in what is known in colloquial terminology as "useless bullshit," and this one was no different. There was a rusty anvil out front that caught my eye, but its five-hundred-dollar (Canadian) price tag kept me from marching it to the counter, even though I'm not entirely sure what they are used for outside of the cartoon universe.

"Seems like a lot for an anvil," Nils said, reading my mind.

"Yeah," I said, just as blown away by this latest development as Nils seemed to be.

I couldn't help but do a bit anvil research on my phone as we continued looking around, and I was surprised to find five hundred dollars (still Canadian), while not exactly a steal* as far as anvils go, isn't a bad price, either. Even so, that felt like way too much to pay for one, considering it would likely just be pushed far under my bed as soon as I got it home.

Nils and I poked around the store for a couple minutes as I kept my eye out for any especially Canadian novelties I might bring back home with me. There were a couple sets of antique wooden sock dryers that I'm still kicking myself for not buying, but other than that, not much in the way of must-have items.

"Can I help you guys?" asked the man behind the counter—who

---

* Or should I say "steel"? Thank you. By the way, please consider these footnotes as bonus content. You are not required to read a single one of them—to be fair, at least one in three exist solely as an attempt to chip away at my contractually-agreed-upon word count. That said, I do recommend that you read most or all of them if you would like to really get your money's worth and experience this book in all its one-quarter-Canadian glory.

appeared to be about seventy and had an electrolarynx, one of those robotic-sounding trachea devices that help people who have lost their voicebox to speak—as we milled around the store.

"We're just looking around, mostly," Nils told him.

"Are you from here in town?" the man asked.

"I live just a few blocks away," Nils told him. "My friend here is visiting from New York City."

Nils and the man continued talking for a couple minutes after that, and I stood there watching as my mind drifted back to my childhood, when my dad took my brother and me to a Cleveland Indians baseball game. My dad ended up sitting next to a guy with an electrolarynx, something I had never seen or heard before in my life. I was stunned as I listened to my dad talk with this man who sounded just like the Cylon Centurions from the original series of *Battlestar Galactica* well into the seventh inning. I don't know if I'd thought about that day even once since then, but suddenly there I was, standing in an antique shop in Merrickville, Ontario, somehow being magically transported back to my youth. It was nice, in a way, but also weird as hell, and even a bit sad, considering that the Tribe lost that day and I tended to internalize such things in my youth. So, in an effort to beat my feelings back down inside me, I decided to go back out front and ponder the rusty anvil again for a couple minutes until Nils joined me outside.

"Five hundred bucks," I said, shaking my head. "Who knew?"

"Yeah," Nils agreed. "Seems like a lot for an anvil."

We tooled around town for a few minutes after that, stopping into a record store where Nils once regretfully paid twenty-five dollars for a Damn Yankees* T-shirt intended to be worn ironically

---

* Damn Yankees were an American rock "supergroup" comprised of Tommy Shaw from Styx, Jack Blades from Night Ranger and Ted Nugent, formerly the guitar player for the excellent Amboy Dukes and now a right-wing American nutjob whose only positive attributes are being sweet at guitar and having worn a loincloth on stage during much of his solo career. He also reportedly used to shoot a crossbow on stage during Damn Yankees concerts, which also seems kind of cool, but that's it—I'm done talking about that anus.

but ultimately worn with genuine enthusiasm, and passing by the canals in town, which Nils said were cause for great excitement for people of all ages during the high season.

"People like to come and look at them," he explained.

"And then what?" I asked.

"I dunno," Nils said. "Maybe go get ice cream or something."

"I like a nice canal," I told him, even though it's hard to say whether I really do or not. "And ice cream, of course."

A few minutes later, we found ourselves back at Nils's place.

"My wife took the kids to my mom's for the day because she said she wanted us to be able to have some 'guy time,'" Nils said, laughing in a way that let me know that any concerns that he might saw me in half or maybe do something that would be even harder to explain to my loved ones was officially my own hang-up.

"Cool," I said before scratching myself in the way that men do when they know they are in a judgment-free environment.

After I set my bag down in one of Nils's basement guest rooms, he and I did our damnedest to really dig in and have some serious "guy time," first by talking about how Joe wouldn't be able to park his car in the street overnight because of the snow plows, and then about how the plumber was coming the next day to look at the toilet. And when that ran its course more quickly than expected, we decided to head into town to look around a bit more, stopping off first at a shop that specialized in mustard, a reasonably manly condiment, all things considered.

I imagine Nils took the mustard store for granted, what with it being just down the street from his house and all. But, like so many others before me, I'm sure, I couldn't help be lured by the promise of mustard that didn't exactly play by the rules. And the fact that the store's slogan was "We know good mustard" wasn't helping matters. There seemed to be quite a few stores like this in Merrickville, places that were hell-bent on cashing in on a day tripper's willingness to check his or her inhibitions at the city limits when it came to good times all the time, whether they be mustard-related or not. In their day-to-day lives, sure, most people play it close to the vest when it comes to things like mustard or even scented candles. But when you get them cutting loose a bit, next thing you know, they're marching to the counter with a jar of wine peppercorn, beer basil or even chipotle-lime mustard.

"This one is honey-tarragon flavoured!" I said to Nils as I dipped a complimentary pretzel stick into an open jar no doubt intended to seduce me.

"Yup," Nils replied.

"And this one is balsamic and cracked pepper!" I said, sampling another jar.

"Yeah," Nils said, seemingly not as excited as I was about the various mustard offerings. "They have a lot of different mustards here."

"And this one is Canadian maple!" I said, helping myself to a third sample. "I bet this is pretty popular around here. You know, since we're in Canada and all."

"Probably," Nils replied. "You about ready to go or what?"

I could have stayed in there, sampling mustards, all day, but between the annoyed look on Nils's face and the fact that I would have had to check a bag if I decided to bring any artisanal mustard back on the plane with me, I figured it was as good a time as any to head out and see what other adventures awaited us in Merrickville, and—who knows—maybe even beyond. To that end, we headed outside and continued down the block to the Goose, a neighbour-hood bar that Nils said would probably be our best bet in terms of "action" on a Monday afternoon.

The Goose was kind of like the Merrickville version of the bar *Cheers*, as best I can tell. There was a hockey goalie mask mounted on the beer taps and two television screens on the wall, both of which were playing either a hockey game or a show about hockey games, which is usually just as good in terms of giving a place the hockey vibe I rather enjoy.

"Hey, Nils," an attractive blonde woman behind the bar said to him as we grabbed a couple stools. I have to admit, it felt pretty good to be rolling in there with a regular like that.

In the spirit of guy time, Nils and I ordered a couple beers and, since we were both feeling a bit peckish,* began perusing the menus, eventually both deciding on the seafood chowder that came served in a bread bowl. As anyone will tell you, I am generally against the concept of a bread bowl, as I think people need to practise restraint and not eat what is technically serving as a dish for most of the meal. The way I see it, if you are still hungry after finishing whatever was inside the bowl, order something else.** But since I was on Nils's turf and didn't want him to get a reputation for showing up with difficult out-of-towners, I decided to keep this controversial opinion to myself.

"Gary*** got a job in a gold mine in Nunavut," said the blonde bartender, who I soon learned was named Hailey. "Two weeks on, two weeks off."

"What does that mean?" I asked, just trying to join the conversation. "He goes up there and works two weeks, and then comes back here and hangs out for two weeks?"

"Yup," Hailey said, presumably impressed with how easily I pick up on things.

"Well, at least that way, you won't get too sick of him, I guess,"

---

* Admittedly not a very good word to use for any reason whatsoever during "guy time," but I'm sticking with it.

** If you are a Dave Hill completist (and really, why wouldn't you be?), you may remember that I tore bread bowls a new one in my last book, *Dave Hill Doesn't Live Here Anymore*. I realize some people might think laying into bread bowls in writing more than once in one's lifetime is a bit much, but mark my words: as long as bread bowls remain a thing and I still have a voice, I will be putting up with none of them and their bullshit.

*** I can't remember what Hailey's husband's actual name is. I simply choose to believe that his name is Gary because that's where my head is at right now. And if you think I'm going to go to the trouble of calling Nils and asking him Hailey's husband's correct name so I can get it right the one time I mention him in this book, you've got another think coming. I've got bigger fish to fry, thank you very much.

I replied. Needless to say, everyone within earshot laughed a whole bunch after that.

As you can probably tell, things were going really great for me at the Goose, but it was at this point that Joe texted to let us know that he was finally pulling into majestic Merrickville after a long drive from Cleveland, so Nils and I finished our beers and I stopped short of sending my empty bread bowl crashing to the ground to send a clear message about how I feel about them on the off chance that none of the people in the bar that day end up reading this book. Then, Nils and I walked back to his place to meet Joe.

Since Joe is also a regular listener and caller to my radio show, I'm guessing there was enough of a familiarity between him and Nils for Nils to also welcome him into his home for a couple nights. And on the off chance that Nils was still feeling uneasy about things and had only agreed to let Joe into his home because I had mentioned it, I brought up the fact that Joe's dad was a famous television sports announcer back in Cleveland, even though I know Joe gets annoyed by the fact that I do that literally every time I introduce him to someone.

"Joe's dad is pretty much the Don Cherry of Cleveland," I explained as any residual tension slowly left Nils's body. "He was the announcer for the Cleveland Cavaliers and the Cleveland Barons."*

"Awesome," Nils said with a smile.

"Thanks," Joe said, setting his bag down. It was fun to watch them becoming friends so quickly.

Before Nils had a chance to ask any follow-up questions about Joe's dad or Joe had a chance to glare at me for bringing up his dad's status as a local Cleveland celebrity again, even after he had asked me to stop doing that, Nils's wife and kids arrived back home, so we headed upstairs to greet them.

---

* I'm guessing you know who the Cleveland Cavaliers are. But in case you don't know who the Barons are, they were a professional hockey team that played in the NHL from 1976–78.

"How has your guy time been going?" Nils's wife, Jen, asked as she and Nils's children, seven-year-old Anna and four-year-old Huey, sat on the couch, quietly eyeing me and Joe, as young children tend to do when two strange men are milling around their house and coming within close proximity of their toys and stuff.

"Good," Nils said. "It was quality guy time."

"Yeah," I chimed in. "It's good you stayed away with the kids for as long as you did."

Jen looked at Nils and me suspiciously for a moment after that before Nils tried to get his kids in on the excitement.

"Huey does a mean version of the Canadian national anthem," Nils said.

"Awesome," I said, making no effort to hide my enthusiasm for what I believe to easily be one of the top five national anthems out there today, especially when it's sung in French.

"Yeah," Nils continued. "He combines it with 'Can't Help Falling in Love' by Elvis Presley."

"Why does he do that?" I asked while certainly not complaining. "Is it on purpose?"

"I have no idea," Nils answered. "He just does it."

"That's amazing!" Joe said. "Will he sing it for us now?"

"Yeah!" I chimed in. "Sing it, Huey! Come on! Sing it!"

"Let's see if I can get him to do it," Nils replied in subtle acknowledgement of the fact that everyone knows little kids won't do shit unless you beg them for, like, ten minutes first. "Huey, will you sing the national anthem for us?"

Huey just shook his head and went back to watching *Despicable Me* for what Nils estimated was the forty-seventh time.

Shut down, at least in terms of hearing what promised to be the greatest mash-up of a national anthem and an Elvis tune of all time, anyway, Joe and I decided to let Nils have a little family time and headed back downstairs to rest up for my radio show that night, which would be broadcasting live from Nils's garage whether he liked it or not at that point.

I decided to take a nap, and woke a short while later to find Nils bringing Joe and me a cheese plate and a Thermos full of hot coffee to help us fuel up for the three hours of scintillating radio ahead of us. At first, I thought it was strange that Nils brought us an entire Thermos full of coffee rather than, for example, having us just walk upstairs for a refill if we needed one. But after thinking about it for a second, I found it remarkably considerate and very much in keeping with the nonstop guy-time aesthetic we were apparently after, at least as far as Jen was concerned, anyway. In fact, if there is anything more manly than drinking coffee from a Thermos in a basement in Canada in the dead of winter, I'd sure as hell like to hear about it. Then again, he may just have been trying to avoid having me corner his son and beg him to sing the Canadian national anthem again, not that I had any intention of giving up on that anytime soon.

As I was gearing up for my radio show, Nils's friend Paul popped by, seemingly both to say hello and perhaps ogle the foreigners who had commandeered Nils's basement. Paul is a musician, and there was talk of getting together the next night at the home of their other musician friend Steve in nearby Kemptville, the town Nils is originally from.

As is usually the case when musicians hang out in a basement, the talk eventually drifted to music. And since we were in Canada, the music talk then drifted to Canadian bands, a complicated topic. I mean, sure, there's Rush, which most Canadians and Americans can at least agree is the best, as far as being Rush goes. Ditto for Triumph. But then you get into the Tragically Hip, who are held in high regard by all Canadians, but remain a largely confusing entity to most Americans, myself included, at least for the moment.

"Why are they so popular?" I asked.

"You gotta love the Hip," Nils explained.

"Yeah, everyone loves the Hip," Paul agreed.

We all just stared at each other for a few seconds after that, until, fortunately, Paul had to go, thus allowing me to avoid further discussion of the Tragically Hip until I was really ready for it.

As for my radio show that night, you will no doubt be thrilled to read that I made a point of making sure that all the music I played on the show broadcast live from Nils's garage that night was Canadian.* The rest of the show involved Nils, Joe and me hunched over a microphone that was hooked up to my computer, which then beamed our voices to WFMU's studio in Jersey City, New Jersey, where my right-hand man James Fernandez hit all the right buttons required to broadcast it over the airwaves. It was exciting to see the show from Nils's perspective as he and Joe cracked open beers (German and Polish and *not* Canadian beers, I am horrified to note) and took swigs of rum while I did my damnedest to host the show and field phone calls from listeners as I always do. At various points in the program, Nils would get up from the table my microphone and laptop were resting on and alternately smoke a cigarette, ride an exercise bicycle or relieve himself in the driveway—and, at least once during the evening, as I recall, all three at the same time.

Vying for attention on the show that night was a porn star turned author who called in from her parents' house in New Jersey to promote her new book, which I was told focused less on porn and more on the entrepreneurial spirit and general moxie required to be a porn star who plays by her own set of porn rules. But even that wasn't enough to outshine the magic and majesty of broadcasting live from a garage in Merrickville, Ontario, that night.

And as we rolled into the final hour of the show, I broke my own rule of not drinking alcohol during my show** and cracked one of Nils's non-Canadian beers for myself so that I might fully experience my own radio show as Nils does from his garage each week. It was a great feeling, even if a few slices of cheese and a couple pretzels were the only things I had eaten in the last several hours and,

---

* Specifically, I played "Dance with the Devil" by Ottawa's New Swears (don't sweat it, guys); "Tired of Waiting" by Victoria, British Columbia's NoMeansNo; "Turn the Season" by Toronto's Fucked Up; the Pink Floyd song "Astronomy Domine," as interpreted by Jonquière, Quebec's Voivod; "Another Year Again" by Toronto's the Sadies; "Summoned to Succumb" by Toronto's Cauldron; and, yes, "Fly by Night" by Toronto's (and, ultimately, the world's) Rush.

** This is because of my professionalism.

as a result, I was audibly slurring my words—and, according to some reports, at least, adopting a light Canadian accent after just a couple sips.

When midnight rolled around, I signed off for the night as a feeling of great pride washed over me, knowing that I had just completed what I maintain is the first-ever live broadcast of a US-based radio show from a garage in Merrickville, Ontario. And to celebrate that bold achievement, Nils, Joe and I toasted ourselves with shots of rum. I still think we should have had shots of Crown Royal, or least shotgunned a couple Molson's instead, but whatever—sometimes you just gotta make do with what you have.

By this point in the evening, I had already been up for about twenty hours, which I realize isn't enough to land me in any medical journals or anything, but was still enough to leave me pretty exhausted, so I decided it was time to turn in for the night.

"I'll see you guys in the morning," I said to Nils and Joe as I headed back into the house.

"Are you serious?" Nils asked as he relieved himself in the driveway again.

"Yeah, I'm pretty beat," I explained.

"I usually hang out in the garage until about five in the morning after your show each week," Nils said.

"Really?" I asked. "That's awesome!"

"Yeah," Nils agreed. "It is."

"You still could, I guess," I replied.

"Oh, I intend to," Nils said. "Good night."

It was hard not to admire Nils's joie de vivre and even be a bit jealous that he still had the fire to party until dawn on a Monday night in Merrickville, but we had big plans to swing by nearby Kemptville, where Nils grew up, the next day, so I decided it was best to rest up for the red-hot suburban Ontario action ahead.

I awoke the following morning to find Joe pouring a cup of coffee from a fresh full Thermos Nils had apparently just delivered to the basement. I poured myself a cup and then headed upstairs to see if I could convince Nils's son, Huey, who was currently watching

Despicable Me yet again, to sing his particularly inspired version of the Canadian national anthem.

"Hey, Huey," I said, "think you could sing the national anthem for me now?"

He just looked at me for a second before returning his eyes to the TV screen.

"Come on, Huey," Nils urged, "just give us a couple bars."

Still nothing. And with that I returned to the basement, where at least knew I could get myself another cup of coffee if I wanted one.

"The kid won't budge," I said to Joe as I poured myself a fresh cup from the Thermos.

"Because he knows he's sitting on gold," Joe said, sipping from his.

A short while later, the kids went to school for the day, so Nils, his wife and Joe and I headed into town for breakfast at a local diner. By this time, I'd learned to check all Canadian menus for poutine before I did anything else, and I was surprised to find that, despite the fact that we were in a diner in Ontario, the menu indeed featured several varieties.

"I thought poutine was more of a Quebec thing and that it wasn't a good idea to eat it anywhere else," I said to Nils.

"Sort of," Nils explained, "but we're still technically in curd country here, so you'll be fine."

With that, Nils, Joe and I each placed an order.* Not looking to fly so close to the sun that early in the day, Jen refrained.

"A buddy of mine in Cleveland has a restaurant and they serve poutine," Joe said, seemingly just as excited as I was that the phrase "curd country" had just been used.

---

* And I made a mental note to reserve the domain curdcountry.com as soon as possible as I would certainly need it for the chain of poutine-based restaurants called Curd Country I intend to open just as soon as the royalty checks from this book start pouring in. Speaking of which, may I ask that, in the event that you'd like to see Curd Country become a reality even half as much as I'd like to, you please buy an additional copy of this book for a friend or even an enemy?

"Where does he get his curd from?" I asked. "It better be from curd country."

"I don't think so," Joe replied. "I think he gets it from New York somewhere."

"Then that's not real poutine," I said, starting to get worked up.

"It's pretty good," Joe said, holding his ground. "In fact, let me text him and find out exactly where it's from."

"Well, I can't wait to hear the answer to this one," I said to Nils with an unmistable "Can you believe this guy?" look on my face.

Tensions were momentarily eased a couple minutes later when our coffee arrived, followed soon afterward by our multiple orders of poutine. It was at this point that I realized that—aside from my unfortunate poutine encounter mentioned previously in these pages—I had yet to ingest it while fully sober. In fact, it was my understanding that there was a law on the books somewhere in Canada that you had to be at least a little bit hammered to eat any poutine whatsoever.* Still, we dug in anyway, and I was delighted to find that the poutine of Merrickville was of a high standard.

"Well, that's curd country for you," I said, stuffing a forkful into my mouth. "Any word from your friend who makes the bullshitty poutine?"

"Yes, actually," Joe said, eyeing his phone. "He gets his cheese from somewhere outside of Albany."

"Sounds like it sucks then," I said with the bravado only a true one-quarter-Canadian person can muster.

"I'm telling you it's good!" Joe said, not backing down.

"That's impossible," I said, not even looking at Joe by this point. "Don't you agree, Nils?"

In true Canadian fashion, Nils took the high road and avoided the conflict altogether by pretending not to hear me.

---

* Please note that when Curd Country is open for business—and it definitely will be—there will be mandatory breathalyzer tests before anyone is permitted to order any poutine. No blood alcohol level? No poutine for you!

"You guys want to swing by the foundry after this?" Nils asked as we finished our breakfast.

"Sure!" I answered, hoping the foundry was the name of a cool brewery* in town.

As it turned out, however, the foundry was an actual foundry where they made all sorts of metal things. I was hoping to find another cast-iron moose to go with the one I bought earlier in this book, but instead they mostly had candle holders, welcome plaques and whimsical signs someone's aunt might hang in her kitchen. In fact, most of the stuff for sale there seemed to be geared toward someone's aunt. And the more I think about it, I would estimate that a good 75 percent of the stores I'd been in in Canada to this point seemed to be geared toward someone's aunt, selling things like oven mitts, throw pillows, adorable cookie cutters, potpourri decanters and, yes, artisanal mustards I just can't get enough of. After we left the foundry and Jen headed to her job as a massage therapist in town, Nils, Joe and I continued on to some place that sold hand-milled soaps and various skincare products—which only served to further underscore this point. Lest you think I am complaining about any of this, though, rest assured I am not. In fact, I found a great skin conditioner called Phantom Oil at the hand-milled soap place that I use to this day. Did Nils and Joe make fun of me for buying skin conditioner? Yes, they did. But they did back off a little bit once I told them how it was called Phantom Oil. Also, last I checked, it's not like I made them go into the hand-milled soap place with me, so it's not like they're the manliest guys I ever met, either.

After swinging by a coffee shop down the block for some hot chocolate, we decided we'd just about wrung all the fun to be had

---

* Note to self: Open a brewery called the Foundry. This could be a good companion business to Curd Country. People could start the night at the Foundry before heading over to Curd Country for any of the over 700 varieties of poutine we'll have on the menu. Oh, and be sure to hit the gift shop on the way out.

out of Merrickville that morning, so we decided to kick "guy time" up a notch by driving over to Kemptville for a bit.

We rolled into Kemptville proper a few minutes later, stopping off first at a guitar store for a quick look around before swinging by a local coffee shop. I had noticed a bizarre, almost psychedelic painting in Nils's garage that featured lightning, storm clouds and various flying livestock, and I'd told Nils how I'd love to own one like that myself if possible. It had been painted by a local man, and apparently the coffee shop occasionally had a few of his latest works for sale. Nils told the woman behind the counter what I was after, and one of the staff retrieved a handful of canvases from the back of the shop.

"Cowfee," I said to Joe, reading aloud from one of the paintings that depicted a cow drinking coffee. "Not bad."*

There were three or four paintings in total, but none of them achieved the unhinged majesty of the one Nils had hanging in his garage, so, alas, there was no sale for him that day.

As Nils, Joe and I stood at the counter, making small talk with the woman behind it, a curious fact was revealed: apparently, the shop had been voted as having the second-best poutine in town.

"It was in the local paper," the woman explained.

"Second-best!" I said. "That's good enough for me—I'll take one order!"

"But that's the thing," the woman behind counter said. "We don't even sell poutine."

"Then how did you get voted as having the second-best poutine in town?" Joe asked.

"We don't know," she said, her eyes drifting toward the floor. "We just don't know."

You'd think a quiet little Ontario town like Kemptville, this suburban Canadian paradise where Nils had spent his formative

---

* Far be it for me to interfere with any artist's creative process, but it's just occurring to me now that in the corner of the "Cowfee" painting, the artist could have painted a sheep looking on and saying, "Not baaaad." I know I would have liked to have seen it.

years, could exist free from scandal or any of the ugliness, deceit and treachery one might associate with somehow winning a poutine award when you don't even have poutine on the menu, but nope—I guess this sort of thing can happen anywhere, even in Kemptville, a place that—to outside observer, anyway—appears to be nothing short of a Canadian paradise. I finished my coffee in silence as I let all that sink in. Then I told Nils and Joe that I'd meet them back at the minivan and headed for the door.

"The thing is, I really wanted to try their poutine," I said as we drove back to Merrickville.

"Me too," Joe said, staring out the window. "But they don't have it."

"No, they certainly don't," Nils chimed in, seemingly still trying to make sense of it all.

Nils had to pick up his kids from school that afternoon, so Joe and I decided to give him a few hours with the family while we headed back up to the Goose to drink beer and make chitchat with the locals. It was closing in on happy hour, so the place was starting to hop.* Joe and I ordered a couple beers and tried to strike up some conversation with strangers, which was admittedly not that hard, since word had gotten out around town pretty fast that we had done a live broadcast of my radio show from Nils's garage the night before. As a result, the glow of celebrity was upon us, not unlike how it must have been when Liberace happened to roll through Clinton, Ontario.

"You got a radio show, huh?" a burly fellow next to me asked. "What kind of radio show?"

"It's mostly just talking and stuff," I explained. "Sometimes I take phone calls from listeners, a surprisingly large percentage of which seem mostly interested in doing bong hits over the phone."

"I wish I would have known," he said, sipping his beer. "Maybe I could have called in."

---

* In rereading this paragraph sometime after originally writing it, I have no idea why I chose to use the word hop. What am I? A detective from the fifties? It also doubles as a beer pun, I guess, arguably making matters worse.

"I would have liked that," I replied, even though it's really hard to say whether I would have in the end.

"You don't want him calling in to your show!" the guy next to him said, rolling his eyes. "Trust me."

"Okay, I will," I replied. "Anyway, what do you guys do?"

"We work in sales," the burly fellow explained. "I was a hockey player for a while before that."

"Cool!" I said, perking up. "Where'd you play?"

"Japan, mostly," he answered. "Semi-pro."

Since I am both a hockey fan *and* a Japanophile, things couldn't possibly have been going better for me at this point, at least in terms of random conversations with strangers at a bar, anyway. I grilled him for a while on his years playing hockey in Japan before the conversation drifted back to Canada and what the hell I was doing in Merrickville.

"I'm writing a book about Canada," I told the guy.

"Well, it's all about beer and hockey here," he said as he raised his glass, seemingly to toast himself. "That's all you need to know."

Further conversation revealed that the two salesmen were from nearby Smiths Falls, Ontario.

"A weed grower took over the old Hershey chocolate factory," the burly salesman explained. "It used to smell like chocolate all the time, but now the whole town smells like weed."

It was hard to tell whether he was complaining or was simply telling me and Joe because he noticed our rock look and figured we'd enjoy this kind of information. Regardless, I was really starting to like this guy and was even starting to wish he *had* actually called my radio show when Nils showed up, pulled up a stool and informed us of the game plan for the night.

"We're gonna go to my buddy Steve's place back in Kemptville, drink some beers in his basement and maybe do some jamming," Nils explained. "One or two of his musician buddies might come over, too."

It sounded like a solid plan to me. And it felt even more solid when Nils pulled the minivan up to a place called the Beer Store a short while later so we could load up on supplies for the night.

"That's it?" I asked. "It's a beer store, so they just went and called it the Beer Store? Just like that?"

"Yeah," Nils replied. "They got 'em all over Ontario."

"That's awesome," Joe said as we headed inside.

As hinted at in the name, the Beer Store sold all sorts of beer, so we loaded up on a bunch of it while we were there as it seemed crazy not to. It's also worth noting that they sold these cool beer mugs that lit up like a hockey goal light. And as I sit here typing right now, I can't for the life of me think of any reason why I didn't buy one and am kicking myself for not doing just that.

"The Rangers just scored!" I could yell to no one in particular while sitting and watching a game in my living room one evening. "Oh, hang on a second!"

Then I could turn my goal-light beer mug and things would get even more exciting. I guess what I'm trying to say is I really blew it.

Anyway, from the Beer Store, we continued on to Steve's place. We showed up a few minutes later, and I was delighted to find that Steve had a pile of hockey sticks in the corner of his living room, as it was exactly how I'd always imagined a Canadian living room might look. Nils's friend Paul was there, too, seemingly taking the hockey sticks in the living room for granted, and we all headed down to the basement, sat around a table and began drinking the beer we'd gotten at the Beer Store. I couldn't remember the last time I had just gone over to someone's house to hang out and drink beer in their basement like that, and it felt nice. It made me wonder why I'd allowed my life to get so complicated, as certainly this was not a situation that could be greatly improved upon unless Randy Bachman himself had pulled up a chair and cracked one open alongside us.

The five of us sat there, chatting and drinking for a while, before eventually the allure of the guitars, drums and amps set up in the corner became too great and, as is often the case when men in their forties hang out together in a basement, we were overpowered by the urge to rock. Usually, my guitar playing goes downhill after a couple beers, but it really starts to shine after four or five, so since I was sitting in that range by this point, I was especially eager.

"What do you want to play?" Steve asked as he sat down behind the drums.

"I dunno," I answered, strapping on a borrowed Telecaster. "Maybe something in B?"

With that, Steve and Paul, who had picked up a nearby bass, hit a stone-cold groove and I began soloing as fast as my hands would take me after several beers, which is to say not very. After a couple minutes, Nils stepped to the mic and began belting out some lyrics he had no doubt come up with while staying up until five in the morning in his garage the night before. And while I couldn't hear a word of it, I have no doubt it was awesome. This went on for anywhere from five minutes to three hours straight—I'm honestly not sure—until Nils signalled it was time we headed back to his place in Merrickville.

I was still pretty wired from the jam session, so it was hard to get to sleep once we got back to Nils's place. And the fact that I inexplicably drank what was left of the coffee straight from the Thermos before going to bed didn't help matters one bit. Eventually, though, I drifted off to a sound Canadian sleep, no doubt with images of beer mugs that lit up like hockey goal lights dancing in my head.

I woke the following morning to the sound of footsteps and Nils and his family chatting upstairs. I couldn't really decipher any of it until, suddenly, a familiar melody rose above the din, that of the Canadian national anthem as interpreted by Nils's son, Huey.

"O Canada, our home and native land," he crooned, "but I . . . can't . . . help . . . falling in loooove with yoooou."

And it may very well have been the most beautiful thing I'd ever heard in my life.

5

VICTORIA, BRITISH COLUMBIA

Innocence Lost

A FEW YEARS AGO at a gathering of my extended family, the conversation gradually drifted from vague inquiries as to when I might get a "real job" to talk of travel, and my uncle Joe, perhaps the most worldly of my entire bloodline, happened to mention that Victoria, British Columbia, was most beautiful city he had ever visited.

"But isn't Victoria Vancouver's bitch?" I asked him.

"No," Uncle Joe replied before turning his attention to a cheese plate, "not by a long shot."

To be fair, I was just trying to stimulate further conversation when I asked that, and in fact, I had yet to even set foot in either of the British Columbian hotspots at that point in my life and thus had no real opinion on the matter. Still, Uncle Joe's words stuck with me and I knew, author of the world's foremost book about Canada written by a non-Canadian or not, I absolutely had to see Victoria for myself before I died or was forbidden by law to leave the state of New York, whichever came first.

As fate would have it, I had been asked to perform my trademark not-for-everybody comedic stylings in the Seattle area one weekend,* so I figured this would be the perfect time to strike, as Victoria and Seattle are a mere 172 kilometers away from each other.

Joining me on this particular invasion of Canada was my girlfriend, whom I lured mostly with that bit about how my uncle had said Victoria was the most beautiful place he'd ever visited, but also with the promise of distinctly Canadian snacks.

As part of our journey, we had a layover in Seattle before boarding another short flight to Victoria, which turned out to be aboard a prop plane that had a charming, we're-all-gonna-die quality that harked back to a time when people used to get dressed up to fly and the pilot helped with the luggage. Just prior to boarding, my girlfriend began to engage in seemingly avoidable conversation with strangers, as she often tends to do. This time it was an elderly couple who were apparently no strangers to Victoria and surrounding areas.

"Be sure to visit Butchart Gardens," a woman in a sleeveless blouse and golf visor told her. "It's gorgeous."

Since I tend to avoid taking advice from strangers at airports, especially ones wearing golf visors, I made a mental note right then and there to definitely *not* visit Butchart Gardens under any circumstances. As soon as we touched down at Victoria's airport a short while later, however, we were bombarded with further suggestions that we visit Butchart Gardens via advertisements that seemed to cover every flat surface we encountered en route to the car rental desk.

"Maybe we *should* visit Butchart Gardens," my girlfriend said, slowly weakening.

"No!" I told her. "That's exactly what they want—for us to believe that we'd be insane not to visit Butchart Gardens so that they can just take all our money. But guess what—we're not falling for it."

---

* Should you be interested in a bit of bonus content or simply a break from the psychological clutches of this book, the show I was doing was NPR's *Live from Here with Chris Thile* and you can watch the full video of my performance on YouTube. You can go ahead and watch a cat video or something after that.

A couple minutes later, on our drive into town, we passed yet another sign advertising Butchart Gardens, this one telling us to turn right and we'd be there in minutes. It was at this point that we decided resistance was apparently futile and we should just get it over with, bang a right and see what all the damn flower-based fuss was about.

To be fair, we had already encountered a fair amount of the natural beauty typical of the Pacific Northwest*—rolling green hills, impossibly tall coniferous trees of every sort, and other things that make me ever-so-momentarily wonder exactly why I live in New York City. So when the young man on duty at the entrance to Butchart Gardens asked us to each pay thirty-three dollars to sniff around the place, we considered turning things around. But, of course, the only way to turn around by the time you've approached the gate is to fork over the cash and continue on through the entrance.

"See?" I said to my girlfriend as I steered us toward the parking lot. "That's how they get you."

"Well, you could have just told the kid we don't want to pay that much and asked to turn around if you really wanted," my girlfriend suggested.

"And give him the satisfaction of thinking we can't afford to pay a grand total of sixty-six dollars to look at some goddamn flowers?" I replied. "No—not in a million, trillion years. Now let's get this over with."

We parked the car and made our way inside to join what appeared to be mostly Japanese tourists and old white ladies wandering through impeccably manicured grounds where not even a single leaf appeared to have grown without some sort of human intervention.

I remember, when I was a kid, my Canadian grandfather Clarence Blake and his American wife, my grandmother Agnes Blake, maintained an impressive rose garden in their backyard.

---

* Or, since we were now in Canada, were we in the Pacific *South*west? The mind boggles.

During one visit when I was maybe six or seven years old, my dad decided to cut my hair in their kitchen and then proceeded to dump all of my newly shorn hair into the rose garden, something that struck me as strange at the time, and admittedly still seems a bit weird all these years later.

"It'll be good for the roses," he explained as I watched him carry out what, at the time, seemed like some sort of voodoo ritual.*

I was confused, but, not looking for a fight, I just went with it. Anyway, my point is that Butchart Gardens was kind of like my grandparents' (or any grandparents', really) rose garden except that it went on for acres and acres. Oh, and minus all the hair.

As we slowly wandered in and out of the various gardens, standing in each one at least long enough to make ourselves feel like we'd really appreciated it to its fullest, kind of like how people at museums appear to linger in front of a painting as if they are being secretly watched and judged on whether or not they really "get it,"** it occurred to me that, while I truly love and enjoy nature, I guess I prefer it when it's just going about its business, without any humans getting involved to make sure that a shrub, for example, looks like a giraffe or maybe a Disney character—which is admittedly great in its own way, but just not my thing. Still, we'd paid all that money, and my girlfriend was at least pretending to have a nice time, so we soldiered on, following a path into a wooded area where a young family was posing for photos in front of some pachysandra of some sort, when I became suddenly overwhelmed.

"My chest is getting tight," I said to my girlfriend.

"Mine too," she admitted.

"Are we dying?" I asked.

"Not today," she replied.

---

* I am still not entirely convinced this was not, in fact, a voodoo ritual.

** Okay, so maybe it's just me who does this, especially when the art is abstract and you just know everyone else in the gallery is secretly judging you on your capacity to connect with the subject matter.

"Wanna get out of here anyway?" I asked.

"Yes," she replied.

I knew I loved that girl.

On the way back to the car, we slowly filled with pride in the knowledge that we could at once acknowledge the undeniable beauty of Butchart Gardens while simultaneously calling bullshit on it, no matter how many signs and brochures had told us to come here.

"I bet your mom would really enjoy this place," I told her as we climbed back in the car.

"*Anyone's* mom would enjoy this place," she replied.

"But not two fortysomethings with their whole goddamn lives in front of them," I said. "No thanks!"

A big part of our rejection of the place was simply based on the fact that we resented the number of ads we'd been subjected to—it was our way of trying to prove to ourselves that we are immune to the power of advertising. Then again, we'd already been relieved of sixty-six bucks, so it's hard to say whether I'm even slightly right about that.

As we drove through the exit, my girlfriend and I spotted a lone deer wandering the perimeter of Butchart Gardens while nibbling on its well-attended-to greenery, ever so slowly undoing the work of the gardeners on staff and, as far as I'm concerned, anyway, really sticking it to the man.

"Keep up the good work, buddy," I yelled out the window to the deer. I'm not sure he really noticed, though.

We had a little time to kill before our Airbnb apartment was ready, so we decided to head into the city for a look around. There, we encountered so much sunlight and natural beauty that it was hard see what Aleister Crowley, famed occultist and brooding weirdo whose entire legacy built upon embracing the darker things in life, saw in the place. Supposedly, Crowley visited Victoria in 1915 and enjoyed it so much, he decided to live there for a while before returning to England to focus on creeping everyone out over there. (This is information you won't find on the Victoria, British Columbia, Wikipedia page.) Anyway, I guess my point is that Victoria is so universally delightful that even the blackest of souls aren't immune to its charms.

After wandering the streets for a bit, taking in some of the local architecture that I defy you to tell me cannot be described as Victorian, we stopped off for lunch at a place called the Flying Otter, a bar-and-grill type place along the water whose name suggested to us that anything may very well go, before heading to our Airbnb. And yes, I did have the poutine, which was delicious. So there.

As it turned out, our accommodations this trip weren't technically in Victoria, but in an area called Esquimalt, home to the Pacific fleet of the Royal Canadian Navy, among other things. Shortly after we crossed the bridge into Esquimalt proper, we happened to pass an establishment called the Carlton Club Cabaret, whose sign out front advertised that the soup of the day was "whiskey." I'm guessing there are a lot of bars in the world with that same exact sign out front, but somehow I had yet to see one during my years on this planet, so I was understandably amused beyond reason.

"I've got a feeling about that place," I said to my girlfriend as we rolled past.

"Great," she replied.

We arrived at our Airbnb a few minutes later. It turned out to be a guest bungalow tucked behind a family home on a quiet residential street, just a few hundred yards from the Strait of Juan de Fuca, if I'm reading the map right. There, we were greeted by a middle-aged woman in a housecoat and a small dog not unlike Toto from *The Wizard of Oz*, only it had three legs instead of the standard four.

"How did he lose his leg?" I asked, feeling sorry for the pooch.

"He was attacked by a raccoon in our backyard a few months ago," the woman explained. "But he's doing pretty well now."

I couldn't help but respect the little guy. If someone or something had torn off one of my legs, or even just a foot, in my own backyard, I would have serious hang-ups about it, probably for years. But here the little guy was, wagging his tail, yipping and sniffing around at his new visitors just a few months later, as if the whole missing-leg thing was really no big deal at all. Now *that's* what I call bouncing back. As we got settled into the place, I made a mental note to try and have even a small amount of his joie de vivre at all times.

After freshening up a bit, my girlfriend and I grabbed a cab into town. Along the way, we passed the Carlton Club Cabaret again. It still looked pretty quiet, but I couldn't help wondering what sort of thrills might be in store for its patrons later that night. To get a better idea, I decided to pull up some reviews on my phone.

"The place is sloppy at best and pretty grouty [sic] to be honest, but there is some kind of bent appeal, like going to a circus for the blind drunk," read one.

"The clientele are trailer park trash types, low ranking military rowdies, hillbilly hicks who like to wake up the whole streets with drunken after bar fights and arguments," read another.

A third—and my personal favourite—read, "Went here with my girl and some guy started dancing up on my girl. Went up and started dancing with her with my back to him. Didn't square up on him or anything, just wanted to let him know she was with me. Later he got in my personal space & started spitting at me as he warned me not to test him."

In short, I wanted to tell our cab driver to turn our cab around and take us back to the Carlton Club Cabaret immediately. But I had already promised my girlfriend a relatively classy evening with dinner, drinks and little to no risk of anyone "dancing up on her," or any of the other fun stuff I'd just read about.

"We should probably go there at some point before we leave town, though," I stressed to her as we crossed the Johnson Street Bridge into Victoria proper. "You know—for research."

"Maybe," she replied.

After our cab driver dropped us off in town, we began our evening with a drink at a rather fancy establishment with a large wooden bar lined with bright frosted-glass lanterns. It reminded me of pubs I'd been to in Scotland.

"This place used to be a bank," our bartender, a red-haired twentysomething fellow in a crisp white Oxford shirt, told us after bringing us a round of drinks. "It's supposedly modelled after the bars in Scotland."

It felt good to think something and then, just a couple minutes later, have someone confirm that I was absolutely right about that thing I was thinking a couple minutes ago. It made me feel like a grown man who knows stuff instead of the fifteen-year-old who is about to get kicked out of the place—which is what I tend to feel like for the majority of my waking hours.

After a bit more chitchat with the bartender, we knocked back our drinks and sallied forth into the night, walking a block or two before stopping into a restaurant I'd read good things about.* We had a couple more drinks and ordered a bit of food, including a clam-and-sausage-based dish that we asked to be prepared without the sausage since, delicious as it tends to be, we are both off the stuff. When it arrived, however, it appeared to have been prepared instead with *extra* sausage—so much, in fact, that the clams looked more like a garnish than one of the main ingredients. And while I know you didn't come here for my food criticism, I feel it had to be said. Anyway, naturally, this caused both my girlfriend and me to fly into a blind rage—and quietly pick out all the sausage from the dish and set it to the side without saying a single word about it to our waiter. I'm just guessing here, but it felt like the most Canadian way we could have handled things, and we both felt pretty good about it.

"How is everything?" our waiter asked at one point.

"Absolutely perfect," I replied, hoping he wouldn't question the curious mound of discarded sausage sitting in the middle of the table, like some sort of offering to the gods.

---

* Reading up on exactly where to go in a town can be a mixed bag. Often, the places that are recommended in local guides are those "hip" and "happening" places that just so happen to have also bought some ad space. But I find that when it comes to finding those really special local gems where, say, the chef might have stabbed someone once, it's usually best to keep an ear to the streets.

Slightly jet-lagged, a bit drunk, and with our fingertips reeking of sausage, we decided to jump in a cab back to our rented bungalow to rest up before grabbing Victoria by the horns the next day. Along the way, we of course passed the Carlton Cabaret Club again. By now, it appeared to be absolutely rocking and crawling with the "lowlife military rowdies" I was determined to hang out with at some point before we skipped town.

We awoke the following morning and headed back into Victoria proper to have breakfast at a diner I'd read was seriously Canadian, a promise that was delivered on in full, as far as I was concerned, as there were pictures of both the Barenaked Ladies *and* Gordie Howe at our table, something that filled me with so much joy that I threw caution to the wind and ordered marble toast, which everyone knows is the Russian roulette of toasts, but I didn't care one bit, for on this day, I felt alive.

"Is this the point in the story where you tell us how you ordered poutine for the second time in less than twenty-four hours, Dave?" you ask.

And to that I say no, no I did not. Did I want to? Yes, of course. But this particular establishment was serving some sort of newfangled poutine incorporating yams instead of potatoes, and as a poutine purist within reason, I wanted nothing to do with it. My grandfather didn't go work in a shirt factory in Winnipeg before gradually making his way to Cleveland by way of Detroit so that his grandson could just walk into some diner in British Columbia and commit poutine blasphemy. I have a legacy to protect, and protect it I did by just ordering some eggs over easy with home fries instead.

After breakfast, we wandered the streets for a bit, ducking into various shops and keeping our eyes open for anything distinctly Canadian we might happen upon. Somewhere along the way, we passed a couple men walking along the street while chatting about something or another.

"The men sound somehow nicer here," my girlfriend remarked after overhearing a snippet of their conversation.

"They do," I agreed. "It's almost like you can detect a sort of lack of aggression and entitlement I'm suddenly realizing most American males seem to have at least a slight hint of in their voice."

"Yeah," my girlfriend replied. "It's like you can tell that the men here aren't dicks or something."

"Exactly," I said.

I realize I need to be careful here, so as not to throw all American males, myself included, under the bus or anything. I don't think all American guys are dicks or anything. In fact, I would argue most of them are definitely not. It's just that if I had to bet on which of the two countries has more dicks per capita, I would definitely, without question, pick America. I've heard it speculated that a possible reason for this is the American Revolution. In short, Americans kind of expect to be messed with, and this major attitude problem has managed to carry over for centuries now. That's one theory, anyway.

And now, back to our regularly scheduled programming . . .

At some point prior to our visit, my girlfriend had done a bit of Victoria research of her own and stumbled upon something called "the running of the goats," a phrase that instantly rendered me excited almost to the point of requiring medical attention, taking place at a nearby children's zoo. Apparently, twice a day, a bunch of baby goats are led between the area where children and other people with an affinity for goats are allowed to get up in their business to a more secluded area where the goats can eat, sleep and just sort of goat it up without human interference for a spell. While my girlfriend and I both acknowledged that there was something slightly creepy about two childless adults showing up at a children's zoo to hang out for any stretch of time, there was still no way in hell we weren't going to do just that, and as soon as possible, given the kind of goat access the place was promising. Fortunately, the children's zoo was just a mile or so away, so we were there within minutes of my girlfriend first mentioning it to me.

"Two adult admissions," I said to the guy at the front desk upon our arrival.

"Okay," he replied. "And how many children's admissions for you today?"

"None," I told him. "None at all."

I stared into his eyes without saying another word for a good thirty seconds after that, in some sort of psychological game of chicken I am confident I won.

"Enjoy the animals," the guy said with what I'd like to think was at least a hint of defeat in his voice after taking my money.

"Oh, we will," I told him. "We will."

We hadn't walked more than a couple feet before we suddenly encountered a male peacock with its plumage on full display.

"It's mating season," the guy at the front desk called over to us. "He's showing off."

If you're like me, you probably haven't seen the words *attack* and *peacock* in the same sentence before, either, but based on the high-pitched screeches that peacock starting letting loose with as we approached, I was pretty sure that, at that very moment, we were indeed in the presence of an attack peacock, one that was willing to kick my ass all over that petting zoo—in some sort of bizarre display of avian male dominance rarely seen outside of ostrich circles—if I didn't back off immediately. Also, I'm pretty sure he wanted to get with my girlfriend, something I took umbrage at. Anyway, keeping this in mind, I quickly snapped a couple pictures on my phone before grabbing my girlfriend by the hand and running off in the direction of the goat pen. There were other animals at the petting zoo, including some rather handsome pigs and a donkey that was pretty easy on the eyes, too, but goats were the only ones on display that we were allowed to actually touch, so we couldn't wait to get in there and frolic with them.*

As soon as we got inside the goat pen, I took a quick scan of the place and pretty much confirmed my suspicion that we'd be the only childless adults in the place. But that didn't stop either of us

---

* Statistically speaking, whenever you hear of someone getting their ass kicked by a bird, an ostrich is usually to blame. Sure, emus are no slouches either when it comes to handing out a beatdown. But trust me, you see an ostrich coming your way, you hightail it out of there if you know what's good for you.

from getting in there with an enthusiasm that made most of the children present seem like they weren't really all that into goats by comparison. And for the record, there were fully grown goats, baby goats and goats of all other ages. In short, for a guy like me who counts goats as easily among his top five favourite animals of all time, this was a goat-based paradise.

PLEASE DO NOT PICK UP THE GOATS, a large sign inside the goat pen read, suddenly challenging that notion.

"What kind of bullshit is that?" I said to my girlfriend, pointing at the sign.

"You're just gonna have to let the goats come to you," she replied. "And watch your language."

"Fine," I said before sitting down on a nearby bench and hoping for the best.

I noticed several small children, most of whom probably couldn't even read in the first place, completely ignoring the sign and picking up the goats, but I tried not to let that bother me as I sat there, doing the best I could to conjure my inner goat whisperer.

Sure enough, after a few minutes, the baby goats indeed began to approach me and, in some cases, jump right in my lap. One goat whose collar said RAINBOW even began nibbling on my hair. I can't say for sure whether they could indeed sense my goat-whispering skills or were simply able to identify me as a grown man who wasn't going to poke them in the eye or get candy in their hair, as all the children around me seemed to be doing, but I can confirm that the feeling of having several baby goats frolic on and around you at once is exhilarating—life-affirming, even.

As these things tend to go, however, it didn't take long for all the children in the area to get super-jealous of how much more the baby goats seemed to like me than any of them.

"Stop eating his hair, Rainbow," a boy who looked about seven kept saying to the goat trying to make a meal out of my delicious locks. "It's bad for you."

"How do you know eating my hair is bad for him?" I wanted to ask the little brat. "You don't know shit about goats. You don't know shit about *anything*!"

In the end, though, I decided to keep my mouth shut and not say anything at all. Because if there's anything worse than being a childless adult at a children's zoo, it's being a childless adult swearing at somebody else's kid at a children's zoo. Besides, Rainbow was totally ignoring the kid, so I didn't see much point in schooling him, anyway, even though you could probably fill an entire library with what that little prick didn't know about goats.

"I honestly don't care if we ever leave this goat pen," I said to my girlfriend once the annoying little boy finally wandered off—to annoy someone else, no doubt.

"Me neither," my girlfriend agreed.

As much as my girlfriend and I would have been content to sit there with those goats until the authorities finally arrived to physically remove us from the place, there was a lot more of Victoria left to discover, so after about forty-five minutes or so of cavorting, cuddling, and communing with the goats, we finally forced ourselves to climb back in the car and head into town to explore the place further.

Butchart Gardens aside, the one thing we kept hearing about as far as things to do in Victoria were concerned was high tea. I'd heard that this is a bit of an affectation on the part of Victoria, in a bid to clumsily embrace its British roots, sort of like the way an Irish bar in the suburbs of Cleveland will subject its patrons to tin-whistle music to the point where they have no choice but to drink themselves silly as a means of self-preservation. I'm not a big tea drinker, and I tend to call bullshit on finger sandwiches in general, but I figured there still had to be a reason why no one would shut up about the tea in this town, so I decided to really swing for the fences and get us a reservation for high tea at the Empress Hotel,* which was supposedly the best in town, if you're into that sort of thing.

---

* My uncle Joe was kind enough to point out to me that the Empress Hotel—as well as the provincial Parliament Buildings in Victoria—was designed by a British architect named Francis Rattenbury, who lived in British Columbia from 1891 to 1929. In 1935, he was bludgeoned to death with a croquet mallet by his second wife's seventeen-year-old lover. The murder was reportedly one of the biggest scandals in Britain at the time—and, I'm guessing, one hell of a mess to clean up after. Now you know.

Still covered in goat hair and dried baby goat saliva, we strolled into the hotel a few minutes ahead of our reservation.

"May I help you?" a woman at the host counter asked us as we walked in.

"Dave, reservation for two at one thirty," I replied.

"Your reservation is in fifteen minutes," the woman replied. "Can you come back then?"

I couldn't help but notice that the dining room was only half full, and it looked like they could probably seat us and maybe even forty of our friends quite easily, but I admired the fact that this woman was playing by the rules—or, perhaps more accurately, the totally made-up and annoying quasi-British rules—that would require my girlfriend and me to wait awhile for no real reason. It made me feel like this place really had its shit together, something I look for in all establishments, not just high tea joints.

"Sure thing," I told her, before heading out into the lobby to wander around with my girlfriend for exactly fifteen minutes.

Fortunately for us, there was a gift shop in the lobby featuring all sorts of tea-related items, including a ceramic tile with a cool colourful crown on it that you could use to rest your teapot if you happened to have one, which I didn't.

"Should I get one of these?" I asked my girlfriend while pointing enthusiastically at the tile.

"What is it?" she asked.

"I can rest my teapot on it," I explained.

"You don't have a teapot," she replied.

"Yet," I said. "I don't have a teapot *yet*."

"You don't even have room for a teapot," she said.

"Well, I may have to *find* room if I end up buying this tile that's specifically designed for teapot resting," I countered. "Otherwise, what's the point in owning the tile?"

"Put that down," my girlfriend said before dragging me out of the store.

Somehow, we managed to kill a few more minutes before I approached the host counter again at 1:30 p.m. on the dot.

"Hi," I said to the woman. "It's Dave. From before."

"Yes, follow me," she said, leading us into the dining room with just the right amount of swagger in her step, at least for a tea place, anyway.

After settling in at our table, I scanned the room to see who else was about to experience a high-tea service that had been boldly described on the hotel's website as "hot and steamy since 1908," which is just one more thing that understandably had us practically tripping over ourselves to get here. As it turned out, it was almost entirely women, except for this one other dude who quickly looked at the floor as soon as I made eye contact with him. I'm not sure what his problem was. Maybe I made him uncomfortable. Or maybe he was just insecure about the fact that he was one of only two men in the whole place about to enjoy a nice pot of tea, some finger sandwiches and an assortment of dainty desserts for a mere seventy-eight dollars (Canadian) per person.*

As for me, I'm a little more confident in my masculinity, thank you very much, and had zero hang-ups whatsoever about knocking back a pot of Earl Grey, Royal Empress Oolong, White Monkey Paw or whatever the hell else might come my way. In fact, as I sat there waiting for our tea and weirdly miniature sandwiches and desserts to arrive, my mind drifted back to childhood, when my Canadian grandfather would drink tea with milk, something I had never seen anyone else do before. At the time, it seemed borderline insane to me, as that's not how tea drinking tended to go down in America—or at least not Cleveland, as far as I was concerned. But now, here I was, just a few decades later and a few thousand miles away, about to do the very same thing. I realize this may seem like a minor accomplishment to some, but at the time, it felt good. Or, at least, that's what I told myself at the time, as this thrill was costing me seventy-eight bucks—in case I haven't mentioned that already.

---

* A steal, when you really think about it. And when I say "think about it," I mean "accept the fact that we are all hurtling toward death at incomprehensible speed, so nothing really matters anyway."

Our individual pots of tea arrived along with a tiered pedestal of impossibly small sandwiches and desserts, and we did our best to enjoy all of them while casually discussing where we might grab some lunch immediately after we left. Still, knocking back an entire pot of tea on one's own can take a while, so by the time we finished, I realized our parking meter had likely run out and we'd probably get a ticket.

"I wouldn't bother paying any parking tickets while you're here," our waiter told us after I inquired about the likelihood of definitely getting a ticket. "You're not from here, so it's not like they can really enforce it."

It was hard not to admire this outlaw spirit at the time, but less so in hindsight; it turns out that they actually *can* enforce the parking tickets by simply charging the rental-car agency, which in turn just charges the renter—in this case me—for it, which is exactly what ended up happening to me. Still, at the time, his words emboldened me, so from high tea at the Empress Hotel we continued on to another of Victoria's great gems, Miniature World, without giving that parking meter another thought.

As hinted at in the name, Miniature World is a place where everything is smaller than in real life. In fact, the brochure for the place featured totally regular-sized people towering over dioramas of small towns and urban landscapes alike, looking like bewildered giants as they stared wide-eyed at the tiny people, dogs and, in some cases, even chickens, going about their business in their alternate reality.

"Shall we?" I asked my girlfriend as I fished around my pockets for the measly sixteen dollars (Canadian) each that it would take for us to wander around Miniature World—right up until closing, if we so desired.

"Seriously?" my girlfriend asked in that manner people tend to incorporate when they have no idea how awesome something is about to be.

"Do you have a better idea?" I asked.

"We could go on a whale-watching tour," my girlfriend suggested, referencing the whale-watching tour office located right next to the entrance to Miniature World.

"There's no guarantee we'll see whales on a whale-watching tour," I explained. "But at Miniature World, we are 100 percent guaranteed to see miniature depictions of the Great Canadian Railways, the Swiss Family Robinson, something called the World of Dollhouses and any number of other things I've worked for my whole life. Besides, this is much cheaper."

"Fine," my girlfriend said, following me inside with all the enthusiasm you can imagine.

The first thing one realizes upon first entering Victoria's Miniature World is that it's pretty much a licence to print money. The place looks and feels like it was painstakingly assembled sometime in the seventies and then left completely untouched ever since, save for the occasional vacuuming or once-over to make sure none of the tiny townspeople in any of the dioramas had somehow fallen over. Even the pre-recorded narrations accompanying most of the exhibits have a certain frozen-in-time quality to them.

"Isn't it weird to think how the guy talking right now is definitely, without question, 100 percent dead by now?" I asked my girlfriend as we pondered an exhibit that featured an old Canadian mining town undergoing simulated nightfall over the course of what turned out to be the longest thirty seconds of my life.*

"Yeah," she agreed. "This place is kind of depressing."

"Certainly nothing a little trip to Circus World can't fix," I told her.

"Huh?" she said.

"Follow me," I told her while grabbing her hand and leading her down a narrow hallway as if I were a modern-day Willy Wonka

---

* All the lights on the tiny streets and various miniature buildings stay on the whole time in this particular exhibit. And, in fact, only the miniature, old-timey sun turns on and off, something that feels like cheating to this hard-hitting journalist, but whatever—if you want to see what a miniature Canadian town looks like at both night and day while sacrificing a mere thirty seconds of your life in the process, you could do a lot worse.

who just so happened to have absolutely no candy on him whatsoever.

Moments later, we found ourselves standing before a sprawling diorama of Ferris wheels, circus tents, carnival rides and other things that signal instant good times. It was fun to imagine how freaked-out the tiny people glued to the fake grass below probably would have been had two relatively giant people like me and my girlfriend suddenly happened upon the scene, no doubt sending each and every one of them dropping their cotton candy, peanuts and ice cream cones and running for their lives.

"This is just creepy," my girlfriend said, taking it all in.

"Well, you have to remember," I told her, "they're a lot more afraid of us than we are of them."

From Circus World, we continued on to Fantasyland, Camelot and even something called Little Mill's Lumber Company, which claims to be the world's smallest operational sawmill, even though any idiot could see that this place was not actually in the lumber business in any meaningful way. And even though it goes without saying since it's right there in the Miniature World name, it cannot be overstated that each and every one of the dioramas we encountered featured stuff that is much smaller than in real life. You'd think it would end at some point and the museum curators would get lazy and just slap some regular-sized stuff behind glass for us to all stare at, mouths agape, for minutes on end, but it didn't happen.

"If it's on display in Miniature World, it absolutely has to be miniature," you could almost hear the museum's founder saying all those years ago, before the place opened for business. "Now if anyone needs me, I will be in my completely normal-sized office." It was an impressive commitment we could all no doubt learn a lot from.

"I think I like the goats better," my girlfriend said before we pushed through a set of doors and back out into the daylight as if we'd somehow finally managed to escape a decidedly benign funhouse.

"The goats were pretty great," I agreed. "But if you looked closely, you would have noticed that there were plenty of miniature goats glued to fake grass in Frontierland."

In an effort to offset any side effects of wandering around a windowless maze of dioramas for half an hour, my girlfriend and I jumped in the car and drove up the coast for a bit, soaking up as much natural beauty as possible for a solid twenty minutes or so before heading back to our rental place in Esquimalt to freshen up before another wild night on the town. Along the way, we passed another establishment that piqued our curiosity—something balled Bingo Esquimalt. I was certainly aware on some level of the popularity of bingo, and many times I have experienced firsthand the good, clean fun it can provide to men, women and children of all ages, but I truly had no idea the game was popular enough to warrant a brick-and-mortar operation that promised nonstop bingo mayhem every single day of the week. You probably saw this coming, but we couldn't help but pull into the parking lot immediately.

We walked inside to discover a large and extremely brightly lit room that felt like what I imagine it might be like if a bowling alley and the Department of Motor Vehicles* had a baby. There were only a handful of people in the place—maybe five, tops, all of them seemingly alone at the time, but also in the greater sense. And, aside from the fiftysomething mustachioed man calling bingo numbers from an elevated booth along one wall of the place, it was oddly quiet, with none of the usual profanity you expect to hear when a high-stakes bingo game is underway.

"You here to play some bingo?" a guy in his thirties in a golf shirt asked us after he noticed us standing there, awestruck, just inside the entrance.

"Yup," I told him. "We sure are."

---

* Please note that I am guessing there is another name for this sort of place in Canada. But, in case you aren't sure, I am talking about the place you go to get a driver's licence.

"We're in the middle of a game right now," he explained. "But as soon as we start the next one, we can get you in there."

"How many games of bingo do we play?" I asked, not entirely sure what I was hoping the answer might be.

"There are seventeen games in each session," the guy told me.

"Can we try just one game and see how it goes?" I asked.

"I guess you could do that," the guy answered, while looking at me like I was completely insane.

There were a bunch of electronic bingo stations in the place, but since my girlfriend and I are purists when it comes to bingo—and other games we admittedly don't play very often at all—we insisted upon using the classic bingo-card-and-marker setup as we settled into some chairs directly in front of the bingo caller so we wouldn't miss a word.

"You sure you don't want to just use one of the machines?" a sixtysomething woman in a windbreaker asked us. "That way, you don't have to pay attention to the bingo caller—the machine will just mark whatever numbers you get."

"Then what do I do?" I asked her.

"You can just sit there," she said.

"But then I don't get to experience any of that edge-of-your-seat excitement we've all come to expect from the game of bingo," I replied. "No, thanks."

"Suit yourself," she said before heading back to her seat behind one of the machines she was trying to sell me on.

A few moments later, the guy with the mustache began calling out the bingo numbers over the PA system. And then, in case any-one missed it, each bingo ball also appeared on a TV monitor over his shoulder. It was a lot of bingo-based stimulation for a Thursday afternoon. And by the time the game finished just a few minutes later, after some other lady sitting by herself got bingo before the rest of us, I was pretty exhausted.

"Well, that was fun," I said to my girlfriend while slapping the cap back on my bingo marker for emphasis. "Should we head back to the apartment for a bit?"

"Hell, no!" she replied. "I wanna play some more bingo!"

That's the thing about bingo—it's addictive. Also, to be fair, my girlfriend likes to live on the edge a bit more than I do. She goes to casinos, she buys those scratch-and-win cards from the deli, and I even saw her drink milk a day after its expiration date once. In short, she really likes to let it ride whenever possible. Even so, there was no way I could commit to a full seventeen-game bingo session without breaking out into hives or possibly even falling asleep, no matter how much prize money might be on the line, so I convinced her to leave with the promise that we might stop back in a bit later when the place was really jumping.

"I could have stayed there for hours," my girlfriend told me as pulled out of the parking lot.

"I know you could, honey," I said. "I know you could."

Sometimes, when I wind up in a new city where I know absolutely no one, I will make use of modern technology and post something on Twitter, asking if anyone has any has any hot tips on what I might get up to while I'm in town. And after doing just that regarding Victoria, I was contacted by a young man named Kellen, who told me he was a regular listener to my radio show and just so happened to live in Victoria. He kindly offered to show me around a bit, I accepted his offer, and my girlfriend and I made a plan to meet up with him and his wife at a bar in town that evening.

"But Dave," you ask, "aren't you afraid meeting up with a total stranger could result in you being slowly murdered before your body is dumped off in the woods or something?"

And to that, I say yes but guess what, pal—my girlfriend isn't the only one who likes to let it ride. Besides, Kellen isn't exactly a serial killer–type name, so I was willing to roll the dice.

On the off chance my girlfriend and I were, in fact, about to be murdered, however, we stopped off for oysters before heading to meet Kellen and his wife at the bar. My girlfriend loves oysters even more than she likes bingo, so I wanted her to have a great last meal in case things really did go south for us after meeting up with a non-murdery-named guy and his wife.

Again we decided to take a cab into town rather than drive, so when we passed the Carlton Club Cabaret yet again, I asked our driver if he knew anything about the place.

"Don't go in there," he said ominously.

"Why?" I asked.

"You don't want to be in there," he continued, admittedly less ominously than before, but still sounding pretty negative.

"Yes, I do," I said.

"No," he replied. "You really don't."

"Why?" I asked again. "Will someone stab me or something?"

"No," he said.

"Then why shouldn't I go in there?" I pressed.

There was a long pause, during which it seemed like he was trying to speak but somehow couldn't, like he was maybe having a stroke or being possessed by demons, but still weirdly in complete control of the car.

"Your feet," he finally uttered. "They will stick to the floor."

I was pretty sure he was talking in code at this point, but before I had a chance to really crack it, we had reached our destination. So, after telling our cab driver that I was definitely going to Carlton Club Cabaret, sticky feet or not, my girlfriend and I jumped out of the cab and headed into the oyster place, where we knocked back a dozen together with a glass of wine before heading off to meet up with two complete strangers I'd made contact with on the internet, something my Canadian grandfather—as long as I'm connecting the dots between him and me with this book—would never have dreamed possible in a million, trillion years.

A short cab ride later, we arrived at the bar, ducking inside to find a guy with a ponytail racing to get a karaoke machine up and running, presumably before things really started to heat up in the place. As for me, I made a mental note to leave before any karaoke actually started happening, as I believe getting drunk and singing off-key was meant to be a solitary activity, preferably done while slumped against a brick wall in an alley or sprawled out on the gravel in some rail yard.

Kellen and I were able to recognize each other thanks to the magical scourge that is social media. And, after quickly sizing him and his wife, Jaime, up and deciding they were not even the least bit murdery, the four of us slid into a booth with a round of drinks.

"They have pretty good poutine at this place," Kellen told me.

"I knew I had a good feeling about you," I said to him before returning to the bar to place an order for the table.

A piping-hot bowl of poutine arrived a few minutes later, and the four of us began to dig in while chatting about satanic heavy metal* and other stuff people who have just met tend to discuss in an effort to get better acquainted. It was a lot of poutine, though, so my girlfriend, Kellen and his wife set their forks down after a few minutes. I, however, continued shovelling the steamy mess into my face like I hadn't eaten in weeks. This is when I realized I might have a problem. But not enough of a problem to stop.

"Have you guys ever been to the Carlton Club Cabaret?" I asked, hoping to get a further read on the place. "Our cab driver seemed to think it was horrible."

"It's supposed to be pretty horrible," Kellen replied. "Let's go!"

Everything was going exactly according to plan at this point, as far as I was concerned. And with the threat of full-blown karaoke still looming, I suggested we finish our drinks and head to the Carlton Club Cabaret immediately.

Unfortunately, between the goats, Miniature World and everything else, we had already packed in a lot of excitement since

---

* To be fair, anyone with even a cursory knowledge of me and what I am entertained by would know that bringing up satanic heavy metal is a great way to get my attention, and Kellen, to his credit, was no different. In fact, he even brought me a copy of *Dark Years*, an extremely rare album from 1974 by the British Columbia–based band Twitch, who wore corpse paint, sang about Satan and did other stuff I recommend that everyone try at least once. On the back of the record sleeve, the band mentions that the album was "recorded in a cold and drafty work-shed on Harris Road, Haney, BC." And on the front cover, three of the band members appear to be stabbing the fourth—presumably the drummer—in the stomach. In short, it is the best album.

touching down in Victoria the day before, so my girlfriend politely declined to join us for what I, on the other hand, was anticipating to be the absolute highlight of our visit and perhaps this entire book. We dropped her off back at the apartment and continued on to the Carlton Club Cabaret, land of dreams.

"You sure you don't want to come?" I asked her as she got out of the car. "All signs seem indicate this place is gonna be pretty great."

"I'm good," she said, heading toward our bungalow. "See you in a bit."

We pulled into the Carlton Club Cabaret a few minutes later, where we were greeted by a large mural of the late, great Ronnie James Dio,* something I took as further evidence that we had definitely made the right move by coming here.

After taking turns posing for photos next to the Ronnie James Dio mural, we headed inside to find a mostly empty, dimly lit nightclub with a bar, a dance floor, a small stage and a DJ booth containing a DJ who was not playing any Ronnie James Dio music, much to my disappointment.

"Shouldn't the DJ be playing Dio?" I asked an attractive female bartender who appeared to be about thirty. "You know, because of the Ronnie James Dio mural out front that has given me the impression that, on its best nights, this is a Dio-only establishment?"

"Go ahead and ask him," she said with a smile. After ordering for each of us a round of a local beer called Blue Buck and a shot of something bright green and on special, I decided to do just that.

---

* I sincerely hope I've already mentioned and explained who Ronnie James Dio was in these pages. But in the event that I have yet to do so, or you simply need reminding, Ronnie James Dio was one of the greatest heavy metal singers of all time. He was in Rainbow, Black Sabbath and, of course, Dio, among other incredible bands. As I type this, a multitude of personal items from his estate are being auctioned off. Among the various swords, road cases and impossibly billowy shirts, there is an extremely large dragon head from his stage show that I am really hoping winds up in my living room if everything goes according to plan. UPDATE: I was going to wait until the next edition of this book to tell you, but it turns out someone else won the dragon head. Life is bullshit.

"Can you play some Dio?" I asked the DJ, a twentysomething guy in a baseball cap, after sidling up to his booth. "You know, because of the mural out front?"

"Sure!" he said with a smile.

I was admittedly taken aback by his willingness to indulge my request. I don't make a habit of approaching DJ booths—or even hanging out in establishments that have DJ booths, for that matter—but the few times I have done such a thing, it didn't go nearly as well. You probably saw this coming, but I am chalking this up to the fact that this was the first time I approached a Canadian DJ. And if you disagree, please, just let me have this one.

"Thank you!" I said to him before settling into a table next to the dance floor with Kellen and Jaime, where we quickly became fixated on a set of twins, two women of about fifty who we soon learned were named Mo and Jo, dancing together all alone. It was fun to watch them seemingly enjoy each other's company in that way that I'm guessing is only possible after you've spent nine months in the same womb together. And as I sat there, watching them dance to song after song (including, for the record, "Rainbow in the Dark" by Dio) I imagined for a second what it would be like to—if I may use the words of the great wordsmith Billy Idol for a moment— "dance with myself" like that. I'm guessing I'd be pretty creeped out by it. But I really enjoyed watching Mo and Jo nonetheless.

Before long, it was time for another round of beers, so I headed back to the bar, where I met a guy named Ron who seemed to be there all alone. Ron wore a black T-shirt that featured what appeared to be two faceless figures from a crosswalk sign engaged in a sex act incorporating a position commonly known outside of high-tea establishments as "doggie style." The figure on the receiving end was labelled YOUR MOM, and the figure behind it was labelled ME— the implied message, of course, being that Ron has had a special relationship with my mother.

"Nice shirt," I said to Ron, just trying to be friendly.

"You like that?" he asked. "Check this out."

It was at this point that Ron rolled up one of his shirtsleeves to reveal a sloppily executed tattoo of the Pillsbury Doughboy being sexually gratified by a woman kneeling before him. I wanted to ask Ron at what point he decided he needed to get that tattoo, what doubts he may or may not have had beforehand, how his mother— for example—might have reacted to his new ink and, perhaps most of all, why the Pillsbury Doughboy and not the Michelin Man or maybe even the Kool-Aid Man. But, not wanting to rub him the wrong way, I just told him I really liked it before dropping off a fresh round of beers at our table and continuing on to the rest-room, all the while wondering if I could ever pull off that shirt Ron was wearing, or if it's the sort of thing that should be left to the professionals.

My trip to the restroom was uneventful, save for a vending machine I encountered labelled VEND-A-SCENT. As best I could tell, if you had somehow left the house without any cologne on, and at some point in the evening decided that was definitely a mistake, you could make things right again by popping a few quarters into the machine and treating yourself to generic approximations of the fragrances especially amorous types tend to prefer. Since I didn't have any quarters on me at the moment, I just finished my business, washed my hands and headed back to our table, probably smelling of beer, poutine and whatever miniature hotel soap I hap-pened to be travelling with, a failed mission to be sure, but proba-bly for the best.

"That guy over there has a tattoo of the Pillsbury Doughboy get-ting a blowjob," I told Kellen and Jaime while pointing to Ron, in case they had never seen that sort of thing before and felt like rush-ing over to get a look for themselves.

"Why the Pillsbury Doughboy?" Kellen asked.

"I was wondering the same thing," I replied. "I'll probably need to ask him a couple beers from now."

As a few more bodies drifted onto the dance floor, I noticed a silent TV on one wall playing a music video by Calgary's own Loverboy. Meanwhile, the DJ just so happened to slip on the Bachman-Turner Overdrive classic "You Ain't Seen Nothing Yet."

All it took was a few more sips of the Canadian beer in front me before the true Canadianness of the situation had reached critical mass and this full-blown Canadian trifecta was suddenly lifting from my chair and urging me onto the dance floor myself. At first, I lingered on the perimeter, gently moving from side to side as I admired Mo and Jo continuing to do their thing. But then, thanks in part to power of the cowbell in the simply unstoppable chorus of "You Ain't Seen Nothing Yet," I found myself slowly drifting to the centre of the dance floor as the music began to fully have its way with me.

It was at this point that I noticed a woman of about forty rise from her chair and walk across the dance floor until she was standing directly in front of me. She then threw her arms over her head and began to grind her hips suggestively and slowly invade my personal space as the dulcet tones of one Randy Bachman blared overhead like some primal carnival barker.

"Excuse me, miss," I said to her. "Are you 'dancing up on me'?"

"I sure am," she replied while continuing to gyrate in front of me at a distance that shrank more and more with each passing millisecond.

It was in this moment that I suddenly realized that everything I had worked for over the past forty-eight hours had finally come to fruition and the prophecy of the Carlton Club Cabaret's online reviews had been fulfilled. And I wouldn't have traded it for the world.

6

WINNIPEG, MANITOBA

The Paris of Southeastern Manitoba

ASIDE FROM CLINTON, ONTARIO—birthplace of my grand-father Clarence Blake—the place in Canada I was most curious about, and perhaps even felt the most spiritually connected to with regard to my overall Canadianness, was Winnipeg, Manitoba.

"But Dave," you ask, "who *doesn't* feel spiritually connected to Winnipeg, Manitoba?"

And to *that*, I say, please, this is my book, just let me finish.

Anyway, as you may recall from earlier in these spine-tingling pages, Winnipeg was the promised land Clarence Blake set off to as a mere fifteen-year-old after deciding to leave the farming life—and Clinton, Ontario, in general—behind to tear the world of menswear a new one by way of working in a Manitoban shirt factory. I'm not sure if I'll ever quite understand how a teenager just one day thinks, "Menswear—that's for me!" and subsequently moves over two thousand kilometres away from his family like that. Other than going to school, I was lucky if I strayed more than a few blocks from home when I was that age. I did have a first cousin once removed who joined the priesthood at roughly the same age, but people being called by the Lord are like a hot blonde in Hollywood—you can't throw a parking-garage voucher without grazing one on the ankle. Just up and moving from home to work in a shirt factory before you've even finished high school, though—that takes some cold balls of steel. And it occurred to me that, to better understand my late grandfather and exactly what might have called him to Winnipeg, I needed to see the place for myself posthaste.

I must confess that, prior to my journey, I didn't know much about Winnipeg at all. I mean, sure, it's the Paris of Southeastern Manitoba—no one would fight you on that. And as I can do with most Canadian cities, I can easily connect Winnipeg to a bit of hockey trivia: in 1981–82, the National Hockey League's rookie of the year, Dale Hawerchuk, the pride of Oshawa, Ontario, started playing for the Winnipeg Jets.* But that was pretty much it. In short, before I just hopped a plane to Winnipeg, I had some Googling to do.

Unfortunately, my preliminary research on Winnipeg didn't turn up a whole lot more about the place, other than what I've already told you. I mean, sure, Randy Bachman is from Winnipeg, but does anyone else think it's weird how much ink I've already given Bachman-Turner Overdrive in these pages? And, according to Wikipedia, hockey great Bobby Clarke is also from Winnipeg. But any idiot could tell you that's not even remotely true and that the legendary Broad Street Bully was born and raised in Flin Flon, Manitoba, which, last I checked, is a whole 768 kilometres away.

Eventually, however, I stumbled upon something about how Winnipeg is part of the Prairies, the Canadian equivalent of the American Midwest as best I can tell, and that's when the hairs on

---

* A team that, I think we can all agree, had a much cooler logo the first go-around.

the back of my neck really stood up. After all, I was born and raised in Cleveland,* so I naturally thrive in a flatland environment—the fewer inclines of any sort, the better as it makes it easier to scamper about. So, between the distinct possibility that Winnipeg might very well be the Canadian equivalent of Cleveland and all that stuff I was just saying about how my grandfather weirdly moved there as an adolescent, I was suddenly vibrating with excitement and simply could not get to Winnipeg soon enough.

My wingman for this particular journey was my buddy Nils, whom you no doubt remember from my trip to Merrickville, Ontario, where he was kind enough to let my friend Joe and me camp out in his basement for two days while he tried to maintain some semblance of a normal family life just one floor up.

"Why Winnipeg?" Nils asked after I first broached the subject with him.

"I dunno, Nils," I replied with more than a hint of disdain. "Maybe it's because Winnipeg is my fucking destiny."

"Gotcha—just curious," Nils said. "Anyway, I'll tell my wife I need to get out of town for a couple days."

"You're damn right you will," I told him before hanging up without saying goodbye—just like they do in the movies.

As part of my journey from New York, I had a layover in Toronto, where, during a routine scouring of the duty-free shop, I discovered that Wayne Gretzky had gotten into the wine game with a host of offerings from something called the Wayne Gretzky Estates,

---

* As long as we're on the topic, I'll admit that, as a kid, I resented Cleveland, largely overcast paradise that it is, being called a part of the Midwest. "Why can't we say Cleveland is a part of the Mideast?" I would ask authority figures or anyone I thought might have a thing for geography, pointing to Cleveland's greater proximity to the East Coast than to, say, Colorado. It just made more sense to me. Over the years, though, I've come to realize that calling Cleveland a part of the "Mideast" just sounds confusing and weird. And I have, in fact, come to embrace my Midwestern roots and all that goes with them—even the accent some of us allegedly have.

which sounded like the kind of place where vintners would prune the grapevines with knives fashioned from old skate blades and the wine would be sipped from the skate boot itself. I was disappointed to find that Wayne had apparently decided against calling his wine "The Grape One," easily one of the greatest missed opportunities in oenophile circles (or any circles, for that matter), but whatever—it was an attractive bottle just the same. Did I buy any? No—not after what happened after I threw a bottle of Mike Ditka Merlot in my laptop bag that one time. But I figured it might at least give me something fun to talk about on the connecting flight to Winnipeg.

"The Grape One!" I'd tell anyone willing to listen. "It's kind of a play on words, you know, cuz everyone calls hockey's Wayne Gretzky the Great One. Anyway, name's Dave. I look forward to engaging in lively conversation with you for the duration of our flight and straight on up to when we finally and reluctantly part ways at the baggage claim, never knowing for sure whether this friendship could have had wings."

I couldn't wait.

In the end, though, the closest I came to conversation was when the guy next to me asked me if I "wanted his nuts" after the flight attendant brought snacks around, which unfortunately rendered me giggly beyond control and thus incapable of speech despite being a grown man.

I landed in Winnipeg a short while later, where Nils was waiting for me by the baggage claim area. There, we hugged in an excited yet perfectly manly fashion for a few seconds in anticipation of forty-eight hours of nonstop Manitoban action before pulling ourselves together to figure out how we might get into town.

Our original plan was to just use public transportation to get around, but I figured it might be a good idea to rent a car so that we could easily cover some extra ground and, who knows, maybe just keep the pedal to the metal until we hit Flin Flon should the mood strike. Unfortunately, however, there wasn't a single rental car available at the Winnipeg airport, something I took as a sign

that Winnipeg was even more exciting than I had already anticipated and that there was no shortage of folks eager to drink in its
endless and unmistakable magic.

"If my grandfather could only see me now," I thought as Nils and
I headed outside to grab a taxi into town. We found one in short
order and were on our merry way, probably just like my teenage
grandfather had done all those years ago.

As we rolled in the direction of Winnipeg proper, I was struck by
how similar the landscape was to my native Ohio—remarkably flat
stretches of grass-covered land with nary a hint of any serious
incline in sight. The closer we got to the city, clusters of single-
family homes of the usual brick and aluminum siding began to
pop up with increasing frequency.

"This is the Beverly Hills of Winnipeg," our cab driver told us as
we drove past a row of especially fancy houses with manicured
lawns and shiny sedans in the driveway.

"Huh?" Nils and I grunted back.

"Is nice," our cab driver reiterated.

"Oh," I said. "Yeah."

Another thing struck me on our drive into town, and this may
very well be my undeniable feral instincts talking, but I could sense
the mostly landlocked nature of our surroundings: that none of
these roads we drove along were going to lead us to some majestic
ocean inlet where we might watch boats slowly drift toward the
shore beneath a golden sunset. It was one more thing that reminded
me of the American Midwest, where a glimpse of one of the Great
Lakes—and perhaps a whiff of an expired walleye that had washed
up onto some nearby rocks—is usually about as good as it gets.

I had found us an Airbnb rental a few kilometres outside of
town. I thought it might allow us to really see how the
Winnipeggers* live, how they go about their day-to-day business,
what makes them tick, and—who knows—maybe even get invited

---

* As it turns out, this is what they call themselves. I tend to think
"Winnipegians" has a more regal ring to it, but what do I know?

over for snacks or something. Also, all the stuff closer to town was too expensive.

Nils and I were hungry, though, so we asked the cab driver to drop us off in an area a bit closer to the action called Osborne Village. I'm probably going to lose a bit of my hard-earned street credibility by admitting this, but before coming to a new city, I will sometimes do an internet search for "hip neighbourhoods." It's a phrase I have never said aloud and can assure you I never will. But I'm told this is how people who are, in fact, less "hip" than I tend to talk, so it never fails to yield results when trying to pin down somewhere to grab a cappuccino served to you by someone wearing a Misfits T-shirt, no matter where you might find yourself. Anyway, my point is that, when I did this with Winnipeg, the internet told me to head to Osborne Village.

When we got there, we wasted no time in grabbing a table at a café that was doing a brisk business with the lunchtime crowd. I can't remember what Nils ordered, but I ordered some soup that was on special.

"I should tell you the soup is spicy," our waitress warned me. "Not so much in temperature, but in flavour."

I didn't quite understand what she meant by that, and I still don't. But the soup was good, and that's all I was really after, anyway.

Since our waitress had a tattoo, we figured she might be able to tip us off to any wild underground stuff happening in town, but other than telling us about this one bar she likes to go to sometimes, she played it pretty close to the vest as far as hot tips go. She did, however, confirm that Osborne Village was "where all the action is" and that we were indeed "in the right place," something we took as an indication we should at least go window-shopping after lunch.

Nils and I headed outside and began shuffling down the block until we discovered a vintage shop practically begging us to come inside.

"Maybe they'll have something for sale that says 'Winnipeg' on it," I said enthusiastically, in hopes of luring Nils.

It totally worked, and seconds later, we found ourselves scouring aisle after aisle of used coffee mugs, dusty old candle holders and other things I somehow can't resist when the price is anywhere close to right.

"My friend Dave here and I went to a vintage shop where I live," Nils said to a seemingly uninterested lady at the cash register. "They had an anvil for sale for five hundred bucks."

"Five hundred bucks?" the lady replied, perking up a bit. "Where is that?"

"Merrickville, Ontario," Nils said.

"We'd be lucky to get fifteen bucks for an anvil here in Winnipeg," the lady, who looked just old enough to perhaps be Randy Bachman's sister, said matter-of-factly.

"But think of how much you could charge for shipping!" I said, smiling in anticipation of the big laugh I was sure was about to come from pretty much everyone within earshot.

That laugh never came, though, so, after nodding politely a couple times at the woman, Nils and I headed back outside in search of some more hot Winnipegian action.

A couple blocks later, we happened upon a store called Wild Planet, which, based on the name alone, we figured was our ticket to instant and potentially endless excitement, the kind of place where we'd best check our inhibitions at the door. We headed inside to discover various tapestries, smoking paraphernalia and other items that suggested both an affinity for the bohemian lifestyle and a high statistical likelihood that the person buying these items lived in his mother's basement. They also sold an alarming variety of T-shirts advertising the band Slipknot, as well as other bands that must have seen the Slipknot shirts and thought, "Hey, we should probably make some shirts like that."

"Looking for anything in particular?" a leathery man in his fifties asked as we wandered through the shop.

"Do you have Slipknot T-shirts?" I asked.

"Yeah," the guy replied, pointing at the wall. "Right over there."

"Oh, I know," I said, shrugging. "I was just . . . never mind."

"Well, let me know if I can help you," the guy said.

"I'm from Ontario and he's from New York," Nils told the guy in hopes of breaking the ice and moving on from my Slipknot-based inquiry altogether.

"Ontario, huh?" the guy said.

"Yeah," Nils said. "Merrickville."

"I tried to go out east once, but they were too mean," the guy said. "Now I tend to just go west when I travel."

"Really?" I asked.

"Yeah," the guy said, shaking his head.

As you've probably picked up on by now, I've found my experiences with Canadians in every direction to be nothing short of delightful, so I was a bit confused.

"Why were they mean out east?" I asked.

"I dunno," the guy said. "They just were."

"Western Canada doesn't really get along with eastern Canada," Nils explained to me. "It's kind of a thing."

"Yeah, the people in the east just aren't as nice," the guy said.

"Yeah, Nils here aside, I've found the people in the eastern part of Canada to be total pricks," I replied, admittedly just trying to get on his good side by telling him what he wanted to hear. It totally worked, too; even though we didn't end up buying anything, the guy gave each of us a free refrigerator magnet with a marijuana leaf on it when we left, which was great because I had been trying to figure out some way to let all who enter my kitchen know I'm laid back and not the type to have hangups.

"That couldn't have possibly gone any better," I said to Nils as soon as we got outside.

"Probably not," Nils agreed.

We continued down the block and wandered into a shop that sold Halloween costumes, magic supplies and other novelties, the most entertaining of which was a small handbell that had RING FOR SEX printed on it. We took turns standing there, ringing it and giggling to ourselves, until the lady at the register gave us one of those "Please buy something now or leave" looks I have become all too familiar with over the years and we opted for the latter.

By this time, the midday sun was beating down pretty hard on Osborne Village as well as the two handsome strangers who'd shown up without warning there just a short while earlier, so we headed into a bar down the block called Toad's to cool off a bit while we plotted our next move.

"Can you come back in ten minutes?" an attractive thirtysomething woman behind the bar asked us while momentarily looking up from her phone. "We'll be open then."

Not looking for trouble, we decided to grab a seat on the steps out front to watch the traffic until we were allowed back inside. It was then that I saw something that struck me as distinctly Canadian. As a bus approached, I noticed its LED destination sign read NOT IN SERVICE. But what was strange to me was that, immediately before it said, NOT IN SERVICE, it said, SORRY.

"That's bizarre," I said to Nils.

"What's bizarre?" he asked.

"The fact that that bus is just driving around, apologizing to everybody like that," I said.

"What do you mean?" Nils asked.

"It says 'sorry,'" I told him. "I mean, I realize Canadian people say 'sorry' all the time, even when they don't mean it—maybe even *especially* when they don't mean it. But buses? That's some next-level manners."

"The buses don't say 'sorry' when they're out of service in America?" Nils asked.

"No—they just keep driving like nothing happened, like everything is totally fine and no one is being inconvenienced in the least," I said, shaking my head. "We're savages."

It was a simple thing, but the bus sign spoke volumes to me in terms of the difference between the United States and Canada. In the United States, the bus signs would likely tell you to go screw yourself before they'd apologize for making you wait for the next bus to come along.

Fortunately, I wasn't allowed to reflect on this too long and risk going to a dark place where I would be forced to further accept the vast and disturbing differences between our two countries. Our ten minutes were up and it was time to head inside for a drink.

"Hi," I said to the bartender. "We're the two guys from before."

"Yeah, I remember," she said, looking up from her phone again. "What can I get you?"

It's at this point that I usually try to just keep a low profile and simply order a beer like I'm just some totally regular guy who lives down the street and just so happened to wander in on the way home from getting something looked at. But I was determined to dive headfirst into my Winnipeg experience, so I instead asked her if they had any local beers at the bar before telling her that I was visiting from New York and Nils was from Merrickville. I also told her about that RING FOR SEX bell that Nils and I really got a kick out of earlier, but I don't think she was nearly as amused as we were about that.

"The Peg is awesome," the bartender told us before going to the trouble of writing up a list of places we should probably swing by while we were in town.

"The Peg?" I asked. "Is that what the locals call it?"

"Yeah," she replied. "The Peg."

"I can't wait to check out all these places in the Peg," I told her once she'd handed over the list.

"Yeah, we're gonna go all over the Peg," Nils chimed in.

"All over the Peg," I agreed.

"The Peg," Nils said.

"Yup, the Peg," I replied.

The bartender had walked away by then, but the whole thing had gone well enough that Nils and I decided to celebrate with a second beer before jumping in a cab over to our Airbnb to freshen up for the wild Winnipegian night ahead.

Our Airbnb turned out to be a cozy basement apartment on a quiet, residential side street. It seemed like the kind of place you might seek out if you were going on the lam, and I wondered if our host maybe thought we were doing just that. I might have been overthinking it, but even so, Nils and I did our best not to do anything suspicious during our visit.

During my intense pre-trip research, I had read about a place called Bar Italia that was described online as "legendary" and "awesome" and was allegedly the preferred destination of both "bikers" and "lowkey models," and I told Nils we should probably go there when it was time to hit the town again.

"They serve Italian food?" Nils asked.

"I don't know," I replied. "I think it's just a bar."

"Are the drinks Italian?" he asked.

"I don't know that either," I told him. "I'm just gonna need you to trust me on this one."

To save a few bucks and also experience Winnipeg like real Winnipeggers (at least those who don't drive), we decided to take the bus back into town. It felt good. And as we headed down the street, clutching our transfers with all our might, it was hard not to wonder whether my grandfather had ridden a bus down this very road all those years ago, and if maybe, at this very moment, he was proudly looking down on me from the heavens as I cruised the streets of Winnipeg to drink among its bikers, low-key models and whoever else might also be at Bar Italia after we got off the bus a few stops later.

As it turned out, Bar Italia was in the Little Italy section of Winnipeg. And I'm not exactly sure what I was expecting it to be like, other than teeming with local Hells Angels members and models who apparently don't like to make a big deal about things, but it mostly just seemed like your average sports bar. The couple dozen people gathered there, none of whom—with all due respect—seemed to be either outlaws or particularly glamorous, focused their attention on the TVs broadcasting the Golden State Warriors handing out a beating to the Cleveland Cavaliers in the NBA finals.

I don't normally care about basketball, but what with me being a guy from Cleveland, in Winnipeg during the NBA finals, which the Cleveland Cavaliers just so happened to be playing in, I figured it was kind of my duty to at least feign an interest bordering on genuine enthusiasm for at least a few minutes.

"These are my guys," I said to Nils and anyone in the place else willing to make at least fleeting eye contact with me as I nodded at the screen.

But as I did my best to focus my attention on LeBron James and company being dragged all over the court by the Warriors, Nils was slowly falling apart.

"Why is it carpeted in here?" Nils asked, nodding at the worn industrial-grey carpeting covering the floor.

"I dunno," I replied.

"Do you think they vacuum it?" Nils asked.

"I don't know that either," I said. "Probably."

"I hope they do," he replied. "I know *I* would."

"Of course you would," I said. "You're a good man who was raised right."

"But what I'm really wondering is why is it even carpeted in the first place?" he continued. "It just makes no sense."

"Some people like carpet," I tried to tell him.

"I don't," he replied. "Not in a bar!"

"You gotta let go of this," I told him while trying to gently redirect his energy toward the game.

But he couldn't. And sure enough, after we finished our drinks, Nils insisted we catch another bus and head back to Toad's, where, to be fair, I think we can all agree things had gone really great for us earlier. My dad is a big proponent of public transportation, so I was excited to tell him how I had successfully ridden the bus twice in one day in a whole other country. I saved that thought as we rolled into Toad's a short while later, the better to shift our focus on the present.

"Hey, Nils and Dave," the bartender yelled to us as soon as we walked in.

"It's like we're regulars," I said to her with a smile as we grabbed a couple stools in the corner. "Cool!"

"Not really," she replied. "It's just that, you know, you guys were just here a couple hours ago."

"Yeah, well, I guess there's that too," I said. "But it still feels pretty great."

"Okay," she replied. I could tell she was pretty pumped that we were back.

Nils and I ordered another round of beers and looked forward to cementing our status as regulars, whether the bartender liked it or not. But unfortunately, we were getting into happy-hour territory and the actual regulars had begun to show up, shifting her focus from the strangers in the corner to more familiar faces, the majority of them bearded, slowly filling up the joint. I tried ordering some poutine in hopes of further ingratiating myself with her, but it wasn't to be—not tonight, anyway. After another beer, Nils and I set off into the night in search of Winnipeg gold elsewhere.

To that end, we took a cab across town to an English-style pub we'd heard about. Along the way, we passed the Burton Cummings Theatre, which I know I don't need to tell you is named after the lead singer of the Guess Who.*

"Burton Cummings gets his own theatre?" I asked Nils.

"I thought it was weird too," Nils agreed.

"Randy Bachman—yeah, I could see it," I continued. "But Burton Cummings?"

"Burton's no slouch," Nils said, suddenly defending the guy whose eyes, as anyone will tell you, have "seen a lot of love."

"No one's saying he is—he's a major talent," I replied. "I'm just saying if you're gonna name a whole theatre after a member of the Guess Who, you gotta go with Randy Bachman."

"Why's that?" Nils asked, presumably just playing devil's advocate, because why would anyone even ask that?

"Bachman-Turner Overdrive," I told him. "They say lightning never strikes the same place twice. Well, it sure as hell did when it came to Randy Bachman."

"That's true," Nils said, staring out the window into the clear night sky. "That's very true."

I imagine we could have continued that discussion all night, and maybe even into the next day, but soon enough, we were at our

---

* You know, Randy Bachman's old band.

destination, so we headed inside so that I could pretend to care about the NBA finals for a few minutes longer until the game—and, with it, the Cavaliers themselves—was largely over.

"What can I get you?" our bartender, a sandy-haired guy of about thirty, asked us with an Australian accent.

"Australia, huh?" I said, offering up my standard line whenever I encounter anyone from Australia, New Zealand—or even sometimes England or Ireland, if I've had enough to drink.

"Yup," he said with a smile. "Melbourne."

I was admittedly a bit drunk at this point, but I couldn't help but smile back at the young fella as it suddenly occurred to me that maybe he was a bit like my grandfather had been all those years earlier, in that he, too, saw fit to just up and move to Winnipeg one day in the pursuit of his Winnipegian destiny.

"Cheers, my friend," I said, hoisting my drink while giving him a look that I hoped suggested I totally got where he was coming from—and, perhaps more importantly, where he was going. "Cheers."

I'm not really sure what happened after that, but I woke up the next morning with enough of a hangover that I thought it a good idea to wander over to the diner across the street from where we were staying and, yes, order poutine for breakfast. I realize this is a doubly brazen move, as not only was I pretty far west of peak poutine territory—at least, to hear Nils tell it—and it was still morning, a time of day when even the heartiest of Canadians tend to live a poutine-free lifestyle, from what I've heard. And when it arrived at my table, I myself had to wonder whether I was ordering poutine whenever humanly possible as part of some sort of journalistic responsibility, or if I was just looking for an excuse to disrespect my body and ingest a plate of food that, it is my understanding, most reasonable people only eat while drunk. It was hard to know, really, but I can tell you that the poutine was really good.

I had just returned to the apartment a short while later when I got a text from Nils, who had woken up before me to wander the neighbourhood, presumably in search of truth, but maybe a bagel or something, too. "Meet me at Baked Expectations," it read.

My tireless pre-trip Googling had already told me that Baked Expectations was a bakery of some sort, but I guess I could have figured out that from the punny name. Since I am a sucker for both puns* *and* baked goods, I was on the next bus.

The fact that I was able to successfully ride a public bus two days in a row struck me as great progress. As a kid growing up in Cleveland, I tried to take a bus home from a tennis lesson at the local Catholic girls' high school one day, somehow got on the wrong one and wound up in a rough section of town with nothing but my tennis whites and my mother's old wooden racquet to protect myself. My dad had to leave work early to come get me before I fell in with a gang of street toughs or something. I was so shaken by the experience, I walked just about everywhere my parents weren't able to drive me for a good six years after that.

"*Now* look at me," I thought as I sat an admirable distance from the priority seating section. "I am a grown man riding a bus all by himself, and the odds of anything going wrong before I reach my destination aren't very good at all, really. And if, God forbid, something does go wrong, I will not drag my dad into it."

To be fair, some small part of me was hoping maybe I'd gotten on the wrong bus and would soon end up in some magical new corner of Winnipeg I had yet to lay eyes on. But mostly it just felt good to be getting around Winnipeg all alone by bus like that— so good, in fact, that I rewarded myself with a slice of German chocolate cake once I met Nils at Baked Expectations.

"Don't you think it's weird that the Germans used coconut, an ingredient not native to Germany, in their chocolate cake?" I asked Nils, whose father was born there. "It seems like cheating."

"I don't know if it's weird or not," he said. "But yes, it does seem like cheating."

From Baked Expectations, Nils and I grabbed a cab over to a place called the Forks. For the record, I would have preferred to

---

* As long as I'm on the topic, I should tell you my favourite puns are those used in the naming of hair salons. Mane Attraction, Hair Apparent, Curl Up and Dye—gems that will never get old, one and all.

walk, but Nils was wearing flip-flops, something I believe no one should ever do unless they are actually at the beach or, at the very least, can clearly see the beach from where they are standing, but whatever. Anyway, we arrived there a few minutes later.

For the uninitiated, the Forks is where the Red River and the Assiniboine River meet in Winnipeg. It used to be a place where Indigenous peoples, European fur traders and assorted other travellers would gather to do business or maybe just take a load off for a bit. Now there is a restaurant called Baja Beach Club, among other things, housed in a converted railway station. No one saw it coming. Not in a million, trillion years.

Nils and I headed inside and began casually exploring the place. And as we wandered in and around the railway station, poking our head into various shops and watching people eat their lunch, the sort of existential fatigue one tends to feel after sniffing one too many scented candles and eating at least a couple too many free cheese samples slowly began to set in.

"What are we doing?" Nils asked as I finished off a to-go cup of curried something-or-other I'd ordered from one of the many food stands inside.

"I don't know, Nils," I replied. "I don't know."

After a few more minutes of wandering through the Forks shopping centre, we headed outside to have a look at the water. There was a stand selling tour-boat tickets and—more importantly for my purposes—duck food, priced to move at just a dollar a bag, an incredible value, considering that the food could presumably also be used to feed the geese populating the area. I took advantage of the savings and bought a couple bags before puttering off in the direction of the various waterfowl I was hoping couldn't wait for me to offer them some. As for Nils, he grabbed a seat on some rocks near the water so that he could stare blankly at it for a few minutes while I got the duck feeding out of my system.

"See you soon," I told him, heading for the birds.

"Okay," Nils replied, settling in.

I was disappointed to find that neither the ducks nor the geese were particularly interested in the food I was tossing in their direction. I figured it was probably because lots of folks had come along to feed them already that day, but it probably didn't help that I ran away from them while making high-pitched noises every time they got even remotely close to me. Regardless, as soon as I was done emptying the bags of food in the general vicinity of the birds, I turned to find that Nils had been joined by a couple of older men sitting on either side of him.

"Hi, I'm Dave," I said to the men as I approached.

"This is Ben and Harry," Nils said as I grabbed a seat alongside them.

"Nice to meet you," Ben, a bearded man in a fishing vest said to me, extending his hand.

"Nice to meet you," I replied, extending mine.

As for Harry, he was also bearded but vest-free. And instead of shaking my hand, he offered me a fist bump that suggested an air of hipness I honestly hadn't anticipated.

I soon learned that Ben and Harry had both come to Winnipeg from other, more remote parts of Manitoba as young men in search of the kind of exhilaration only the Peg can provide. They had both since retired.

"We just meet up down here and walk around every once in a while," Ben told us.

"Just to see what's going on," Harry added before reaching into the plastic bag at his feet. "Newspaper?"

As best I could tell, Harry had emptied the contents of one of the free newspaper dispensers I'd seen in the area and was now carrying the papers around, offering a copy to whomever he might happen to encounter while walking around with Ben.

"Thank you," I told him as I accepted it. "This will help bring me up to speed on the local goings-on."

"Yup," Harry said.

"Great," I said before opening the paper across my lap and heading straight for the classifieds.

After a bit more chitchat, Harry and Ben wandered off and I sat there a while longer with Nils, mostly staring at the water, but also wondering how long I'd have to carry the free newspaper around with me before I could toss it in the trash.

"Just throw it away now," Nils told me.

"But what if Harry sees me?" I asked. "I don't want to offend him."

"We can't worry about that right now," Nils reasoned. "Besides, it's not like he can keep tabs on every paper he hands out. It's out of his control now, and he knows it."

"Yeah," I replied. "You're probably right."

As I watched Ben and Harry disappear along the river, it occurred to me that perhaps they were Winnipeg's answer to *Waiting for Godot*'s Vladimir and Estragon, two vagabonds just looking to pass the time until further stimulation happened to arrive. And as Nils and I sat there, contemplating the river for a few more minutes, trying to decide what we might do next, I began to wonder the same about us.

"Portage and Main," Nils finally declared. "Let's go there."

"What's that?" I asked.

"*Portage and Main, fifty below*," Nils half-said, half-sang. "It's from a song Randy Bachman and Neil Young did together."

It was all I needed to hear, and with that we were on our way.

On the cab ride over, Nils explained that Portage and Main was actually an intersection in Winnipeg reputed to be the coldest and windiest in all of Canada. I couldn't wait to experience it for myself. When we got there, though, it didn't seem to be either one of those things.

"Maybe we're standing on the wrong corner," I said to Nils as I flapped my arms a bit in hopes of sensing some sort of imminent cold breeze.

"I'm not sure if that will help," Nils replied. "It *is* June, after all."

Nils had a point. And I did feel a bit foolish for thinking that the legend of Portage and Main might somehow be experienced all year round, as if it were some sort of bizarre meteorological phenomenon that existed independently of the seasons. Anyway, since there didn't seem to be much else happening on that corner at that given moment, we decided to take advantage of the air conditioning in a bar and restaurant we were standing in front of.

"Two Bloody Caesars," Nils said to the bartender, a man in his forties dressed in a crisp white shirt and a black vest, as we hopped up on a couple stools.

"You like them spicy?" he asked.

"Yes," I said, "not so much in temperature, but in flavour."

"Huh?" the bartender asked.

"Yes, we like them spicy," Nils said, restoring order.

"Good," the bartender replied. "I get my hot sauce from the cook at a restaurant down the block. He makes it at his house. Secret recipe, lots of kick, and you can't get it anywhere else."

I liked the idea that our drinks would be getting a little extra boost from a hot sauce that had a bit of street credibility, almost as if it had been acquired on a hot sauce–based black market and wasn't just some bullshitty, store-bought kind that you could get anywhere.

"Here you go," the bartender said, proudly presenting our drinks to us a few moments later.

"You from around here?" I asked the bartender in a manner I hoped suggested I was looking for some real scuttlebutt on Winnipeg.

"No," he replied. "I moved here about a year ago from San Francisco."

"What made you decide to come here?" I asked.

"I'm originally from Canada, but I was bartending in San Francisco for about fifteen years," he explained. "Then, one day, I got a call from the Canadian government."

"What did they say?" Nils asked.

"Well, I was adopted, and it turned out I'm actually First Nations," he replied. "I was part of the Sixties Scoop."

I had no idea what he was talking about, but, as he explained it (and also according to Wikipedia), for a few decades starting in the 1950s, the Canadian government removed roughly twenty thousand

Indigenous children from their families and placed them either in foster homes or up for adoption so that they could become better suited to join "mainstream society."

"That's horrifying," I told him.

"Yeah," he replied. "Anyway, the government ended up giving a lot of the children a settlement, including me, so I came back to Canada for that, and eventually wound up here in Winnipeg."

As much as I couldn't quite wrap my head around the Sixties Scoop and everything it entailed, I also wondered what it must be like to adjust from life in San Francisco to the relatively quieter environs of Winnipeg.

"When you're someplace like San Francisco, there's all sorts of stuff to do," he explained. "But here, there's not as much to do, so you start to learn a lot more about yourself instead. For example, I learned that I like watching airplanes."

"How'd you learn that?" I asked.

"I live by a Royal Canadian Air Force base," he told me. "And I just started going out there to watch the planes land and take off and stuff."

I liked the idea of that. It sounded almost meditative to me. And even if reaching some sort of higher consciousness wasn't necessarily in the cards, at the very least, watching planes *is* pretty cool, no matter what, so there is that.

After Nils tapped on our empty glasses with his index finger—the international signal for "Another round, please"—the bartender returned with two more Bloody Caesars, which, for the record, were delicious and definitely seemed to benefit from the mysterious hot sauce referenced earlier.

Our cocktails in hand, the conversation gradually wended its way toward the Canada Child Benefit, something else I'd never heard of.

"The government will basically give you money if you have kids," the bartender said.

"Really?" I asked.

"Yeah," Nils said, nodding between sips of his Bloody Caesar.

"Yeah," the bartender continued. "I could just have kids and get paid for it if I wanted."

"Wow," I replied. "Do you have any kids?"

"Well, I'm not bragging or anything, but I've gotten a lot of pussy," the bartender then told us, lowering his voice and leaning in a bit for emphasis in that way that people often do when saying things like that. "But I always wear condoms, so I don't have any kids."

It was right around this time that Nils and I figured it was probably as good a time as any to ask for the cheque and wander back out to the corner of Portage and Main to see if anything might have somehow changed there in our absence—and maybe catch a cab, while we were at it.

"The bartender was pretty nice," I said to Nils as we rolled back toward Osborne Village.

"Yeah," Nils agreed. "And I'm glad he let us know he's gotten a lot of pussy."

"Yeah," I agreed. "Otherwise, how would we ever have known?"

"We wouldn't," Nils replied. "We'd be forced to just wonder forever."

Not entirely sure what to do next, we headed back to Toad's, the bar where, since this would be our third visit in less than thirty-six hours, we were not just regulars, but regulars I imagine the staff was beginning to get a bit concerned about.

"Hey, Nils and Dave," the bartender we'd met the day before yelled to us from behind the bar as we walked in.

"Hey!" we yelled back in a manner I'd like to think held an implied, "It's us again!"

I realize that you're wondering whether I ordered another poutine at this point. And I am happy to report that yes, yes, I most certainly did.

"The thing is, they don't usually get the cheese curds right this far west," Nils said, once again judging my cavalier attitude toward poutine intake. "They don't squeak like they should."

"Yes, I've heard that, many times, in fact," I replied. "But squeak or no squeak, I'm enjoying the poutine in Winnipeg just fine, anyway."

"Okay," Nils said. "I just wanted to make sure you know that a lot of people would judge you for eating so much poutine this far from Quebec, and with good reason."

"Fine," I said, digging into the piping-hot pile of fries, cheese curds and gravy like a man with nothing left to lose. "Let 'em! See what I care!"

Things got quiet for a bit after that until Nils suggested we move closer to the television to get a better view of the Cleveland Cavaliers finishing the job of handing over the NBA championship to the Golden State Warriors.

"You should probably have an OV beer while you're here," Nils told me as we settled into a booth near the TV.

"What's that?" I asked.

"It's *super*-Canadian," Nils explained before leaving the booth, only to reappear a few moments later with two bottles.

"Cheers," Nils said, setting a bottle down in front of me. "Let me know what you think."

As I recall, the OV tasted pretty good. But I wish I had known then what I know now: that OV—which, it turns out, stands for Old Vienna—was originally brewed in Ohio, not Canada, and only became a "super-Canadian" beer after it was acquired by O'Keefe (now part of Molson), which moved operations north of the border. Then I could have told Nils how it was weird to be drinking OV this far from Ohio, which would have no doubt shown him that I can dish it out just as well as I can take it. Instead, I just sat there and slowly drained the bottle.

I had hoped we'd stumble into the night for continued adventures in the Peg, but between the OV, the poutine and the Cavs' humbling defeat, it seemed like it might be hard to ring more fun out of this particular night so we packed it in.

I awoke the next morning a bit groggy and figured that perhaps a killer run around Winnipeg was just what I needed to reset my clock before my flight back to New York. I threw on my running outfit* and shoes and hit the streets at a brisk (for me) pace.

After a few blocks, I happened upon a set of railroad tracks leading God knows where. I followed the tracks for a few hundred metres before making my way down a residential side street, where a couple dogs barked at me as I passed and a sweaty man in a tank top and shorts appeared to be reading a broken-down lawnmower its last rites.

I continued a few blocks more until I happened upon an old kitchen table, standing alone on a treed lawn, with a sign taped to it that said TAKE ME. It seemed like the perfect souvenir for this trip, and I actually thought about it for a second before realizing how hard it would be to fit into the plane's overhead bin.

I then ran some more until I stumbled upon an outdoor ice rink, now covered in grass, presumably until the next change of season. As a kid, this would have been the kind of thing I could have only imagined in a fever dream, as Cleveland lacked both the necessary cold and enthusiasm for a hockey rink to be just sitting there at the end of a suburban street like it was no big deal at all. I stopped and stared at the rink for a minute, imagining it in the dead of winter, a youth hockey game raging on as parents and various other neighbourhood folks peered excitedly through the chain-link fence around the rink at the action on the ice, cheering with all their might before heading home to perhaps eat some poutine and down a couple OVs in front of a warm fire.

From there, I continued on for a few more blocks, passing row after row of single-family homes lining sleepy suburban streets and putting as much impossibly flat land behind me as I could before eventually stopping to catch my breath for a moment. And it was

---

* Don't worry—it's just an old, paint-spattered pair of track pants and a T-shirt. I'm not one of those annoying buffoons in the spandex hot pants— I am a man of the people. Were you to see me out running one day, you'd swear it was laundry day and I was merely in a hurry and in no way engaged in any sort of cardiovascular activity whatsoever.

then that I finally realized something: outdoor ice rink aside, just as I'd hoped, Winnipeg really *was* Cleveland. And Cleveland was Winnipeg.

And suddenly I felt more at home in Canada than I ever had before.

7

HALIFAX, NOVA SCOTIA

Axe Crazy*

I FIRST BECAME AWARE of the charms of Nova Scotia through my friend Mike Belitsky, a drummer from Halifax who now plays with the excellent Toronto-based band the Sadies. I briefly played bass in a band with Mike in New York City's East Village, way back in the post-grunge nineties—a simpler time when we both had effortlessly incredible if infrequently washed hair and it seemed like anything was possible.

Anyway, when we weren't busy rocking with authority in some dank practice space somewhere, Mike would thrill me with tales of his exotic hometown. He made Halifax sound like some seaside paradise where pickup hockey games would break out on almost every street corner at the drop of a toque, salmon would leap right

---

* In the interest of full disclosure, I should tell you that I have borrowed the title of this chapter from a song by the New Wave of British Heavy Metal band Jaguar, which as best I can tell is a song about guitars and not actual axes, which is to say it is pretty cool but not quite as cool as what I'm about to tell you.

out of the water into your fish-loving arms if you even looked in their direction, and walking around with an axe wasn't considered weird at all.* To be fair, Mike didn't necessarily describe it that way, but he did mention something about salmon and the fact that he, like most Canadian guys I've met, grew up playing hockey, and that was enough for me to jump to my own conclusions.

As these things often go, however, I eventually left Mike's band to try and tear rock 'n' roll a new one with a band of my own, and with that, my dreams of one day seeing Halifax in particular, and Nova Scotia in general, for myself slowly faded. When I began work on the definitive book on Canada written by a non-Canadian, however, I knew it was time to make things right and be sure to visit what the guy at the car-rental desk in the Halifax airport told me was also known as New Scotland, something I probably should have figured out for myself before I got there, as it was pretty much hiding in plain sight, but whatever.

Oh, and before we go any further, I suppose I should also mention that Halifax figures heavily into my very existence in that it's where my great-great-grandparents Timothy Blake and Ellen Leydan first arrived in Canada from Ireland before settling in Clinton, Ontario. So, aside from all that stuff I just mentioned about my buddy Mike, by visiting Halifax I would also, in effect, be living my family history.

"Isn't that a lot of pressure, Dave?" you ask.

You're damn right it is. But I didn't get where I am today by taking the easy way out, so I threw a couple pairs of underwear in a bag and hopped on a plane.

Anyway, as always with these strategic hits on Canada I've been making in the name of researching this important book, before I hopped a plane to Halifax, I tried to figure out at least some plan of attack for my visit—the things I should probably make a point of

---

* Also, the band Sloan is from Halifax, and all these years later, I maintain that the opening drum fill on "Underwhelmed," the first song on their debut album, *Smeared*, is one of the coolest things that has ever happened. Released in 1992, *Smeared* is ranked #86 in Bob Mersereau's book, *The Top 100 Canadian Albums*. Take that, *The Way I Feel* by Gordon Lightfoot (#98).

seeing, how I might blend in with the locals, and what strange laws might be on the books that I should avoid breaking.

As fate would have it, I was doing my friend Wesley Stace's excellent variety show, *Wesley Stace's Cabinet of Wonders*, in New York a few days before my trip, and, as is often the case lately when I'm in the midst of a bit of casual green-room chitchat, I happened to mention to anyone within earshot that I was in the midst of writing the most definitive book about Canada ever written by a non-Canadian, which caused not one, but two Canadians in the room to perk up and make themselves known in that low-key, entirely non-egocentric way Canadians tend to behave in such situations.

One of these Canadians was none other than Halifax native David Myles, a stellar singer-songwriter and, on that night, anyway, a veritable ambassador for Halifax who provided me with an excellent list of things to see and do while I was in town, most electrifying of which was a place where I would supposedly be legally allowed to drink beer and throw axes at the same time, something I simply could not wait to do.* David also saved me some embarrassment by letting me know that the people of Halifax were not known as Halifaxians, as I'd been wrongly calling them in my frequent and often heated discussions about Halifax and its natives over the years, but as Haligonians, which is totally nuts and makes zero sense, but whatever.

Joining me on my invasion of Nova Scotia—a Canadian province that, for the record, most Americans would not be able to find on a map if their lives depended on it—was my girlfriend, who had originally decided to sit out the mission until I told her that thing David Myles told me about the axe throwing.

"They just give you an axe and let you throw it right there in the bar?" she asked incredulously.

"That's what David, my new *Haligonian* friend, told me," I assured her.

---

* Please note that this particular journey took place prior to the North American Axe-Throwing Craze, a point further elaborated upon shortly.

"What's a Haligonian?" she asked.

"You're about to find out, dammit," I replied. "You're about to find out."

As excited as my girlfriend and I were to explore Halifax and its surrounding areas upon our arrival, things went south as soon as we arrived at the Halifax airport, when a woman on our flight who just so happened to own a royal blue suitcase nearly identical to my own—the one I'd just purchased with the false hope that it would be damn near impossible to confuse with any other suitcase on Earth—walked off with mine before my girlfriend and I even managed to get off the plane.

"Someone took my blue suitcase!" I said to the flight attendant at the end of the jetway in a manner that I hoped would suggest we had a real caper on our hands.

"Here it is!" the flight attendant said with a smile as he gestured to what turned out to be the woman's nearly identical suitcase that I had already opened to discover contained a hairbrush, some lingerie and a handful of other things I tend not to pack when travelling to Canada—or anywhere, really.

"No, this is a woman's suitcase," I explained.

"Yeah, I guess it does kind of look like a woman's suitcase," the flight attendant replied. "What does yours look like?"

"Exactly like this!" I told him as a wave of emotion washed over me.

Our conversation went on from there, but the long and short of it was that, while my girlfriend and I went through customs, the flight attendant chased down the woman who had mistakenly walked off with what I choose to believe was my completely unisex blue suitcase, exchanged it with hers and returned mine to me before I'd even had the chance to fully explain to the customs guy why I was so excited to drink beer and throw axes at the same time. And while the Canadian reader might view all of this as a perfectly normal way for the flight attendant to have handled the situation, I am confident that any American reading these pages right now will agree with me that, had the case of the mistaken blue luggage occurred at JFK, for example, the flight attendant likely would have shrugged at best after I explained to him what had happened, leaving me to spend the rest of the weekend making do with whatever the blue suitcase–having woman in question happened to have packed for me that weekend. I tried to thank the Canadian flight attendant and point out some of the more masculine features of my suitcase after he returned it, but he was long gone before I had the chance, no doubt already cheerfully assisting someone else with a pressing air travel–based matter.

My girlfriend and I found an Airbnb located in Halifax's North End, which was convenient to all sorts of bars and restaurants, including but not limited to the axe-throwing place I apparently won't shut up about. In short, with the Haligonian Unisex Luggage Caper behind us, everything was suddenly going our way and then some. We parked our rental car, dropped our luggage inside and decided to explore the neighbourhood a bit. And we had only walked a block or two when we happened upon a marijuana dispensary, with a hand-painted sign depicting a marijuana leaf and everything, on the sidewalk out front. I don't smoke pot myself,* and my girlfriend doesn't make a habit of it, either, but in the spirit of "cutting loose," she wanted to have a look inside.

Since I didn't want to seem like one of those weirdos who just like to look at pot and not smoke it, I decided to wait out front while she got it out of her system. After a minute or two, however, I grew bored and decided to head in myself. I entered what turned out to be a completely empty retail space, save for a young woman playing video games behind the counter. My girlfriend was nowhere in sight.

"Hi," said the young woman behind the counter, momentarily looking away from the video game monitor. "You looking for your wife?"

"Slow down there, missy—she's just my girlfriend," I explained. "But yes, I am."

---

* Please know, however, that I am "hip," "with it" and all for the legalization of marijuana use for everybody but dogs and children.

"She's in the back with my boyfriend," the young woman said.

"Wow," I replied. "This is a real 'anything goes' kind of town, I guess."

"Huh?" the woman said.

"Nothing," I said, shrugging. "What are they doing back there?"

"He's showing her the product," she explained.

If I didn't know any better, I'd say it sounded, you know, kind of like a drug deal was going down, which seemed a bit strange to me, since I'd assumed the reason there was a marijuana dispensary with a sign out front and everything was because marijuana was totally legal in Canada. But apparently this wasn't exactly the case.

"It's not legal *yet*," the young woman's boyfriend explained to me after he and my girlfriend returned to the front of the store a few moments later as if nothing weird had just happened at all. "Not until July."*

"Is that why you have nothing but empty shelves in the front of the store?" I asked.

"Yeah," said the boyfriend, who had piercing blue eyes and a crude tattoo of a crucifix on his face. "We had all kinds of stuff for sale up here, but then the cops came and we had to get rid of everything."

The boyfriend then gave us a crash course on marijuana in Canada, explaining how it had just been legalized for recreational use, but that the law wasn't in effect yet. As a result, marijuana dispensaries apparently weren't technically legal, but had still begun doing business in a way that allowed them to sell marijuana as long as the authorities didn't actually have to see it happening—or something like that, anyway. But at the very least, it kind of explained why he and my girlfriend disappeared into the back room of the place while I shared a few awkward exchanges with the girl out front.

"So," my girlfriend asked, "you guys married?"

"No," the girl answered. "But we've got a couple kids."

---

* At least this was the case at the time. In the end, recreational marijuana was not legalized in Canada until October of 2018. Deal with it.

"Two kids already?" I asked, just making conversation. "You guys seem pretty young to have two kids."

"We're both twenty-four," the girl said. "He has six kids altogether."

"You mean four more in addition to the two you have together?" I asked. "That's amazing."

"Yup," the boyfriend said with a smile. "A couple of them are twins, too."

"It would be kind of weird if just one of them was a twin," I replied.

"Huh?" the boyfriend said.

"Nothing. Anyway, how did you manage to have four other kids already?" I asked in a totally non-judgmental way.

"We split up a couple times," the girl explained. "It happened then."

"You really make the most of your downtime, huh?" I asked the boyfriend.

"Yeah," he said, blushing a bit. "I was in prison for a while, too, so it wasn't easy."

"Six kids," I mused while doing my best to resist asking any follow-up questions about the whole prison thing. "That's gotta be expensive."

"Yeah," the boyfriend said, "but I don't pay the child support."

"You don't pay the child support?" I asked, at this point not making any effort to not sound shocked, but still not being the least bit judgmental, I swear. "That's crazy!"

"I know, right?" the boyfriend replied as if he had suddenly morphed into a third person involved in our conversation and was just as shocked as I was that he was neglecting his child-support payments. "I don't know how I get away with it sometimes."

"Well, you guys are together now, and that's what's important," I said, trying to stay upbeat about things. "You guys seem to have good heads on your shoulders, so I'm sure everything will work out great for everybody in the end."

"Yeah," the girl said, smiling. "We've got each other."

"We're not really back together at this point, though," the boyfriend replied, seemingly not ready to leave the awkward woods.

The girl and I just looked at him after that, at which point it admittedly felt like time to go. As for my girlfriend, in an effort to both help the young couple and their six kids in total and also not feel weird about not buying anything after we'd hung out in the store a little too long by our estimation—kind of like how I always feel obligated to buy a pack of mints or something after reading an entire magazine at a newsstand—she decided to buy some sort of giant marijuana-infused gummy bear on our way out.

"Just eat a small piece of it," the boyfriend cautioned, pressing the gummy bear into my girlfriend's hand. "Or you could eat all of it, I guess—it's up to you, really."

We wandered the neighbourhood a bit more after that, stopping into a few shops, before eventually grabbing a drink and a snack at a wine bar, where we sampled some cured fish that, based on the description, anyway, might have spent time in a duffle bag but actually tasted pretty great, before eventually giving in to the inevitable and swinging by the axe-throwing place to see what was what.

I should probably mention at this point that the more I travel, the more I tend to want my destination to deliver on whatever stereotypes or preconceived notions I might have in my head, at least in terms of good, clean fun (and/or scenarios where I might send a weapon hurling through the air). For example, in Norway, I want to go plundering with Vikings;* in Japan, I want to be attacked by Ninjas; and in Brazil, I want to wake up in a bathtub full of ice with my liver missing. The fact of the matter, though, is that the more I travel, the more I find that everything tends to be pretty much the same wherever you go: people hang out in coffee shops, go shopping and occasionally step outside for some aggressive vaping or a phone call conducted in a voice I usually find a bit too loud.

---

* I would like to stress that I personally frown upon the raping and pillaging that usually goes along with plundering. But plundering I can generally go either way on.

In light of this, I was thrilled that the axe-throwing place did its best to cater to my admittedly unreasonable expectation for Canada to be a place where people in flannel shirts hang out while drinking beer and throwing axes pretty much all the time. Even some of the walls and fixtures in the place had been painted to look like they, too, were wearing flannel. In short, it was the best. And while a bit of research has revealed that North America appears to be on the brink of an axe-throwing craze on par with the unfortunate resurgence of swing dancing in the late nineties, this was the first I'd heard about it, so as far as I was concerned, my girlfriend and I had simply stumbled upon a quaint Halifax bar where Haligonians just drunkenly whip axes around at their leisure like it's no big deal at all.

Unfortunately, however, crazes being what they are, the axe-throwing place was already doing a brisk business, and we soon learned that if we wanted to drink beer and throw axes instead of just drinking beer while watching other people throw axes, we'd have to try coming back tomorrow, as they were fully booked for the night. That didn't stop us from at least watching a bit of axe throwing, which was fun at first, but ultimately frustrating, because if there's anything that gets you fired up to drink beer and throw axes around all willy-nilly, it's sitting there, watching other people drink beer and throw axes around all willy-nilly. Before long, the urge to try it ourselves was too great, and we decided to leave before we did something that might make international headlines.

We walked the few blocks back to our rental apartment, keeping our eyes open for anything seriously Canadian that might be happening along the way, but came up mostly empty, unless you count the young couple with the marijuana concern closing up shop for the night. Still, we were determined to get our Canadian on during this trip, so we hit the main drag near our apartment in search of something called a donair. David Myles had told me a donair was a must-have food item for anyone visiting Halifax, especially if they were kind of drunk. Since I met both of those qualifications at this point in the evening, it seemed like as good a time as any to go in search of one.

We ended up finding a pizza place that also sold donairs just a block or two away from the weed dispensary—which is a smart business plan, the more I think about it. But as it turned out, a donair is kind of like a gyro, and unfortunately my girlfriend and I had both given up red meat fairly recently, so we had no choice but to opt for pizza instead. I don't mention this to suggest we are virtuous or better than anyone because we stopped eating red meat. In fact, it's quite the opposite. Here we were, both half in the bag, a time when a steaming pile of meat of indeterminate origin slathered in sauces of equally indeterminate origin is just the ticket. But instead, we were forced to scarf down slices of pizza that tasted like they'd been sitting under the heat lamp since there were only six teams in the NHL.

As disappointed as we were by our near-donair incident, things began to heat up on the Canadian front again once we got back to the apartment and noticed that our host had left us a box of maple leaf cookies on the kitchen table. These weren't the same as the homemade maple leaf cookies I had encountered back in my grandfather's hometown of Clinton, Ontario, either—these were the fancy, store-bought kind, complete with a fancy box depicting maple leaf cookies in idyllic, maple tree–adjacent surroundings, presumably a glimpse into their life before making it into the hands of the consumer. I figured they might be entirely different from the ones I had already (mostly) regretfully encountered, so I reached for them.

"What are those?" my girlfriend asked.

"Maple leaf cookies," I replied.

"What's a maple leaf cookie?" she then asked.

"It's the official cookie of Canada, as best I can tell," I explained. "It's kind of like an Oreo, only instead of two chocolate cookies with a creme filling, there are two mostly bland, maple leaf–shaped cookies with a mysterious maple-flavoured filling in between."

"Those don't sound anything like Oreos," my girlfriend said.

"Oh, they're not," I clarified. "Not even close."

With that, I opened the box, handed my girlfriend a maple leaf cookie and took one for myself. We then both took a bite.

"These are disgusting," my girlfriend said, a look of deep disappointment washing over her face.

"Totally disgusting," I agreed.

"Do Canadian people really like these?" she asked, throwing the remainder of her cookie in the trash.

"I'm not really sure," I said, powering through the remainder of mine, "but, as evidenced by the fact that our Canadian host left us a box of them, we can only assume they are a point of great national pride."

In spite—or perhaps because of—our maple leaf cookie encounter, my girlfriend and I drifted off to sleep shortly thereafter. We woke early the next day, ready to tear Halifax a new one as we fired up the rental car in search of breakfast. We only made it a few blocks, however, before we found ourselves stuck in heavy traffic. As best I could tell, the cause of the traffic was some light road construction going on at an intersection up ahead. It hardly seemed to be enough to cause the traffic to back up for blocks, but upon closer inspection, I began to notice something—the cars already in the street were repeatedly stopping to let cars pull out of driveways and parking lots and into the road.

"What the hell are they doing?" my girlfriend asked.

"I dunno," I replied. "It looks like the drivers in the street are noticing that people are trying to pull into the street ahead of them and they are actually *letting them*."

"Like, *on purpose?*" my girlfriend asked.

"It appears that way," I said, dumbfounded. "It's like everyone is just letting each other go, like that's totally fine with them or something."

We couldn't believe it. Under similar circumstances in America, the person trying to pull out of a parking lot or driveway and into heavy traffic would likely have to force their way onto the road to the point of threatening to hit the other cars so the drivers already in the road would have no choice but to either let them in or risk getting into an accident. Here in Canada, they were willingly letting each other pull back onto the road with no threat of collision or even name-calling for that matter. It was absolutely bizarre.

My girlfriend and I were momentarily warmed by this discovery of seemingly routine Canadian kindness. But after a couple more minutes, we realized that this Canadian courtesy was actually making the traffic worse, as just about every driver in the road would stop to let someone trying to pull back into traffic go ahead of them. We attempted several detours, in fact, and found that, as a result of this remarkable shared courtesy, the traffic was backed up for blocks in every direction—all because a couple workmen were patching a hole in the road.

"These Canadian people are insane!" my girlfriend said.

"Completely insane," I said, shaking my head. "Don't they have anywhere to be?!"

What felt like hours later, my girlfriend and I finally arrived at a diner for a breakfast that didn't seem particularly Canadian. They didn't even have poutine on the menu. And, making matters worse, they allowed us to pay with American dollars. We were grateful for the convenience, of course, but it's worth noting that Canadians would never be allowed to pay for anything in America with Canadian money, even if the conversion rate had been factored into the transaction. In short, it's time to bring the hammer down, Canada, even if it's a hassle for me, Dave Hill, probably the most pro-Canadian non-Canadian you will ever meet in your whole, entire life.

Our unofficial Halifax tour guide in absentia, David Myles, had suggested we check out something called Dartmouth while we were in town, so after breakfast, we headed over that way. David had mentioned we could take a ferry over, but not being particularly seafaring types, at least not on this day anyway, we opted to drive. It's also worth mentioning that, as I write this, news has just broken that a man walked into a Tim Hortons in Dartmouth, told the staff he had a gun and demanded they hand over all the their money. The man then boarded the ferry and used it as a getaway vehicle to

Halifax proper. Police called the ferry and demanded they turn it around, back to Dartmouth, where the man (who, in true Canadian fashion, didn't really have a gun after all) was apprehended and presumably given a stern talking-to. I guess my point is that, between this and the incident with my suitcase at the airport, Halifax is apparently a wildly unpredictable place where just about anything can and will happen, so if you decide to visit for yourself one day, watch your back.

Anyway, it was on the drive over to Dartmouth that we encountered even more extremely bizarre Canadian behaviour. There was a toll bridge to get to Dartmouth, which cost one Canadian dollar. As mentioned previously, we had no Canadian money with us, so when I pulled up to the toll booth, I explained to the guy inside that I only had American money.

"That's fine," he said. "We'll take that."

"Great," I replied, handing him one US dollar.

He then handed me a coin, which I assumed was change of some sort since—not to be a dick about it or anything—the US dollar is worth slightly more than the Canadian dollar (or at least it was at the time of the incident). I tucked the coin into my pocket and proceeded to drive toward the gate. Naturally, I expected the gate to raise as I approached, but it didn't. We sat there momentarily, waiting for the bar to raise, when suddenly the toll booth operator yelled to us.

"Did you put the coin in the basket?" he asked.

"No," I said. "I thought that was our change."

"No," he replied. "That was a Canadian dollar for you to toss into the toll basket."

"Sorry about that," I said. "Should I just back up and toss the coin into the basket?"

There were no cars waiting behind and there was plenty of room to back up and pay the toll—in fact, I probably could have made a day of it, so this seemed like the perfect solution. The toll booth operator, however, had another idea.

"Just go ahead," he said with a smile. "Don't worry about it."

With that, the toll bar raised and we continued on, free of charge,* to Dartmouth. I realize this may not seem strange at all to the average Canadian. But had this happened in America, the toll booth operator in question would most likely have made some disparaging remarks about all the women important to me in life, multiple cameras would have captured the fact that I didn't pay the toll, and I would have eventually been mailed a ticket for an amount of money that would really hurt my feelings. But here in Canada, it was no big deal at all. And it scared us.

"What the hell was that all about?" my girlfriend asked.

"I don't know," I replied. "It was really weird."

"It was totally weird," my girlfriend agreed.

A bit shaken, but still safely in Dartmouth—*and* one Canadian dollar richer than we should have been—my girlfriend and I began tooling around town, stopping into coffee shops and other destinations people with nowhere in particular to be tend to frequent, before ultimately swinging by a pizza place that David Myles had told us was somehow famous not for its pizza, but for its fried clams despite having the word PIZZA right there on the sign. There, we dined like kings on fried clams and other items put through the deep-frying process without incident before hopping back into our car to wander farther—which is, of course, when we were subjected to still more bizarre Canadian behaviour. Our plan was to take a left out of the parking lot of the fried clam–specializing pizza place. Unfortunately, however, there were two lanes of traffic heading in the opposite direction, each backed up with at least ten cars each. In America, this would naturally mean that we'd have to wait for all twenty or so cars to pass before we could safely (or even unsafely) make a left turn into the road. Here in Halifax, however, we were stunned to find that both lanes of

---

* Unless, of course, you consider the fact that I basically traded an American dollar for a Canadian one, leaving me about 30 cents Canadian in the hole by my most likely squirrely calculations.

oncoming traffic stopped entirely to allow us to pull out ahead of them and make a left turn into the road.

"This is like *The Twilight Zone* or something," my girlfriend said as I casually pulled into the road as though there were no danger of being completely T-boned whatsoever.

"Yeah," I agreed. "I don't feel safe."

From there, my girlfriend and I cautiously continued on to something called Conrad's Beach in nearby Lawrencetown. David Myles had told me it was a hard-to-find, "best-kept secret" kind of place, which I guess may also explain why, as I also learned upon further investigation, Conrad's Beach is also a piping plover breeding area. A piping plover is a small, sparrow-like bird that nests and feeds along coastal areas in North America, something I just looked up on the internet.

Anyway, apparently the piping plover also likes to get down to business on Conrad's Beach. It was admittedly nice to have the heads-up about this sort of thing, but to be fair, my girlfriend and I were mostly just hoping to have a quiet, bird sex–free walk along the beach. Whatever those piping plovers were getting up to was really none of our concern, if you must know.

As promised, Conrad's Beach was a bit tricky to find, but damned if we didn't find it, park the car, and go for a lovely stroll along the sprawling, sandy and reasonably damp beach. And as much as we had anticipated that the scene at the beach would be something straight out of a piping plover–based *Caligula* or something, if there were any piping plovers having their way with each other while we were there, they certainly kept quiet about it. And for that, I thank them.

Coincidentally, among the hot happenings in Halifax the weekend we were in town was the Halifax Pop Explosion, a festival featuring bands, comedians and other stuff, too, I bet. As part of the festival, it turned out my friend Walter's psych rock band, Dead Heavens, was playing at a club a few blocks from our rental apartment that night, so I made a plan to swing by for some hot rock action. Before we could do that, however, my girlfriend and I were absolutely determined to get in some axe throwing. With that in mind, we swung by the axe-throwing place again to see if we might whip a few around while half in the bag. Unfortunately, however, the axe craze remained out of control, so we had little choice but to sit there and have a couple drinks while talking to the locals about how badly we wanted to throw some damn axes—or even just a single axe, if it really came down to it.

"I'm just here to drink," a guy in his fifties who seemed like he'd been doing that for a while already told us.

"You from Halifax?" I asked him.

"No," he replied. "I just moved here from Flin Flon for work."

"Flin Flon!" I said excitedly. "That's where Philadelphia Flyers great Bobby Clarke was born."

"Yeah, I know," the guy replied, seemingly not nearly as excited about this bit of trivia as I was.

"Pretty cool, huh?" I continued.

"What is?" the guy asked before burping.

"The thing about Bobby Clarke being from Flin Flon," I said. "You know, the hockey great."

"Yeah, I guess," the guy said, nodding in a manner that suggested he was really thinking about it.

It felt like talking to a guy from Flin Flon about Bobby Clarke was about as exciting as it was gonna get for us at the axe-throwing place that night, so my girlfriend and I finished our drinks and headed off into the night in search of dinner and wound up sitting at the bar of a bistro just a few blocks away. To the naked eye, there wasn't anything particularly Canadian about the place. But I took care of that in no time by ordering a Bloody Caesar for myself.

"You can really taste the clams!" I yelled to the bartender, hoping to sound in the know.

"Cool," he said, momentarily looking up from a concoction he was in the middle of preparing.

It was hard to tell whether the bartender really had "Bloody Caesar Fever," as I like to call it, but either way, we were having a really nice time, and I'm pretty sure no one could tell we weren't from there. It was a great feeling.

"Want to try my drink?" I asked my girlfriend. "There's clam juice in it."

"No," she replied, seemingly not suffering from the Fever, either.

As it turned out, my girlfriend was pretty wiped out from all the red-hot Halifax excitement we had already taken in that day, so I dropped her off at home after dinner, helped myself to another maple leaf cookie to see if it was a taste that I might acquire over time,* and headed back into the night in the direction of the rock club where my friend Walter's band was playing.

I had been in touch with him earlier that day to wield what I like to call "the Power of Rock" and see if he might be able put my name on the guest list—something he, of course, agreed to, probably more because we were friends than anything to do with that "Power of Rock" thing I was just talking about. When I arrived at the club, however, my name wasn't on the list. Even so, they let me in for free.

By this time, you are probably assuming I will chalk this up to Canadian kindness, and you're not wrong. Might I have weaseled my way inside without paying under similar circumstances in America? Maybe. But more likely, they'd have asked me to get a hold of Walter somehow and tell him to tell them to let me in, something I wouldn't have bothered to do and instead just forked over the cover charge without incident, unless you count swearing under my breath as I obsessed over whether or not Walter had knowingly left me off the guest list.

Once inside the club, I quickly found Walter, neglected to mention the guest list incident because I'm a class act, and instead just bonded with him over our shared enjoyment of Halifax. Walter also introduced me to a handful of his Canadian friends who had come out to the show.

"What brings you to Canada?" Walter's friend Ray, who was visiting from St. John's, Newfoundland, asked.

"I'm writing the definitive book about Canada by a non-Canadian, so I'm just trying to see as much of it as I can," I told him, hoping to

---

* As it turns out, it's not.

set off the usual pandemonium that occurs when I break out this sort of information.

"How are you finding it so far?" he asked.

"I love it!" I told him. "Canadians are so nice. In fact, Americans are total dicks compared to Canadians."

"Really?" Ray replied. "I find Americans to be delightful."

I was admittedly extra harsh about Americans in hopes of instantly ingratiating myself with Ray, and was kind of hoping Ray would pile on with some equally negative talk about my fellow countrymen, to which I would reply with something or other about how I see myself actually living in Canada someday, which in turn would surely only make him like me that much more. But the fact that he instead countered with talk of how nice Americans are only served to further underscore the fact that I have so far found Canadians to be ridiculously nice—so nice, in fact, that they pass on an invitation to trash-talk Americans, a particularly popular international sport at the time of this writing.

I made a bit more chitchat with Canadians in my general vicinity until the first band of the night came on: Ottawa's New Swears, a band I am hoping is grateful for, or at least curious about, their repeated mentions in these pages. This was my first live exposure to the band, and they have what I like call a "hot sound," something that probably dooms them in terms of mass appeal, but at least guarantees that I'll listen to them every couple weeks or so like clockwork.

Walter's band, Dead Heavens, was up next. They played a great psych rock–inspired set—so great, in fact, that between that and the Bloody Caesar I'd had earlier in the night, I found myself weary from all the good times I'd packed in, and I headed back to the apartment shortly after they finished in hopes of resting up for continued Nova Scotian mayhem the next day.

On tap the following morning was a trip to Lunenburg, an adorable little port town about an hour and a half from Halifax that David Myles had also suggested we not miss on our trip here. The hope when visiting places like this is that you'll stumble upon the discarded belongings of some sailor who went lost at sea or drank himself to death priced to move at a secondhand shop right there in town, but, like the rest of Canada in general, it's usually just a bunch of shops once again catering to someone's aunt, and Lunenburg was no different.

The drive to Lunenburg, however, delivered in spades. Not only was it chock full of natural beauty, but along the way, we spotted an actual hitchhiker, handmade hitchhiking sign and all, slowly thumbing his way down the roadside, like something out of a movie. It was a sight I hadn't see in America since the late eighties, at least.

"Wanna pick him up?" my girlfriend asked.

"No!" I said. "That's the one thing you're *not* supposed to do with hitchhikers."

"But this is Canada," my girlfriend replied. "Hitchhikers aren't murderous here like back home."

"Really?" I asked.

"Yeah, hitchhikers are nice here," my girlfriend said. "I read about it."

I slowed the car down a bit as we approached the guy, who appeared to be in his thirties and had a look in his eye that suggested he was up for anything in the way that both hitchhikers and serial killers historically tend to be.

"I don't know," I said, hitting the gas again. "What if he murders us? The cleaning fees on the rental car alone would be a disaster."

"Fine," my girlfriend said, huffing. "I still think we should, though."

It was then that I realized that I'd had a pretty nice life so far, and even if it all ended that day, I really didn't have that much to complain about. And with that, I finally pulled the car over a good hundred yards down the road from the hitchhiker. I figured he'd spot us easily, grab his rucksack, toss his hitchhiking sign into the brush and come running down the road after us. But instead, he just kept waving his thumb at oncoming traffic, no doubt hoping to find a ride with someone of greater conviction.

"Oh well," my girlfriend said as we pulled away. "We tried."

"Yeah," I replied. "I still think he would have killed us."

"Probably," she agreed. "But think of the story."

As we continued down the road, it occurred to me that perhaps, despite my lineage, my girlfriend was in fact more Canadian than I was, given the way she was about to let a total stranger into our rental car like it was no big deal at all. And it was indeed beginning to mess with my head a bit until I spotted a sign in the distance that read, CHRISTMAS TREE CAPITAL OF THE WORLD. I wouldn't necessarily call myself a Christmas guy, but I'm not made of stone, either. And since Christmas was indeed mere weeks away and we'd most likely be spending it on the grey and rainy outskirts of Cleveland, this felt like our best chance to really get in the spirit of the holiday season as we took in the majesty of that sign. And who cares if it was a bright and sunny day with not a single snowflake on the ground? The air was clean and there were pine trees—and, I'm sure, other trees that I simply mistook for pine trees—as far as the eye could see.

"Should we stop and take a picture in front of the sign and make a Christmas card out of it or something?" my girlfriend asked.

"No—we gotta keep moving," I replied like the future old man I now had a much better chance of becoming, what with not being murdered by that hitchhiker and all. "I want to get to Lunenburg in time for lunch."

I'll admit the sign was fun to take in while it lasted. Despite my inexplicable hurry, however, we did happen upon a flea market at an intersection just outside of Lunenburg. And since I'm a sucker for any and all roadside bullshit, I was definitely pulling the car over for that.

"You don't need any more stuff," my girlfriend groaned as I put the car in park.

"Come on—it'll be fun," I told her. "We can fraternize with the locals."

As these things go, most of the wares on sale were of the lone ice skate and discarded vacuum cleaner part variety, but as fate would have it, I did manage to find for myself a small pin that said CANADA. A little on the nose, maybe, but at two bucks Canadian, it was priced to move. My girlfriend scored even bigger, however, buying a couple tubes of homemade skin lotion that, according to the lady selling them, anyway, were "a whole lot better for you than anything you're gonna find in the stores, I'll tell you that much."

It's worth noting that, since that day, I've not had to rush my girlfriend to the emergency room as a result of using the stuff, and my Canada pin looks great on just about everything, so we're both still feeling pretty good about pulling over to the side of the road on the way to Lunenburg that day.

As for Lunenburg itself, we rolled into town shortly after the Canada pin/skin lotion score. Set along what I'm choosing to call a bay but I'm guessing there is another name for, Lunenburg, with its tall boats and quaint little shops and restaurants along the water and all, reminded me a bit of one of my favourite places in the whole world: Bergen, Norway, minus the ominous Nordic skies, and with nary a Lars or Olaf in sight. It also called to mind Morrissey singing about "the seaside town that they forgot to bomb" in his song "Every Day Is Like Sunday," but that feeling was quickly swatted out of mind as we stopped into a café where "Oh Sherrie" by former Journey front man Steve Perry was soft-rocking the lunch crowd into submission. There, we dined on a chowder of some sort before wandering in and out of shops for a bit. And in keeping with the aforementioned theory that most stores in Canada seem to cater to someone's aunt, we found a great pine-scented candle and a dish mat for the kitchen that promised to dry dishes much faster than all those other totally sucky dish mats that most people have.

Satisfied with our Lunenburg invasion, we pointed the car back in the direction of Halifax and the axe-throwing place we were determined to have our way with. We arrived a short while later to find the place had just opened. As a result, we were the first ones in the joint.

"We're here to throw axes," I said to the lady behind the bar.

"Great," she replied.

It happened just like that.

You probably saw this coming, but they make you sign a waiver before they let you just start whipping axes around the room like you're gonna live forever or something. I didn't read it too closely, but the gist of it was that if you injure or kill yourself or anyone else while throwing axes, you won't give the place a bad Yelp review or anything like that. I couldn't sign it fast enough. It's also worth noting that there was a sign on the bar saying that there had not been a single "axe-ident" since the place opened a little over a year ago, something I got a big kick out of and am chuckling a bit over right now as I think about it again. And it sure was fun to imagine the thrill that whoever came up with it must have felt when it first popped into their brain.

"Axe . . . accident . . . AXE-IDENT!" they must have thought. The endorphin rush one must get from that sort of thing would kill a lesser person.

Anyway, to help keep up the death-free streak, my girlfriend and I were assigned an axe-throwing instructor, a dark-haired woman named Pam from Saskatchewan with an attractive yet gruff look that suggested an affinity for any and all weaponry.

"You're gonna wanna swing the axe behind your back like this," said Pam, carefully demonstrating the ideal axe-throwing technique to my girlfriend and me after we'd each grabbed an axe that seemed to go best with our outfits from the pile on hand. Then Pam let loose with the axe, sending it hurtling through the air, end over end, before it lodged itself with a satisfying thud in the tree stump mounted to the wall about twenty feet away. Of course, if you do it wrong and throw the axe like my girlfriend and I both did, the axe just hits the wall sideways and falls to the ground like a wayward salmon at a fish market. And the sound that goes with that unfortunate technique is a much louder *thwack!* that lets everyone in the place know just how badly you suck at axe throwing, and, by extension, the lumberjack lifestyle in general.

After a few more tries, though, we were whipping axes around the room like a couple of bearded mountain men, managing to lodge our axes in the tree stump at least every other try, which felt pretty good, what with us being a couple of city folk when it gets right down to it. The problem, however, is that once the initial thrill of throwing axes around a room while half in the bag wears off, the realization that you are essentially playing a larger-scale version of darts sets in. And since I find darts mind-numbingly boring, the thrill wore off almost immediately after I'd posted a few shots of me successfully throwing an axe to Instagram in an effort to let the world know that I was currently throwing axes in Halifax and they weren't. And from the looks of the photos, anyway, axe throwing in Halifax is probably my favourite thing in the whole wide world, so I'm choosing to remember it that way, in case anyone ever asks.

With the axe throwing finally out of our systems and the drinks wearing off shortly after, my girlfriend and I spent the rest of the day wandering the streets of Halifax some more in search of more distinctly Canadian fun. At one point, we happened upon an antique shop. We went inside to find the main floor packed with the usual dusty artifacts that looked like they'd been salvaged from someone's basement, or perhaps a dead loner's van.

"This looks pretty good if you don't have hang-ups about the chipped rim or missing handle," I said to my girlfriend as I held up a coffee-stained mug with some slogan or another on its side that advised not bothering the person drinking from it until they had finished its contents.

"Put that down," she said. "Now."

I was momentarily upset, but quickly moved on from that as I discovered that the shop also had a basement. I headed downstairs to discover a low-ceilinged room absolutely crammed with folk art, all of which was by Canadian artists, or so the sign suggested. For the uninitiated, folk art is kind of like regular art, only it's really, really shitty in a way that I just can't get enough of.

"Was this painted by a five-year-old?" someone with an untrained eye might ask of one of folk art's great masterpieces.

"No," the folk art expert replies. "That was painted by a fifty-three-year-old man with a wife and kids, a house and a mortgage, the whole deal."

It's the best.

Anyway, I was puttering around for a couple minutes when, suddenly, the shopkeeper, a fortysomething man in a winter coat and knit hat despite the springlike weather, appeared at the bottom of the stairs just as I was appreciating a collection of small clay sculptures depicting people engaged in various activities like eating dinner or watching TV, as well as a couple of activities that were less exciting. They were primitive yet charming, looking like they'd be equally at home on the mantel or in the trash, depending on your mood.

"The guy who makes those is really big," the shopkeeper said, gesturing at the sculptures.

"You mean he's popular on the Canadian folk art scene?" I asked.

"No," the shopkeeper replied. "He's, like, 450 pounds."

I left the antique shop with a much lighter wallet that day.

My girlfriend and I caught an early morning flight back to New York the next day. We both planned to head straight to work after we landed. At the time, I had a writing gig on a TV show for a few weeks, and it occurred to me that it might be nice to surprise my co-workers with a gift from the wilds of Nova Scotia, this mysterious land to the north that, I would no doubt have to explain to at least some of them, was part of Canada. Just down from our gate at the Halifax airport, I spotted a large box of maple leaf cookies, the very same kind our host had left for us at the rental apartment, on display and priced to move. I decided to snatch up a box. When I arrived at work later that morning, I set the box of maple leaf cookies in the centre of the conference room table where the writers congregate for a few hours each day to hammer out dick jokes together.

"These are the official cookie of Canada," I announced to the room. "And I got them for all of you because you're my friends and I care about you. A lot."

They were gone by noon.

Maybe the problem is me.

8

MONTREAL, QUEBEC

Dieux du Métal*

AS ANYONE WILL TELL YOU, I love heavy metal. You may not
know it from my author photo, but I'm probably the most metal
mofo of all time. I'm so metal that when I go to the airport and the
security agent says all metal objects must go through the X-ray
machine, I just lie down on the conveyor belt.

Yeah, I know—that's pretty darn metal.

As it turns out, Canada is pretty darn metal, too. In fact, according to a map I found on the internet that details which countries
have the most metal bands per capita, Canada is second only to
Scandinavia as far as being seriously metal goes, which is just one
more thing I love about my grandfather's homeland.

Of course, I was fully aware of Canada's long and storied heavy
metal history long before I looked at that map on the internet. For
example, as mentioned earlier in these pages, one of my favourite
heavy metal bands of all time, Voivod, hails from none other than

---

* Metal Gods.

Jonquière, Quebec. And I'd be remiss, bordering on just plain insane, if I didn't tell you that I played guitar for none other than Canadian muscle-metal rocker Thor for exactly one show in Texas in 2015.*

In light of all of the above, it should come as no surprise that, as soon as I got word that the heavy metal festival Quebec Deathfest would be happening in Montreal during the period I'd be research-ing and writing this book, I wasted no time in conning my publisher into paying for the trip so that I might headbang French-Canadian style for the weekend.

When I told friends of my plans to go to Quebec Deathfest, they, of course, all wanted in.

"The people of Quebec really like to rock out," my friend Nick Flanagan, a comedian from Toronto, told me. "It's weird. It's, like, a *thing*."

"What do you mean it's a *'thing'*?" I asked him.

"I mean if someone is playing loud guitars on stage, the people of Quebec will be there,**" Nick said. "You'll see."

Keeping that in mind, Nick, no stranger to both Canadian and non-Canadian metal himself, made plans to hop a bus into town and join me for the weekend. Also joining me would be my friend Greg from New York and Nils from Merrickville, Ontario, the latter of whom you should already be familiar with by now from his

---

* Get Googling—the outfits alone are worth it. There are even videos of this show on YouTube, if you really want to lose part of your day. And let the record show that Thor himself, ever the gentleman, gave me an authentic Vancouver Blazers hockey jersey as a special thanks for my six-string service. Sometimes, I wear it with nothing else at all and walk around my apartment. It's an incredible feeling on many levels, though I'm just now realizing I probably shouldn't have told you that.

** It's worth noting that since I originally wrote this chapter, Montreal City Councillor Craig Sauvé managed to push through a declaration to dub Montreal a "heavy metal city." Give that man a raise! Also, maybe some sweet gauntlets and a battle vest.

earlier exploits in this incredible book. To be fair, I don't think Greg or Nils will take offence when I say that neither of them is particularly metal, per se, at least not in terms of the music they listen to, but they do like to drink large quantities of beer in a shirt-optional environment, so when I told them there would be plenty of opportunities for that over the course of the weekend, they were in. Big time.

Adding to the mayhem would be the fact that two of my friends' bands would be playing at the festival too: Autopsy from Oakland, featuring my buddy Chris on drums and vocals, and Exhorder from New Orleans, featuring my buddy Marzi on guitar.

And if all of that weren't enough for this to be the sickest weekend of all time basically, Canada would be making recreational marijuana officially legal just a couple days prior to our arrival, which I could only assume would absolutely add to the festive atmosphere in town and, ultimately, across the entire country of Canada.

Unfortunately, I had a prior commitment to rock some people of my own in New York, so I wasn't able to make it to Montreal until the second day of the festival. But that was okay because that was when both of my friends' bands were playing, anyway, so I simply made a commitment to myself to pack two days of French-Canadian heavy metal mayhem into just one while tacking an extra day onto the back end of the trip to assimilate back into regular society, where things are unfortunately not nearly as metal as I'd like them to be much of the time.

I flew to Montreal early Saturday morning with Greg. As we ate breakfast burritos at a restaurant bar at LaGuardia, a man talked extraordinarily loudly into his cell phone just feet from our heads.

"You can tell he's one of those obnoxious Americans," I said to Greg in an attempt to do a little shit-talking in anticipation of our trip north of the border. "And not the least bit metal, either."

"You got that right," Greg agreed. "We're definitely not going to run into this problem in Canada."

"Not a chance," I told him. "Not a chance in hell."

We glared at the cell phone guy for a bit after that before hopping a plane to lovely Montreal, where, upon our arrival, Nils informed me via text message that he was already wandering the streets of the Gay Village in search of poutine, beer and adventure. And as it turned out, that's the exact same neighbourhood where I had found us an Airbnb rental, so things couldn't possibly have been going better for us at that point.

"It's all coming together!" I wrote to Nils.

"Yeah, whatever," he replied. "Just get over here."

I could tell he was excited.

After picking up our rental car, Greg and I headed over to the Gay Village, dumped our car on the street near our apartment and headed over to meet Nils, who was already up to his elbows in some elaborate poutine that involved at least five more ingredients than should be legally allowed, in my opinion. A purist just looking to blend in, I ordered traditional poutine and a local Boréale beer.

"Back when I was a beekeeper, we used to shake hands with each other while cradling a bee so it would sting the other guy," Nils suddenly told us between forkfuls of poutine. "We called it a 'buzzer.'"

"You were a beekeeper and I'm just now finding this out?" I asked.

"Yeah," Nils said. "Anyway, another prank we'd do is to throw a bunch of bees into another guy's mask and then smack his head a few times to get the bees all mad so they'd sting him."

"Wouldn't that really hurt the other guy?" Greg asked.

"Oh yeah, definitely!" Nils said. "But you get used to it after a while."

"You mean you'd pull that prank on the same guy more than once?" I asked incredulously.

"Yeah," Nils replied. "But it was funny every single time."

Between the poutine, beer and Nils's bee prank stories* that I

---

* Please rest assured that Nils's bee-prank days are now behind him and that they took place in a simpler time, when enlisting innocent bees to harm your friends was just business as usual. Today, however, Nils is a man of wisdom who harms no living things—unless you count the one or two times he has unintentionally hurt my feelings.

honestly never saw coming, the trip had already paid for itself, as far as I was concerned. But when a couple guys in heavy metal T-shirts strolled in after a few minutes, I was reminded that we had other business to attend to—the business of heavy metal, dammit.

"Look, there are two guys in heavy metal T-shirts," I said to Nils and Greg. "I should probably go over to them and say hello."

"Please don't," Nils said, urging me toward the exit. "Just let them eat their lunch."

As I headed for the door, I tried to give the guys in the metal T-shirts a knowing glance to let them know that I, too, was a slave to metal who was ready to do its bidding wherever and whenever, regardless of personal ramifications, but they didn't seem to notice. Also, at this moment, I was wearing a sweater with baby sheep on it and some periwinkle-blue corduroy pants that had come back from the dry cleaner with weird creases in them, so maybe it was for the best that we didn't share a moment just yet. And yes, I think it's weird that I got corduroys dry cleaned too. As I sit here typing this right now, I can't for the life of me think of what possessed me to do such a thing. I guess I just wanted to feel special for a change.

Since our Airbnb wouldn't be available for another hour, Greg, Nils and I continued from the poutine concern to a nearby blues bar for another beer. There, as we settled around a table, an older fellow I assumed to be a regular glared at me from a barstool, which I took as a sign we were in a bar for real Quebecois and not someplace for some random tourists to just come strolling in, looking to kill a little time.

"This is the real deal," I said to Nils and Greg. "In fact, I'm pretty sure that guy over there wants to kill me."

"Yeah, French Canadians can get territorial sometimes," Nils said.

"What do you mean?" Greg asked.

"Some of them hate people who aren't from here," he explained.

"Wow," I replied. "That's awesome."

I'm honestly not sure why I tend to have more respect for people who dislike me than for those who welcome me with open arms. In fact, it's probably a topic I should save for another book entirely. But as far as sitting in that blues bar went, it definitely enhanced the experience.

With our Airbnb finally ready and, as we were nearing happy hour, the threat of a blues jam increasing by the minute,* we figured it best to finish our drinks and get out of there. Along the way, we stopped off at a beer store specializing in Canadian microbrews. I probably could have done without any more beer for a bit at this point, but as a journalist, I figured it was my responsibility to load up. To that end, we picked out a dozen or so random beers and headed to the Airbnb, which was just a few blocks away.

As soon as we got inside the Airbnb apartment, I learned a hard lesson about real estate photography.

"This is a real dump," Greg remarked as he set his bag down.

"I'll say," I replied.

When I'd looked at the place online, it appeared to be a sprawling two-bedroom with a pullout couch in the living room. There was an island in the middle of the kitchen, where I imagined fun conversations over a cheese plate might take place. There was even talk of a terrace we might enjoy at sunset, presumably while enjoying even more cheese.

"This seems like the perfect place for a friends to create lasting memories over the course of a heavy metal–centric weekend in Montreal," I thought as I booked the place.

But in person, the apartment told a different story. In fact, it didn't feel so much like we had a fun heavy metal weekend ahead of us as it felt like we were on the run from something and this apartment was where we'd lie low, subsisting entirely on ketchup packets until we got orders from some crime boss somewhere to

---

* Don't get me wrong—I enjoy blues music almost as much as the next guy. It's just that, in the wrong hands, it can get out of hand very quickly. If you're not careful, you could find yourself watching some dentist in a fedora and sunglasses attempt a harmonica solo while some guy wearing jean shorts and a fanny pack stands next to you, cheering for more at the top of his lungs.

gather our things and steal into the night. Everything in the place was a different and entirely depressing shade of grey, except for the walls, which had been painted a bright white at some point, but were now stained in a way that suggested some sort of extended, violent struggle had taken place in the apartment, the kind where at least a couple people leave in duffle bags—if they leave at all.

"I think this might be some sort of stash pad," Greg said while inspecting a deep-red stain of unknown origin on one wall.

"What's a stash pad?" I asked, perhaps revealing a bit of my Midwestern innocence.

"*This* is a stash pad," Greg replied.

"It's a really shitty apartment where people hide drugs, weapons and other illegal stuff," Nils clarified. "You know . . . a *stash pad.*"

"But the description on Airbnb said this place was adorable," I said.

"It *is* adorable," Greg replied, "but just in a stash-pad sort of way."

As often happens when something becomes too much to comprehend, Nils, Greg and I decided to distract ourselves with more alcohol, cracking open a few cans of the whimsical-looking microbrews we'd bought earlier and draining them with metal abandon before pulling on our coats once more and making our way to Quebec Deathfest.

"Is it bad that I'm not wearing all black?" Greg asked as we headed out the door.

"No, not at all," I told him. "In fact, it's a power move."

"What do you mean a 'power move'?" Greg asked.

"By *not* wearing black, you're letting people know you walk alone and don't follow trends like some kind of sheep," I said. "Why do you think I'm wearing a green plaid jacket, blue suede boots and a really fun scarf right now?"

To be fair, the real reason I thought it was good that none of us was wearing black was that it would make it easier to find each other in the crowd when it came time to leave the heavy metal festival and go have an early dinner at a lovely wine bar my chef friend Riad had arranged for us. But I didn't have the heart to tell Greg that at the time. I wanted him to feel dangerous, not practical, dammit.

"What about these khakis I'm wearing?" Nils asked.

"They're a statement," I assured him. "And believe me, a lot of people will take notice."

Quebec Deathfest was being held in a number of venues in downtown Montreal, but the main venue was the unfortunately named MTelus theatre on St. Catherine Street. We took a cab over to the area and, before heading inside, took a quick stroll around the neighbourhood, during which the impact of the recent marijuana legalization was especially evident as plumes of blue smoke rose above the heads of seemingly half the people we passed on the street.

"I heard the local weed shops have already run out of inventory," Nils said.

"There'll be riots," I told him.

"It's too late for riots," Nils said. "Everyone is too stoned already."

Up first at the MTelus that night was Exhorder, the legendary New Orleans–based heavy metal band considered to be a huge influence on Pantera, Lamb of God, White Zombie and many other bands that went on to sell a lot more T-shirts than they have. They are a great band who definitely didn't get their due back in their heyday in the early nineties, in my 100 percent expert heavy metal opinion. There are some who speculate that the fact they titled their debut album *Slaughter in the Vatican*, with an illustration of the Pope being led to the gallows on the cover, is largely to blame for this, but I just don't see it.

Anyway, my friend Marzi, who shreds like the wind,* had recently been enlisted to replace one of the band's original guitar players, so I was especially excited to see them play at Quebec Deathfest. There's just something special about being able to stand in the crowd and elbow strangers during the show and say stuff to them like "That's my close personal friend up there. It's funny—just the

---

* My point here is that he is a very accomplished guitarist and can play really fast and stuff.

other day we were just chatting and laughing at inside jokes you could never understand if you tried," or even "I bet if I ever needed a kidney or seventy bucks or anything, the guy up there on stage right would give it to me without even thinking about it." To that end, we rushed in and grabbed a spot for ourselves on the ground level, in an elevated area a safe distance from the pit, where there would have been too great a risk of getting my shoes dirtied.

Exhorder took the stage only moments later and were just a couple songs into their set when I noticed the two metalheads we had seen at the poutine place, sitting on some stools just a few feet away. This was my chance.

"I saw you guys at the poutine place earlier," I yelled to them over the excellent groove-oriented thrash metal we all seemed to be really enjoying at the moment.

"Huh?" one of them said, momentarily pulling his eyes from the stage.

"The poutine place!" I repeated. "You guys had poutine earlier at a poutine place, and I saw you there because I was having poutine at the poutine place, too!"

"Oh, yeah," the guy said before turning his eyes to the stage again. "That's cool."

It was a pretty sick hang.

Anyway, Exhorder played an awesome set that whipped the thousand or so people in attendance into a heavy metal frenzy. It had totally primed Nils, Greg and me for hours more headbanging, too, but as mentioned earlier, we had a lovely dinner at a wine bar planned, which was going to be extremely metal in its own way, so I had no choice but to reluctantly gather Nils and Greg and get us all into a cab posthaste.

"But I was just getting the hang of things," Nils said as we walked out of the theatre. "I was even started to headbang a little, and a lot of people were noticing."

"It's okay," I assured. "Once the headbanging is inside of you, it will never leave you. In fact, something tells me it was inside of you all along."

"You really think so?" Nils asked.

"I do," I replied, just telling him what he wanted to hear. "I really do."

We arrived at Vin Mon Lapin on Rue Saint-Zotique in Little Italy a short while later.

"Are you Dave?" a twentysomething restaurant employee asked me as soon as we entered.

"Yes," I told him. "Yes, I am."

"Excellent," he replied. "Would you like to grab a drink at the bar while we get your table ready?"

I swear to you it happened just like that. And while I'd like to think it was because my reputation preceded me, it was more likely because I cut to the head of the line and told him we had a reservation for six-thirty. Even so, it still felt great.

We sat down a few minutes later and proceeded to dine on a mélange of small plates consisting mostly of seafood, vegetables, cheeses and a few delicious things I struggled to identify in the place's tastefully dim, yet extremely metal lighting. To wash it down, we had a few too many glasses of biodynamic red wine, the most metal of all wines, and you can ask anyone.

"I feel like I would really love living here in Montreal," I said as a busboy cleared our empty plates.

"You seem drunk," said Nils.

"What—you don't like Montreal?" I asked.

"I love Montreal," Nils replied. "But I'm just saying you seem kind of drunk right now."

To be fair, Nils was probably right. But I couldn't worry about it right then because I had research to do. And while the focus of my trip was to hear extreme heavy metal played in a distinctly French-Canadian environment, the Montreal Canadiens were also playing the Senators in Ottawa that night, so it seemed crazy not to at least try to catch a period before we descended upon the metal festival once again. Besides, hockey is the most metal of all sports, and you can ask anyone that too.

Keeping all that in mind, we made our way to the nearby Bruno

Sports Bar, which was showing the game on perhaps the largest TV screen I have ever seen in my entire extremely metal life—it stretched from floor to ceiling and was at least the length of two mid-size sedans parked bumper to bumper. It's also worth noting that there was a large deli case, something you don't see every day in a bar and something that really impressed me at the time, mostly because I think Nils was probably right about me being at least a little bit drunk. Anyway, we settled around a table in the back to catch what was the left of the third period.

"Looks like Ottawa's got this one," Nils said as the clock wound down.

"Do you think this place could turn violent?" I asked.

"Yes," Nils said. "But not because of the game, but because you've been sitting directly in front of the screen and obstructing everyone's view this entire time."

I mumbled something or other about Rocket Richard in hopes of getting on everyone's good side, but it didn't seem to help as the Senators handed the Canadiens a 4–3 loss. Besides, my friend Chris's band, Autopsy, was going on soon, so we needed to get back over to the MTelus theatre.

"*Bonjour!*" I said to a few folks as we headed for the door. They all seemed to appreciate it as best I could tell.

We arrived at the MTelus theatre a few minutes later and bought a round of Molson tall boys to enhance our overall Canadian experience. I was pretty tired or drunk at this point, depending on whom you ask, so we decided to sit up in the balcony during Autopsy's set so I wouldn't get jostled, or perhaps even passed around the venue against my will or anything.

For the uninitiated, Autopsy are gods as far as death metal and being nice fellows in general goes. They formed in the Oakland area in 1987. My buddy Chris is the drummer and singer. Chris also played on the first album by Florida death metal legends Death,* *Scream Bloody Gore*, when he was just seventeen years old.

---

* Yes, in the event that you are unfamiliar, I realize this name is a little "on the nose," but just keep reading. I don't have time to get into this right now.

The album is considered by many to be the first death metal album.*

"Why did you quit Death?" I once asked Chris.

"Because I promised my mother I would come home and finish high school," he told me.

It doesn't get much cooler than helping to create an entire subgenre of music while still respecting the importance of getting an education, if you ask me. He's not Canadian or anything, but we could still all learn a lot from Chris.

Anyway, Autopsy played a great set that included all their hot hits, including "Twisted Mass of Burnt Decay," "Charred Remains," "Service for a Vacant Coffin" and the many others that have pretty much made them the Rihanna of the death metal scene, as far as I and a lot of other people are concerned. And while death metal played by even the best of the best, like Autopsy, may not be for everybody, it cannot be denied that seeing and hearing it performed live is a spectacle to behold, even when you've been drinking all day in Canada with your friends and may or may not have fallen completely asleep in the balcony for at least a couple of songs as a result.

"You guys are the best at death metal!" I screamed from the balcony before belching a couple times. I'm not sure if anyone in the band heard me or not, but I did get a few stares from the floor when I screamed it a few more times after Autopsy had already vacated the stage and security was trying to get everyone to leave.

The Autopsy show—and, with it, Quebec Deathfest—completed, I grabbed Nils and Greg, found my buddy Nick from Toronto, and we headed backstage for a quality death metal hang with my buddy Chris, his bandmates, and any other metal-type people who might have been around at the time.

"That's a nice sheep sweater," Chris remarked to me as we cracked open a couple beers. "Pretty metal."

-----

* Yes, metalheads reading this, I know some people think the first death metal album was recorded by the Possessed or Necrophagia, but this is my book and I am calling things as I see them. Also, I am right. So there.

"Yeah, I know," I told him. "That's why I wore it. Because it's metal."

Chris and I continued our heavy metal–based conversation for a while after this, which is when I managed to witness what I am now convinced is the most Canadian thing that has ever happened.* I don't want to speculate on whether there was a lot of marijuana being smoked backstage because marijuana had just been legalized in Canada or because we were just backstage at a heavy metal festival, but whatever the reason, there was no shortage of joints being passed around among folks other than me. And while one such joint was being smoked by one of the many heavy metal musicians who had played that day, I happened to witness a young man with an extremely strong Canadian accent ask him, "Should I ask for some of that joint?"

Had I heard this question asked in the United States, I might have dismissed it as just kind of weird. But that night in Montreal, it sounded so impossibly polite, so asking-without-actually-asking, so ridiculously Canadian, that the thought of it had me laughing so hard, most people would have thought I was the most stoned person in the room, despite the fact that I hadn't touched the stuff. I suppose I could have had a "contact high," given the amount of pot smoking going on backstage, but to be fair, the same could probably have been said about anyone on St. Catherine Street, or maybe even the entire population of Canada by that point, assuming the rest of the country was celebrating the weed legalization like the people of Montreal appeared to be. And for the record, the guy succeeded in getting "some of that joint" in the end, so there's that.

Having sufficiently partied within reason with the members of Autopsy, Exhorder and everyone else backstage at the MTelus theatre that night whether they liked it or not, Greg, Nils and I grabbed

---

* Yes, I know I have described several things in this book as "the most Canadian thing that has ever happened" by this point, but this time, I really mean it. At least until something else comes along that is even more Canadian, at which point the Canadian baton will be passed.

a cab back to the stash pad, where I would like to let the record show that I let them each take a bedroom while I embraced the harsh realities of the pullout couch in the living room—which was also the kitchen, now that I think about it. Under different circumstances, I might have viewed this is as a less-than-ideal compromise, but as I drifted off to sleep that night, it all felt pretty metal to me.

"If only Ronnie James Dio could see me right now," I thought as I turned off the lights and pulled a worn-out, undoubtedly-slathered-in-DNA comforter over my torso, which had become rather bloated from a solid work day's worth of drinking and eating.

I awoke the next morning still reeking of beer and Canadian marijuana decriminalization to find a light snowfall descending upon the Gay Village. Nils, a serial early riser, had already woken and headed to the corner diner for breakfast, so Greg and I got dressed and met him for a cup of coffee before he headed off to catch his bus back to Merrickville.

"You don't wanna encounter a moose when he's in his rut," I remember Nils saying, seemingly from out of nowhere, not unlike the bee talk from earlier in this chapter, as I slowly reconstituted myself at our corner table.

"What's a rut?" I asked. "You mean like when the moose gets stuck in some sort of pattern in his life that's difficult to change despite his best efforts?"

"No," Nils said. "I mean when a moose wants to get laid."

"Everyone has needs, I guess," I replied.

"Yup, even moose," Nils said. "Only they take it out on *everybody*."

"Even non-moose?" I asked.

"*Especially* non-moose," he replied.

Nils went on to describe the various times in his life when he'd found himself confronted by an amorous moose. It was more often than Greg or I could have possibly imagined, and I probably could have listened to him talk about it all day, but Nils had a bus to catch, so instead, we all piled into a cab to drop him off before Greg and I went to meet Nick for breakfast at Bagel Etc. on Boulevard

Saint-Laurent, as I continued to imagine Nils in various moose-related states of compromise.

We were about halfway to the bus station when I remembered that I had rented a car for exactly this sort of occasion, but as I wasn't in the best of shape at the moment, I didn't have the heart to give myself too hard of a time about it.

"We can drive the car later," Greg assured me. "Just as soon as you remember where you parked it."

As for Bagel Etc.,* supposedly it was one of Leonard Cohen's old Montreal haunts. We arrived there a few minutes later to find the Sunday brunch line already spilling out the front door, and Nick bringing up the rear like a boss.

"Huh," I said. "I guess *everybody knows* about Bagel Etc."

I was hoping for a bigger reaction from everybody in the line to what I am confident is one of the stronger Leonard Cohen reference–based jokes you'll hear all year, but no one really seemed to notice, or if they did, they weren't willing to acknowledge my genius.

"Please keep the door closed," a waiter asked after squeezing down the line toward the exit. "It's letting in too much cold air."

"Canadians can be really pragmatic," Nick explained after the waiter pulled the door shut, leaving us on the sidewalk until our table was ready. "Just watch how hard they try to make sure that door stays shut now."

Sure enough, everyone working at the restaurant, as well as everyone waiting to get a table at the restaurant, joined in solidarity for at least the next fifteen minutes or so to make sure the door remained shut. It was an impressive sight to behold, and I imagine the joint effort continued long after that, but with our table for three finally ready, Greg, Nick and I headed inside to do our best to guess what Leonard Cohen would have recommended,

---

* I probably shouldn't be getting into this right now, but shouldn't it be called *Bagels* Etc.? If I think about this for too long, my brain starts to hurt, but I leave this here for you and future generations to ponder.

which—as I far as I was concerned, anyway—turned out to be bagels with lox. And since this was quickly turning into one of those "anything goes" sorts of weekends, I washed it down with both coffee and a chocolate shake, something I'm not proud of, but figure I am obligated to tell you out of journalistic integrity. Then again, the more I think about it, it is a pretty metal beverage combination, so I should probably just own it, dammit.

"*Hallelujah*," I said with a knowing glance to Nick and Greg after finishing my shake. "That's another famous Leonard Cohen song."

"Yeah, we know," Nick said. "Should we grab the cheque?"

"Sure," I replied, while making a mental note not to waste my genius on Nick and Greg for at least another couple hours.

With breakfast behind us, we took to the streets, where Nick headed off to do some writing in a nearby café and Greg and I drifted in the opposite direction down Boulevard Saint-Laurent. We didn't get far before we found a shop that sold, among other things, heavy metal records and pants—which, of course, ticked a couple boxes of personal interest, as I had come to town for the primary purpose of harnessing the power and majesty of heavy metal *and* I was currently sporting a pair of unfortunate pants. So, I headed inside to right some wrongs, at least as far as my pants went, anyway, and bought a pair of work pants that weren't too short and didn't have weird creases in them like the pair I'd worn to the airport the day before. Since I didn't feel like carrying around an extra pair of pants, though, I decided to simply wear the new ones over the old pair—a controversial move, to be sure, and definitely one that inspired some strange looks from the guy behind the counter, but in the end is something I choose to view as luxury living. I mean, think about it—my grandfather Clarence Blake made his way from Clinton, Ontario, to the United States in the early twentieth century in search of a better life. And now, here was his grandson, roughly a hundred years later, walking around his native Canada wearing not one, but *two* pairs of pants *at the same time*. It was hard not think of how proud he would have been to see me walking down Boulevard Saint-Laurent with all that fabric bunched up between my legs.

"Don't they chafe?" Greg asked of my pants we headed back outside.

"You're damn right they do," I answered proudly.

Greg, my two pairs of pants and I continued down Boulevard Saint-Laurent in the direction of our Airbnb, stopping off along the way to buy a vintage cowl-neck sweater I thought might help complete my look and also help me blend in with the locals a bit more, as I'd like to think it made me look like I'd just returned from a relaxing weekend by the fire in the Laurentian Mountains or something, a look I am confident would have hit home even more so had I removed the price tag.

"*Bonjour!*" I said to no one in particular as we continued down the street. It felt good, like I was a real French-Canadian person just walking down the street in a French-Canadian sweater, as is my wont.

Farther down the road, Greg and I stumbled upon a heavy metal department store of sorts. And, still coming down from Quebec Deathfest the night before, we couldn't help but head inside for a look at all the black T-shirts, black coffee mugs featuring heavy metal band logos, and other black things they had for sale there.

"Hi," an attractive young woman in a heavy metal T-shirt standing behind the counter said to us as we entered.

"Don't let my cowl-neck sweater fool you," I replied. "We were at Quebec Deathfest last night."

"Oh," she said before tending to the register.

I could tell she was pumped. Even so, things quickly went south after Greg looked at a T-shirt for the Norwegian black metal band Darkthrone*, a band whose logo is particularly hard to read to the untrained eye, and tried to read that logo out loud, with mixed results, in front of the whole store, thus outing himself as a guy who really isn't all that metal when it gets down to it. Sadly, I had

---

* It seems crazy not to mention here that Darkthrone have a song called "Canadian Metal" that appeared on their excellent 2007 album *F.O.A.D.* It is arguably the best song on the topic I have ever heard.

no choice but to quickly usher him out the door and get away as quickly as possible before I was subject to any guilt-by-association judgments the woman at the front counter—or any of the other slaves to metal inside the store—might cast upon us.

"Why do we have to leave?" Greg asked as I shoved him out the door.

"You wouldn't understand," I told him.

The shame of Greg's heavy metal band name mispronunciation mostly behind us, we finished the walk back to our Airbnb. We were feeling a bit peckish by then, so it seemed like a perfect time to check out a place called Poutineville, which was just around the corner from where we were staying. What with us being in Montreal and everything, it seemed insane not to go to a place that was called that.

"Isn't all of Montreal a Poutineville of sorts, if you really think about it?" I said to Greg as we headed inside. I had no choice but to take his silence as an affirmation that I'd just completely blown his mind.

As hinted in the name, Poutineville's specialty is poutine. They make everything from traditional poutine to poutine where you can choose your ingredients and make the poutine of your dreams, even if that's a really bad idea. Say, for example, you wanted poutine made with sweet potato fries and a pile of mozzarella cheese–covered General Tso's chicken dumped on top of it like you thought you were going to live forever or something—you could totally do that.

"What if we opened a place right across the street called Poutineria?" I asked Greg as we each made light work of a bowl of traditional poutine.

"Why?" Greg asked between bites.

"You know—just to mess with their heads," I told him.

Greg just ignored me after that, but I'd still like to think he was really into the idea and only went quiet because he was trying to figure out how we might finance this bold new curd-based venture.*

---

* Between this and Curd Country, I'm about to be a very busy man.

We returned to what, by now, we were pretty sure was a murder bunker, no matter how many flattering adjectives had been incorporated into its Airbnb description, for a brief respite before meeting back up with Nick and his friend Maryanna at a coffee and dessert shop called the Cardinal on Boulevard Saint-Laurent. It was here that the heavy metal debauchery of the night before, as well as—if I'm honest—the challenges of wearing two pairs of pants all day, were really starting to catch up with me. I tried to revive myself with some hot chocolate and a slice of squash cheesecake pie that was about a thousand times more delicious than it originally sounded to me, as I generally tend to lead a squash-free life, but it was no use. Until, that is, Maryanna mentioned the possibility of swinging by a fast-food restaurant called Lafleur that she claimed was owned by Montreal Canadiens great Guy Lafleur, at which point my fire momentarily returned.

"Are you serious?" I asked her. "You mean we could dine on fried things with one of the greatest wingers in the history of the NHL lurking nearby, maybe even secretly watching us from behind the deep fryer or something?"

"Well, I don't know about that last part," Maryanna replied. "But he does own the place."

"So strange," I thought. "How did I somehow never hear about the fact that Guy Lafleur was a fast-food impresario?"

It is at this point that I got curious and did a bit of internet research on Guy Lafleur and any connections he might have to the fast-food game. And it turned out he was, in fact, not involved with the chain of restaurants sharing his last name.

"Dammit!" I said, slamming the table. "Guy Lafleur has nothing to do with this Lafleur restaurant you speak of!"

"Are you sure?" Maryanna asked.

"I'm positive!" I replied. "And here I was, absolutely looking forward to enjoying some fries, and maybe a medium Coke, in a family-friendly atmosphere with the great Guy Lafleur himself no doubt eventually sauntering over to the table to ask if he might join us for a bit of light chitchat before he headed back to the kitchen to help out with things like the down-to-earth guy he is—pun intended—and now it's never gonna happen!"

"I'm sorry," Maryanna said. "I really thought it was his restaurant."

"Sorry isn't gonna cut it, sister," I told her.

It was a bit much, maybe, but with that I stormed out of the café and back to our rental apartment once again. We did make plans right before that to meet up a bit later for a nice dinner, but I'm still pretty sure that Maryanna, Greg, Nick and everyone else in the place knew full well that I was completely enraged at this point and that they had better think twice before lying to me about a restaurant—or any small business—supposedly owned by an NHL Hall of Famer ever again.

Back at the apartment, Greg, Nick—who would be taking the bed vacated by Nils that night—and I each took a short nap in hopes of better preparing ourselves for whatever French-Canadian debauchery might be in store before meeting up with Maryanna once again for dinner at a cozy little restaurant downtown. It was there that Nick and Maryanna began to school me on the art of Quebecois profanity, something I didn't realize how much I really needed in my life until then.

"*Tabarnak* is a big one," Nick said. "It means 'tabernacle.'"

"Tabernacle?" I asked. "Why would someone say that?"

"French-Canadian profanity is mostly based on church things," Maryanna explained.

"*Sacrament* is another one," Nick said. "I like that one a lot."

Having been raised Roman Catholic, I took to French-Canadian profanity in a manner not unlike the way a newborn fawn just gets up and starts running around all of a sudden, and I couldn't wait to start using it all the time. In fact, having been grounded on many occasions during my youth for having used more traditional American profanity around the house, I felt like I needed to make up for lost time.

"*Tabarnak!*" I said as soon as I finished my drink. "I need another drink. *Sacrament!*"

"I don't think you get how this works," Nick said.

"Yeah, I do," I replied. "It's like you just say regular church stuff to swear, and that way you don't get in trouble like you do when you drop F-bombs in front of your aunt and stuff, and all of a sudden, you're eating Thanksgiving dinner in the garage again."

"Sort of," Maryanna said, "but also not really."

"Man, I wish I knew this stuff last night when we were at the heavy metal concert," I continued. "*Tabarnak!*"

As it turned out, like most things in life, there was a bit of a learning curve when it came to incorporating French-Canadian profanity into everyday life, but I was excited to get the hang of it in the days, weeks and even years to come.

"I guess we'd just like to ask you to take it slow at first," Nick added. "Until you get the hang of it."

And with that, I made a mental note not to use any more French-Canadian profanity, at least until we got outside again.

"There's other Quebby stuff we could teach you besides that," Maryanna said once I'd officially calmed down.

"'Quebby'?" I asked. "Does that mean stuff that's distinctly French-Canadian?"

"Yes, Dave," Maryanna said. "Yes, it does."

"Cool!" I said. "As it turns out, I love Quebby stuff!"

And with that, we got the cheque and headed off to our next destination, which I was assured was one of the most Quebby places in town: the Cheval Blanc brewery.

"I get so mad when I see poutine outside of Quebec," Maryanna told me there after I finished telling her about all the other provinces I'd had poutine in so far.

"Me too," I told her. "I've just been eating it in all those other places to remind myself how much better it is here in Quebec. You know—to teach myself a hard lesson."

To tell you the truth, I've enjoyed poutine literally every time I've eaten it,* from Halifax to Victoria and everywhere in between, so I was just saying that to get on her good side. But there is something

---

* Except for the very first time, I guess, when, looking back on it, my system just wasn't ready for the good times ahead.

especially nice about having it in the place it was invented, while also rattling off various church terms for no apparent reason whatsoever.

"*Tabarnak!*" I suddenly shouted, just trying to stay in practice.

"What did we tell you about that?" Nick said.

"Sorry," I replied.

I don't know if it was because of my newfound and 100 percent awesome penchant for French-Canadian profanity, or the fact that everyone was just kind of tired, but we called it a night shortly after that and Greg, Nick and I headed back to the apartment for some much-needed sleep. And while I'm thinking about it, I should tell you that if you've never slept while wearing two pairs of pants at the same time, you should give it a shot. It is a form of decadence like no other, and it comes in especially handy while sleeping on a pull-out couch in the middle of some strange kitchen in Montreal where it seems as if your life could very well be snuffed out at any moment.

We awoke early the following morning feeling robust again, so much so, in fact, that if there were, weirdly, a heavy metal festival that somehow started on a Monday morning in Montreal, we would have headed there immediately. Since that wasn't the case, however, we instead hatched a plan to meet Maryanna for bagels in the Mile End section of town.

Living in New York, I am of course fairly biased when it comes to bagels—not because I necessarily have a strong opinion on the matter, or even eat bagels very often when you get right down to it, but more as a point of pride and civic responsibility. So when Nick and Maryanna came at me with what I perceived at the time to be "Montreal bagels are the best" bullshit, I was a bit reluctant to get on board. Still, in the name of journalistic integrity, I felt obligated, so I drove us to Saint-Viateur Bagel, one of Montreal's finest bagel establishments.*

---

* And yes, I realize that some Montreal bagel enthusiasts will say I went to the wrong place and I should have gone to *their* favourite Montreal bagel place instead and to those people I say "*Tabarnak!*" with the confidence of a man who has been using French Canadian profanity for a solid 24 hours straight at least.

My original plan was to get an everything bagel or two. But when we got there, the sesame bagels were fresh out of the oven, so Nick and Maryanna urged me to get one of those, even though everyone knows sesame bagels are bullshit.

"But they're warm," Maryanna said.

"That makes them better," Nick explained further.

Not looking for trouble, I bought a couple warm sesame bagels along with a room-temperature everything bagel and a rosemary bagel. It seemed aggressive to eat four bagels for breakfast, but I figured if I was gonna do this, I was gonna do this. Plus, how metal is it to eat four bagels in one sitting? Pretty metal, last time I checked.

"How do you like it?" Maryanna asked me as I devoured the first sesame bagel out on the sidewalk moments later.

"It's fine," I replied, not wanting to admit how completely delicious it was. "You know, if you like sesame bagels, which I definitely don't."

As for the difference between New York bagels and Montreal bagels, New York bagels are bigger and fluffier and make you want to tell someone to hold all your calls immediately after eating one. Montreal bagels are smaller and denser and, as a result, more suited to the on-the-go lifestyle. For example, Nick and I each ate our bagels while walking down the street like it was no big deal at all. In New York, eating a bagel means stopping in your tracks and maybe even setting your belt back a notch or taking off your pants altogether—whether you are wearing a second pair at the time or not. Then again, that might just be me and a few problems I need to work through.

Farther down the block, we stopped into a coffee shop full of older French-Canadian men who seemed to have even more disdain for me than that one guy at the blues bar a couple days earlier. I tried to win them over by trying out some more of my new French-Canadian swear words on them, but it only seemed to make matters worse, so I decided to cut my losses. Greg and I said our goodbyes to Nick and Maryanna, and we headed for the airport.

After we got settled at our gate, I decided to fish another sesame bagel out of my bag and wolf it down right then and there as we waited to board our plane.

"You're making a mess," Greg said to me with a furrowed brow as he noted the myriad of crumbs and sesame seeds in my lap, my chair, and on the floor all around me.

"But it's totally metal," I replied, just trying to own things.

"It's metal to make a mess while eating a sesame bagel at your airport gate?" Greg asked.

"Yes, it totally is," I told him. "And you wouldn't understand it in a million, trillion years."

Then I got up and walked off in search of a Tim Hortons and some napkins.

9

ST. JOHN'S, NEWFOUNDLAND*

In the Shadow of the Big Stick

OUT OF ALL THE PLACES in Canada I set my sights on visiting
for the purposes of this gravity-defying book, the one I was perhaps
most excited about was Newfoundland.

"Is that because of Newfoundland's rich and storied history with
regard to the elusive codfish?" you wonder.

No. In fact, with all due respect, I don't even like cod all that
much, when it gets right down to it.

"Well, then, it must be because Newfoundland is where Cluny
Macpherson, inventor of the gas mask, was from?" you suggest.

---

* Rest assured, Newfoundland and Labrador natives and current residents,
I am well aware that you have to use both dog names when properly referencing your fair province. I only left off the Labrador part in this chapter
because that's what everyone in Newfoundland did when I was there. I'm
sorry you had to hear this from me, Labradorians. I promise you, though,
that when I finally make it to Labrador one day, I will intentionally leave
off the Newfoundland part in an effort to make things right between us.

Nope. It's not that, either, though I will be the first admit that that's pretty cool.

No, the reason I was so excited to visit Newfoundland was that it is the place where the Newfoundland dog, arguably the greatest dog of all time,* is said to have originated. On the off chance you don't already know, the Newfoundland is a massive, magnificent and—perhaps most of all—drooling beast that could probably pass for a couch if it could ever manage to hold still long enough. It's so large, in fact, that one half expects it to suddenly stand upright and reveal that it was actually a grown man in a dog suit, just playing a really great prank on you this whole time. To this day, on the rare occasion I encounter a Newfoundland walking down the street, I am instantly filled with absolute joy, forget all my problems and proceed to press my face deep into the Newfoundland itself until its owner practically has to drag me off the thing.

In light of this, the mere thought of finally visiting Newfoundland had me just plain giddy, as I assumed it must be some sort of dog-based utopia where Newfoundlands of every variety** roamed the land freely, wandering into local butcher shops to help themselves to whatever they damn well pleased, napping in the middle of the street and relieving themselves wherever and whenever the mood struck—sort of like I've heard cows do in parts of India, minus that thing about the butcher shop, of course.

You can imagine how devastated I was to find out this wasn't even slightly the case. My buddy Reed, who's spent a fair amount of time in Newfoundland, was the one to break the news to me.

"I've been there a bunch of times," he said, "and I don't think I've seen even one Newfoundland dog running around."

---

* To be fair, technically speaking, *all* dogs are the greatest dog of all time, especially my sweet girl, Luci, a boxer-pit bull-hellhound mix who has actively tried to stop me from writing this book every step of the way. I do hope you are grateful that she failed, though I accept that there have to be at least a few of you out there who wish she had tried a little harder.

** As if the Newfoundland weren't already awesome enough, it comes in black, brown, grey, and white with black spots. Collect all four!

"Are you sure?" I asked him. "Not even one, Reed?"

"Not even one, Dave," he replied.

Regardless of this news, I wanted to see the place, as I still figured the odds of running into one of those awesome dogs had to
be at least slightly better than in New York City, where I'm lucky
to happen upon one every six months at best.

As far as the people of Newfoundland go, I'd heard they were
pretty cool, too, and were, in fact, so outgoing and welcoming
that it could very well prove difficult to leave when it came time to
do so. As fate would have it, my buddy Reed, mentioned earlier,
was friends with a whole family of them, so when I told him I had
booked myself a trip to St. John's* to snoop around, he put me in
touch with the matriarch of the family, a lovely woman named
Rose. My first interaction with her was when she called me up
without warning the day before my trip and told me I wouldn't be
renting a car to get around, as I'd originally planned, because she
and her husband, Gerald, would be picking me up from the airport whether I liked it or not.

"But I already rented the car," I told her. "I even paid for it in
advance so I could save six dollars."

"Now, I won't be hearing any of that," Rose told me in a
Newfoundland accent that turned out to be actually pretty light
compared to the ones I would soon be hearing. "You'll be able to
spot me and my husband at the airport because we'll be wearing
matching brown sweaters. How will we be able to spot you?"

"I'll be wearing a green plaid jacket," I told her.

"Great," she replied. "Oh, and my husband is in a wheelchair, so
you could look out for that, too."

I wanted to tell her that even one of the details we'd just
exchanged would probably be enough for us to find each other at
the relatively small St. John's airport, but in the end, it didn't

---

* I almost booked a flight to Saint John, New Brunswick, instead. Just imagine, Saint John, New Brunswick: this chapter was a mere mouse click away
from being about you!

matter, as Rose and Gerald's son Duane's girlfriend, Erin, and their young son, Isaac, ended up grabbing me from the airport the next day instead.

"We were at the Christmas parade today," Erin told me as we pulled onto the highway and headed in the direction of town. "Do you know what bologna is?"

"You mean the popular sandwich meat?" I asked.

"Yes," she replied. "Anyway, there's a big bologna that marches in the parade."

"Do you mean people march in the parade while carrying a big bologna?"

"No," she said. "The bologna does the marching himself."

"Do you mean it's a guy in a bologna costume, then?" I asked, looking for clarification. "Is that what you're saying?"

"Yes," she replied. "They call him the Big Stick."

Assuming the guy in the bologna costume had long since climbed out of it, probably leaving the larger-than-life processed-beef disguise crumpled on the ground in a corner where it would likely stay until called into action the following year in anticipation of the birth of the baby Jesus, it was hard not to feel like I'd already missed the real action on this trip. Still, I tried to keep an open mind as Erin and Isaac dropped me off a short while later at a pub in nearby Quidi Vidi* called the Mallard Cottage, where Duane was playing guitar at his weekly gig, a Sunday session where he and an accordion player have their way with Newfoundland and non-Newfoundland folk tunes for several hours at a time.

"Hi," I said to the hostess as I entered. "I'm looking for Duane."

"Yup," she said. "He's in there playing now."

I headed into the bar area, where Duane, a fortysomething fellow with a black beard and longish hair to match, was seated at a table in the corner, playing what sounded like a jig of some sort with a similarly bearded accordionist working the buttons across

---

* Pronounced "kitty-viddy," as it turns out, which is much more fun than it looks on the page.

from him. Duane and I had never met, but I approached the table and gave him a wave to let him know I had arrived, like some weirdly friendly assassin in a spy movie or something. He kept playing, but managed to smile and nod back as if to say, "You must be Dave, that American guy. Too bad you missed the giant, anthropomorphic bologna that was walking around town earlier today. It was quite a sight, one we're not likely to see again in these parts for some time."

Then I grabbed a seat at the bar and ordered a beer from a bartender beautiful enough for me to imagine a whole new life for myself, together with her in Newfoundland, after just a few sips. I also ordered some fries and chicken wings while I was at it. And, yes, I realize that was a mistake, since there were plenty of great local seafood dishes to be had, but after a long day of flying, I was pretty exhausted and wanted something I could easily shovel into my face as I sat there, enjoying the stone-cold folk jams and doing my best to blend in.

The pub was an especially cozy one, with a dozen or so tables of people eating, drinking and soaking in the guitar and accordion-based jams along each wall. At the centre of the room was a table piled high with desserts. In short, things couldn't have possibly been going better for me at this point. And after another beer, I worked up the courage to go sit at the table with Duane and the accordionist so I could see the hot session action up close and perhaps chat with them a bit in between songs. It can be difficult to sit at a table, stuffing your face with fries and wings while the other two people play jaunty folk tunes, but I'd like to think I really nailed it as I sat there, watching Duane play Django Reinhardt–worthy licks up and down the neck of his guitar while his accordion-playing partner, Aaron, worked his instrument as if he were practising some sort of accordion-based witchcraft.

"Is this your first time in Newfoundland?" Duane asked me in between songs.

"Yup," I told him in between bites of chicken wings. "I heard I missed the Big Stick."

"Yeah," he said with a heaviness that seemed to acknowledge my disappointment. "But there's probably some other stuff we could show you here."

I wasn't sure how anything was going to beat a guy walking in broad daylight dressed as a giant tube of questionable meat, but I decided to take his word for it, anyway. And speaking of words, Duane and Aaron both spoke theirs with a Newfoundland accent as well, which to my ears sounded like a mix of Irish, Scottish and American Southern accents, with perhaps a dash of Cajun thrown in there for good measure. It was pleasing to my ear, sort of like a warm sweater, a thick sandwich and a shot of off-brand whiskey in aural form.

"My parents got rid of their accent," Aaron told me. "But I kept mine."

"I'm glad you held your ground," I told him. "It sounds great."

At around 7:30 p.m., the session came to a end, I gave the bartender a wave I hoped would let her know that, in an alternate universe, I would have done my damnedest to make her the happiest woman in all of Quidi Vidi, and Duane and I headed outside to grab a cab back into St. John's proper. And it's at this point that things got really crazy—at least in terms of me trying to understand a thick Newfoundland accent, anyway.

"Yeah, it's a really nice place," Duane said to our cab driver in response to what I can only guess was a question he'd asked about the pub we'd just left.

Our cab driver was a fireplug of a man in his fifties with a shaved head and a raspy voice that sounded like he gargled with live bees every morning. And since Duane and his guitar had filled up the back seat, I rode shotgun, which gave me the opportunity to not only hear what he was saying, but also to watch his lips move as he did it. But even that didn't help me any when it came to understanding a word he said. He might as well have been speaking in tongues. The only words coming from his mouth that I understood completely were "cut of meat," which I could only assume must have been yet another reference to the Big Stick that I was still kicking myself for missing earlier that day. Everything else he said, I just had to guess at, based on whatever Duane said immediately before or after the cab driver spoke. And the way Duane and the cab driver seemed to understand each other perfectly, despite my confusion, kind of reminded me of *Star Wars*, where C-3PO, R2-D2 and Chewbacca all spoke to each other in different languages, but somehow it all worked out just fine, anyway.

"What was *that* accent?" I asked Duane when we jumped out of the cab.

"That was a townie accent," Duane told me.

Our first stop in town was the Ship Pub, one of Duane's regular haunts. Tonight was their spoken-word night, and given what I'd just experienced on the cab ride over, I braced myself for further confusion, since we were now technically in town—you know, the place our cab driver was presumably from—so I assumed everyone would be talking, confusing and at times even scaring me like that. As it turned out, though, all of the performers that night sounded more like they were from my native Cleveland than like the cab driver. There was one spoken-word artist who had a flute accompanist, which kind of felt like cheating to me, but other than that, our time at the Ship Pub was largely without incident. Once the flautist had fully cleared the stage, Duane and I knocked backed whatever was left of our drinks and headed off into the night in search of further St. John's adventure.

"That's where they used to have the hanging tree," Duane said, pointing to a hillside along Water Street a couple minutes later.

"Hanging tree?" I asked in that way one tends to do after someone has mentioned a hanging tree. "What do you mean, 'hanging tree'?"

"It's where they used to hang people," he clarified.

"Used to?" I asked. "Where do they hang people now?"

"Oh," Duane said. "They don't do that anymore."

There's now a tapas restaurant across from where the hanging tree used to be, so it's not like torture has left the area altogether, though.

Anyway, as we continued down Water Street, looking out at the boats along the dock and at various bars and restaurants that Duane told me had popped up fairly recently in an attempt to cash in on the innate human desire to get hammered near large bodies of water, I was struck by how much St. John's reminded me of various seaside towns I've visited in Norway. I will admit that this is partially because I am a simple man, and pretty much all it takes is for a town to have a harbour and some cold weather and I'll start comparing it to Norway so much, you'd swear I was being paid to do it, but I'm still sticking to it.

Somewhere along the way, Duane and I wandered past a former church that is apparently now home to a strip club. It felt a little too easy if you ask me, like whoever took ownership of the church after the clergy and congregation decided to move on must have sat down and thought, "Hmmmm, now what's the absolute worst possible thing I could do with this beautiful old building?"

"A tapas restaurant?" his partner probably suggested.

"Nah," the first guy might have replied. "One of those just went in over on Water Street."

"What about a strip club?" the partner might then have asked.

"Perfect!" the first guy must have then replied. "We'll have private lap dances in the confessionals, a drink special called Holy Water, the whole deal!"

You might be disappointed to hear we didn't go inside the church-turned-strip-club, even though, as a journalist and all, I guess it was sort of my obligation. But I learned long ago that strip clubs are actually a lot like churches in a way: it can be kind of fun to poke your head inside one as long as you're in the area, but it tends to get boring quickly, and if you don't get out of there fast, sooner or later, someone's going to hit you up for money.

Keeping all of that in mind, we instead made our way over to George Street, the main drag in town in terms of nightlife.

"What's all this about getting 'screeched in'?" I asked Duane as we walked.

"I don't think you really need to do that," Duane replied.

The reason I brought it up is that my buddy Reed had mentioned I should get screeched in while I was in town. I had no idea what he was talking about, but I did a bit of internet research and read that getting "screeched in" involves doing a shot of dark rum and kissing a cod. The website I read this on also said getting screeched in is "non-obligatory," something I was relieved, yet still kind of disappointed to hear. I mean, how cool would it be if everyone visiting Newfoundland has absolutely no choice but to kiss a cod when they come to town?

"How was Newfoundland?" your friend might ask upon your return.

"It was great until they made me kiss that cod," you'd reply.

"What do you mean they made you?" your friend then asks. "Couldn't you say no?"

"No," you'd explain. "There's absolutely no getting out of it."

"Wow," your friend would then say. "Tough place."

"It sure is," you'd reply, while staring off into the distance, perhaps trying to forget the whole thing. "It sure is."

We continued working our way through town, popping into various local watering holes before we eventually wound up at a dimly lit bar on Water Street, where a handful of people were wringing the last bit of fun out of Sunday night and the odds of me having to kiss any sort of seafood whatsoever didn't seem very good at all. It was already pretty late at this point, and after a long day of travel and at least a couple too many drinks, I was feeling a little vulnerable. No doubt picking up on this, a woman in a fur hat and thick-framed glasses sauntered over to me in the way that one does when fresh meat of the Cleveland variety has rolled into town.

"You look like an interesting person," she said. "Are you a graphic designer?"

I was conflicted. On the one hand, I was flattered to hear that I looked "interesting," or that she even wanted to talk to me in the first place. But despite the fact that I can't resist a nice font and also happen to know my way around Photoshop pretty well, her graphic designer comment somehow rubbed me the wrong way, even more so after I caught my reflection in a mirror and realized I do sort of look like a graphic designer when it gets right down to it. Regardless, I took it all as a sign it might be time to call it a night.

"Good evening to you, ma'am," I said to the woman, doffing an imaginary cap and heading for the door. "We must be on our way."

I felt bad just leaving her hanging like that, but I had a big day ahead of me tomorrow in the form of driving around with Rose and Gerald in their minivan, and as such, it was time for some much-needed rest.

I awoke around nine the following morning and went for a quick run around town. It's one of my favourite things to do when visiting a new city, as you can see a lot of stuff more quickly than if you were just strolling around.* It also helps lift the fog a bit, whether you've been screeched in or not. Anyway, I was jogging past the Mile One Centre, home to the ECHL hockey team the Newfoundland Growlers, who were sadly not playing while I was in town, when a woman of mature years who happened to be sitting on the ground, smoking a cigarette, began screaming in my direction.

"Go! Go! Go! Go! Go!" she yelled, as if I were secretly running my own private marathon.

It was hard to tell whether she was rooting for me or openly mocking me. And I was admittedly equally delighted at either possibility. Part of me wanted to double back and ask her which one it was, but then I remembered that thing about the people of Newfoundland being so friendly and outgoing and just decided it was probably that first one. Besides, Duane's parents were going to be pulling up in front of my hotel any minute, and I needed to hustle.

"Thank you," I yelled to the woman as I kicked things into something resembling overdrive.

After a quick rinse, I pulled on some clothes and went downstairs to meet Rose and Gerald, who were parked in front of my hotel.

"Whatta y'at, Dave?" Rose said to me as she gave me a big hug.

"What?" I asked, hugging her back.

---

* You know, because of the running.

"It means 'How's it going?'" she explained as I hopped into the back seat.

"Oh, really great," I told her. "You know, minus the thing about how there aren't really any Newfoundland dogs here."

"What's that?" she asked as she threw the minivan into drive.

"I was sort of kidding," I explained. "It's just that I used to think that Newfoundland had Newfoundland dogs running around everywhere."

"You might see one," Rose told me, most likely just humouring me, but still giving me at least some glimmer of hope.

As for Gerald, he was in the passenger seat and, as promised, was wearing the same brown sweater Rose was.

"I like your sweaters," I told him.

"Rose made them," Gerald replied.

As Rose explained to me as we drove, Gerald suffered a brain hemorrhage about twenty years earlier, shortly after retiring from his career as a schoolteacher. As a result, he spends much of his time in a wheelchair. And while he remains a man of great intellect, he is also a man of few words. That was okay, though, because, in the way that all great couples tend to balance each other out, Rose was a real talker.

"This is Jellybean Row," Rose told me as we drove down a street lined with brightly painted townhouses. "Everyone here has to paint their house bright colours like this."

"It's really helping my mood," I told her.

"Why?" she asked. "Are you sad?"

"Well, you heard how I missed the Big Stick, didn't you?" I asked.

"What's that?"

"Oh, nothing."

The big plan for the day was to take me outside of St. John's proper so that I could see what Newfoundland was really like, away from the hustle and bustle of the big city.

"We're gonna take you out round the bay," she told me as we pulled onto the highway.

"What's that?" I asked.

"Around here, you either live in town or you're out round the bay," she explained.

As we put some kilometres behind us, the conversation gradually drifted to politics.

"We have some bumps in the ice as you skate around," Rose said of the current political situation in Newfoundland.

I can't remember the exact context of that statement, but I do remember being so delighted by how impossibly Canadian it sounded that I nearly hugged Rose from the back seat as she sped down the highway. Not wanting to cause an accident, however, I controlled myself and instead just made a mental note to start incorporating ice-skating analogies into my own daily lexicon immediately.

Our first stop as soon as we got "out around the bay" was Port de Grave, a peninsula big on fishing and, at least on the day of our visit, grey skies and a light drizzle. Gerald was born and raised there,* and he and Rose were excited to show me around. First, we swung by the harbour, where Rose told me they have a boat-lighting ceremony that's cause for great local excitement during the holiday season. And while I didn't get to see that, I did manage to pick up a pamphlet about how to survive in freezing water, in case that should be in my future. As it turns out, you're not supposed to panic and flail around as much as humanly possible while making high-pitched noises and regretting most of your life choices, as I had originally assumed.

I had intended to read further, but before I knew it, we had pulled into the driveway of Rose and Gerald's friend Mona, a Port de Grave native who had spent most of her life there, save for a few years when she moved away to teach kindergarten. Now in her seventies, she lives there with her daughter, who operates the family crabbing business.

---

* For more on Port de Grave, look no farther than Gerald's wonderful book on the place, *Heritage of a Newfoundland Outport: The Story of Port de Grave*.

Rather than having us go to the trouble of getting out of the van, Mona instead threw on a raincoat and came outside to hang out with us in the backseat for a bit.

"Nothing irritates us more than when someone mispronounces Newfoundland," Mona told me, her teaching instinct still alive and well.

Since I was outnumbered by Newfoundlanders, three to one, and given the odds of anyone ever thinking to look for my body in Port de Grave, of all places, I wanted to make sure I got it right. And as it turns out, I and pretty much everyone one else I'd ever heard try to pronounce *Newfoundland* prior to my visit have been pronouncing it all wrong this whole time. The emphasis isn't on the first syllable, as I'd always thought, but on the last (at least when Rose says it). And you don't want to see the daggers Mona will shoot you if you pronounce the second syllable as "fin." Instead, the *found* part is pronounced "fun," and the *d* in *land* is kicked to the curb altogether. And when said properly, it should kind of/sort of rhyme with the word *understand*.*

Not wanting to incur the future wrath of anyone in the van, or even within a hundred kilometres of it, I began to practise saying Newfoundland out loud so many times, you would have sworn I had developed some bizarre form of Tourette's syndrome. And while I'd like to think it amused them at first, after about a half hour of this, Mona couldn't take it any longer and politely excused herself to head back into the house.

"I really think I'm getting the hang of it," I said to Rose and Gerald as we pulled back out onto the road. "Newfun*lan*! "

"Yup," Rose said, keeping her eyes on the road. "You sure are."

It's hard to say whether she really meant it or not, but it didn't matter because we had bigger fish to fry—almost, but not quite literally in the form of the Port de Grave Fisherman's Museum, which Rose and Gerald's friend Vern, a Port de Grave native in his eighties, was somehow affiliated with. I say "somehow affiliated

---

* Minus that pesky *d* at the end, of course.

with" because I know Vern at least had keys to the fisherman's museum. And while I'm pretty sure he explained to me exactly what his role with the museum was, his Newfoundland accent was so thick, I could honestly only understand about 5 percent of what he was saying and had to just guess at the rest.

"Go have a look around with Vern," Rose said to me as he led me down the grassy path to the museum, which resembled a barn from the outside, most likely because it was at some point. "We'll wait for you in the van."

The Fishermen's Museum was founded by a New York artist named George Noseworthy. Noseworthy visited Port de Grave in the sixties with his wife and was apparently so taken with the area, he decided to stay and teach the locals to paint, and he set up the museum while he was at it.

As you might have guessed, the Fishermen's Museum consists mostly of old photos and paintings, along with even older fishing equipment, including but not limited to spears, hooks, scales (for weighing the fish, not the kind that are actually on the fish. You understand.) and at least a couple pair of what appeared to be historically accurate underwear. Vern led me around the space for twenty minutes or so, pointing at the various objects and presumably explaining to me exactly what they were. But as hard as I tried to make sense of it—not unlike my experience with the cab driver the night before—I could barely understand a word, which left me no choice but to fall into my default state for such situations, where I kind of smile and nod as if I'm just happy to be out of the house. That said, I love looking at old stuff that once belonged to long-since-dead people, so I could have spent hours smiling and nodding at Vern in that place.

"That was fun yet extremely confusing," I told Rose and Gerald as we got back on the road a short while later. "What language was he speaking?"

"That was pure Port de Grave," Rose told me with a laugh.

"But still English?" I asked.

"Yes," Rose replied. "Mona was intentionally speaking slowly so you'd understand her, but I wanted Vern to give you the full treatment."

It was hard not to wonder if Rose and Gerald were intentionally speaking slowly to me, too, but I tried not to worry about it as we moved on from the Fishermen's Museum to lunch in nearby Mad Rock, a town named for its allegedly irritable rock formations along the shore. There, we would meet Rose and Gerald's friend Winnie for a local dish called fish and brewis, which they pronounced as "fish and brews," which in turn caused me to be perhaps more excited about lunch than I should have been.

We parked in front of a small roadside café a few minutes later, and Rose walked to the other side of the van to get Gerald out of the passenger seat and into his wheelchair.

"Can I help you?" I asked Rose as she began the routine.

"You think I need help?" Rose said with a smile. "I've been doing this for twenty years."

Except for some time Gerald spent in the hospital and subsequent rehabilitation, Rose has been Gerald's round-the-clock caregiver since he suffered the brain hemorrhage, which is no small feat, any way you slice it. Still, I was amazed at the ease and grace with which they both seemed to deal with the situation and enjoy each other's company above all else. I'm usually a mess if I even have to deal with an especially stubborn ketchup packet.

As Rose, Gerald, Winnie and I settled around a table inside, I was disappointed to learn that fish and brewis was not fish and beer, as it had sounded to my ears, and we would not be happily throwing the day away to day-drinking, as I'd originally assumed. Instead, fish and brewis is a dish involving fish, hard bread, crackers and something called scrunchions, which it turned out is a bit of salted pork fat. Since I'm off pork these days, I asked our waitress if I might just have my fish and brewis without the scrunchions.

"I don't think you wanna do that," our twentysomething waitress told me.

"Yes, I do," I assured her.

"No, you don't," she replied.

The discussion continued as everyone else at the table weighed in, and it became clear to me that the scrunchions were doing the heavy lifting when it came to fish and brewis, and without the scrunchions, I would simply be left with a mushy plate of fish and hard bread that is about as tasty as that sounds.

"Pea soup and fish cakes it is," I told the waitress.

My lunch also came with something called a touton, which sounded like it might actually be some kind of hat, and probably could have doubled as one in a pinch, but turned out to be a local pastry that was not unlike a slightly less dainty croissant.

"Some people put butter on top and some people cut it open and put the butter inside," Winnie told me as I stared at the large slab of fried dough on the plate in front of me.

"And I like mine with molasses," Rose said as she squeezed a tube of the stuff onto her touton.

In the end, I went all in with butter and molasses in my cut-open touton. Was I flying a little too close to the sun? Maybe. But I didn't come all this way to take the easy way out. And if you think I didn't drench my fish cakes in molasses, too, while I was at it, guess again, dammit. And while it was pretty tasty, it was hard not to wonder what all those dead fishermen whose stuff I'd smiled and nodded at back at the Fishermen's Museum with Vern would have thought of all this. I guess it didn't matter, since I wouldn't have been able to understand a word of it, anyway.

After lunch, we took a quick spin by Mad Rock's namesake rocks and stared at them for a second in hopes of getting at least some sense of their rare majesty before heading back to St. John's proper, where I crawled into bed for a much-needed nap after my day "out round the bay."

A couple hours later, Duane swung by my hotel and we hit the mean streets of downtown St. John's in search of further good times, first settling in at the bar of a seafood restaurant on Water Street. There, I brought Duane up to speed on my day with his parents, and he in turn told me a bit more about his family.

"Part of my dad's condition comes down to his state of mind," Duane told me, referring to his father's brain hemorrhage.

"What do you mean?" I asked.

"Well, he's in a wheelchair," Duane said. "But sometimes he'll be left alone and I'll find him somehow upstairs."

"No one sees him walk up there?" I asked.

"Nope," Duane replied. "Another time, my mother left him in the van and they found my dad a few blocks away in a gas station parking lot, eating a yogurt."

"Where did the yogurt come from?"

"We don't know," Duane told me. "We don't know."

It was nice to hear how, despite some health issues, Gerald still had a few tricks up his sleeve. I also couldn't help but think back to earlier in the day, when Rose pointed out to me that Gerald didn't live *in* a wheelchair, but *from* a wheelchair. I'm not sure if she was consciously hinting at the yogurt incident, but it suddenly started making a whole lot more sense to me.

As fate would have it, the restaurant we were at happened to have beer on tap from the Dildo Brewing Company of Dildo, Newfoundland.

"How's the Dildo?" Duane asked the bartender while I stifled a laugh.

"You guys want to try the Dildo?" the bartender, a bearded fellow in his thirties, asked us.

"Definitely!" I said while doing my best to hold it together.

Duane and I each tried a sample of the beer, agreed it was delicious, and decided to order some pints.

"We'll take a couple Dildos," Duane said to the bartender.

"Yes, a Dildo for him and a Dildo for me," I added, piling on. "We love a good Dildo!"

By then, I had fully given up trying to suppress my laughter and instead just gave in to the simple joys of laughing at the name of an unusually named Newfoundland town, even though I am technically a grown man. Still, I'd like to think Duane and the bartender let out a chuckle or two as well. And as I sit here, thinking about it,

I'm not sure how that bartender ever manages to get through a shift without giggling himself silly as long as that beer is on tap.

"I can't wait to put this Dildo in my mouth," I said as I raised the glass to my lips. "Bottoms up!"

I probably could have closed the place making similar jokes all night long, but there was more to see, so Duane and I knocked our beers back and headed back out into the night.

Our next stop was a place called Shamrock City, which, as hinted in the name, is an Irish bar. Duane's friends were playing some traditional Irish tunes there that night. We walked inside to find the place teeming with fresh-faced young people, many of whom appeared to be just minutes past legal drinking age, milling about the place, seemingly in search of love in its various forms and whatever drinks might be on special. The sight of it didn't necessarily make me feel old, but it did have me cringing a bit as I thought back to when I was roughly their age, hunched over in some loud bar as I did my best to somehow fit in, yet stand out at the same time, in hopes that I might catch the attention of some beautiful lass with that perfect combination of questionable taste and poor judgment. I also wondered what the future might hold for these young revellers, and whether they'd one day find themselves walking out to a minivan in the rain and trying to explain to some guy from Cleveland how to pronounce *Newfoundland.*

"Wanna get out of here?" Duane shouted to me a short while later, above the din of arguably one Irish singalong too many.

"Sure," I told him as I took one last, wistful glance at the pageant of youth in front of me before shuffling toward the door.

From Shamrock City, we moved on to a place called Christian's, which I'd read was a popular location for getting "screeched in." I was feeling pretty wobbly by this point and figured if I were ever going to cozy up to a cod, it might as well be now, dammit. Even so, I had a look around when we got there, and there wasn't a cod in sight. I ordered a shot of rum and knocked it back in hopes that this might cause a cod to somehow magically appear, but it didn't seem to do the trick, not even after a trip to the men's room. I'm honestly not sure what happened after that. All I know is I awoke the following morning in my hotel room—with my shoes still on—to a text message from Rose saying that she and Gerald would be pulling up to my hotel in about twenty minutes. Keeping that in mind, I splashed some water on my face, gathered my things and stumbled outside to find them parked out front, this time wearing matching blue sweaters, also courtesy of Rose.

"Whatta y'at?" I said as I slid into the minivan.

"Whatta y'at, Dave?" Rose replied with a laugh. "You're really getting the hang of it."

"I know," I told her. "And it feels great."

After less than forty-eight hours in Newfoundland, I really did kind of feel like I was settling into things and getting a feel for the place—so much, in fact, that the winter hat with CANADA on it that I had bought in Montreal in hopes of appearing more "local" suddenly felt out of place. Newfoundland, more than anywhere else I had been to in Canada thus far, truly felt like its own place and was unlike anywhere else I'd been in my grandfather's home-land. In light of this, I took off my hat, threw it in my bag and made a mental note to grab a hat that said NEWFOUNDLAND as soon as possible.

The plan for this morning was for Rose and Gerald to show me around town a bit more before dropping me off at the airport. Our first stop was Signal Hill, which overlooks St. John's Harbour. It's where Marconi received the first transatlantic wireless transmission back in 1901. It's also worth noting that the final battle of the Seven Years' War was fought here, in 1762. Today, however, it was mostly just Rose, Gerald and me, circling around in the minivan as a light mix of rain and snow fell from the sky, threatening to destroy whatever progress I'd made on my hair that morning as soon as I stepped outside.

At the top of Signal Hill is Cabot Tower, constructed in 1989 to commemorate the four hundredth anniversary of John Cabot's discovery of Newfoundland, something he supposedly wouldn't shut up about.

"In the summer, there are busloads of people getting dropped off here to have a look at the tower," Rose told me.

Today, however, it was just me crawling out of the back of the minivan as Rose threw it in park so I could trudge up the hill in hopes of having a look inside, only to be told by a young woman standing outside of a minivan of her own near the entrance that Cabot Tower was closed for the winter, so I should probably walk back down the hill. It was okay, though, as Rose had other excitement in store for me.

With that in mind, we drove back down from Signal Hill toward the harbour, where Rose steered into what appeared to be a construction site with a confidence I had slowly come to envy since first meeting her just the day before. There, we pulled around a couple dump trucks, and at least three men in hard hats and reflective vests, until Rose suddenly threw the van in park once more.

"What are we doing?" I asked.

"Remember how I told you might see a Newfoundland dog while you were here?" Rose replied.

"Yup," I said.

"Well, he's right over there," Rose said, pointing through the windshield.

Sure enough, just ahead, there was a statue of not only a giant Newfoundland dog, but also a Labrador retriever, which I guess originated just to the north in Labrador, which is pretty cool, but still not nearly as awesome as the Newfoundland dog, as far as I'm concerned.

"Go have a look," Rose told me.

I got out of the van once more and climbed up to the stone platform the two dog statues stood upon. I had a quick look at the Labrador dog statue as I passed it, in the interest of being thorough, before walking over to the awesome Newfoundland dog, which, despite being a mere statue, still filled me with some semblance of the joy and excitement I feel whenever I encounter the real thing. I stood about ten feet in front of it and found myself staring it in the eyes, when suddenly, I couldn't help but think of my own dog, Luci. And then my girlfriend. And then my family and everyone else I love. And then I began thinking about Rose and Gerald, parked just a few metres away, and the love between them that I'd had the pleasure and honour of witnessing in action over the past couple of days. Then, suddenly, I found myself thinking of those kids I'd seen the night before at Shamrock City.

And I wondered if any of them ended up getting lucky. And if any of them ended up throwing up. And if any of them had ever come down, right where I was by the harbour, and stood there, crying in front of a dog.

MOOSE JAW AND REGINA, SASKATCHEWAN

In the Land of Dreams

ONE OF CANADA'S many endless charms is, of course, its wonderfully named cities and towns. And while lesser men may gravitate toward the cheap thrills provided by a Punkydoodles Corners, Ontario, a Ball's Falls, Ontario, or even a Head-Smashed-In Buffalo Jump, Alberta, my personal favourite has always been Moose Jaw, Saskatchewan. To me, it always sounded like some sort of Canadian utopia, a place where every man, woman and child wore a trapper hat all year round, the air smelled of some intoxicating mix of pine needles, peameal bacon and bulk Crown Royal, and cars would be backed up for blocks on end as a result of actual moose crossing the street whenever they damn well felt like it. Add to that the fact that, in order to visit Moose Jaw, I would be required to fly into Regina, Saskatchewan—a city whose name, when said out loud, provides another form of entertainment I know I shouldn't enjoy nearly as much as I do, but don't plan on tiring of any time soon as best I can tell.

I first became aware of Moose Jaw, of course, because it is the hometown of the legendary New York Islanders left wing Clark Gillies.* And while the fact that Clark was six foot three and 210 pounds most certainly gave him an edge out on the ice, it's hard not to think that being from a place called Moose Jaw couldn't have hurt, either. I mean, think about it—I'm from a place called University Heights, Ohio, and I never even made it to the minor leagues. You tell me. You. Tell. Me.

Anyway, my point is, in light of all of the above, it has been nothing short of a lifelong dream of mine to witness the magic and majesty of Moose Jaw for myself one day, walk among its people and, who knows, maybe even stand outside of Clark Gillies's boyhood home just long enough to at least get the current residents to close the drapes.

In the interest of full disclosure, I had originally planned to visit Moose Jaw and surrounding areas the previous March. But still recovering, at least emotionally, from a wonderful yet excruciatingly cold January visit to Quebec City, I woke up the day before I was scheduled to go to Moose Jaw, saw that it was currently minus-17 Celsius there and made a mental note to forget to set my alarm for my flight the next day. I felt like a bit of a wuss at the time, sure. But knowing I would ultimately need these fingers to write this book, it felt like the better part of valour.

In the end, I chose a couple weekdays in September to fly to Saskatchewan, as it was, at the very least, light jacket weather then, which can still look reasonably manly in pictures if you get the collar just right. Still, manly or not, the idea of travelling to Saskatchewan at all felt good, as I would wager that 99 percent of Americans have never set foot in the place and never will. In fact,

---

* As a young hockey fan, I of course made it my job to have a stalker-worthy level of knowledge about all my favourite National Hockey League players. In the pre-internet years of my youth, this would mostly be done by memorizing every page of *The Hockey News*'s annual yearbook, which my father brought home to me from the newsstand at the start of each season until I was able to roam the streets of Cleveland all on my own.

I felt like a bit of a trailblazer for even booking that first flight I neglected to show up for.

I had to fly through Toronto to get to Regina. I ran into a friend, the musician Rufus Wainwright, at my gate at LaGuardia, something I mention partly to give you as much detail as possible in this book, but mostly just to do a bit of good, old-fashioned name-dropping, one of America's greatest pastimes.

"You're flying to Toronto, too?" Rufus asked.

"Yes," I said, "on my way to Regina."

I'm not sure how long we both laughed after that, but it was definitely a while, well into the boarding process at least.

After a brief layover at Toronto Pearson, notable only for the fact that I witnessed a man getting his white sneakers shined at the shoeshine stand—something I know I will try and fail to make sense of some sleepless night in the near future—I continued on to Regina, which is when things really started to heat up in terms of my ability, or lack thereof, to keep a straight face whenever someone said that city's name out loud. I knew I needed to get over it. And I know I need to get over it now, or at the very least, put a cap on the number of words dedicated to the subject in this chapter, but please know that I can't promise either of those things will ever happen, not even in the inevitable follow-up to this book, when, buoyed by the overwhelming success of this book, I will bring up Regina several times on the very first page.

Anyway, I slept for most of the three-hour flight to Regina, but even so, a flight attendant made a point of leaning over and telling me that we were almost there. It was nice to know my excitement was palpable to others, even with my eyes closed.

Since I'd be flying out of the Regina airport at the ridiculously early time of 5:30 a.m. a couple days later, and as a result would likely be barely functioning, I made a point of taking a look around a bit once we landed. For the record, it's a tiny airport that would likely register as a bus station at best in most cities.

First, I swung by Tim Hortons for a cup of coffee, so that I might blend in a bit better, before continuing on to a shop called Rumour,

Inc., which sounded like it might be a strip joint, but turned out to sell woven hats and various locally made tchotchkes. I had hoped to find a hat with moose antlers on it to help me seem like a local during my visit, but was shocked to find they didn't carry anything even half as fun, so I had no choice but to continue on, hatless, to pick up my rental car.

"Are you sure it's reserved under the Buffalo Sabres account?" I overheard the sales representative at the rental-car desk ask the man in line ahead of me as I approached. It occurred to me that he might be an NHL scout swinging through Moose Jaw to chat with one of the Moose Jaw Warriors junior hockey players—perhaps some young upstart who'd dreamt of living the sweet life in Buffalo ever since his peewee-league days—about coming up to the pros soon. I was delighted to witness something so mundane, yet impossibly and thrillingly Canadian at the same time. In my youth, I had dreamt on many occasions that one day an NHL scout would struggle to reserve a rental car at the Cleveland airport, just so he could come talk to me, a scrappy left wing from University Heights, so I was admittedly a bit jealous, too.

A few minutes later, I was behind the wheel of my rental car and steering in the direction of Moose Jaw. It was a brisk yet sunny day and I was instantly struck by the bright fall colours in the surrounding landscape. Somehow, I had always imagined it was winter all year round in Saskatchewan, yet here were impossibly blue skies and not even the slightest hint of frost on the ground. As I drove along the Trans-Canada Highway the seventy or so kilometres to Moose Jaw, I felt like I was drifting through an Andrew Wyeth landscape. Somewhere along the way, I noticed a trio of utility poles cutting the horizon, the crosses of Calvary suddenly creeping into view. For a moment, I was worried I might be finding God, an inconvenience on any road trip. Then, suddenly, a fourth utility pole broke across the horizon, and I lost Him just as quickly.

Farther down the road, I saw a sign advertising paintball. I thought about stopping off for a quick round before realizing how creepy it might seem to show up at a paintball facility and ask to play all by yourself.

"But who will you shoot the paintballs at?" I imagined a confused employee asking me.

"Oh, you'll find out," I'd reply with a crazed look on my face. "You'll *all* find out."

The thought of it kept me wildly entertained for at least the next few kilometres.

Since this would be my first Canada trip for the purposes of this book that I would be making all on my own, I figured it might be a good idea to rest my head somewhere I might have at least an off chance of running into another human being, so that I didn't wind up having some sort of Poe-worthy descent into madness or anything during my stay. To that end, I booked myself a room at a bed and breakfast located a couple kilometres from downtown in a house said to be the oldest one still standing in Moose Jaw, dating back to 1902.

As I found my way to the house, I passed a factory with a sign out front boasting that its employees had gone 714 days without a "lost time accident." I was excited for them as I thought about the fact that they'd gone nearly two years without anyone losing a limb or falling into a vat of some flesh-eating something-or-other. But then I wondered about what might have happened 715 days ago—or, perhaps worse, what a blow to their collective pride it would be after the next accident, when someone would have to go out front and reset the sign back to zero.

"Let's not beat ourselves up too much—we had a good run," I imagine the sign changer saying. "And whaddya say we try and track down those missing fingers before lunch, okay?"

Farther down the road, I saw a sign for a place called Chateau St. Michael's, which sounded like somewhere I might stop off for a glass of Chardonnay and a cheese plate until I passed it by a couple minutes later and discovered that Chateau St. Michael's was a retirement home and it would probably be kind of weird if I tried to do that there.

"I don't care if Mr. Mitchell needs his damn insulin," I'd say. "I want some goat cheese and a half carafe of Kendall-Jackson now!"

A couple blocks later, I pulled up in front of my bed and breakfast which was located at the corner of a dead-end street. The hosts had let me know that they'd likely be out upon my arrival and had left a key for me to get in. I let myself in to discover that the interior of the place looked alarmingly similar to the house from *Misery*—you know, the film adaptation of the Stephen King novel about an author who ends up being held captive and tortured for months inside some old house in the middle of nowhere. Fortunately, I love that movie, so I was mostly just excited about the similarity rather than fearing for my life. Besides—dying in Moose Jaw, what a way to go!

Anyway, I headed upstairs to my room and was dumping what few things I'd brought with me when it suddenly occurred to me that I'd yet to see a single human being—or even a dog or cat, for that matter—anywhere since I'd pulled into Moose Jaw proper a short while earlier.

"Maybe no one actually lives here, and I'm the sole living being in some sort of post-apocalyptic Canadian ghost town that just so happens to come with a complimentary breakfast and fresh coffee around the clock," I thought for a second.

But then I heard footsteps and a pair of voices coming from downstairs, so I decided to head to the ground floor and either confront the undead or meet my bed and breakfast hosts, whichever came first.

"Hi, I'm Lois," said a dark-haired woman of about sixty, dressed in a bright blue track suit, as I descended the stairs. "Are you Dave?"

"Yes," I said, offering my hand.

"Please help yourself to anything you'd like during your stay," Lois said, shaking my hand.

At this point, I saw a bit of motion in an armchair in an adjoining sitting room. For some reason, I figured it must be a dog, so I craned my neck in its direction, smiled wildly and began to frantically wave in that way people tend to do when trying to make some sort of connection with a domestic animal. Unfortunately, I quickly discovered that it wasn't a dog in that chair at all, but a grown man, who I would later learn was Lois's husband, John, watching television. Not wanting to seem like some sort of weirdo, though, I just committed to my smiling and waving frantically and continued to do so until he stopped paying attention altogether.

The introductions out of the way, I decided to head into town for a look around. Naturally, my first stop was to see Mac the Moose, a sculpture I'd read about with understandable excitement in my pre-trip research. For the uninitiated, Mac is a large steel-and-concrete moose built by a Saskatoon artist named Don Foulds, allegedly in an effort to attract more visitors to Moose Jaw. As already documented in this book, I'm a sucker for a moose sculpture of any size. Even so, I'm not convinced that building a large moose would be enough to get someone out of their chair to come all the way to Moose Jaw. Then again, here *I* was, endangering lives as I drove as quickly as possible from my bed and breakfast to get a look at Mac the Moose for myself, so who knows—maybe Don was onto something after all.

Mac the Moose is conveniently located at the edge of the parking lot for the Moose Jaw tourism office. It was almost like a trap.

"The way I see it, we lure them in with the moose," I imagined someone at the local chamber of commerce saying to a co-worker. "Then, next thing you know, they're loading up with pamphlets, T-shirts and whatever else we can stick 'em with inside the tourism office!" It was the perfect plan.

I parked my car not far from Mac's hindquarters and approached with unnecessary caution, given the fact that Mac wasn't an actual moose but merely a large replica. And I was instantly struck by a few things. First, Mac wasn't nearly as large as I'd hoped, standing at just 9.8 metres tall, it turns out, no more than twice the size of an actual—if extremely large—moose, by my calculations. Impressive, sure, but I had hoped for a moose that could be seen from outer space, like they say you can with the Great Wall of China, India's Statue of Unity or a King Diamond concert—if you're gonna do something, *do* it, I figure. Second, there is a fence surrounding him, making my hopes of getting a stranger to take my photo as I posed with Mac for any number of giant moose-based sight gags an impossibility. Apparently, Mac had been vandalized on several occasions in the past—some nutjob painted him blue, for example—so now we're all paying the price.

"I hope you're happy now," I imagine the police must have said to the delinquent moose painter as they led him away in cuffs. "Now no one will be able to enjoy full moose access."

A third detail about Mac I noticed is that—at least from behind, anyway—he appears to be anatomically correct, something I'd like to think gives him a uniquely European flair. And as long as I'm on the topic of Europe, a bit more research on Mac the Moose revealed that he had a solid thirty-one-year run as the world's largest moose sculpture until some pricks in Stor-Elvdal, Norway, decided to build their own moose and deliberately made it thirty centimetres taller than Mac, presumably just to give Moose Jaw the finger. You'd think Stor-Elvdal could just let Moose Jaw go on holding the title of home of the world's largest moose sculpture, but no—they had to take that title away from them, like some sort of grade-school bully tripping one of the younger kids out on the playground for no good reason. Get it together, Stor-Elvdal—you're better than that!*

After snapping a couple photos of myself with Mac that weren't nearly as cool as they could have been had I been allowed on the other side of that damn fence, I headed inside to the tourism office, where an actual train car was being guarded by a cardboard

---

* If you're anything like me, you'll no doubt be thrilled to hear that in the time since I first wrote this chapter, the people of Stor-Elvdal have come to their senses and reached a truce with Moose Jaw, agreeing to let Mac the Moose get a new, larger set of antlers that will put him back in pole position once again. For its part, Moose Jaw will heretofore acknowledge that Stor-Elvdal does indeed have a "pretty awesome-looking moose." The whole thing has got me thinking—if Stor-Elvdal and Moose Jaw can get along then—hey—maybe we *all* can get along.

cutout of a conductor with a sign asking that no one climb on the actual train car. To be fair, I hadn't really thought about climbing on the train car at all until I saw the sign about not climbing it, at which point my rebel spirit kicked in, and suddenly, it was all I could think about. Not looking for trouble, though, I quickly turned my attention to some paintings by local artists for sale on the opposite wall of the place. Among the landscapes and various depictions of local landmarks was a colour portrait of a Japanese geisha that had been curiously titled *Chinese Beauty,* a steal at just seventy-five dollars (Canadian). For the time being, I resisted the urge to snap it up and instead bought a refrigerator magnet with Mac the Moose on it to commemorate my encounter with what turned out to be only the world's *second*-largest moose sculpture thanks to those needlessly competitive Norwegians, as well as an enamel pin with crossed Canadian and Saskatchewan flags I figured would dress up just about any outfit.

And as long as I'm on the topic, may I say that the Saskatchewan flag is one of the most attractive flags of any sort I've seen in recent memory—so much, in fact, that I also considered buying a patch of the Saskatchewan flag before realizing it was more of a commitment to the area than I was ready to make just yet.

"Are you from Saskatchewan?" I imagined someone with a keen eye for recognizing the flags of the various Canadian provinces asking me.

"Nope," I'd answer.

"Do you live in Saskatchewan?" they'd then ask.

"Nope," I'd say.

"Did you use to live there?" they'd continue.

"Nope," I'd reply.

"So what's up with the Saskatchewan patch?" they'd finally ask.

"I dunno," I'd tell them. "I just went there once."

It just felt kind of weird, like something a guy who goes to play paintball all by himself might do.

I did consider buying a bag of sunflower seeds they had for sale there, too, as I assumed they must be native to the area, but after checking the label and finding they were from Manitoba, I set them back down out of principle. Besides, I hadn't eaten sunflower seeds since the nineties, at least, so it seemed crazy to break the streak like that.

"Can you recommend any local places a fella might stop off for a drink and perhaps a bite to eat?" I asked the young woman at the information counter as she rang up my items. I'm not sure why I said "fella," as if I might be asking for someone other than myself, but I did, and I don't apologize for it.

Anyway, she rattled off the names of a few places in town a fella like me might wet my whistle, and I headed to downtown Moose Jaw to see what was what.

Something that struck me about downtown Moose Jaw as soon as I rolled up to it was how easily I could see the flat land around it seemingly stretch out for miles, almost as if all the buildings, shops and restaurants had just dropped from the sky one day, sort of like the movie-set version of a town in the Old West. I liked that because it made the place seem manageable to me, like I wouldn't later find out I had been hanging out in the wrong neighbourhood the whole time or something.

"What were you doing in *East* Moose Jaw?" a Moose Jaw insider would ask me. "Everyone knows the real action is in *Southeast* Moose Jaw." File under the last thing I need.

Anyway, I parked my rental car in front of Casino Moose Jaw, threw not quite enough change into the parking meter, and ducked into the Salvation Army thrift store down the block. I'm not sure what it is about other people's old bullshit that I just can't seem to stay away from, but I am drawn to it like a moth to a damn flame. There's just something about throwing down a buck or two for some stained coffee mug with its handle missing, or an ashtray I'll later fill with things I have even less use for, that I take comfort in knowing my next of kin will likely just throw in the trash immediately after I've moved on to that great Southeast Moose Jaw in the sky. On this day, however, I would come up empty, instead just taking a quick lap I would like to think at least slightly alarmed everyone else in the place, what with my carefully cultivated "not from these parts" look and all.

From the Salvation Army, I continued on to Main Street, the place where I figured I'd find the most surefire action. There, I spotted a vinyl record store that also sold bongs and accoutrements of the "anything goes" lifestyle and headed inside, as I figured this would be the place to find out about where all the really cool, off-the-beaten-track stuff in Moose Jaw was going down. I took a quick lap around before spotting a binder full of rock band patches, the kind the type of guy who hangs out in a store that sells bongs might sew onto his jacket in his spare time. I flipped open the binder and feigned interest in a patch for the death metal band Cannibal Corpse in an effort to set the scrawny twentysomething guy behind the counter at ease.

"Saw these guys in '96," I said him. "Really brutal, you know, in a good way."

"I bet," he said, momentarily looking up from his phone.

I was pretty sure I had won him over by that point, so it seemed like a good time to hit him up for a few local tips.

"Can you recommend anywhere a fella might get a drink in this town?" I asked. "And when I say 'fella,' I mean me specifically, lest there be any confusion whom I'm talking about here. I don't need a repeat of what happened to me over at the Moose Jaw tourism office."

"Huh?" he asked.

"Nothing," I replied.

I was hoping he'd tell me about some crazy underground Moose Jaw speakeasy of some sort, the kind of place where I'd need a password or have to show my worst scar or even expose myself before gaining entry, but instead, he just named most of the same places the woman from the Moose Jaw tourism office had told me about. Still, I guess it felt good to know that the woman at the tourism office, who was arguably the town's front line as far as visitors go, and the guy working at the place that had its own bong room were in agreement on where I should hang out later.

Aside from wherever I might end up having a drink later, one of the biggest attractions in Moose Jaw is, of course, the Tunnels of Moose Jaw, built in the early twentieth century for some sort of underground heating system that was never completed. As the story goes, the tunnels were initially used to hide Chinese railway workers, who lived there with their families under far-less-than-ideal conditions. Then, in the 1920s, the tunnels experienced a renaissance during Prohibition, as they were a great place to keep rum-running and other not-exactly-legal activities running smoothly and out of sight of the local authorities (or at least the ones not in on the whole thing). Legend has it that it was during this period that famed (and, let the record show, syphilis-riddled) gangster Al Capone supposedly spent time in Moose Jaw when things got a little too hot down in Chicago. That said, not a single photo of Capone in Moose Jaw exists, and the way I see it, you get a famed mobster hanging out in your town, you break out a camera and see you if you can't get his good side. I guess what I'm trying to say is I call bullshit on the notion that Al Capone ever set foot in Moose Jaw, or anywhere in Saskatchewan, and I don't care who knows it.

Capone or not, however, as is usually the case when something has supposedly enjoyed a criminal past, the tunnels are now a tourist attraction, where curious visitors can fork over a few bucks to wander the tunnels themselves for a bit before hitting the gift shop for some memento of their time spent underneath Moose Jaw. I made a mental note to tour the tunnels myself before I split town, out of journalistic integrity. But as a guy who was mostly in town to see what the actual people of Moose Jaw—who I was shocked to find are called Moose Javians,* of all things—get up to on the regular, I was admittedly more excited about the bars two out of two Moose Javians had so far recommended to me that day. With that

---

* I'll be honest—at this point in the book, I should probably just admit to myself that I'm not very good at guessing what the people living in various Canadian locales call themselves and move on.

in mind, I decided to head back to the bed and breakfast and rest up for the hopefully wild Moose Javian night ahead.

Before jumping back in the car, however, I quickly popped into a combination furniture store/coffee shop/Asian food café across the street from the tunnels for a quick bite. As I sat down at a table in the corner, it was hard not to think of the young woman I mentioned at the very beginning of this book, who tried to entice my former bandmates and me all those years ago with promises of "Saskatchewan" food that turned out to actually be Szechuan.

"Maybe she was onto something after all," I thought as I wolfed down an order of curried vegetables with rice a few minutes later in the heart of Saskatchewan. "Maybe she was onto something after all."

By the time I got back to the bed and breakfast, the sun had begun to set, making the interior look even more like the house from *Misery*, which, aside from provoking fear I might die at any moment, continued to tickle me, as it's not every day you get to live out a Stephen King novel. I took a quick nap before heading back into town for whatever adventures might lie ahead, walking this time, as downtown was close enough to reach on foot. I started walking along the roadside before cutting through a wooded area, at which point, I realized I had no idea what sort of wildlife might inhabit this part of Canada—or, more specifically, which ones might want to kill me just to break up the day a little bit.

"Will I be mauled by a bear?" I wondered. "Or will I be set upon by a pack of hungry wolves, at least one of which will no doubt feel the need to maul me as a means of proving to his fellow wolf pals that maybe he should be allowed to lead the pack every once in a while, too?"

In the end, a couple of small birds that flew near my head were as close as I came to death before I found myself back in downtown Moose Jaw. My first stop was a place called Bobby's, a Scottish-themed bar I had passed earlier in the day. I had hoped it was going to be pretty rocking, at least for a Wednesday, but it was instead rather quiet, with just a few tables of people having drinks and food.

I bellied up to the bar and ordered a beer while perusing the food menu.

"Can I get the chicken wings, please?" I asked a woman of about thirty behind the bar.

"Okay, but they're frozen," she told me, "so it might take a while."

I wanted to tell her how I kind of assumed they were probably frozen at some point, and how, if I were her, I would have just left that part out, as it seems that highlighting that fact can only dampen the customer's chicken wing–eating experience. But instead, I just said, "Fine," and began scanning the bar with a look on my face I hoped suggested I was open to making friends. It's a move I admittedly try often when sitting alone at a bar, and statistically, it seems to work for me roughly 1 percent of the time, something I chalk up mostly to the carefully cultivated "crazed drifter" look I tend to go for when preparing for a night on the town.

After finishing another beer I'd ordered in hopes that it might give the impression that I was in for the long haul and was willing to wait as long as it might take for my chicken wings to appear in front of me, I ended up just giving up and asking for my cheque before heading off into the night in search of human contact, or at least someplace that might have some wings in the back that had already been thawed out. To that end, I found a sports bar a couple blocks away that had NHL pre-season hockey on at least four different TV screens, something I took to mean that distinctly Canadian good times awaited me inside. I bellied up to the bar, ordered a beer and looked around to find that there were only four other customers in the place, all of them dudes sitting together at a table in the corner.

"Is this a gay bar, or just a really great place to watch the game?" I thought to yell out in an effort to make friends, before ultimately thinking better of it and ordering some wings again instead. They showed up this time, and I devoured them quickly, all alone at the bar. And when I looked up to show off my empty plate to the bartender in hopes of making some sort of connection, I realized I was the last person in the place and the staff were waiting for me to leave so they could maybe go someplace and have some beer and wings, too.

"Cheque, please," I said, not wanting to be physically removed from the place.

I quickly paid my tab and headed back into the Moose Javian night. As I walked down Main Street, I got a text from a friend I'd yet to meet in person, a First Nations filmmaker from Regina named Trudy. Trudy had seen some of my Instagram posts from my previous Canadian travels and suggested I get in touch when I got to Saskatchewan in case I needed some boots on the ground. As much as one can build a psychological profile from someone's Instagram feed, I surmised Trudy wasn't a serial killer or anything and made a plan to meet her at a place called Cask 82, which the woman at the tourism office had warned me was going to be "absolutely crazy" tonight.

Since Trudy was driving in from Regina, I had a bit of time to kill at this point, so I decided to pop my head into Casino Moose Jaw for a few thrills. I'm admittedly not much of a gambler, unless you count that earlier instance where I didn't put enough money in the parking meter, but I at least like the promise of a casino, that idea of glitz, glamour and nonstop good times, where anyone could strike it rich at any moment—or, in the event that that doesn't work out, perhaps squander his life savings in a mere forty-five minutes before drinking himself silly on complimentary booze while bumming off-brand smoke after off-brand smoke from a stranger. I also liked that the place was called Casino Moose Jaw, which somehow made it sound classier to me than if they had just called it the Moose Jaw Casino.*

I headed inside to find a few dozen folks, most of whom were on the back nine of life, hunched over slot machines, poker tables

---

* I mean, think about it: would eggs Benedict seem so delicious if they were called Benedict eggs? No—you'd wolf them down and get on with your day as if it had never happened.

and other devices designed to make them part with their money. I was in the midst of a quick spin around the room to bask in all the flashing, coloured light when I realized how sad it was to be walking around a casino all alone, the scent of buffalo wings still fresh on my fingertips—and most likely my breath, too. It was in that moment that I realized I should probably leave the folks milling around the place to their fun while I headed back outside to breathe in a heady mix of cool night air, second-hand smoke and what I feared may very well be urine.

From Casino Moose Jaw, I headed over to Cask 82, which turned out to be a small pub located beneath some other bar whose name I didn't catch. As I mentioned, I had been warned that this place was going to be "crazy," so I was surprised to walk in to find just four or five people in the place.

"Where is everybody?" I asked the bartender, a woman of about forty, as I grabbed a seat. "I was expecting it be mobbed in here."

"That was earlier, for the drawing," she explained. "But everyone was gone by seven or so."

I looked at my phone to see that it wasn't even 10 p.m. yet. And as I had already been to three bars and one casino in Moose Jaw so far this night, and none of them were the least bit crowded, it was hard not to wonder where all the people were. At the very least, I had hoped to run into the guy from the Buffalo Sabres organization I'd stood in line behind at the airport car-rental counter, but I guess even he had called it an early night.

I was a few sips into my beer when Trudy showed up.

"Hey!" I said, offering her a chair.

"Hey!" she said, sitting down.

One of the few things I like about the internet, aside from all the humorous cat videos, is that you can meet a person for the first time and still feel reasonably comfortable as a result of having seen what each other's dogs and salads look like in advance and all that. If there's ever an awkward silence, you can just ask, "How's the dog? You know, the one with missing eye and the cable-knit sweater!" or whatever and everything is just fine again.

As it turned out, Trudy was a part of the Sixties Scoop I first learned about from that bartender in Winnipeg. She is from the Cree tribe and, like the Winnipeg bartender discussed earlier in these pages, was adopted by a white couple in the seventies.

"That's some messed-up shit," I said, once again stating my usual spot-on assessment of the Sixties Scoop.

"Yup," she agreed before taking a sip of some sort blueberry concoction that was on special.

As much as my mind was blown by the Sixties Scoop and all it entailed, it was when Trudy began to tell me about the residential school system in Canada that my eyes really began to widen. I realize I'm late to the party on this one, but I had admittedly never heard of it. In the event that you are clueless on the matter like me, not unlike the Sixties Scoop, the Canadian residential school system was a bunch of boarding schools for Indigenous or First Nations children in Canada, ostensibly designed to help them become better indoctrinated into "dominant Canadian culture." A simpler way of putting it would be to say that the Indigenous children were pretty much ripped from their families so that they might learn to be more like white folks. All told, roughly 150,000 Indigenous Canadian children, or about a third, were placed in residential schools over a period of more than a hundred years, ending in 1990. Oh, and it's estimated that between three and six thousand Indigenous Canadian children died from residential school–related causes during this period, so, uh, there's that, too.

As if it weren't hard enough keeping the mood light while Trudy taught me about the Canadian residential school system, it wasn't even 10:30 p.m. and it was last call. We finished our drinks and, as wise as it would have been of me to call it a night at that point, in the interest of further journalistic adventure I suggested we continue on to a place I'd read about called the Canadian Brewhouse, which I was sold on entirely because of its name, which suggested it would deliver in spades as far as providing me with a ridiculously Canadian experience that just so happened to involve even more beer, the last thing I needed but the first thing I wanted at this particular juncture.

I'm guessing some folks might know this already, but the Canadian Brewhouse is a chain of bars where virtually every vertical surface is covered in a big-screen TV. To be fair, you'd have to drug me, duct-tape me from head to toe and stuff me into an extremely large duffle bag to get me into a place like this in the United States, but what with it being in Canada and all, I figured that what they would be showing on those TVs was hockey, the one sport that has any effect on my heart rate, and this just might be a place worth checking out.

With pre-season NHL hockey in full swing, I figured the Canadian Brewhouse would be packed with Moose Javians taking turns drinking Old Style Pilsner straight from the tap, but there were only a handful of people in the place. Still, that didn't stop me from ordering some poutine and chicken wings like I was getting the chair in the morning as soon as we settled into a booth.

"I think I have a problem," I said to Trudy. "A poutine problem."

"Is that bad?" she asked.

"No," I told her. "Not by a long shot."

As a relative lightweight, I was beyond overserved by now, so I have no keen observations about the Canadian Brewhouse, aside from the fact that I was extremely impressed that they had forks with hockey-stick-shaped handles. And in my poutine-enhanced state, I knew I needed to have one for my very own. I considered conveniently sticking the one I'd been given to eat my poutine into my pants pocket, residual gravy and all, but, not wanting to cause any sort of international incident, I asked our waitress if I might instead just buy one.

"Sure thing," she said.

A few minutes later, she reappeared with a full set of silverware for purchase. There was, of course, the hockey-stick fork I was after. But with it, there was also a baseball-bat knife and golf-club spoon.

"Any chance I could just get three hockey-stick forks instead?" I asked her.

"No," she replied in a manner that suggested she'd been asked this sort of thing one too many times before.

"Can I just buy the fork then?" I then asked.

"No," she said. "It's kind of an all-or-nothing thing as far as buying the silverware here goes."

I told her to go ahead and put the sports-themed silverware set on my tab. I can't remember exactly what it cost, but given the fact that I insisted that Trudy take the knife and spoon and get them out of my sight immediately, that hockey-stick fork is definitely the most expensive fork I will buy in this lifetime. I'm also ashamed that, while I still beam with excitement every time I see it in my silverware drawer, I find it not nearly as enjoyable to use at home as it was at 11 p.m. on a Wednesday in a mostly empty sports bar in Moose Jaw.

I woke around 9 a.m. the next morning to the sounds of breakfast in full swing in the first-floor dining room. I pulled myself to the side of the bed, pausing briefly to marvel at the odd, hockey-stick-shaped fork on my nightstand before remembering how determined I had been to have it mere hours before. Then I reluctantly put some pants on and headed downstairs.

"Good morning," Lois, seated at the head of the table, called to me. "Have a seat and I'll get you some breakfast."

Already digging into a stack of pancakes were a couple other guests at the house, Marty and Sara, a couple in their sixties visiting from Edmonton. Sara was a member of the Canadian version of the Red Hat Society,* and they were headed to Regina for a gathering later that day. Exciting as that was, however, it was when Marty mentioned he'd had a run-in with the Hells Angels back when he and Sara were living in Detroit years ago that I really started to pay attention.

"I heard they can be real jerks," I said while digging into some fruit salad.

"That's one way of putting it," Marty said.

---

* Those ladies who run around in the purple dresses and red hats. Look it up.

Marty had worked in the railway business for years and I guess it's not uncommon to run into trouble with Hells Angels—and other groups of people not exactly crazy about obeying laws—when you're working on the rails. When things started to get especially unpleasant, he and his wife figured it might be time to head north again, and now here they were, having breakfast with me, Lois and her husband, John, at least one of whom* wasn't exactly crazy about laws, either.

"Have you ever had chokeberries before?" Lois suddenly asked me.

Given the conversation, I thought maybe "chokeberries" was a euphemism for some crazy thing the Hells Angels get up to now and again. But it turned out they were a fruit of some sort, and the syrup on my pancakes had been made from them. And while I was disappointed that our Hells Angels discussion had effectively ended, I was delighted by the chokeberry syrup, which is delicious on pancakes and also sounds like a great name for a band, the more I sit here thinking about it.

"And did you think those were blueberries in your fruit salad?" Lois continued.

"Uh, yeah," I said, worried she was about to tell me I had just been the victim of a prank.

"Those were actually Saskatoon berries," she explained.

I was admittedly relieved. And, for the record, I bet the Saskatoon berries would be pretty great in syrup form, too, if anyone has the time to get on that. Ditto on the band-name thing, too, the more I think about it.

"We went to the Tunnels yesterday," Marty said, effectively bringing the red-hot Canadian berry–based conversation to an end.

"How were they?" I asked.

"I didn't like the Al Capone one," he explained. "Too many skits."

"Skits?" I asked.

---

* Let's be clear: I'm talking about me here.

"Yeah, they've got all these people dressed up in old-timey clothes and they act out skits for you," he said.

"That sounds stressful," I told him.

"Yeah," he agreed. "But the Chinese one was good."

"There are two different tours?" I asked him.

"Yeah. But there aren't any skits in the Chinese one," Marty said. "I liked that one better."

"It sounds better," I told him, in full support of his anti-skit stance. "How long are the tours?"

"They're each an hour," Marty said. "So two hours total."

Two hours struck me as a long time to be stuck underground in Moose Jaw—or anywhere, really—so I made a mental note to move the idea of taking a tour of the tunnels later that day from the "possibly" column over to the "probably not" column. Besides, I figured Marty telling me about the tunnels was probably just as good as forking over the money to go on the tours myself. The man had a way with words.

After pouring myself more coffee, I began to tell everyone about my night out in Moose Jaw, including the part about how I paid a lot of money for a fork and how my new friend Trudy was an Indigenous filmmaker, which in turn inspired Lois's husband, John, to leave the room and appear moments later, wearing some sort of First Nations ceremonial garb made of bones, leather and fur that hung around his neck and covered his chest. I imagine there's a shorter name for it, but I guess it was meant to protect the wearer from arrows and whatever else might come his way, back in the days when that sort of thing might be cause for concern.

"A First Nations buddy of mine made it for me," John explained before momentarily disappearing again.

When John returned, he was wearing a buckskin jacket with foot-long fringe hanging from each sleeve.

"Did your First Nations buddy make that for you, too?" I asked.

"No," he said. "Another buddy of mine made this for me in prison."

"You were in prison?" I asked, just making conversation.

"No," he replied. "But my buddy was."

"If I had a jacket like that, I would never not be wearing it," I told him, in hopes that he would respond by insisting I take the jacket with me when I hit the road later. That didn't happen, but he did insist that I wear the jacket and the First Nations chest protector and pose for a picture in the living room.

As I stood next to the fireplace, grinning from ear to ear, I hoped this was a special occasion and that not every guest got to wear John's fringe jacket and First Nations ceremonial garb. But then I thought about it some more and figured it would be even better if every guest had no choice but to pose for a photo in the living room with this stuff on, whether they liked it or not.* Here's to never really knowing for sure.

"Thank you for breakfast," I said, gently removing my new outfit before slowly heading back upstairs to gather my things.

Given my beer-and-chicken-wing intake, I thought a quick run before I headed to Regina for a look around might be in order, so I threw on my running gear and headed out the back door into what I believe is known in those parts as the Wakamow Trails. It was the same area where I had worried about being mauled by a bear or some other beast that might not be exactly crazy about Dave the night before. But in the daylight, as I ran along dirt paths through assorted greenery and along rivers and streams leading who knows where, I found it all very peaceful, beautiful and inspiring. And at one point I wondered, what with me being in Moose Jaw and all, what exactly my chances might be of running into an actual moose as I attempted to sweat the hops, barley and Buffalo sauce out of my system. And if I did run into an actual moose, I wondered about the chances that I might climb upon his back, tame the antlered beast and perhaps ride him into town. It was a momentary delusion most likely caused by dehydration more

---

* Between this and the cod-kissing thing in Newfoundland, I guess I've got a thing for forced tradition.

than anything else, and I'm not ashamed to admit that I enjoyed it very much. But then I thought about what a pain in the ass parking the moose might be should I decide to stop into a shop or two once I got into town, the fantasy abruptly ended and I began to focus on the path in front of me once again.

My killer run complete, I returned to the bed and breakfast for a quick shower before saying my goodbyes and pointing my car in the direction of Regina, a city whose pronunciation—several thousand words into this chapter—is still completely hilarious to me and always will be. I had already driven a few kilometres when I suddenly remembered the painting of the Japanese geisha I had seen the day before at the Moose Jaw tourism office, and after some brief deliberation in which part of me thought I probably didn't need to spend seventy-five dollars (Canadian) on a Moose Javian geisha painting that just so happened to be titled *Chinese Beauty*, I made an illegal U-turn along the Trans-Canada Highway and headed back to the Moose Jaw tourism office for a second time in less than twenty-four hours—a world record, I can only assume.

"I'd like to buy the geisha painting, please," I told the same woman I'd seen behind the desk the day before. "And thanks again for the bar tips—this fella really enjoyed them."

"You're welcome," she said before ringing me up and sending me on my way.

For the record, I also bought a bag of those Manitoban sunflower seeds I'd seen the day before. Talk about bullshit—I tried to eat a handful in the parking lot before spitting them out and leaving the rest on the ground for whatever birds decided to hang out with Mac the Moose later.

A short drive later, I found myself in Regina proper. It was grey and rainy as I pulled into town, and for at least the first few blocks or so, virtually every person I saw wore a hoodie and looked to be about nineteen, something I chalk up to it being a university town. Things took a quick demographic turn, however, when I passed a hospital and saw a body covered in a sheet being wheeled out on a gurney. I'd like to think the person underneath was very much alive and that the sheet was there just to keep them dry, but that's mostly because I didn't need a dead body ruining an otherwise delightful visit to Saskatchewan—a province I don't plan on associating with random dead bodies any time soon, the local populace will no doubt be pleased to hear.

I'd found an Airbnb not far from the university and, after a quick nap, met up again with Trudy, who had promised to show me the Regina ropes.

We started with a trip to the First Nations University of Canada, whose main campus building awesomely features a massive teepee as part of its structure. Behind the building was an art installation featuring about a dozen real teepees in a small field, housing paintings by various Indigenous artists. Some of the paintings dealt with various First Nations traditions and spirituality; others dealt with the residential schools and the Sixties Scoop. And as Trudy and I made our way from teepee to teepee, she told me more about First Nations history and culture.

"I think I can speak for the majority of Americans when I say that I didn't really know about any of this stuff," I told her.

"Yeah," she replied. "A lot of Canadians don't, either."

One of the more fun facts I learned is that North America is referred to as Turtle Island by First Nations people.

"It's because it's shaped like a turtle," Trudy explained.

Of course, this begs the question of how the First Nations people of old knew this without having an aerial view, but I only mention it because Trudy told it to me first while we were checking out all the teepees. As a guy who still doesn't fully understand electricity, I admittedly can't spend too much time worrying about this one.

From the First Nations University of Canada, we continued on to the MacKenzie Art Gallery for a quick lap around the place. My favourite piece was a collection of skateboard decks featuring paintings depicting the residential school system and the Sixties Scoop by Cree artist Kent Monkman, who paints beautifully in a style reminiscent of the Old Masters. The skateboards were at once fun and not very fun at all. But more than either of those things, they were absolutely gorgeous, and had there not been any guards in the place, I would have yanked at least a couple of them from the wall and made a run for it.

The gallery was also holding a reception of some sort, featuring a young man playing an impossibly loud electric guitar as guests sipped wine from plastic cups while doing everything in their power to get as far away from him as possible, a de facto performance-art piece I decided to call *Hey Trudy, Can We Please Leave Now?*

With that, we got back into the car and headed downtown.

"Is there somewhere in town, like a popular tavern or some-where, that I can observe the locals in their natural habitat?" I asked Trudy.

"There's the Victoria Tavern," she replied. "Wanna go there?"

It felt a little on the nose, what with the fact that it had the word *tavern* in its name and everything, but I said yes anyway. There, we had a beer and ate various fried things while I tried to pick up on anything distinctly Saskatchewanian that might be happening right in front of me, or perhaps gain some insight into why, for example, the people of Saskatchewan never change their clocks, in effect observing daylight saving time all year round.* It was admittedly hard to crack. I did see a table of guys wearing heavy metal battle jackets,** and since I, too, am a slave to metal, I tried to give them a knowing glance in hopes it might lead to conversation, but they didn't seem to notice, so Trudy and I just paid our tab and headed out into the night in search of further Saskatchewanian fun.

"To be honest, we could just stand out here on the sidewalk and I could keep saying 'Regina' out loud," I said. "That would keep me going for hours and hours."

---

* It's true. I'm not saying I understand it, but I did look it up.

** For the uninitiated, these are the sleeveless denim vests with all the heavy metal patches sewn onto them that metalheads like to wear so they can more easily identify each other when out in the world. They are awesome, and everyone knows it.

"Let's not do that," Trudy, who as a resident had presumably already gotten this sort of thing of her system, said.

Anyway, just down the street was the Hotel Saskatchewan, and what with the fact that it looked old and had the word *Saskatchewan* right there in its name and all, it seemed crazy not to go in terms of my quest for a distinctly Saskatchewan experience.

I had hoped the Hotel Saskatchewan would be crawling with lumberjacks and, who knows, maybe even Clark Gillies himself, but it was mostly just well-dressed folks milling about in the hotel's elegant cocktail bar. There, Trudy and I bellied up to the bar and I ordered the hotel's signature drink—you guessed it—the Hotel Saskatchewan.

"It's for my book," I said to the bartender as I ordered.

"Huh?" he replied.

"I'm writing a book about Canada and figured it would be good to try the local cocktails as a means of better understanding the country of Canada and its wonderful, wonderful people," I continued. "You know, because I'm an author who is writing a very important book."

The bartender seemed pretty blown away by this last bit of information, so much, in fact, that he said nothing in reply, instead just setting my drink in front of me a moment later and slowly backing away. I don't remember what was in the drink, or even what it tasted like, but I do remember wanting to wrestle at least half the people in the joint after just a few sips—a mark of quality, if ever there was one.

After a bit more chitchat, most of which involved Trudy trying to discourage me from talking to various bar patrons I was convinced were looking at me funny, she dropped me off at my Airbnb and I slept for a bit before I had to wake up for my criminally early 5:30 a.m. flight back to New York by way of Toronto. While sending my belongings through the X-ray machine at security at the Regina airport, I somehow lost my passport.

"I swear I just had it," I explained to the security agent as I desperately patted myself down in hopes of finding it.

As it turned out, it had somehow gotten knocked out of its tray as it went through the X-ray machine.

"Here you go, sir," another security agent said to me a few moments later as he handed it to me. "I found it underneath the conveyor belt."

"Thanks," I told him. "I was worried if I didn't find it, I was gonna be stuck in Regina forever."

There was a lot of giggling immediately after I said that, but to be fair, it was only coming from me.

I arrived back in New York City that afternoon, and after dumping the contents of my bag all over the living room floor, I quickly set about finding a spot on the wall for my Moose Javian geisha painting. She now hangs proudly above the couch, among all sorts of other things suitable for framing. But unlike all those other things, her eyes seem to follow me, greeting me each morning, bidding me goodnight at the end of each day and, not least of all, watching my every move. Sometimes, I'll stop and lock eyes with her for a moment. And in that moment, a message is shared. And it is the same message every time: "We'll always have Moose Jaw."

CALGARY, ALBERTA

All Alone in Stampede City

TO BE HONEST, when I first agreed to write this book, I had
secretly hoped my research would double as a tour of every single
hockey arena in Canada, where I'd scarf down plate after plate of
nachos, catch a few stray pucks and, who knows, maybe even enjoy
some quality hang time with the players after the game, knocking
back cold ones and engaging in heated arguments about Gretzky
and stuff. After all, as you may recall the former minor-league
hockey player at that bar in Merrickville, Ontario, telling me,
"Canada is all about beer and hockey."

While I feel like I've done more than my share as far as investigating the first part of that statement goes, somehow, despite a
solid ten separate trips to my grandfather's homeland for the
purposes of this timeless, Canada-themed literary classic, I had
somehow failed to catch even a single period of a hockey game in
person. I'm not entirely sure how I let this happen; at least mentally, anyway, I had already earmarked every single dollar of the
travel stipend my publisher gave me for hockey games and hockey

games alone. But the fact remained: after a year and a half of visiting Canada, I still had yet to do arguably the most Canadian thing there is and get to a damn game.

As it turned out, the above realization coincided with another insight: that I'd yet to even set foot in Alberta, home not only to one of the best-named cities in the country, Medicine Hat,* but also—more importantly, in terms of everything I just said—home to not one, but two National Hockey League teams. Which are, of course, the Edmonton Oilers and the Calgary Flames.

As a kid, I'd completely idolized the Oilers. I was so obsessed, I even talked my dad into driving me and my friend Kevin all the way to Pittsburgh to see them play the Penguins when I was twelve. I still have the program from that game, signed outside of Pittsburgh's Civic Arena by a young and frazzled Wayne Gretzky, who was absolutely mobbed upon his arrival at the players' entrance, as were his teammates Mark Messier, Jari Kurri and Paul Coffey, who, to be fair, were at least slightly easier to get to at the time.

Keeping that in mind (and with all due respect to the Flames and the people of Calgary in general), I decided to check the Oilers' schedule first, and when I saw they'd be on the road the week I was hoping to invade Alberta, I looked at the Flames' schedule, saw they'd be playing a game at home, and booked myself a flight to Calgary instead.

I had hoped to fly direct, but ended up having a layover in Toronto, where, after several delays and one unfortunate wrap sandwich, I eventually boarded a crowded four-and-a-half-hour flight marked primarily by the relentless farts of a man who had stopped caring long ago.

---

* As it turns out, Medicine Hat is named after the Blackfoot word for a headdress worn by medicine men. It had also occurred to me that it would make for a great name for a band that isn't exactly shy about getting caught up in a full-on blues jam from time to time. And as fate would have it, Washington State's very own Medicine Hat has apparently been fulfilling that prophecy for some time now—and has the fedora-wearing harmonica player to prove it. For further distraction on this topic, I point you to www.medicinehattheband.com. You're welcome, guys.

We finally touched down in Calgary* around 11 p.m. As soon as I got off the plane, I spotted a guy sitting at my gate in a cowboy hat, thus fulfilling the promise of Calgary in the first ten feet, as far as I was concerned, as I had been told it was kind of the Wyoming of Canada.

"Howdy," I said to the guy in the cowboy hat.

He just looked at me, but it was late, so I let it slide.

After picking up my rental car, I headed for my Airbnb apartment just a few kilometres outside of downtown Calgary. And despite the fact that it was just November, winter—or at least what passes for it in the comparatively balmy United States—appeared be in full effect, with snow, ice and at least a hint of despair already covering the ground and doing its best to creep into my very soul.

I passed through downtown along the way, and as I caught my first glimpse of the skyline, I was struck by how bustling Calgary appeared to be, compared to most other places I'd already visited in Canada. I realize I'm probably stating the obvious, but after you've spent an entire twenty-four hours hunkered down in Moose Jaw, for example, lovely as it most certainly is, this sort of stuff tends to jump out at you. In fact, on first glance, Calgary sort of reminded me of Dallas—an absolutely freezing Dallas where, if God forbid you should get locked out of your house or car for an unreasonable amount of time, you would definitely die.

Anyway, of particular excitement was the Saddledome, which, true to its name, indeed looked like a large horse saddle jutting out from the urban landscape. Personally, I would have finished the job and had a giant horse underneath the saddle, and maybe even a giant cowboy or cowgirl on top of that saddle, but this is probably why I write books and do other stuff that doesn't have a whole lot to do with architecture or city planning. Then again,

---

* It was probably my exhaustion talking, but it occurred to me shortly after I got off the plane that a good mnemonic device for the Calgary airport code, YYC, is to remember that it's just like the Toronto airport code, YYZ, if it were said out loud by the kind of person who pronounces the word *jazz* as "jass." I hope you enjoy this helpful tip, airport code buffs.

think of the tourism boost a giant horse in full gallop, absolutely sprawling across ten city blocks, would be for the wonderful city of Calgary. Picture it for even a second, and it's all but impossible to tell me I'm wrong. And as a guy who made two separate trips on two consecutive days to see the Mac the Moose in Moose Jaw, Saskatchewan—who, despite his undeniable greatness, doesn't hold even half the majesty of the giant horse scenario I've just described to you—I'm pretty sure I would know.

I pulled up to my Airbnb around midnight. It was on an impossibly quiet residential street also home to something called the Calgary Japanese Gospel Church. As a guy who is fascinated with Japan almost as much as with Canada, and who also enjoys a bit of gospel music from time to time while he's at it, I couldn't believe my good fortune. I said a brief prayer that they might somehow be holding weekday services to coincide with my visit. And with my Airbnb being directly across the street, I delighted at the possibility of being woken the next morning by the sound of gospel songs sung in Japanese.

"No man should be this lucky," I thought as I approached the bungalow I'd be sleeping in the next couple nights. "I just don't deserve this."

There were no street or outdoor house lights on, so I had to rely on the light of the moon to guide me as I walked the icy path to the front door of the house. And I was no more than ten feet from it when I noticed a man in a hooded down jacket, sitting in a folding chair next to the front door. I assumed he must be outside in the freezing cold to have a cigarette, but upon closer inspection, he wasn't. He was just sitting there. Staring at me.

I don't want to tell anyone how to live their lives or anything, but if I were him and a strange man—in this case, me—were approaching my house at midnight on a Tuesday, I'd speak up and maybe say "Hello" or "Can I help you?" or maybe even ask something along the lines of "You haven't come to kill me, have you, sir?" But he didn't say a word or even let out so much as a grunt, so the burden of initiating human interaction was on me.

"Is this the Airbnb?" I asked him.

"Yup," he replied. "It's around back."

I imagine it takes either a lot of confidence, a complete lack of options, or perhaps some wild combination of both to wind up just sitting there in a folding chair, doing absolutely nothing at midnight on a Tuesday in the freezing cold on a quiet residential street across from a Japanese gospel church in Calgary, but I tried not to think about it too much as I made my way behind the house and let myself into the basement apartment of the house while also trying to make sure I hadn't been followed and, shortly thereafter, be made a victim of something that would undoubtedly make the news.

I had hoped to maybe head into town for a look around, and maybe even a nightcap, before turning in, but as soon as I set my bags down in the apartment, fatigue quickly got the best of me, so I decided to lie down for a moment and catch my breath. It was at this point that I began to hear loud noises coming from the floor above me, presumably being made by the man I'd just encountered in front of the house a couple minutes before, as he seemed to be stomping around, opening and closing drawers and slamming doors in the way that someone does when they're looking for just the right ordinary household item to kill you with.

"This is how it all ends," I thought momentarily as I lay there, staring at the ceiling. "Not just the book, but me, my life, everything."

To be fair, I suppose part of this momentarily grim mindset might have been the product of the fact that there is just something inherently depressing about being all alone in a nondescript basement apartment on some dark side street at midnight, whether it be in Calgary, Paris or even my glorious hometown of Cleveland. Still, I'd had a nice life up until this point, and unlike most folks, I'd had the rare pleasure of actually seeing quite a bit of Canada while I was at it, so if it all ended right then and there, who was I to complain?

"I have been to Winnipeg," I thought. "And that has made all the difference."

Then again, if I didn't turn in this book in its entirety to my publisher before dying, I wouldn't get paid, so it was with this in mind that I decided to sleep with my clothes on that night, in the event that running for my life might be in my immediate future. To be fair, I was also feeling a bit lazy and figured that if I woke the next morning already dressed, it would be that much easier to get the day started.

I rose early the next morning with delusions of going for a run, but after a quick look out the basement window, I realized Calgary was still pretty committed to this whole winter thing and ultimately decided against it in the interest of survival. Instead, I climbed behind the wheel of my rental car and, after confirming that the Calgary Japanese Gospel Church was, sadly, not holding services that morning, pointed it in the direction of a neighbourhood I'd read about called the Beltline in search of a cup of coffee.

I arrived in the Beltline a short drive later and spotted a small diner with not one, but two tables of construction workers seated in the window.

"I've hit the jackpot," I thought. "I can't wait to go in there and rub elbows with a bunch of salt-of-the-earth Calgary workingmen who will no doubt be thrilled to let me squeeze into their booth, get inside their heads and really find out what makes the average Albertan tick."

But as much as I'd hoped this would happen, the line to get in was way too long, so I was left with no choice but to dine alone on coffee and something called the "Southwestern quiche" at a coffee shop across the street. Adding insult to injury, the coffee shop in question was connected to someplace called Party Central, which, given that it was not even 10 a.m. at this point and I was sitting all alone, thumbing through an outdated arts weekly, seemed to be mocking me more than anything else, as the party potential—as well as my own capacity for partying at that point—didn't seem very good at all.

At some point during all of this, I received a text message from my buddy Nils in Merrickville, Ontario. Nils had spent some time in Calgary while working in the oil industry a few years back.

"Go see the Olympic ski jump," Nils told me as I sat there, trying to make the most of my sad, solo breakfast.

Naturally, I assumed he was talking about a large ski jump, in use at that very moment by actual Olympic ski jumpers, right there in the centre of town. The thought of it excited me, as I imagine it would just about anybody with a pulse. There's just something about the sight of another human hurtling down a steep, snow-covered hill before flying into the air, and then either landing smoothly or—preferably, in terms of overall entertainment—smashing themselves to bits just as soon as they make contact with Earth again.

Keeping all that in mind, I got back in the car and drove to the closest thing to "Olympic ski jump" that came up on the map on my phone when I typed it in, the Olympic Plaza, where I arrived just a few minutes later to find that, while very pretty and all that, it appeared to mostly be just the sort of plaza where people enjoy a cup of soup and maybe a Snackable or something while on a break from the office. In fact, there wasn't a single person clad head to toe in spandex in sight.

"WTF?" I texted to Nils once I got there. "There's no ski jumping going on here."

"The Calgary Olympics were in 1988," Nils texted back.

"Thanks for wasting my time," I replied before making a mental note to never listen to anything Nils told me ever again.

My trip to the Olympic Plaza was admittedly a bit deflating, so I pulled the car over alongside the nearby Bow River to compose myself and decide what to do next. While doing so, I noticed a man jogging along the river in shorts and a T-shirt. Since it was just 1 degree Celsius outside, it was hard not to feel like a bit of a wuss by comparison for forgoing my own run, even though I'd packed enough winter clothes to go ice fishing in a blizzard. I guess what I am trying to say is that you Canadians are of hearty stock, and I salute you for it. When the rapture comes, the smart money is on you.

Anyway, once I pulled myself together, I threw the car into drive again and headed over to nearby Kensington Village, as I'd been told it was a "hip" and "happening" area. It's also worth noting that it was at this point that I discovered my rental car was equipped with heated seats, a luxury I usually avoid, as it tends to make me feel like I am about to soil myself—or just have, and will never get my deposit back. But after witnessing that guy running in the freezing cold in a T-shirt and shorts like that, I decided I was never going to live life to less than its absolute fullest, and I cranked the heated seat as high as it could possibly go.

My hot butt* and I arrived in Kensington Village a short while later. And while it pretty much just looked like your average strip mall to my untrained eyes, I did notice a music store and decided to pull over for a look. It's something I pretty much have to do whenever I'm in a new town, as the hope, of course, is that some rare gem of a guitar—or a Stradivarius, perhaps—is inside, has somehow been mislabelled and is priced so far below its value that it would irresponsible not to buy it immediately and steal away before the error has been discovered. On this day, however, the closest I came to this sort of larceny was a ukulele with six strings instead of the usual four, which I ultimately fought the urge to buy, since I could already hear the flight attendants on the plane the next day, asking me to play a tune for them, and I couldn't bear the prospect of it.

"I guess you're the in-flight entertainment today," they always say with a laugh when I fly with my guitar, which is often. And while it was definitely funny the first couple hundred times, that 201st time—and every time after that—just kind of rubbed me the wrong way. But I digress.

---

* In between this paragraph and the last, I decided to do a bit of Googling to see if anyone else out there feels like they are going to shit their pants while sitting in a heated car seat. And though it appears I may be alone on this one, I did find no shortage of people openly talking on the internet about experiences they've had with incontinence while driving. Also, fellas, heated car seats apparently do no favours for your sperm count, but I guess we all saw that one coming.

From Kensington Village, I began to just drive around aimlessly for a bit in hopes of getting a better feel for the city and perhaps stumbling upon something so quintessentially Calgarian that my car would have no choice but to throw itself into park so I could jump out and have a look for myself. It was at this point that I also happened to discover a feature on the map on my phone, allowing me to choose a vehicle for the icon showing me exactly where I was instead of using the default—and no fun—arrow icon. I decided to go with a bright green pickup truck, a choice that somehow added to my delight as I wheeled around town. It was fun to imagine that I was driving the bright green truck, and that I was even the kind of guy who might drive a bright green pickup truck in the first place.

"Hey, there's Dave in his bright green pickup truck!" I imagined the locals on the sidewalk thinking as I passed. "He is a fun, approachable guy who gets invited to parties!"

I even honked my horn a couple times, which really added to the fantasy.

I guess what I'm trying to say is that I really wasn't sure what to do next. So I just tried to keep the old saying "You make your own fun" in mind as I tried to make a decision in that regard. And somehow, at that very moment in time, that meant pretending I was driving a bright green pickup truck for at least a few blocks on a cold Wednesday in Calgary.

After snapping back to reality a short while later, I happened upon a "vegan boutique" and decided to pull the car over once again—not because I am a vegan or think that veganism might be a defining characteristic of Calgary, but because the store had an adorable goat in its logo, and—as hinted at during the Victoria chapter—I am a sucker for those little guys. I also figured it would do me good to actually talk to a human being and maybe get a little inside scoop on the area.

I was in the vegan boutique less than a minute when I realized I was wearing suede boots, and that that sort of thing may very well be frowned upon in a place like that. Still, I was determined to engage with another human, so I figured the best thing I could do would be to walk right up to the front counter of the store so that I could talk to the woman working there while hiding my feet from her sight. And who cares if I had to buy a twenty-five-dollar scented candle to make the whole thing seem more believable? It worked like a charm.

"So," I began, "can you recommend any neighbourhoods in town I might check out to really see how the local Calgarians go about their business—somewhere a bit out of the way, perhaps, where no one would expect an internationally renowned author to just stroll up without warning?"

Okay, those may or may not have been my exact words, but that was certainly the gist of it.

"You might try going to Bowness," said the woman behind the counter, an attractive thirtysomething woman with black hair that greyed ever so slightly at the temples in the way that one's hair sometimes does when one works at a vegan boutique.* "That's a pretty interesting area."

"Cool," I said. "And then I was gonna go to the Flames game later."

"That should be fun," the woman behind the counter said.

It is at this point that it occurred to me that maybe I should ask this mysterious vegan woman to go to the Flames game with me in exchange for her giving me her keen insights into Calgary—and the entire province of Alberta in general—which I would in turn quote verbatim in these pages. I could buy the tickets and everything. But then I put myself in her vegan shoes for a moment and realized what it might feel like to have some suede boot–wearing creep who pretends to drive a bright green pickup truck around town, even when it's really just a Nissan Sentra, ask you to go to a

---

* Yes, I know this is a gross generalization, and I'm sorry. My point is that, in my limited experience, people who work at vegan stores of any sort seem to be genuine folks who tend not to get caught up in superficialities like covering up a bit of grey hair as much as us suede boot–wearing monsters tend to do. I guess what I am trying to say is, I meant it as a compliment.

hockey game with him when you're just trying to get through your shift at the vegan boutique, and I thought better of it.

I did, however, take her advice about Bowness and drove there, with my twenty-five-dollar scented candle in tow, immediately afterward. It was a charming little hamlet, notable—at the time of my visit, at least—for a man standing all alone on a street corner, laughing uncontrollably to himself. I stared at him momentarily, wondering what it would be like to feel that kind of joy even once in my life other than when saying Regina, Saskatchewan out loud, before I became unreasonably distracted by the realization that—like just about everywhere else I've been in Canada since the country's legalization of recreational marijuana—it seemed you couldn't throw a maple leaf cookie in Bowness without hitting a marijuana dispensary. But since that's not personally my thing, I decided to keep moving in my quest to fully grasp the magic of Calgary, the city *The Economist* ranked as the fourth most livable in the world.*

And since the Southwestern quiche I'd had for breakfast didn't fully deliver, I decided it might be time to stop back at a place I'd spotted in the Beltline that was advertising poutine for a mere six dollars, like it was 1942 or something. Given the poutine addiction I seem to have developed while researching this book, it seemed downright crazy not to take advantage of the savings and head there posthaste.

I arrived at the poutine concern a short drive later without incident, bellied up to the lunch counter and ordered myself a steaming pile of the stuff. As I ate it, I noticed a TV with the sound off on the back wall of the place. Justin Trudeau was on the screen. And while I realize opinions on your prime minister vary—wildly even, depending, in my experience, on how much one has had to drink—it still can't be denied that he is much easier to watch on TV with the sound off while eating poutine than the orange American equivalent. But I digress.

---

* Take that, Toronto, you measly #7!

Anyway, I finished my poutine in record time and headed up the block to a chocolate shop I'd spotted while parking and ordered myself a spicy hot chocolate.

"Wait, Dave, you mean to tell me you drank a spicy hot chocolate after eating a plate of discount poutine?" you ask.

You're damn right I did. The way I see it, you either go big or go home. Then again, I'd be lying if I said I didn't regret this decision immediately afterward, given what I said earlier about the heated seats in my rental car. Even so, that didn't stop me from getting back in the car anyway and puttering around town a bit more until I spotted an antique shop and got out of the car once again to have a look around. The hope, of course, was that I would find some magical remnant of the past that would scream "Calgary!" (or, who knows, maybe even "Medicine Hat!") to me and perhaps give me some rare glimpse into what this place is really all about beyond that one guy I saw at the airport wearing a cowboy hat. The closest I came to something particularly Canadian in the place, however, was an old vinyl record with Guy Lafleur on the cover, simply entitled *Lafleur!* The jacket copy was all in French, however, so I have no idea what was on that record. Still, it was fun to think that, during his tenure as one of the greatest right wingers the National Hockey League has ever seen, Guy found time for a side gig as a recording artist.

"Now *there* is a man without limits," I thought as I stared at the album cover for a moment before setting it back down again. And while this might normally be the sort of thing I'd save for a footnote, I feel like what I'm about to tell you demands inclusion in the main text of this book, as it has forever changed me.

Thanks to the endless magic of the internet, I have since learned that the slab of magic entitled *Lafleur!* that I so foolishly failed to march to the register that day in Calgary turned out to be a full album of French-Canadian disco tracks, over which Guy Lafleur gives instruction in French on the finer points of such ice hockey basics as facing off, skating and checking—the subjects discussed, in that order, in the three tracks contained on side one of the disc—and power play, shooting and scoring, the subjects discussed in that order in the three tracks contained on side two.

On the face of it, the *Lafleur!* album could be interpreted simply as a sort of lazy attempt to cash in on the popularity of both disco and Guy Lafleur in one extremely awkward and totally weird swoop. However, once you've listened to this album in its entirety on YouTube—as I have roughly fifteen times now—you will no doubt agree that it is nothing short of a Dadaist masterpiece that future civilizations will almost certainly cite as not only one of the crowning artistic achievements of the twentieth century, but also a bit of hard evidence that, every once in a while, humanity gets it right.

I could go on at this point and tell you how the *Lafleur!* album also came with an opportunity to join the Guy Lafleur fan club for a mere two dollars (Canadian), in exchange for which one received, among other things, not one, but *two* letters from Guy himself, or that the inside of the record sleeve features a beefcake shot of a shirtless Guy smiling while lacing up his skates, thus confusing things even further from where I am sitting, but I have not come here to drive you absolutely insane today, so let's not even get into that right now. Instead, I will end this Guy Lafleur disco digression by simply telling you I have righted wrongs by ordering a copy of *Lafleur!* for myself on eBay, and it is on its way to my loving arms and ears at this very moment.

Anyway, the weird Guy Lafleur record aside, I came up empty at the antique mall. So, after stopping briefly to thumb through the December 1973 issue of *Playboy* I spotted near the entrance—as a salute to my inner fifteen-year-old, since I am now a grown man and there is absolutely nothing anyone can do to punish me for such behaviour in this life or the next—I got back in the car and headed back to my Airbnb for a quick rest before the main event: the Calgary Flames home game I would be attending all by myself.

Prior to my visit, I asked my Twitter followers if anyone had recommendations for things I should do in Calgary. I got exactly two replies, both of which said I should go to a bar called Ship and Anchor. I should probably also mention that I told my alternate-universe Flames game companion at the vegan boutique about this and she said, "Yeah, that's pretty much the bar to go to if you want to hang out with Calgary people."

Keeping this in mind, I took a cab from my Airbnb to the Ship and Anchor a couple hours before the opening faceoff of the Flames game and grabbed a seat at the bar, which was already bustling with a happy-hour crowd.

"May I have a local beer?" I asked the bartender, a twentysomething fellow who appeared to have punk rock leanings. "You know, something a local person might drink."

I can't remember exactly what he poured me, but I remember it tasted just fine as I spun around on my stool to have a look at the bar, which was full of attractive young people with their whole lives ahead of them, as well as at least a couple dudes in player-grade Flames jerseys, which only added to my excitement. One of my favourite bands, T. Rex, was even playing on the stereo, so, aside from the fact that I was all alone and had had almost no meaningful human interaction all day—unless you count the December 1973 issue of *Playboy*—things were going really well for me.

Things went south shortly thereafter, however, when T. Rex was followed by that Bruce Springsteen song from that movie *Philadelphia*, which seemed to bring the mood down with it being a ballad and all—so much, in fact, that the punk rock–leaning bartender couldn't help but get involved.

"If this song is bothering you, I can skip it," I heard him say to the two young ladies I had hoped might spontaneously engage me in conversation while sitting next to me at the bar.* "It's kind of a weird choice for this place, y'know?"

And while I didn't hear what, if anything, the ladies said in response, I took this as an opportunity to get involved myself.

"I couldn't help but overhear you talking about this song," I said.

---

* They didn't.

"Huh?" the bartender said, turning to me.

"This song," I replied. "You must turn it off immediately."

"No problem," he said before walking back to whatever device was playing the offending Springsteen composition* and forwarding to the next song, which, to my ears, sounded like fellow Cleveland natives Pere Ubu.

"Is this better?" the bartender asked.

"Yes," I said. "It sounds like Pere Ubu."

"It is," he said, looking down at the playlist. "I don't think I know them."

"They're a great band from Cleveland," I told him. "That's where I'm from."

It's not easy to school a punk rock–leaning bartender in a bar that at least two people on Twitter and a woman in a vegan boutique had recommended to me, but in that moment, I was pretty sure I had done just that, and it felt good.

"What are you doing in Calgary?" the bartender, now humbled and seemingly at my full mercy, asked me.

"I'm writing a book about Canada," I told him. "I'm gonna go to the Flames game after this."

"That's cool," he said.

"Yeah," I replied. "I was gonna take the girl from the vegan boutique, but she was busy."

"Huh?" he said.

"Nothing," I said back.

I'm pretty sure this kid was in awe of me by this point, but I never found out for sure because he suddenly disappeared into the back, never to return, and another bartender took his place. I ordered another beer from that guy, but it felt like too much work to start over in establishing myself as the coolest guy in the place, so I slammed it quickly and grabbed a cab to the Saddledome.

---

* I realize it is at this point that some readers might think I am anti-Springsteen. I am not. I am, in fact, pro-Springsteen. Not as much as my sister Miriam, for example, but I still like him just fine.

It's just occurring to me the amount of stress I may have filled you with, dear reader, by not yet addressing whether or not I actually had a ticket to the hockey game at this point in our story, and for that, I apologize. I guess I may have been unconsciously trying to build suspense. Or maybe I just forgot. Either way, the fact of the matter is that the Flames were playing the Dallas Stars, who were thus far having what might be described in street parlance as a "sucky season." And it is because of this, I'm guessing, that there was no shortage of seats to choose from for some guy from Cleveland who was just planning on wandering into the Saddledome all by himself mere minutes before the opening faceoff.

"One ticket, please," I said to the lady behind the glass at the ticket office. "And don't worry—my life is going great and you and your co-workers back there do not have to be concerned in the least by the fact that I am attending this game all alone."

"Okay," she replied before telling me to pick a section I'd like to sit in.

In the end, I decided on a seat in the upper-level orange section, behind the goal in the Flames' attacking end, above the fancy people on the lower level, but not quite in the nosebleeds, where I might get stabbed by street toughs or something.

Once I got through the turnstiles, I decided to have a look inside one of the arena's many gift shops so that I might buy some Flames souvenir or another that would help me mix more easily with the hometown crowd, the majority of whom wore Flames jerseys of varying authenticity. And while that was a commitment level I wasn't quite ready for, I was immediately drawn to some Flames socks they had for sale by the counter. There were several varieties, each with a different Flames player from the current roster embroidered at about calf level, where folks could get a good look at him. And since I wasn't entirely familiar with any of them, as I am more of a "lover of the game" than a "guy who knows teams and players and stuff," I was about to pick a pair for myself at random when suddenly, I spotted a box of socks with none other than legendary Flames alumnus and Hockey Hall of Fame inductee Lanny McDonald, possessor of perhaps the greatest mustache ever to appear on the ice, on them.

"Are those Lanny McDonald socks the same as those other socks with guys I've never heard of on them?" I asked the woman behind the counter, since the Lanny McDonald ones were entirely obscured inside the box, no doubt to protect them from the casual gaze of mere mortals.

"I believe the Lanny McDonald socks are of higher quality than the other socks," the woman replied.

"Of course they're higher quality," I told her. "They have Lanny McDonald on them!"

And with that, I bought myself a pair. I didn't see what they cost, and I didn't even care. They could have been five dollars or five thousand—it didn't matter. I just knew I wanted them on my feet immediately. And as soon as they were in my possession, I dropped to the cement just outside the gift shop and tore into that damned box of Lanny McDonald socks like a hobo who had just pilfered a ham from a butcher shop window. I then removed the socks I was wearing at the time, threw them in the trash and pulled the Lanny McDonald socks, the socks of the fucking gods, bearing the mighty visage of Lanny himself on each calf, onto my unworthy feet. Then I got up and practically levitated in the direction of my solo seat in Section 219.

As I made my way to section 219, I just so happened to stumble upon a bar dedicated entirely to the selling of Bloody Caesars, the delicious Canadian beverage that, until that very moment, when I read it on a nearby sign, I had no idea was actually invented in Calgary fifty years ago. Anyway, I couldn't believe my good fortune and marched myself over to the bar immediately.

"I'd like one Bloody Caesar, please!" I said to the bartender, a young woman who seemed not entirely prepared for the level of enthusiasm I was bringing to the proceedings.

"Classic?" she asked.

"You bet your hat it is," I told her.

"No," she replied. "I'm asking if you want a regular Caesar or one of our other kinds."

"Oh, yeah," I said. "The regular one. Sorry."

As I marched away moments later, Bloody Caesar in hand and my feet clad in Lanny McDonald socks while at an actual Calgary Flames home game, I realized I'd found what I'd been searching for all day and had finally reached something one might call "peak Calgary." Perhaps the only thing missing was a cowboy hat, but I've yet to meet a man capable of handling that kind of excitement.

I settled into my seat a couple minutes later to find a sports team of some sort called the Calgary Stampeders walking out onto the ice for some reason. The one-quarter Canadian in me is embarrassed to admit that I genuinely had no idea what sport they played. Was it lacrosse? Curling? Or maybe even hockey, like the Flames, but just in some other league? It was impossible to tell, but I still clapped along with everybody else in celebration of something called the Grey Cup that they had apparently just won and even managed to bring out onto the ice with them while they were at it.

"Those guys are my favourite," I said to the guy next to me, just trying to be supportive. "The Stampeders are the very best at the sport they play. Ask around."

He just sort of half-smiled at me after that, but I'd like to think he was impressed with my enthusiasm for the Stampeders and the shiny trophy they were holding out on the ice at the moment.

A few minutes later, the puck dropped for the opening faceoff. And I was genuinely thrilled with the fact that I was finally watching a hockey game in person in Canada, especially my inner twelve-year-old, the one who couldn't believe it when my dad finally caved and got us cable television and I could watch *Hockey Night in Canada* in our family room in suburban Cleveland the way Rocket Richard, Bobby Orr, Gordie Howe and all the other greats had no doubt intended. But more than any of that, my Bloody Caesar was already starting to run low, so after the next whistle, I squeezed past everyone in my row and made my way back to the bar for another.

It was at this point that I also realized I had forgotten to have any dinner. And with two beers and one Bloody Caesar already coursing through my delicate system, I realized I should probably get something to eat along with my second Bloody Caesar so that I didn't wind up wrestling anyone in my section or anything, so I grabbed a bag of peanuts while I was at it. I also decided to get another beer as a chaser, so I wouldn't have to leave my seat again so quickly and miss more of the game.

Shortly after I got back to my seat with a fresh Caesar, a beer and some dinner, the Flames got their first goal of the night, immediately after which, I am thrilled to report, real flames shot out from the giant video screen hanging above centre ice. I could actually feel the heat as it happened, and I'm pretty sure I lost a bit of eyebrow in the process, but it was totally worth it, for on this night, I had lived. In fact, I couldn't wait for the Flames to put another puck in the net so I could really lean into it and have my face melted clean off. Unfortunately, however, the next goal was scored by the Stars, so I instead decided to choose a course of empathy and try to be at least half as upset as everyone else in the Saddledome appeared to be.

"Dammit," I said to the guy sitting next to me. "It appears that the team from Dallas has managed to score a goal for themselves despite the Flames' best efforts to keep that from happening."

"Uh, yeah," he replied, no doubt taken aback by my level of engagement with what was happening out on the ice.

During the first intermission, I decided to go for a stroll around the concourse, which is when I realized what a truly weird feeling it is be at a sporting event all alone in a strange town in a whole other country with nearly twenty thousand other people—all of whom seemed to know at least one other person in the place, as best I could tell. And if it weren't for the fact that I was at least a little bit tipsy at this point and was wearing Lanny McDonald socks while I was at it, I might have let that ruin my night. Instead, however, I decided to grab another beer. And I wasn't more than a couple sips in when a table of complete strangers, all of whom were wearing Flames jerseys, invited me to sit at their table on the concourse with them.

"Thank you," I said to them as I took them up on their offer. "I'm actually in town working on my new book about Canada, and am attending this game all by myself, so I am absolutely thrilled with the kindness you have just shown me."

They had all gone back to talking with each other by then and didn't respond to anything I had just said. Even so, their showing of what I choose to believe was trademark Calgary hospitality warmed my heart to no end.

I returned to my seat for the second period, which was slow on action other than the Stars scoring another goal and upsetting everyone in my row to the point where they seemed extra annoyed when I had to get up to use the bathroom again. But on the plus side, there was a shirtless guy with a trumpet a few sections over, whipping everyone into a frenzy with his trumpet playing mostly, but also with his shirtlessness, as I'm not sure there's a better display of commitment to rooting for the home team than taking your shirt off in front of almost twenty thousand people, especially when yours is a build that benefits from a bit of modesty.

When another shirtless guy with a trumpet appeared in a whole other section of the Saddledome a few minutes later, I put my glasses on to try and confirm whether or not it was, in fact, the same shirtless trumpeter I had seen earlier. And while I still couldn't decide whether it was or not in the end, I chose to believe that it was a second shirtless trumpeter, as that, dear reader, is the world I choose to live in, one where a shirtless trumpeter may very well pop up at a moment's notice and pick up where the first shirtless trumpeter had left off, in hopes of pushing the home team across the finish line to victory.

As for tonight, however, multiple shirtless trumpeters or not, victory didn't seem to be in the cards for the Flames, as the Stars pulled ahead to a 4–3 lead in the third period that didn't look like it was going to budge, since the players, the fans and—perhaps most of all—I were losing steam with each passing second on the clock. And with that realization, I decided to take my leave, mostly to beat the rush of Flames fans trying to get out of there, but also because, being a "lover of the game" and all, in the end I didn't much care who was going to win that night. The very fact that the game had been played at all was enough to make my one-quarter-Canadian heart swell with joy.

The bartender I had completely dominated back at the Ship and Anchor earlier had told me that it would be *the* place to be in town after the game, especially if the Flames had won, so in the hope that I would end up being wrong about the fact that this one was going to the Stars, I decided to grab a cab back to the Ship and Anchor for something at least somewhat resembling post-game revelry.

I arrived a short while later, and after reclaiming my seat at the bar, ordered some poutine with curry sauce, which I fully realize would be considered downright blasphemous by some. But with a flight back to New York first thing in the morning, I knew my time in Calgary was drawing to a close, and as a result, I was feeling downright reckless.

"I'm just coming from the Flames game," I said to the bartender as he delivered my poutine to me.

"How did our guys do?" he asked.

"They were down 4–3 and I couldn't bear to see our guys lose, so I got out of there early," I told him. "You know, because I'm one of the biggest Flames fans there is."

"Me too," the bartender replied. "Me too."

It felt good to bond over the Flames right there in Calgary like that, even though I honestly still couldn't name a single player on the team's current roster as of this writing. Even so, the nonstop Calgarian action I'd experienced over the last twenty-four hours was starting to catch up with me, so after knocking back about half my poutine with curry sauce—which was delicious, by the way, despite whatever some purists might tell you—I decided to call it a night and head back to my Airbnb apartment.

I arrived back at the apartment a short cab ride later and was relieved to see that the guy who had been waiting for me on the front steps the night before, perhaps indeed to kill me, was nowhere in sight. And while I did momentarily consider the possibility that he was, at that very moment, sitting in the dark in the middle of the apartment I was renting, probably wearing some weird animal mask and just waiting for me to return so that he might rise from his chair and slowly choke the life out of me, giggling maniacally all the while, that didn't happen, either. In fact, I walked inside, crawled into bed and almost immediately fell asleep.

I had to head to the airport at around five the next morning, a time of day when it seems only paperboys and serial killers are on the streets, though I'm starting to think the second part of that statement might just be my own hang-up, the more I keep rereading all of this.

I touched down at Newark airport around two that afternoon. And as I headed outside of arrivals in search of a cab a short while later, I couldn't help but notice a young, athletic-looking fellow standing curbside, wearing a baseball hat that said something along the lines of CALGARY STAMPEDERS—GREY CUP CHAMPIONS 2018. On top of his suitcase was a shiny football helmet with the same Stampeders logo I had seen on the Jumbotron at the Flames game the night before, when the Stampeders came out onto the ice with their trophy.

"You play for the Stampeders?" I asked him after putting two and two together, like a damn detective or something.

"Yup," he said with a smile.

"Congrats on winning the Grey Cup," I told him.

"Thank you," he replied.

"So," I continued while nodding at the football helmet, "you guys are a football team, huh?"

"Uh, yeah," he said, the smile on his face replaced with a look of confusion.

"That's cool," I said.

"Thanks," he replied.

"I have Lanny McDonald socks," I then decided to tell him.

He just looked at me after that. But as I walked away, I'd be lying if I said I didn't feel at least a few inches taller.

EPILOGUE

In Which My World Is Turned Completely Upside Down

THIS IS WHERE I'd hoped to wrap things up, come to some sort of dramatic conclusion (within reason), summarize my findings with just the right amount of profanity and ride off into the literary sunset until the demand for the inevitable follow-up to this one-quarter-Canadian classic becomes too great to ignore any longer. I was going to start by owning up to the fact that, over the course of my tireless research for this book, I definitely drank too much beer and ate way too much poutine. And I was going to immediately follow that admission by acknowledging that, as a proud one-quarter Canadian, I'm also fully aware that it's pretty much impossible to do either one of those things.*

From there, I would confess to the many glaring omissions in this book—like, for example, how I failed to make it to Yukon, Nunavut, the Northwest Territories, New Brunswick or Prince Edward Island, and how, if any residents of those places had already thrown this book into the fire or even a snowdrift in disgust by this point, I would completely understand. In fact, in the event that they hadn't,

---

* Though I think we can all agree that I ate poutine with absolutely no discretion whatsoever, with the possible exception of when I put my foot down in Victoria, British Columbia, and refused to eat sweet-potato poutine—a true Norma Rae moment, if I've ever had one.

I would damn well insist upon it. And don't even get me started on the fact that I didn't make it to Edmonton or Vancouver! How hard could it have possibly been?!*

Finally, I was going to admit the great shame I have brought upon my partly Canadian family and even felt through every page of this book by not setting foot on the ice wearing either skates or elusive curling shoes even once during my time in Canada. In retrospect, this should have been Job One.

I was going to talk about all of that stuff I just mentioned, and then we could all just get on with our lives—you, me, the entirety of Canada, and any non-Canadians who'd had that rare combination of good sense and spare time to strap themselves in for this journey as well.

But then, something unexpected happened, something none of us, not even I, could have possibly seen coming.

It all started when I sent an email to my uncle Joe, prodding him for clarification on a few details about some family history as I prepared to put this volume to bed.

"I assumed this project was dead," Joe replied reasonably, since I had not mentioned the Canada book directly to him in a while.

"No, it's not," I told him, while reflecting internally on the joys of family. "Not by a long shot."

Anyway, it was during our correspondence that he suggested I give a call to my aunt Kay, wife of my uncle John and daughter-in-law to my Canadian grandfather Clarence Blake, to answer some of the tough questions.

"Now, remind me what this book is about again," Kay said after we had gotten the pleasantries out of the way.

"I told you already—it's the most definitive book about Canada ever written by a non-Canadian," I said. "And part of it, of course,

---

* Then again, in my minor defence, it's worth noting that, whenever I'd tell a Canadian about someplace I'd been to in their country other than Toronto, Montreal or Vancouver, more often than not, they'd respond by saying something along the lines of "Eh, never been there."

has to do with the fact that my grandfather—and your father-in-law, Clarence Blake, the undisputed menswear authority of the east side of Cleveland—was from Canada, which kind of makes me one-quarter Canadian if you really think about it. Which I have. A lot. Some would argue too much."

"Well, it's not just your grandfather who was from Canada," Aunt Kay replied. "Your grandmother's father, Henry Theodore Kelley, was from there, too."

"What the hell did you just say?" I replied.

"Watch your language," she warned. "Anyway, yeah, your great-grandfather on your grandmother's side of the family was from Amherstburg, Ontario."

This news rendered me instantly speechless. After all, here I was, a guy who had lived over forty years of his life assuming he was merely one-quarter Canadian and who was just about to complete the definitive book on that very subject, when, in fact, I had been *three-eighths* Canadian *this whole time*! It was a lot to take in. And I immediately found myself re-evaluating the world around me, as well as my place in it. After all, I had been living a lie—not just for this entire book up until this very page, but for my *entire life.*

"Who am I?" I wondered. "And has my whole life been a sham?"

As much as my mind was completely blown by all this, I realize it is at this point that you may also be flying into a blind rage at this latest revelation, pounding your fists on the glass at some ice rink—or perhaps even shaking them at the sky in the parking lot of that same ice rink—as a result of having been duped for tens of thousands of words now, regardless of how absolutely gripping, poetic, and subtly erotic they may have been. Believe me when I say that I completely understand—so much, in fact, that I would insist you also destroy this book immediately, just as the entire population of Iqaluit no doubt already has, because if there is anything more disturbing than thinking you are one-fourth Canadian your entire life, only to find out that you've been three-eighths Canadian the whole time, it's thinking you're reading a book by a one-fourth-Canadian person, only to find out you've been reading a book by a three-eighths-Canadian person this whole time.

If you are, against all odds, still reading even now, please accept my sincerest apologies. And if it's any consolation, I've thought long and hard about this and have come to the conclusion that, regardless of the pain it has no doubt caused, my bamboozlement over how Canadian I have actually been this whole time doesn't really affect the thoughts and opinions expressed on the pages herein much at all. Is it, however, just further evidence of the fact that life is nuts and none of us is really safe at any time? Yes. Absolutely. And for that, I definitely and sincerely apologize. Still, on the upside, I'm even more Canadian than I originally thought, which only adds to the gravity of the words collected here, if you really think about it, so there's that, too.

Anyway, getting back to my phone call with my aunt Kay: as it turned out, my grandmother Agnes Kelly's dad, Henry Theodore Kelley,* who would eventually move to Cleveland and become a ship captain on the Great Lakes, was born and raised in Amherstburg, Ontario, just a couple hours south of Clinton in an area that's known in cartography circles as the "sweet, sweet Canadian nugget between Detroit, Michigan, and Toledo, Ohio."** I had assumed he had originally come from Ireland, as most of my relatives of his generation had. I had learned in one brief phone call, however, that I was wrong. Dead wrong.

And now, armed with this knowledge, my world has suddenly and forever changed. For starters, I'm going to have to make a trip to Amherstberg as soon as possible as part of my new journey as a three-eighths-Canadian person. And as long as I've got gas in the tank, I suppose I should swing by Yukon, Nunavut, the Northwest

---

* According to my uncle Joe, the spelling of the family name varied, largely depending on mood.

** Okay, I admit it—I totally just made that up. Then again, look at a map and try to tell me I'm wrong.

Territories, New Brunswick, Prince Edward Island—and, what the hell, even Edmonton and Vancouver, while I'm at it.

And while I definitely, 100 percent intend to do all of that just as soon as humanly possible, I also realize that doing so will likely only serve to further underscore what I already know: that Canada is a beautiful land full of even more beautiful people,* many of whom are a lot more stoned than they were when I first started this book. And that, yes, despite your proximity to the United States, from which I write these words, Canada is a whole other place altogether, an arguably kinder and gentler place where people are much better at hockey, ice fishing and going about their business in the absolutely freezing cold in general. Is Canada perfect? No.** But indeed, it's a place we could all learn a lot from, if not from what I believe to be the obvious merits of the Canadian health-care system, gun laws, etc., then at the very least from the fact that, if you simply swap out the tomato juice with Clamato and throw a little celery salt around the rim the next time you try to make a Bloody Mary, you'll have yourself a vastly superior, if much grosser-sounding, beverage. And holy shit, Guy Lafleur made a disco record!

I also recognize that Canada and its sheer multitudes can neither be contained nor done something even close to resembling justice in a mere book. But through the simple act of trying to do just that, I, Dave Hill, have become a better person, and along the way, have fallen in love with the country my grandfather simply wouldn't shut up about.***

I suppose it is at this point that I should point out that I'm also a person who has not one, but two exceptional moose sculptures in his possession.

---

* Yes, even those pricks in Toronto.

** In fact, I could probably write an entire book on those impossibly lame and cruel Canada Goose jackets alone.

*** Yes, even Winnipeg, where I fully intend to build a new life for myself in the event that I suddenly need to disappear at some point.

You'll hopefully remember the moose I ended up procuring from that charity shop in Clinton, Ontario, after a bit of Ugly American persistence. And you'll hopefully also remember that my friend and accomplice on the Clinton excursion, Joe, a highly accomplished artist, promised to sculpt me a moose, since, as far as he knew anyway, I never did succeed in getting those ladies at the charity shop in Clinton to cough up that moose in the window.

You'll be happy to hear that, a few short weeks ago, a mysterious package arrived at my apartment. It was a large box stuffed with an impossible amount of bubble wrap and Styrofoam peanuts and accompanied by a highly detailed handwritten note on how, after I'd waded through all that bubble wrap and Styrofoam peanuts, I might safely remove the delicate sculpture without breaking it.

I followed the instructions closely to reveal an absolutely glorious moose sculpture. Not only was it larger than the moose I'd gotten from Clinton, but emblazoned on its side was the Canadian flag. And while my original plan, in the event that the auxiliary moose sculpture did finally materialize, was to place it in a room separate from the original moose sculpture so that I might enjoy moose access in two separate rooms of my apartment, in the end, I decided to place the two moose sculptures at opposite ends of *the same room.*

And now, through no small amount of patience and perseverance—and, I guess, at least some small amount of lying to my friend Joe about that first moose, in that I neglected to ever tell him that I bought it—I am now a guy, sitting here in my living room as I type this, with two reasonably large moose sculptures standing guard on either side of me.

And if *that's* not the most Canadian thing that has ever happened, then I don't know what is.

ACKNOWLEDGEMENTS

MOST PEOPLE THINK writing a book involves one person sitting down in a chair, knocking back a bunch of off-brand liquor and maybe a couple bags of circus peanuts, and just writing away until all the hurt is gone. And while that's pretty much how it goes, it's also simplifying things a bit, especially when it comes to this particular book, the creation of which would no doubt have killed a lesser man, especially after he found out he had to go back and add the letter "u" to a whole bunch of words like "colour," "flavour," and "glamour" so they'd look more Canadian on the page. Anyway, keeping all that in mind, I wanted to thank the following people for providing me, however directly or indirectly, with the love, support, guidance and/or other stuff needed to write the most definitive book on Canada ever written by a *three-eighths*-Canadian person: Tim Rostron, Scott Sellers, Lloyd Davis, all the fine folks at Penguin Random House Canada and Penguin Random House (the totally non-Canadian version), Kirby Kim, Kara Welker, Conan Smith, Kathy Kato, Miriam Hill, Luke Simon, Nick Simon, Libby Manthei, Jeff Manthei, Blake Manthei, Bob Hill Jr., Janyce Murphy, Anna Hill, Eamon Hill, Katy Wallace, Rob Wallace, William Wallace, Lilah Wallace, Nils Rusch, Joe Blake, Kay Blake, the Blake family in general, Bob and Barb Kato, Malcolm Gladwell, Dick Cavett, Tom Papa, Sam Bee, Joe Tait, Carl Arnheiter, Trudy Stewart, David Rakoff,

John Herguth, Walter Schreifels, Greg Wands, Nick Flanagan, Reed Mullin, Sandy Mullin, Korri Santillan, Gerald and Rose Andrews, Duane Andrews, Erin Power, Fred Wistow, Todd Barry, the Hill People, Phil Costello, Eddie Eyeball, Rob Pfeiffer, Tim Fornara, Jason Narducy, Bill Dolan, the Tanous family, Curtis Stigers, Pete Caldes, Jim Biederman, Riad Nasr, Dava She-Wolf, the Laurent-Marke family, Adam Resnick, Trish Nelson, Erika Osterhout, Tom Beaujour, Jodi Lennon, Dave Wyndorf, Maryanna Hardy, Lou Hagood, James Fernandez, Binky the Clown, Chris Reifert, Nancy Reifert, Chris Gersbeck, Shaina Feinberg, Tim Parnin, Tony Kellers, Pat Casa, Jim McPolin, Dan Dratch, Sarah Hochman, Kathy Huck, Alison Strobel, Kellen Ross, David Myles, Wesley Stace, the mighty Witch Taint and, perhaps most of all, you—especially if I should have mentioned you by name above but forgot because of the fumes.

Additional thanks go to Randy Bachman, Guy Lafleur and the power trios Rush and Triumph for unwittingly doing a lot more heavy lifting in this book than any of us could have ever anticipated.

An extra special thanks goes to my parents, Bob and Bunny Hill. Mom, I love and miss you every day. And the typing lessons you made me take the summer after eighth grade helped make this book much easier to complete. And Dad, I think this book has the least profanity of any book I've written so far, further proof that I am shaping up to be a fine young man as a result of your endless positive influence.

Finally, I would like to thank my sweet hellhound Luci, who, when not trying to get me to do anything else besides work on this book, slept and farted mere feet from me as though it was her job, through each and every draft, the very definition of teamwork.

Your man,
Dave Hill